BLINI

Jay Giles

Blindsided

Reagent Press
Published by Virtual Press, Inc.

Cover design & illustration by Reagent Press
Cover illustration copyright © 2006 Reagent Press

ISBN 1-57545-104-2

RP BOOKS WASHINGTON
REAGENT PRESS
WWW.REAGENTPRESS.COM

BLINDSIDED

Jay Giles

DEDICATION

For Donna, with love.

CHAPTER 1

It felt like what it was—a cage.

The room was ten by ten at most, lit by strip fluorescent tubes, furnished with a rectangular gray metal table, four straight-backed wooden chairs. On one wall was a door, on another, a one-way-glass observation window. The ceiling was acoustical tile with a big square ventilation diffuser in the middle. Despite the size of the vent, the room was muggy, the air stale. It was quieter than a tomb.

If you were a murderer, rapist or felon, it was the room where you were interrogated.

I was none of those things, but I was in the room anyway.

The police lieutenant "interviewing" me had stepped out to confer with his associates. In his absence, I paced. I had to.

I had been the sole witness to gruesome execution-style killings and the horror was still ricocheting around in my mind. Guns had blazed all around me. I could still smell the gunpowder, see bullets destroying faces, hear the thud of bodies as they hit the concrete floor.

As frightening as it had been, I had a sick feeling in the pit of my stomach that it wasn't over. I'd had that feeling before—the morning Joe Jesso didn't arrive at my office. The morning all of this started.

I'd been right about Joe.

I was afraid I'd be right about what else was about to happen, too.

CHAPTER 2

That morning, I'd camped at the lobby window, waiting, watching. Where was he? Worry, whipped by guilt, had me panicky. In the parking area, heat simmered from the asphalt where Joe Jesso's ten-year-old beige Cadillac should have been parked. Repeatedly, I scanned the approaching traffic for a glimpse of his car. Saw nothing.

My anxiety grew as the minutes ticked by. Why hadn't I done something to safeguard him? Why hadn't I had his new wife investigated? Why hadn't I insisted on a postnuptial agreement?

I'd done nothing. I'd let him down. Upset with myself, I strode quickly to a phone, dialed his number. It rang four times. The recording kicked in. "You've reached Joe and Janet," a female voice said. "We're out having fun. Leave a message."

I slammed the receiver down in frustration, went to my office, grabbed the car keys off my desk, returned to the reception area. "I'm going over to Joe's," I told Rosemary Shears, my receptionist and assistant. " If he calls or shows up, get me on my cell." I opened the front door and held it for Eddie, my Springer Spaniel and constant companion. He scooted through, raced to the car.

Rosemary stood at the door. "Call. No matter what."

"I will," I yelled over my shoulder as I ran down the walk. I wouldn't have chased off like this for just anybody. I thought of Joe more as a favorite uncle than a client.

Eighteen months ago, not long after I opened, Joe had walked into my Sarasota brokerage and asked my advice on what to do with a little money. He must have liked what he heard because he kept coming back, giving me more money to invest. Somewhere along the way, we'd settled into a routine of spending Wednesday mornings talking about his passion—stocks.

Nothing—not faulty alarm clocks, car trouble, illness, even the threat of hurricanes—kept him from arriving promptly at 8:00 a.m.

Twenty long minutes had passed since 8:00.

My mind kept coming back to the only reason why Joe would be that late. He was dead.

I opened the Saab's door. Eddie bounded up and over the driver's seat, landed in the passenger seat in one jump. I slid in, shut the door, turned the key, and pulled out of our parking garden into the traffic on Palm Street.

My thoughts were memories. I pictured Joe carrying a mug of coffee over to his spot on the leather sofa opposite my desk, settling in, talking in a soft voice about price/earning ratios, growth opportunities, potential splits. At seventy-eight, Joe's mind was razor-sharp. It was his face that had aged. It was thin and heavily lined, and his head was covered with more age spots than hair.

Gold-rimmed aviator-style glasses almost hid kind brown eyes. The pencil-thin moustache didn't hide his usual smile.

He wore Florida old-man clothes. Pale, short-sleeved shirts with epaulets on the shoulders. Off-white shorts held up with a white belt. Dark socks pulled up high, tan soft-leather shoes. The ensemble varied a little each week. Three things, however, stayed the same: he always wore a white captain's hat with an insignia on the front, had a nail file sticking out of his front shirt pocket, and carried a beat-up old brown-leather briefcase.

One other thing never varied. Even though Joe came to talk stocks, he was always concerned about me. If I was having a tough time, he'd put his arm around my shoulder, talk to me the way my father used to do.

All the Wednesdays we'd laughed together and talked together ran through my mind as I drove to his condo, a twenty-to-thirty minute drive. A long time to dwell on a friend's death. And the woman who'd killed him.

CHAPTER 3

A week ago, as he was leaving, Joe had said casually, "Matt, I've got some news I want to share with you. I've gotten married." I'd been stunned. He'd never mentioned a woman, much less that he was contemplating marriage.

Rosemary, of course, had wanted all the details. Joe had been evasive. All Rosemary learned was the woman's first name—Janet. All I learned was that there had been no prenuptial agreement. I wanted to feel happy for him. But with Joe's stock portfolio worth over two million, I had a bad feeling about this marriage.

I talked to Joe a couple of times on the phone following his announcement. He'd sounded happy, as if married life agreed with him. I decided I'd panicked, was being overly protective. As I drove to his condo, I replayed each of those conversations in my mind, searching for indications this was coming, adding the questions I now wished I'd asked. I should never have assumed he was okay. I should have made sure. I slammed my hand on the steering wheel. Why hadn't I?

I flew by a wrinkled little man driving an ancient Buick, eased through a yellow light, and accelerated past a strip mall to the entrance of the community where Joe lived.

Laurel Lakes Condominiums was a single street curved around a small lake, the condos in twos, left and right units sharing a common wall. Every unit the same brown, the same two-car garage in front, garage door after garage door.

I wasn't watching the garage doors, however. I was watching the identical mailboxes, looking for one with the name Jesso at the top. I found it and pulled the Saab into the driveway. Joe's was the unit on the left. I got out, walked to the front stoop, and rang the bell. Eddie added a rare bark, as if to say, "Hey, I'm here, too."

I waited. Waited. Didn't hear anything. Rang the bell again. Waited. Waited. Waited. Nothing. I turned and headed back to the car. As I passed the garage window, I noticed Joe's car inside. From behind me came the sound of a door opening. My spirits soared. He'd probably overslept.

I turned, expecting Joe in his bathrobe. Instead, I saw a square-faced, dark-haired man wearing a white shirt, loose at the collar, suspenders holding up dark blue suit pants. He stood on the stoop, barefoot, holding the screen door open. "Can I help you?" he asked irritably.

"I'm a friend of Joe's. I was looking for him."

He eyed me for a minute, finally said, "I'm his brother-in-law." There was a pause—seemed like minutes, probably only seconds—before he said what I knew was coming: "Joe died last night."

I felt a knot tighten in my stomach. "How did it happen?"

He shrugged. "Died in his sleep. Old age, I guess."

"I'm sorry. He was a good friend." Through the door, I caught a glimpse of a blond woman. Didn't look like she had any clothes on.

"Yeah, a good guy," the brother-in-law agreed flatly as he started to close the door.

I stepped forward, offered my hand. "I'm Matt Seattle."

Awkwardly, he held out his hand. "Greg Nevitt."

Now I knew who the enemy was. "Give your sister my condolences."

His eyes narrowed. "Yeah, I will."

I heard the screen door swing shut as I walked back to the car. I backed slowly out of the driveway, aware they were probably watching me. As soon as I left Laurel Lakes, I was on the car phone.

My first call was to Rosemary.

"Seattle on Stocks," Rosemary's British accent was one of our trademarks.

"Rosemary, it's me. It's what we feared."

"Oh, dear."

"He died in his sleep last night."

"Did you talk to the doctor?"

"No, his brother-in-law. Fellow by the name of Greg Nevitt."

"Are you coming back to the office?"

"I'm on my way now. Can you give me Julian's direct line?" Julian Ockerman was my attorney.

She read me the number. I hung up and juggled the phone and the steering wheel as I dialed. It rang twice before he picked up.

"Julian, it's Matt. I've got an emergency. How soon can we get together?"

I heard him flipping pages in his book. "I've got a deposition at ten, filing at noon. How about two? Does that work?"

"I'll be there. Thanks."

Two o'clock found us sitting in Julian's office high atop Sarasota's only true skyscraper—One Sarasota Place. The office was impressive—an elaborate desk, expensive furniture and carpet, subdued lighting, fancy media wall. Normally, I enjoyed the panoramic view of the bay, the Keys, the Gulf. That day, I could have cared less.

Julian slouched on the sofa opposite me, arm over the back, feet up on the coffee table between us. He was tall and lanky, with dark brown hair slicked back, deep-set eyes, a hooked beak of a nose, and strong pointed chin. A face that could be intimidating. At that moment, however, it was inquisitive. "Tell me about this emergency."

Eddie sat on the floor next to me, watching Julian.

I leaned forward. "One of my clients, a guy named Joe Jesso, died last night. I think he was murdered."

"Why?"

"For his money. Joe married a week ago. Suddenly, he's dead. That can't be a coincidence."

"Let's step through this," Julian said calmly. "How old was this client?"

"Almost eighty."

"How old is the wife?"

"I don't know. All he'd tell me about her was her name—Janet."

"What makes you think Janet was after his money?"

"He was eighty years old. What else would she be after?"

He got up from the sofa, paced around the office. Eddie watched him as he paced. "Well, if this Janet woman is seventy, she might have been looking for companionship. If she's twenty, likely she was looking for money. That's why I asked her age."

I shook my head. "I didn't think to ask him that. I should have."

He waved his hand dismissively. "Don't worry. We can find out. What we've got is a fairly common scenario: an older guy who's lonely, probably feels he doesn't have all that much longer, wants somebody to keep him company and look after him. In short, he's vulnerable. He meets a woman who's nice to him, makes him feel good. Before you know it, he'll do anything she wants."

"Are you talking sex?"

He shook his head. "Sex isn't the big issue. It's companionship. Someone to watch television with. Talk to over dinner. Go to a movie."

"That doesn't sound so bad."

"It's not if the woman's older, too. Then it's usually beneficial for both." He grinned. "But remember, we're guys. Would you go for the seventy-year-old blue-haired matron? Or the thirty-year-old blond with fake boobs?" He didn't wait for my answer. "You'd go for the eye candy. We men are such swine. I had a client, a widower about the same age as your friend with three grown children, worth maybe six million. He decided he wanted to marry the maid, a twenty-four-year-old girl from Venezuela who hardly spoke any English. I guess they'd played footsie. He liked it, wanted more. When he died less than a year later, the new wife inherited half the estate. The kids fought it, of course, but the judge said it was legal and ruled in her favor."

"You're kidding me."

"You'd be amazed how often this happens. When guys get older, they don't care. The rules change." He shook his head. "There are a lot of unscrupulous women out there preying on lonely old men. Especially here in Florida with our large population of senior citizens."

"So there's a good chance she was after his money?"

"A very good chance." He stopped, looked at me. "Do you know if he had a prenup?"

I shook my head. "He didn't. I talked to him about a postnup, but."

He made a dismissive gesture. "Postnups are useless. If it ever went to court they'd say she was intimidated into signing it." He resumed pacing. "And you don't know anything about her other than her name?"

"Not a thing, but I did meet her brother, Greg Nevitt, at the condo this morning. He's the one who told me Joe'd died."

He frowned, ran his hand through his hair. "What do you know about Joe? Any family? Children? Trusts?"

As close as Joe and I had been, I knew damn little. Perhaps because I didn't like people asking me about my personal life, I'd never questioned Joe about his. We talked about things that were safe. Guy stuff. Work stuff.

"I can tell by that look, you know squat."

"It's not—"

"Squat."

I sighed. "Okay, squat. What do we do?"

"Well, I think we need to know more about Janet." He walked to his desk, started going through his rolodex. He found what he was looking for, pulled a Mont Blanc fountain pen from his breast pocket, wrote something on a piece of paper. "Here's the name of a private investigator I've used. Give her a call, get her looking into this."

He walked over, handed me the paper. On it was Tory Knight, a local phone number.

I stared at it, unsure that this was the right direction. "Shouldn't I be going to the police, demanding an investigation, an autopsy?"

"Not yet," he said sternly. "You have suspicions. You don't have proof. If the death is ruled natural causes and a physician signs the death certificate, it'll be tough to challenge."

"Can't we demand an autopsy?"

"Not without cause."

"A millionaire married a week suddenly and inexplicably dies. Isn't that cause?"

He plopped down again on the couch opposite the one where I sat, looked directly at me. "It's an implicit accusation of murder and as such could be actionable. She's legally the wife. She has rights. You float that accusation and she'll take every penny you have." Rebuke finished, he stood. "Have Tory look into the cause of death and the wife's background, see what she turns up."

I stood, tucked the piece of paper in my pocket. "Thanks, Julian. I'll keep you posted."

"Do that," he said as he walked me to the door.

Back in my car, I used the car phone, punched in Tory's number, got a recording. "You know the drill. Leave a detailed message. I'll get back to you when I can."

Julian had neglected to tell me Tory had an attitude.

CHAPTER 4

I was hoping that Tory would call while I was at the office. When I hadn't heard from her by seven, I locked up the place, put the top down on my Saab 9-3, and headed home. In the winter, when the snowbirds were in residence, the commute took forty-five minutes; during the summer it only took fifteen.

I negotiated downtown Sarasota streets in virtually no traffic, took the Ringling Causeway off the mainland, an expanse of blue water on either side. A few sailboats were out on the bay; closer to shore were sailboarders and jet skiers. The causeway deposited me on St. Armand's Key with its exclusive circle of upscale shops and restaurants. I slowed as I navigated the circle. People have the right-of-way, and tonight, like most nights, they were out and about. Strolling, shopping, stopping for a bite to eat, taking advantage of a balmy evening. Past the circle, I drove over the New Pass Bridge to Longboat Key.

My condo was a couple of miles down the key at the Watergate Club. I turned into the drive, slowed at the guard gate. Given the name of the place, I'd nicknamed the two security guards Haldeman and Ehrlichman. Haldeman was on. Eddie barked as we drove past; I waved and continued to my parking space.

The Watergate Club was a fourteen-story rounded tower on the gulf side of the key. Eight units to a floor. A separate clubhouse building housed a lobby, meeting rooms, and an exercise facility. The pool was on the Gulf side of the clubhouse; the tennis courts on the street side.

I rode the elevator to the twelfth floor, headed down the hall to my two-bedroom, two-bath affair. I had spectacular views of both the Gulf of Mexico and downtown Sarasota.

An older couple from Syracuse who had decided it was time to go into assisted living sold it to me at a fair price. They'd had a taste for flocked wallpapers, sculptured carpet, and heavy, upholstered wood furniture. The kitchen with its avocado appliances and burnt-orange countertops looked like what it was—something left over from the sixties.

I'd brought in a decorator who in turn brought in a crew of contractors. They got rid of the wallpaper and carpet, reworked wall configurations, completely redid kitchen and baths. The place was transformed. White walls, bleached hardwood floors, modern furniture. The second bedroom had been turned into a library with floor-to-ceiling bookcases. The kitchen was all granite countertops and stainless steel appliances. It had the feel of Manhattan.

On good days, I was pleased with how it turned out. On the bad days, I could have cared less.

I let us in the front door. Eddie trotted into the kitchen and returned, holding his dish. I fed him, made a salad for myself. He finished his bowl and sat patiently as I ate. As soon as he saw me carry my plate over to the sink, he went and got his leash. We went for a walk in the yard followed by a run on the beach.

I spent the rest of the evening reading, waiting for the phone to ring. Eddie sat next to me, his head resting on my thigh. I rubbed his ears, stroked his head. At eleven, when Tory still hadn't called, I showered, went to bed and tossed and turned before going to sleep. With sleep came the dreams.

It was autumn. The leaves were changing. There was a nip in the air. The sky was bright cobalt blue, the grass a vivid green.

Claire and I stood on the sidelines of a soccer match. She held a mug of coffee, a blanket wrapped around her shoulders.

On the field was a shark-feeding frenzy around the ball. For the players in the eight-to-ten-year-old league, the concept of passing had yet to sink in. Our ten-year-old son, Michael, was in the middle of the turmoil. Blond hair, yellow shirt, green shorts, knee-high yellow socks. Wait. Kick. Run. A bit tentative, even though he was one of the older boys.

"Kick it out, Michael," I heard myself shouting.

"You can do it," Claire called.

Next to us on the sidelines, Sarah watched her younger brother disdainfully. She was in the twelve-to-fourteen-year-old league. What she saw happening on the field was beneath her. Eddie sat at my feet, watching Michael carefully.

A whistle sounded. Penalty kick. Michael's team, the Comets, lined up to defend. The boy from the other team got off a good kick, but it sailed high. Another shark frenzy followed the throw-in; then all of a sudden, Michael had the ball on the wing.

"Go, Michael, go," I heard myself shouting. He ran twenty yards before a player from the orange team intercepted him. If he could get five more yards, he'd have a shot. The two boys fought for the ball. Michael got it past the other boy, kicked. Not enough oomph. The ball dribbled across the field right to their goalie.

"Good try, Michael," Claire shouted.

The whistle blew. Game over. It belonged to the Comets. Their first win of the season.

Michael charged across the field, jumped up, and hugged me. "Did you see that kick, Dad? I almost scored."

"You were awesome, Michael."

We headed to the concession stand. Michael ran ahead to rejoin the team, Eddie at his heels. Sarah's friends started arriving for her game. I had my arm around Claire's shoulder. I was happy. Life was full and rich and good.

I woke.

My family was gone. Again.

The emptiness was excruciating. I felt the pain swell and overwhelm me. I would have done anything to have them back; I could do nothing. I felt my eyes fill with tears. At the side of the bed, Eddie put his head on my hand as if to comfort me. I rubbed his ears. It was all I could do as emotions flooded me.

It had been over two years now since the accident. I was in a hurry that morning, an early meeting. Other Merrill Lynch division heads were in town. As the division head for Detroit, it was my responsibility to host the group. I dressed quickly, swung through the kitchen on my way to the car, the kids bickering at the breakfast table. Claire was standing at the kitchen counter getting their lunches ready for school. Normally, I dropped Sarah and Michael off on my way to work since it was on the way. That morning, because of the meeting, Claire was taking them.

"You going to be on time?" she asked as I kissed her good bye.

"Should be. 'Bye, kids." Still arguing, they didn't respond. I was out the door and into the car.

Our division meeting, a two-day affair, was being held at the Detroit Renaissance Inn. We'd worked our way through the pre-meeting continental breakfast and chitchat and were listening to the divisional VP, Frank Cates, when a woman from the hotel staff walked out on the stage and interrupted him for a brief huddled conference off mike. I remember seeing Frank's shoulders sag, seeing him search the faces in the group until his gaze found mine.

He walked over, head down, the woman trailing uncertainly behind. When he reached me, he steered me away from the group to a corner of the room.

"Matt," he said quietly. "There's been a traffic accident. A bad one. I hate giving you this news, but they tell me your wife and son are dead. They've taken your daughter to the hospital. They'll have someone drive you to her. I'm sorry."

The woman from the hotel stepped forward. "Please come with me, Mr. Seattle." She led me out of the room. A police cruiser waited outside the hotel's front doors. On the ride to the hospital, I asked the officer if he knew what had happened.

"Not much, sir," he'd answered politely. "We believe your wife's car was hit head-on by a vehicle attempting to pass at a high rate of speed. They're still investigating."

He put the siren on and soon deposited me at the hospital emergency entrance where a doctor told me briefly about Sarah's condition—multiple broken bones, severe internal trauma. When I started to ask questions, he cut me off, saying he'd rather talk after they'd made a better assessment of her injuries. He said her chances were not good.

You learn what's really important sitting in a hospital waiting room grieving for your wife and child, praying for your other child in surgery. It's not money. It's not your lifestyle. It's not your job. I would have traded all that to have Sarah better. Gladly. I'd have given my life for her to live. For my wife and son to be brought back to life.

Six hours after Sarah went into surgery, the doctor came and told me they'd done all they could. The injuries were more extensive than they'd thought. Time would tell. She was in God's hands.

They let me see her after she'd been moved to intensive care. She looked small and fragile on the big hospital bed, her face swollen, discolored, a ventilation tube in her nose. Her breathing came in short gasps.

She tried. I know she was trying. She held on for six days. I stayed by her bedside, praying I'd see her eyes flutter open, her hand move. I heard her labored breathing stop. Immediately, machines started making noises and staff hustled me out. A nurse came and told me she was gone. They hadn't been able to revive her. She said it was probably a blessing.

I didn't know if I could keep going, probably wouldn't have if family and friends hadn't taken over. My parents, who had flown in from Chicago, watched over me. My bosses at Merrill Lynch provided a paid leave of absence. Friends brought casseroles. But as kind as everybody was, they had to go back to their own lives eventually. When that time came, I assured everyone I was okay.

Only Dr. Adelle Swarthmore, my psychologist, knew I wasn't. I was a mess, a knot of exposed emotions that I couldn't untangle. Twice a week I saw her, poured out my heart. She helped me understand that grieving was a human process with known stages and unknown timetables. With her help, I'd gotten through denial, bargaining, and anger, but depression overwhelmed me. Acceptance seemed impossible.

Reminders of what I'd lost were everywhere. One of Sarah's blue barrettes on the cooking island in the kitchen. Michael's soccer shoes by his chair at the kitchen table. A book Claire had been reading, open on the sofa in the family room. Each held a memory, a link to what I'd lost.

Eddie saw my slide into depression. Once Michael's constant companion, Eddie never left my side. In his way, he watched over me. He'd bring me his leash and take me for a walk when I became melancholy. He'd bark when I didn't get up in the morning. He'd bring me his bowl, reminding me I had to eat. He'd put his head under my hand, letting me know I wasn't alone. Often, Eddie would go in Michael's room and just sit—head down, tail still. He missed them, too. Michael most of all. Watching him, I saw my own hopelessness.

To help me cope, Dr. Swarthmore recommended a support group for traumatic death survivors. In an odd way, it worked. The mutual help—the sharing, talking, listening—grated on me, but it made me realize I needed to take action.

I tried the recommended approach of separating personal items into groups to be kept and discarded. When I couldn't do it, I knew that we had to leave the house. I didn't have the courage to deal with a barrette, far less whole rooms. Someday, maybe. Not now. Again, friends came to my aid. They boxed up the personal things for me, and I put them in storage. I sold the house and furniture. I took only what I could fit in the car—two suitcases of clothes, the family photo albums, and Eddie.

Dr. Swarthmore felt I was running away. Maybe I was. But I was doing something, taking action, and even she agreed that was good.

In our final session, she gave me a card with phone numbers where I could reach her twenty-four hours a day. "I'm going to see you through this," she said. "Call me when you need to talk, even if it's the middle of the night." Eddie and I drove out of Detroit, leaving the life we'd loved. We had no idea where we were going, but we knew what we were seeking. A life we could live with.

I fell asleep again thinking we'd found that. Sort of.

CHAPTER 5

I awoke with a start, the dreams still in my mind, looked at the bedside clock. Five-fifteen.

Eddie put his nose on the bed to let me know he was there.

I patted him, knew I was through sleeping for the night. "It's okay, fella."

I threw off the covers, got up, and walked to the bathroom. Eddie padded along behind me. I rested my hands on the sink counter, leaned forward, looked in the mirror. It was the same face I saw every morning. Salt-and-pepper curly hair, blue eyes, ski-slope nose, broad mouth, dimpled chin. Handsome and refined was the way Claire had described it. This morning, it looked lost.

I shaved, showered, dressed. Eddie and I had a bite of breakfast and a leisurely walk. It was six-thirty when we returned, too early to call Dr. Swarthmore. Seven would be better.

At six-forty, the phone rang. I picked it up in the kitchen. "Matt Seattle."

"Hello, Matt. This is Tory Wright. I got your message. I don't know whether Julian told you, but I don't work for anyone toxic."

"Toxic?"

"Anyone I don't get along with. So before I say whether or not I can help you, I'm going to need to meet you. That okay?"

"It'll have to be. When and where?"

"Eight-thirty at the Pier Grille on Anna Maria?" She named the island just north of Longboat Key.

"Sure. How will I know you?"

"Easy. I'm the woman in black."

At seven exactly, I called Dr. Swarthmore in Detroit. "Hello, Adelle. It's Matt," I said when she came on the line.

"Matt, good to hear from you. Are things going well?" I heard the rustling of papers, probably my file.

"I think I've been doing pretty well. Last night, though, I had dreams again."

Papers rustled briefly. "It's been a little over a month since their last occurrence. That's good. Tell me the specifics." I recounted the dream for her.

When I finished, she said, "We dream to help process information, to attach meaning and feeling, which is part of the grieving process. So this dream was positive in that regard. I'm curious. What do you think triggered the dreams last night?"

It had to be Joe's death. I shared that news with her, let her know Joe and I had become close. Two lonely men with a common interest.

"I'm sorry to hear about your friend, Matt, but I'm pleased to hear you're forming friendships. Each friendship will make you stronger, more whole." Papers rustled again. "I notice your friends all seem to be male. Have you made any female friends?"

I knew what she was really asking. Was I seeing anyone? "I have female friends," I said a little defensively. "Nobody special yet."

"You can't stay walled-up in yourself, Matt. You've made progress in allowing people into your life. Joe, for example. Most of these people seem work-related, which is fine. However, you need to find friendships at a personal level. Male and female." She continued, gave me advice, the name of a book to read. I heard a door open and close. "My patient has arrived for her session, I'm going to have to go, but keep calling me, Matt. You are making progress."

I hung up, walked into the living room, picked up a framed picture of Claire. Progress was great, but I wasn't ready to let go of Claire.

The phone rang again. I walked back to the kitchen, picked it up. "Matt Seattle."

"I'm at the Pier. My meeting just finished. Any chance you could get here earlier than eight-thirty?"

I looked at my watch. Seven-twenty. "I'm on my way."

The Pier Grille was a white clapboard building adjacent to the Anna Maria fishing pier. It didn't look like much, but the food was good, the prices cheap.

I found a spot in the parking lot and pulled in. Eddie got up, circled in his seat, ready to get out. "Sorry, fella," I said. "I'm afraid you're going to have to wait in the car." He didn't complain, just settled back down. I rubbed his ears. "I won't be too long."

Inside, the place was packed. Locals mostly. Northerners went to Firstwatch and Starbuck's. It was crowded, but she was easy to spot. Black is not the color most worn in August in Florida.

"Hello, Tory," I said when I got to her booth. "I'm Matt Seattle."

She put down her coffee cup. "Thanks for coming early. Have a seat."

I slid in the other side of the booth and sized her up. She had dark brown hair, shoulder length, curled under at the ends. An oval face with green eyes and strong features, a long straight nose, wide mouth, high cheekbones that made all her features come together attractively. Even sitting, I could tell she was tall, five eight or so, trim and fit. I put her age at around thirty.

She was probably sizing me up, too. "Well, what do you think? Do I pass the toxicity test?" I asked casually.

I got the beginnings of a smile. "Let's hear what you want first." She dug a legal pad and pen out of a black shoulder bag.

"I'm a stockbroker. One of my clients, Joe Jesso, a wealthy, older man married a—"

Our waitress, a young girl in a white uniform, arrived. "What can I get you?"

"Just coffee," I said.

Tory shook her head. Remnants of her breakfast were still on the table. Our waitress gathered them and departed.

"Joe gets married, a week later he dies. I want to know the cause of death. Was it natural causes or something else? And I want to check this new wife's background. I have this feeling Joe may have married a black widow."

Tory nodded. "It's possible. How old was Joe?"

"Seventy-eight."

"How about the wife?"

The waitress returned, poured me a cup of coffee, departed.

"I don't know for sure," I said after she'd gone. "I heard her voice on their answering machine, though, and she sounded much younger than Joe."

"Define younger? Are we talking twenty or fifty?"

"Older than twenty. Not over thirty five."

"I gather this wedding was a surprise?"

"Sure was. Every Wednesday, Joe spent the morning with me talking stocks. He never told me he was seeing anyone. He never acted any different. I mean, he didn't act goofy because he was in love or anything. He was always calm, deliberate, organized. Then, a week ago, almost as an aside, he told me he'd gotten married."

"Did he tell you about his new wife?"

"He was evasive. That's one of the things that made me suspicious. All I got was her first name. Janet."

"No information about where they met, how long he'd known her, her background—any of that?"

I finished a sip of coffee, shook my head. "I asked if he had a photo of her; he told me she didn't like having her photo taken. I asked if I could take them out to dinner to celebrate. He said she didn't like meeting new people. Which made me wonder how she met him. Where does a seventy-eight year old man meet a thirty-year-old woman? They don't travel in the same circles."

She made a note on her pad. "That's something I can find out for you."

"I thought I'd meet her the morning I went to Joe's place to check on him. But it was her brother who met me at the door, told me Joe was dead."

"How old was the brother? Might give us some idea about her."

"Mid-thirties, I guess."

She looked over at me. "What else can you tell me about Joe? Past history? Employment? Family?"

I shook my head. "Other than he was retired, not much. When we got together, we talked investments. He never offered anything about his personal life. I never pressed."

"How about social security number? Address? That kind of stuff."

I fished my Blackberry out of my pocket, found Joe's information and gave it to her.

When she finished writing it down, she said, "What makes you think foul play was involved?"

"Joe was never sick. Didn't smoke. Took good care of himself. He marries—a week later he's dead. It's the timing. I think she killed him. How, I have no idea."

"It could be as simple as a push or a fall. Withholding medicine is common—"

"Common? You make it sound like this happens all the time."

"You'd probably be surprised how often it does happen. I looked into the death of an older man, virtually bedridden, who married his nurse. He was eighty-five, she in her late forties. His children said when he told them about the marriage, they supported it, thinking their father would get better care. Instead of giving him better care, she didn't give him his medicine. He suffered a seizure and died."

My jaw must have dropped.

"Worse, some of these women go from victim to victim."

"Don't these men—these victims—see what's going on?"

She shrugged. "All they see is a beautiful young wife."

"Poor Joe," I said, a bit overwhelmed by it all. Lawyers and private investigators accumulated some pretty grim data.

"Let's not jump to conclusions. It's possible this woman's a black widow. It's also possible this marriage was harmless and aboveboard. We'll know more once we find out what happened to him." She paused, looked directly at me. "I'm assuming you want me to begin investigating?"

I met her gaze. "I'm assuming I've passed the toxicity test?"

This time I got the full smile. "Admirably."

"The sooner the better."

Her face turned serious. "It's hard to say how much an investigation like this will cost. I charge a hundred dollars an hour. Did you have a limit on how much you were willing to spend?"

I shook my head. "No."

"Okay. To start, I require a retainer of a thousand dollars. Check's fine. I'll give you an itemized accounting."

"How long will this take? When should I expect to hear from you?"

"Depends on who and what we're dealing with."

"Are we talking two days? A week?"

"We should know something in two to three days."

That was acceptable. I got a check out of my wallet and wrote it for her retainer. I gave her one of my business cards with all my phone numbers—office, home, car, cell—on it.

She took the check and the business card, looked at the check, handed it back to me. "Before I take your money, some ground rules. Don't call and ask how I'm doing. Don't pester me or push me to go faster. When I have something to report, I'll call you. The only time I want you calling me is if you have new information that might be helpful. Got that?"

"The don't-be-a-pain-in-the-ass part? Yes."

She smiled. "Good. Then we both know our roles." She plucked the check out of my hand, dropped it in her bag. She reached across the table and shook my hand. "I'll be in touch," she said with a smug smile, slid out of the booth, and left.

I finished my coffee, left money on the table, walked out to the car. Eddie started circling excitedly when he saw me. I got in the car, patted him, put the key in the ignition. "Let's go to work, fella."

My office was a recently-restored historic Spanish-style stucco building in downtown Sarasota, burnt orange with a sign above the front door that included a white, round life preserver as the O in S.O.S. On top the life preserver read: Seattle On Stocks. On the bottom it continued: Sound Advice Can Be a Real Lifesaver.

I parked the Saab in the five-space parking garage to the side and strolled along the walkway to the front door. Eddie ran ahead of me. As soon as I opened the door, he scooted in.

"Good morning," Rosemary said as I closed the door behind me. She looked at me, made a face. "Are you all right? You don't look so good."

From the kitchen, I heard Eddie lapping water from his bowl.

I stopped, perched on the arm of the lobby sofa. "I didn't sleep well. I had dreams last night. When I talked to Dr. Swarthmore this morning, she wasn't very sympathetic. She chided me for not being Don Juan."

"She didn't."

"She wanted to know if I was seeing anybody. When I said I wasn't, she said I wasn't trying."

"Rebecca is coming over. Dan and I think the two of you would hit if off." This was a recurring conversation. Rosemary and her husband, Dan, wanted to fix me up with Rebecca, Rosemary's sister. I'd seen pictures of Rebecca. She and Rosemary could have been twins. Same round face, blue eyes, button nose. The difference was Rosemary was blond, her sister redheaded. Fortunately or unfortunately, Rebecca still lived in England.

"Maybe," I said vaguely. "The other thing that's troubling me is Joe. I just met with this investigator Julian wanted me to hire. What if she finds out Joe's new wife killed him? What do we do then?"

The phone rang. Rosemary shrugged, reached for the receiver. "Seattle on Stocks."

Eddie ambled into the lobby from the kitchen, looked at me, yawned, and headed for my office. I followed. Enough worrying. Time to get to work.

I'd just settled behind my desk when Rosemary buzzed. "Mr. Ballack on one." The start of a busy day. Oil prices had spooked the market. The Dow dropped two hundred points. I made a few buys for clients who saw this as an opportunity and grabbed a quick burger for lunch, but most of my day was spent reassuring my equities clients the drop was an aberration. By six-thirty, the calls had trickled to a stop. I turned off my computer, stood, stretched.

Eddie was asleep in his spot at the side of my desk. "Wake up, fella, let's go get something to eat." He roused himself, stood, stretched. Made me laugh. It was almost as if he were mimicking me.

We had dinner at a little place by New Pass Bridge called the Salty Dog. The manager kept Eddie's favorite dog food and a dog-food bowl on hand. We were regulars. I had the Grouper. You know what Eddie had.

After dinner we went for a walk on the nature trail, I changed clothes at the condo, and we headed to the exercise room. I did an hour running on the treadmill, an hour on the weights. That was enough. We went home and crashed.

That night, I slept well. No dreams. Had I known what was about to happen, I wouldn't have slept at all.

CHAPTER 6

The call came at work the next afternoon. Rosemary buzzed me. "There's a Tony Wright on two."

I picked up. "Hello, Tory."

She didn't bother greeting me. "I've learned some things. We need to meet immediately."

"What did you—"

"Not over the phone. I can be at your office in thirty to forty minutes. Will you be there?"

"I'll be here," I said to myself. She'd already hung up.

I stood, went out to the lobby. "That was Tory Wright. Not Tony. She'll be here in half an hour or so. When she arrives, would you show her back, please."

"Surely. My hearing must be going; you'd think Tory would be a word I'd understand."

"I only mention it because, as you'll discover, she's got a bit of an attitude."

She arched an eyebrow.

I nodded and went back to my office.

Not forty minutes later. Not thirty minutes later. Maybe not even twenty minutes later, I heard the door open. So did Eddie. His ears perked up, and his head turned toward the door. Suddenly, he trotted out to the lobby.

"You must be Ms. Wright," I heard Rosemary say in her most

polite voice.

"Matt's expecting me."

"I'll show you back."

Eddie ambled in first, altogether pleased with himself. Rosemary came next. "Right in here," she said, offering a smile and extending an arm. As soon as Tory walked past her, Rosemary crossed her eyes and left.

I almost missed the eye bit. I was busy looking at Tory. She had on a Day-Glo orange top that left her midriff exposed. Skin-tight black stretch pants. She had her big black bag over her shoulder. Her hair was pulled back in a ponytail. Sunglasses hid her eyes.

I stood. "Come in. Have a seat."

She sat in one of the visitor's chairs, took off her sunglasses, and leaned forward. "I don't want this to be interrupted. Can you cancel any appointments you have for the next hour, have her hold your calls?"

I reached for the phone, hit the intercom. "Rosemary, would you cancel anything I have for the next hour, hold all calls?"

"Would you like something to drink?" I asked Tory.

"A Diet Coke would be great."

I buzzed again. "And could you bring us two Diet Cokes? Thanks, Rosemary."

Moments later she brought in the drinks. "Would you like me to shut the door?" she asked as she left.

"Yes," Tory answered for me.

Rosemary crossed her eyes again, closed the door with just enough of a slam to make Tory jump. I could tell these two would never be best buds.

Eddie, on the other hand, obviously liked Tory. He sat next to her, rested his head on her thigh. She got a folder out of her bag, put it on the desk, found what she wanted, then reached down and absentmindedly stroked Eddie's head.

"Let's start with Joe Jesso's death." Her tone of voice said she wasn't going to sugarcoat anything. "It was natural causes, no doubt about it."

"How can you be sure?"

She frowned. Obviously didn't like being interrupted or questioned. "Oh, I'm absolutely sure. I talked to his primary care physician, Dr. Flores. Seems Jesso had been having angina for over a year and a half. Flores had him do a stress test and discovered two of his major arteries were eighty percent blocked. Flores wanted to schedule bypass surgery, but Jesso wouldn't agree to it."

She paused and took a sip of her drink. "According to the doc, Jesso had a real fear of hospitals. Lots of older people are fearful of going to the hospital, but Jesso must have been adamant. According to the EMS logs from the night he died, they responded to a frantic call from Jesso's wife saying he was having severe chest pain. One of the paramedics told me that when they loaded Jesso into the ambulance, he complained he'd never had such bad pain. It must have been the early stages of a heart attack. The paramedic said he thought Jesso suffered a massive stroke on the way to the hospital. As hard as they worked on him, there wasn't anything they could do."

"So there isn't any doubt it was natural causes?"

"None. I asked the paramedic if he thought there was any chance of foul play. He said what he saw was a heart attack in progress. With Jesso's medical history, it was just a matter of time."

"They why would Joe's brother-in-law have told me Joe died in bed?"

She shook her head. "I don't know. That's not the way it happened. Makes me wonder about this guy." She reached into a bag and pulled out a photo, handed it across the desk to me. "Let me tell you about his sister, your friend's wife. This is a rare photo of Janet

Wakeman—that's her maiden name. You have no idea how hard that photo was to come by."

I stared at the grainy enlargement. It showed an older, balding man in a plaid sport coat, his arm around the waist of a flashy blonde.

"That's Janet with her first husband, Harry Kemper," Tory continued. "I don't know whether it was her idea or his, but right after they were married, Harry footed the bill for a lot of cosmetic surgery. Janet had a nose job, breast augmentation, laser vision correction. She went from a mousy, nondescript brunette to a Pam Anderson look-alike in less than six months."

I could see what she meant. In the photo, three things stood out. Harry's leer and Janet's breasts.

"Janet was twenty-two, Harry seventy-five at the time. I'm told Harry liked to show off his attractive young wife. I'm also told that Janet—somewhat shy before her makeover—loved the attention. She was suddenly desirable and took full advantage of it, using sex to get what she wanted. One of the men she had affairs with was Harry's attorney, Greg Nevitt—"

"That's the guy who said he was her brother."

She frowned, shook her head again. "He may have said that, but he's not. We'll get to him in a minute." She glanced down at her notes, took another sip of her drink. "Harry was worth a little over three million when he died of pneumonia in 1995. Janet probably thought she was going to inherit it all. Surprise, surprise. Harry's money was tied up in trusts. Janet received a bequest for a paltry hundred thousand."

"She didn't have Nevitt alter the trusts for her?"

"No. I don't think Janet really thought about manipulating the inheritance until after her experience with Kemper. I think that's when she realized how much money she could get if she had a lawyer who could make the estate and inheritance laws work in her favor."

"So she hooked up with Nevitt."

"That's what I think. Janet remarried, almost immediately, an older man, Walter Remminger. This time, with Nevitt helping her, Janet had the will altered leaving everything to her. On that six-month marriage, she made close to half a million. Three months later, they struck again. Janet married husband number three, Sol Hecht. Nevitt restructured Hecht's estate so his three grown children received nothing and Janet received property and securities worth just under a million."

"Didn't the kids fight it?"

"Of course, but everything Wakeman and Nevitt had done was legal. It was a legal marriage. It was a legal will. The courts may not have liked it, but they had no choice."

I got up and paced around a little. "You're saying there's nothing anyone can do to stop her?"

"If she's careful, probably not. She's not doing anything illegal. In fact, as a professional trophy wife—an invention of the macho male culture—she's filling a niche."

"You sound like you're on her side."

She made a face. "Only because you're applying double standards. It's okay for a guy to have a trophy wife. But being a trophy wife is bad."

"That's not what—"

"Please, don't tell me about men," she said, her voice bitter. "They'll fuck you and forget you in a heartbeat, but if a woman takes advantage of a relationship, well now, that's wrong."

"You don't think what she did to Hecht's kids was wrong?"

"All I'm saying is she supplies what men demand. You can't put all the blame on her."

"I'm not looking to fix blame. I'm looking to fix the problem. I want to know how to stop this woman. I think Joe'd be alive today if it weren't for her."

"I didn't find any evidence that she hastened his death."

"The fact that their marriage and his death were so close together was a coincidence? I know coincidences do occur, but there's something in the back of my mind that says this one was made to happen."

She laughed, her anger dissipated. "You don't know how wrong you are. We've talked about her. Let me tell you about your friend, Joe. He wasn't the innocent old geezer you made him out to be."

I sat back down. I had a feeling I wasn't going to like hearing this.

CHAPTER 7

"Did you ask him anything about his background? Who he worked for? What he did? Any of that?"

"Of course," I said defensively. "I know he worked in loan approval at Shore Bank and Trust until he retired."

"Do you know anything about Shore Bank?"

"Not really. It's a small—"

"Do you do any business with them?"

"No. Banks—"

"You're positive you don't know anything about them."

"No." I said irritably. "What's so important about Shore Bank?"

"Didn't you think it was strange that Jesso worked for years at Shore but wrote you checks on a Northern Trust account?"

"I never thought about it."

"Do you know who owns Shore Bank? Who runs it?"

"No. I assume—"

"Never assume. Here's what you needed to know. Shore Bank is run by Don D'Onifrio. Chairman and CEO, he personally owns eighty-three percent of the bank's stock. Dee—as he likes to be called—works for the Menendez drug cartel. The only reason that bank exists is to launder drug money."

"Can't be," I said, stunned.

She grinned. "Thought that might rock you. Now you understand why I asked you all those questions. I had to be sure you weren't involved with Shore."

"Just because the bank's dirty doesn't mean Joe was. He was only a loan officer."

"Jesso made at least five trips to South America in the three years before he retired, maybe more. I didn't research farther back than that. Maybe those trips were innocent, but I think they indicate he knew the bank was in the drug business and was actively involved."

I heard the words, but they didn't compute. I visualized Joe pulling annual reports out of his battered brown briefcase. Showing me what had him intrigued about a company. The slight shake to his hands. The excitement of the chase in his voice. The whimsical smile as he decided what he wanted to do.

"No," I said adamantly. "He may have worked there, may even have made trips, but Joe wasn't the kind of person who would have been mixed up with drugs."

"I can imagine this is hard for you to accept," she said, not unkindly. "He was your friend, but Jesso was a key player in the Shore organization. He knew what he was doing. The question now is did the organization know what he was doing with you?"

"I'm not following you."

"Jesso's bank accounts were at Shore, with the exception of the account at Northern Trust he used for his activities with you. What I haven't been able to determine is where the money in the Northern Trust account came from."

"I'm still not following you."

"His accounts at Shore had regular activity—deposits, withdrawals. I didn't find any transfers to Northern Trust. The Northern Trust money was deposited to the account in large chunks, sixty-to-seventy thousand each, over the two-year period before he retired. I can't find where that money came from. It just appears there."

I didn't like where this was headed. "Are you saying it wasn't his money? That it was stolen?"

She took a sip of her soda, nodded, set the can back down. "I think it's possible he took those funds, yes."

The knot that had been forming in my stomach yanked tight. "How can we find out?"

That got a small laugh. "Well, we can't call D'Onifrio and ask if he's missing any money."

"I realize that, but what can we do?"

"If it were up to me, I wouldn't do anything. We don't know for sure it was Menendez money. If it was, they may not know it's missing."

"Isn't that taking a hell of a chance?"

"I think poking around in this—in any way, shape, or form— would be taking a hell of a lot bigger chance. As soon as I saw what was happening, I backed away. Fast. I don't want one of D'Onifrio's men visiting me in the middle of the night."

"That's what they do?" I surprised myself with how frightened I sounded.

She smiled. "I don't know what they do. I was just saying I don't want anything to do with those people."

"Well, even if it is stolen money, even if they find out he invested it with me, the money is in Joe's estate. There's nothing I can do about that."

She smiled again. "That's the other problem I need to tell you about."

CHAPTER 8

"Maybe you already know this." She gave me another one of those quizzical looks. "I made the assumption, because you know so little, you wouldn't know this either."

The lady really knew how to dish out a compliment. "Know what?" I asked peevishly.

"You're executor of Jesso's estate."

Boom. Blindsided again.

She read the bewilderment on my face. "You didn't know."

"No. He never mentioned anything about that. I knew he had very specific thoughts about where he would leave his money—a cancer institute in memory of his mother, a burn hospital, Meals on Wheels. He never shared anything about my being his executor." An interesting thought hit me. "I'm surprised I'm executor. You'd think he'd have named Nevitt or his wife. In fact, knowing what we know about her, you'd think she'd have insisted on it."

"They were married only what—a week? She probably didn't have a chance to get it changed. This probably caught her by surprise, too. Another reason I think his death really was from natural causes."

That made sense. I nodded.

She studied me for a minute. "Are you going to be able to deal with this?"

I knew where she was going. As executor, my job would be to hand over Joe's assets to Janet. I was going to be working for her. The thought made the knot in my stomach pulse.

She drained the last of her Diet Coke, closed her notebook, tucked it in her briefcase, and stood. "Well, that's all the good news I have to share today." She smiled. "Looks like it's all the good news you can handle."

She was right. I didn't need any more.

"If I hear anything else, I'll give you a call. But I think my inquiries are finished. I'll send you a memo along with an itemized statement."

"That's fine," I said wearily.

"Call me if you need anything else."

I nodded, only half hearing her, my mind scrambling for answers. Why hadn't Joe told me I was his executor? He'd hidden his background from me; what else was he hiding?

"I'll see myself out."

How much trouble was I going to have with druggies from Shore Bank? How much from Janet? That reminded me of something. "Tory, before you go, I have one other question. Were you able to find out how Joe and Janet met?"

She stopped in the doorway. "They met at A.A. Usually sat together. Often went out for coffee together after meetings."

Alcoholics Anonymous. Great place to find a vulnerable older man. "Thanks."

She continued to watch me. "You okay?"

"Just a lot to deal with. I'll be fine."

She left.

Eddie knew I was low. He came over and put his head on my thigh, stared up at me. I reached down and rubbed his ears. "We'll get through this, Eddie. We've been through worse."

Rosemary stuck her head in the door. I motioned to her. "C'mon in."

"I hope you're not mad at me," she said, sitting in the same visitor's chair Tory had just vacated.

"Why would I be mad at you?"

"I left the intercom open and listened in. I heard every word. It's horrible."

"I'm shocked. I still can't come to grips with Joe being involved in drugs." I faltered, not knowing how to put what I was feeling into words.

"I know you two were close, and I know it looks bad. But as me mum used to say, 'It's always darkest before the dawn.' Things will get better; I'm sure of it."

"What worries me is something my dad used to say."

"Oh?"

"For things to get better they must first get far worse."

Her eyes widened. "Oh, dear."

I had the feeling my dad knew more than her mum.

CHAPTER 9

That night I didn't sleep well. I had new things to give me nightmares. Somewhere around two-thirty in the morning, as I paced the condo, one brilliant idea did come to me: call Julian and see if he could get me out of being executor. That was the only bright spot in a bleak night.

Unfortunately, Julian wasn't sitting in his office waiting for my call. I tried him early, mid, and late morning, at lunchtime. He was in meetings, depositions, then court.

By two that afternoon, hope was all but extinguished. I gave up on him.

"Hold the fort," I told Rosemary as I headed out. "The Power Squadron is holding a memorial service for Joe. I should be back by four if anybody needs to talk to me."

"The Power Squadron? What would that be?"

"Tell you later," I said as Eddie and I went out the door. It would have taken too long to explain. The Power Squadron was a good-boating-practices service organization. Although Joe had never owned a boat, he'd belonged to the organization for years. I suspected it was an excuse for a group of geezers to get together, swap stories, have a few highballs, feel important. I knew Joe took the organization very seriously. He had served on the luncheon, welcoming, and burial-at-sea committees.

Power Squadron headquarters turned out to be a white, one-story, flat-roofed, concrete-block building with few windows and fewer nautical touches. On the plus side, it did have a generous parking lot. I cruised the lanes looking for a spot, my Saab an alien in the land of Florida Fords. I parked and followed a stooped man with a cane into the building.

Inside, I found a large, dimly-lit room, two dozen older men and one or two women, all chatting and milling about. Card table chairs had been set up in rows facing a lectern. I'd entered at the back of the room. As I glanced around, getting my bearings, I saw Janet Wakeman and Greg Nevitt talking to a bald man in what looked like a naval uniform complete with insignia and ribbons and gold braid on the sleeves.

I watched as he motioned Janet and Greg to seats in the first row and stepped up on the raised platform and walked to the lectern. He adjusted his glasses, got them to his liking, surveyed the audience. Apparently, he found it to his liking also. He banged his gavel on the lectern. "Please take seats and we'll get started."

I found a seat in the back and counted heads. Thirty-two.

"We're here to pay tribute to one of our own, Joseph Jesso, a sailor who has made his final voyage. We'll begin with a prayer. I call on Chaplain Richard Greier."

The Chaplain stepped up and recited—in a high, sing-song voice—the seaman's prayer.

I joined in the "Amen" at the end, sat back, and listened as the guy in the fancy uniform stepped back to the podium and delivered a few terse remarks. He kept glancing past me. I looked back and discovered what he was watching for: the bar was now open.

He quickly finished his remarks about "our shipmate Joseph," presented a proclamation encased in a cheap, thin wooden frame to Janet, and declared the memorial service adjourned. He strode confidently from the podium toward the bar, shaking hands as he went.

That was enough for me. I stood and headed for the door. I was just reaching for the doorknob when a hand on my shoulder pulled me to a stop. I turned. Nevitt.

"I didn't expect to see you here, Seattle," he said with a sneer. "But it saves me the trouble of calling you. I'm having you removed as executor. I want you to know that."

The confrontational way he said it made me angry. I took a deep breath, forced myself to reply calmly. "I can understand that as a lawyer, you're probably more qualified to handle things. That's fine with me. Give my condolences to your sister." I turned to go.

"I want the money back you cheated Joe out of," he said belligerently. "You ripped off the old guy. You're not getting away with it."

"What are you talking about?" A crowd was beginning to form around us.

"You kept buying and selling his stocks so you could run up commissions. You made a lot of money at his expense. You stole his retirement."

"I did not."

"Yeah, right. Tell that to the N.A.S.D."

Mention of the National Association of Securities Dealers hit me like a Mike Tyson uppercut. They were the group that looked into securities fraud. With them, you were guilty until proven innocent. "Tell what to the N.A.S.D.?"

"I filed a complaint charging you with churning, and I demanded damages. You're not going to get away with preying on the elderly."

Some of the geezers in the crowd were beginning to nod, say, "Yeah."

"I didn't do anything Joe didn't want done," I said defensively and left.

I got in the Saab, drove out of there. I was too agitated to drive while I was using the car phone, so I pulled into the parking lot of a convenience store and dialed Julian's number. Amanda, his assistant, answered.

"Amanda, I need to talk to him. This is an emergency." In a moment, Julian was on the line.

"Listen, I know I should—"

"Forget about that. I've got big trouble. Nevitt just told me he's filed a complaint against me with National Association of Securities Dealers."

"What kind of complaint?"

"Churning. He's demanding damages."

"What's churning? Why is he demanding damages?"

"Churning is when a broker buys and sells stocks rapidly to make more commissions. The faster the portfolio is churned, the more money is made. Accusations of churning are reviewed by a mediator who has the authority to award damages."

"Okay, I understand what it is. But you didn't churn this guy, Matt. What are you worried about?"

"I bought and sold a lot of stocks for him. He liked to get in and out of things quickly. Could be close to 400% a year. If it is, I'm dead. The N.A.S.D. automatically pulls your license."

"Oh."

"Even if it isn't, I'm going to look guilty. This is bad. Really bad."

"What do you think he's looking to get out of this?"

"That's easy—money. I think he's going to try and get back every commission Joe ever paid me and then some."

"Has he already filed charges?"

"He said he had. He said he was going to get me removed as executor and had filed charges with the N.A.S.D."

"Removed as executor? He said that?"

"He sure did."

"That's what this churning charge is all about. He's going to use that as grounds to have you removed. Hang on a minute."

He was gone a long time. I watched traffic whiz past, aware that my life had come to a screeching halt.

Julian returned. "Here it is—removal of a fiduciary. There are sections of the revised code that require probate court to 'remove a fiduciary found guilty of having concealed, embezzled, conveyed away, or been in the possession of moneys, chattels, or chouses in action of the trust estate.' That's got to be what he's up to."

"Julian, I don't care about being executor. I'd prefer not to be. But these N.A.S.D. charges scare the hell out of me. They could put me out of business."

"Let me look into it," he said soothingly. "Maybe we can get them dismissed."

"Can't you file a countersuit or something?"

"Let me look into it. He's trying to scare—"

"He's succeeding." Nevitt was at least two steps ahead of me. His sloppy appearance had caused me to underestimate a devious mind.

"Stay tough," Julian said and hung up.

I replaced the car phone in the cradle. Eddie, in the passenger seat, watched me. "We've got to stay tough, Eddie." I gave him a pat on the back, put the car in gear, and headed back into traffic.

Going to the memorial service had been a bad idea. I was the one who got buried.

CHAPTER 10

Three days later, at two in the afternoon, the N.A.S.D. arrived at my office. There were four of them: two suits, two grunts. Eddie took one look at them and wrinkled his nose, his way of letting me know they were trouble.

One of the suits introduced himself as Jack Fowler. He was a thin man with a thin, taciturn-looking face, thinning hair. He was wearing a dark blue pin stripe. The suit in charge.

"Mr. Seattle," he said politely, "we're from the N.A.S.D. I'm assuming you know you've been accused of securities violations?" He gave me a thin smile.

I was so nervous I could hardly talk. "Violations? I knew about the churning accusation. I didn't know there were more."

Second suit—a younger version of Fowler—said, "Try and stay calm, Mr. Seattle. This isn't a witch-hunt. We're not here to frighten you. We're only here to expedite an adjudication."

"In matters like this," Fowler continued, "our role is to collect data, which means we're going to need your transaction records."

Second suit nodded in agreement. "It would be in your best interests to cooperate with us fully. While this isn't a witch-hunt, in these types of situations you are guilty until proven innocent."

"I'm going to cooperate," I assured them eagerly. They'd reduced me to an obedient child. I wanted them to like me, to tell me it was going to be all right. "I haven't done anything wrong. I don't have anything to hide. Tell me what records you need and I'll get them for you." I hated myself for being so frightened.

Fowler gave me another of his thin smiles, plopped a wad of papers in my hand with a slap. "It's all detailed in there. Nothing personal, you understand. We're just doing our jobs." He looked over at the grunts. "Start with the computers. Then the paper files."

I'd expected them to ask me for Joe's account file.

The grunts unplugged Rosemary's computer. Rosemary began to cry.

"What are you doing?" I demanded anxiously. "Why are you taking that computer? I'll get you copies of the records you want."

Eddie, who had been watching the strangers, must have heard the concern in my voice. He growled. Low, threatening growls.

Second suit eyed Eddie carefully.

"It's okay, Eddie," I said. The growling stopped.

Second suit gave me a patronizing smile. "Those documents," he indicated the wad of papers Fowler had handed me, "are a court order. It's all spelled out in there. We have authorization to take all your files."

The grunts went back to work. I stared at the top sheet of papers. It was a subpoena. I didn't look further. I felt sick as I watched them carry Rosemary's computer out the door to their truck. The two grunts came back in, found my office, and disconnected my computer.

"Why do you need to take both computers? They have the same information. You don't need them both."

"Please, Mr. Seattle, don't make it worse than it has to be," Fowler said in a keep-a-stiff-upper-lip tone.

"When will I get my stuff back?"

Fowler frowned. "Hard to say. Depends on the arbitrators, what they decide."

The grunts began wheeling out my lateral files.

"How do they expect me to service my clients when you're taking away everything?"

Fowler came over, stood very close to me, said, "Mr. Seattle, our job is to make sure abuses within the brokerage industry are curtailed. It's not our fault your customers are being inconvenienced. I'll remind you that it was your customer practices that triggered this investigation."

I couldn't believe he'd said that. I lost it. "You pompous bastard, how dare you accuse me of bad practices. The fellow I made these trades for approved every one of them. If you were doing your homework instead of harassing me, you'd have found out this is a totally false, self-serving complaint by an outsider who didn't know anything about these trades."

Fowler never blinked an eyelid. "Are you finished?"

"Of course, I am," I shouted in his face. "I can't do anything if you take all my records."

Eddie picked up the anger in my voice, started barking. A rare display.

Neither the shouting nor the barking seemed to faze Fowler. He looked over at second suit. "Note in our report that Mr. Seattle threatened me and was abusive." He looked back at me. "We're not to blame here. You brought this on yourself. Your behavior now only makes matters worse."

"That's all the file cabinets," one of the grunts said.

Fowler smiled. "Good. We'll be leaving then. I advise you to read those papers carefully, Mr. Seattle. You're in serious trouble. Serious trouble indeed."

I stood there—stunned. As I watched them drive away, my anger dissolved into depression. The internal questioning began: Why had I lashed out at them? Why hadn't I treated these people like my new best friends? Why hadn't I learned more about the charges?

"This is so unfair," Rosemary said angrily, standing behind her desk. "You were so nice to Joe. All those times you tried to put him on fee to save him money."

She was right. There was irony in this. One of the few things Joe and I had argued about was commissions. Joe'd insisted I charge him by the trade. Since I bought and sold a lot of equities for him, those commissions added up. What I would have preferred to do was charge him a percentage on the assets I managed. I'd even put together a comparison, complete with pie charts, that showed moving to a 1% fee made sense for him.

He'd smiled benignly, dismissing my efforts on his behalf. "Matt, I'm more comfortable paying you when you do something for me, and that's the way it's going to stay."

We'd argued over it enough it had gotten to be a sore point with him. If I even looked like I was about to mention a fee, he'd cut me off, change the subject.

The phone rang. "What do I say?" Rosemary wanted to know.

"Tell them I'll call them back," I said.

Forced to come up with a plan of action. I did. "I'll go buy new computers; we'll load the programs off the back-up CDs in the fireproof safe. We should be back up and running in a couple hours."

It was closer to four. At the computer store, I was like a kid in a candy shop. A year ago, when I'd bought the computers, I'd bought basic utility. Now, I had the opportunity to upgrade. I got something stylish for Rosemary. A system with a black, flat-screen monitor, larger hard drive, more functionality. For myself, I chose a system with large-screen monitor and the ability to sync to a new laptop and my Blackberry. I loaded it all in the Saab, feeling like I'd gotten every bell and whistle.

I hoped I'd stay in business long enough to use all these toys.

CHAPTER 11

Back at the office, I had a pile of pink phone message slips waiting for me. I ignored them, picked up the phone, dialed Julian's number. Amanda answered. "He's taking a deposition. I expect him back around eight. Want me to have him call you?"

I looked at my watch. It was seven. Enough time for me to run out, bring back a bite before he called. "Sure. Tell him I'm at the office."

There was a Chinese place, Hop Luck's, a block away. I got an order of chicken fried rice, carried it back. In the office kitchen, I fixed Eddie a bowl of dog food, and we ate in silence. When we were finished, he went and stood by the back door.

I let him out, stood on the back stoop while he sniffed around to find the perfect spot. It was nice out. The heat of the day had passed, the noise of downtown commuted to the suburbs.

Inside, the phone rang. I left the door open for Eddie, hustled in to take it in my office.

"Matt, it's Julian. Amanda said to call as soon as I got in."

"I had the N.A.S.D. here this afternoon, Julian. They took all my computers, my files. Can they do that?"

"They'd have to have a subpoena to impound your property."

I picked up the wad of papers Fowler had handed me. "They did."

"That means they had this approved by a judge and the arbiter. They're moving this along. Usually, in this kind of case, the other side tries to wear you down by asking for more and more information. With you, they wanted it all at once."

"What's that mean?"

"I'll have to talk to the N.A.S.D. to find out for sure."

"Ask for Fowler. He was the guy in charge."

I heard a click. Probably the top coming off his Mont Blanc. Scratches as he wrote down the name. "I'll call first thing in the morning. My guess is Nevitt is posturing for your removal as executor."

"Can we cut a deal here? Tell him I won't be executor if he'll drop these churning charges?"

"I called him, floated something like that to see if he'd go for it. He didn't. He wants money. Specifically, return of all brokerage fees and damages for malfeasance."

"Damages? How can he expect damages?"

"If the N.A.S.D. rules in Nevitt's favor, he's set to file a complaint on behalf of the estate seeking damages for malfeasance."

"Can he do that?"

"I'm afraid he can. There's precedent for a malfeasance suit. He can cite good case law supporting his position. But if the N.A.S.D. rules in our favor, Nevitt doesn't have a case. Let me call this guy, Fowler, sound him out, see what we're up against. I'll call you as soon as I hear something."

"Thanks, Julian." I hung up, walked to the back door to check on Eddie. He was lying in a patch of grass, the last of the day's sun on his back. "Tanning, huh?"

He looked at me, yawned, put his head back down.

I did the dishes, hooked the computers to the network, loaded the software and data. Once I had it all put together, I called up Joe's account and ran the numbers. In the six full calendar quarters we'd worked together, the percentages were: 43, 61, 90, 130, 86, 78.

Considering that Joe often bought stocks and sold them a few days later, the numbers weren't as bad as I feared. High, but not over the magic number.

I looked at my watch. Ten to ten. I turned off the computers, the lights. Tried to turn off my mind. I couldn't stop worrying. Especially when I realized there was something Julian hadn't told me—the amount of the damages Nevitt wanted.

I got a chance to ask him next morning. He called at nine. "I just got a fax from Nevitt. We have a hearing Thursday morning at ten o'clock. Judge Nancy Ott's court."

I entered it in my Blackberry. "Why so soon? Why isn't he waiting until after the N.A.S.D. hearing? That doesn't make sense."

"Sure it does. Ott is one of those judges who favor women. All she has to hear is the suggestion that you've wronged Janet Jesso, and she'll rule in her favor. On the other hand, if you're found innocent in the N.A.S.D. arbitration, Nevitt doesn't have anything. It's the suggestion of impropriety he wants."

"What do you think will happen?"

"They got lucky when they drew Judge Ott. Based on her past rulings, she'll side with them. She'll remove you. That's not all bad since you don't want to be executor. On the other hand, removal will add credence to Nevitt's malfeasance suit."

"Did Nevitt tell you what he wants in damages?"

"No, and I didn't ask. Judging by the way he was talking—compensatory and punitive damages—I think he's going for the moon."

"Julian, do we need to bring in a junkyard-dog attorney for this?" Julian was a good corporate attorney. He wasn't a litigator.

"I'm working on that, I know a litigator who can give Nevitt a run for his money."

"Get him, quick."

"Her," he said.

"Would that help us with Judge Ott?"

"Might. I'll call you back when I know more."

At eleven, Rosemary buzzed me. "Julian again." I picked up.

"Fowler called me back. I introduced myself, said I'd be representing you, played a little dumb. Here's what he told me. Nevitt filed the complaint against you the day after Jesso's death. Their compliance people felt—even though the marriage was only a week old—it was a valid marriage, hence a valid complaint. He said that based on the allegations they feel an investigation is warranted. They'll listen to arguments for dismissal only at arbitration. I asked for their date for arbitration so we'd know how long we have to prepare. They told me two to three weeks from now at the earliest."

"Why so long?"

"Apparently, the N.A.S.D. doesn't move quickly. Which is good. We need time to prepare for this probate court appearance. I've arranged for Amy Quell to litigate for us. You'll be impressed. She's terrific."

He wasn't wrong. Julian, Amy, and I met twice at his office to prepare. Amy was short and wide, with a chubby round face, long stringy black hair, and a booming voice. She had an exceptionally quick mind and seemed to have an answer for everything. I left our meetings actually feeling confident.

My confidence ebbed Thursday as I entered the Sarasota County Courthouse. Nervous, I'd arrived too early. I loitered in the lobby with most of the city's known felons.

At precisely the appointed time, Julian swept in, Amy in his wake. "You look a little green," she said to me.

I nodded. "I'll be glad when this is over."

Amy studied me. "You know the drill? You didn't forget? I answer all questions."

I nodded nervously.

"Let's head on in," Julian said.

I followed them into Judge Ott's courtroom. Amy talked to the bailiff.

"We're on in ten minutes," she told us.

I used the time to get a sense of Judge Ott, an older woman with wispy, gray hair and a shriveled-prune face. She was reading someone the riot act, her voice shrill, penetrating.

"What's going on?" I asked Amy.

She snickered. "Looks like this guy can't account for all the assets in the estate. She'll crucify him; just watch."

I did. It was painful. All I could think about was that could be me up there.

"Jesso vs. Seattle," a male voice called out.

Suddenly, it was me up there. We stood at our table in front of the Judge. Nevitt and the widow Jesso were at their table. The bailiff read the complaint. Judge Ott peered down from her bench, squinting at them, squinting at us.

"Counselor," she said, indicating Nevitt. "I want to hear from you, succinctly, why you believe I should remove Mr. Seattle as executor."

"Your Honor," Nevitt began, "my client learned from her husband—"

"Hearsay, your Honor," Amy bellowed.

Judge Ott looked at Amy, frowned. "Overruled. I want to hear this. You'll get your say."

"Thank you, your Honor," Nevitt said gracefully. "My client's husband felt his stockbroker, Mr. Seattle, was cheating him, that he was buying and selling Mr. Jesso's stocks to run up the commissions he earned. This rapid buying and selling of stocks is called churning. Mr. Seattle is now under investigation by the National Association of Securities Dealers."

Ott squinted at me. Her frown deepened. "That's disturbing."

"Yes it is, your Honor. My client is fearful that, as executor, Mr. Seattle will churn the estate further to create even more income for himself. Since Mrs. Jesso is the sole beneficiary of the estate, there's no reason to subject her to that threat. We ask that under the Florida revised code," he read a series of numbers and sites, "Mr. Seattle be removed as fiduciary and the Court appoint an executor to serve in that capacity. Thank you, your Honor."

Ott's head pivoted. She stared at Amy. "Counselor, let's hear your side of it. Again, be respectful of the Court's time."

"We will, your Honor," Amy said confidently. "Mr. Seattle was Mr. Jesso's stockbroker for over a year and a half. At any time during that period, Mr. Jesso could have stopped using Mr. Seattle's services. He didn't. The fact is, Mr. Jesso had a very good relationship with my client, often spending long periods of time at his offices discussing stocks. I think that's important because it shows Mr. Jesso was a stock enthusiast, a man who liked to buy and sell. Mr. Seattle didn't churn Mr. Jesso's account. Mr. Jesso liked to move quickly in and out of the market. Your Honor, if you were to look at trading records of stock enthusiasts like Mr. Jesso, I believe you'd see even more frenetic patterns of trading. The churning charges filed by Mr. Nevitt are a self-serving ploy—"

"Objection, your Honor," Nevitt said quickly.

"Overruled. I heard what you had to say. I want to hear what she has to say—without interruption."

"Thank you, your Honor. We believe the churning charges filed by Mr. Nevitt were trumped up to give grounds for Mr. Seattle's dismissal. We ask you to look past this ploy. Further, the Jessos were married only a week before Mr. Jesso's death. This was Mrs. Jesso's third marriage—that we can uncover—all to wealthy, older men. Because this marriage was only a week old, Mrs. Jesso hadn't gotten control of her husband's money. We believe that's what this fiduciary removal request is about—getting Mr. Seattle out of the way so Mrs. Jesso can gain exclusive control of Mr. Jesso's estate. We ask, your Honor, that Mr. Seattle be retained as fiduciary."

Judge Ott scowled. All the wrinkles in her prune face shifted. She glanced back and forth at us, at them, then consulted a large book, using her index finger to flip noisily through the pages. She found what she wanted, squinted at it for a minute, flipped around further, found something else.

The tension was killing me.

Finally, she looked up, made a loud, sucking sound as she took a deep breath. "Mr. Nevitt, I find no evidence that supports your contention that Mr. Seattle took advantage of Mr. Jesso. In fact, the evidence supports quite the contrary. It appears that Mr. Jesso and Mr. Seattle had a beneficial long-term relationship, a relationship strong enough that Mr. Jesso named Mr. Seattle his executor. Why you would choose to attack Mr. Seattle rather than work with him is not clear to me. However, you have chosen this course of action and have undoubtedly incurred the animus of Mr. Seattle. I see no reason why Mr. Seattle should be punished to serve your ends. I see no reason why he should be asked to administer a hostile estate, especially since Mrs. Jesso is the only beneficiary." She sucked in more air in another of those deep breaths. "Therefore, I am removing Mr. Seattle from his obligation as executor and will name an officer of the court to serve as executor. Do you understand my ruling, Mr. Nevitt?"

"I do your Honor. I have one small concern."

"Speak up, Mr. Nevitt. Let's hear it."

"With all due respect, your Honor. There is considerable indication Mr. Seattle substantially overcharged for his services. We are preparing to file criminal charges to recover those monies. I'm concerned that an outside executor might complicate this process."

"Don't talk around the issue, Nevitt. Say what's on your mind."

"Your Honor, I'd like you to appoint me executor of the Jesso estate."

"Objection, your Honor," Amy yelled in outrage. "As executor, he'd be able to orchestrate the facts to suit his case."

"Not true," Nevitt corrected her matter-of-factly. "What's happened has already been recorded. The N.A.S.D. has that information and will issue their own verdict on malfeasance. That's not the issue. The issue is Mrs. Jesso. She's the sole beneficiary of the estate. As the sole beneficiary, she would like me to serve as executor, both to make sure the assets are properly administered and to make sure she isn't denied justice in recovering what has been wrongly taken from her."

"Your Honor," Amy snorted. "Mrs. Jesso was married to Mr. Jesso for one week. Hardly enough time for her to understand Mr. Jesso's stock portfolio, much less—"

"Be quiet," Judge Ott ordered.

Amy was.

"Mrs. Jesso, do you want Mr. Nevitt as executor of the estate?"

"Yes, your Honor," she answered meekly.

Ott looked over at me. "Mr. Seattle, would you feel at risk if Mr. Nevitt were executor?"

I looked at Amy for direction.

"I don't want her opinion, I want yours, Mr. Seattle"

"I wouldn't feel comfortable with him as executor," I answered honestly.

"I'm not comfortable with it, either," Judge Ott said reflectively. "Mr. Nevitt, the best I can do for you is make you co-executor with an appointed officer of the court. That officer will report to me. If he senses any impropriety, you'll find yourself in front of me again, and it won't be pleasant. Understand?"

"Yes, your Honor," Nevitt mumbled.

"All right," she concluded. "Mr. Seattle, you are excused, through no fault of your own, from serving as executor of Mr. Jesso's estate. That will be noted on my ruling. Mr. Nevitt, you are appointed co-executor. The court will be in contact with you with the appointment of the other co-executor."

She looked at her watch, then the bailiff. "Next on the docket."

We were dismissed.

We turned to leave, and I caught a glimpse of a young blond man in a flashy green sharkskin suit staring at us.

"I thought it went pretty well," Amy said when we were back in the lobby.

"It did, thanks to you," I said. "You did a wonderful job."

She smiled, obviously pleased. "Don't tell me that," she warned. "I bill accordingly." She patted me on the shoulder. "Just kidding."

"We're not finished yet," Julian said soberly. "This suit concerns me. We need to begin preparing for that as soon as possible." He looked over at me. "I'll have Amanda call both of you and schedule a time to begin. Is that okay?" We nodded. "See you both then." He waved as he walked off.

I thanked Amy again and headed out of the building to my car. The man in the sharkskin suit fell in step next to me. He looked over at me. "Mr. Seattle, can I talk to you for a minute?"

I stopped, turned to face him. He was young, thin, not too tall. With hard black eyes, close-cropped blond hair, weak chin. The gaudy sharkskin suited him. The way he looked at me, I could tell the kid had an attitude. "This isn't a very good time. What's it about?"

He grinned, revealing crooked, pointed teeth. "Joe Jesso's stocks."

"What about them?"

"It'd be better to talk in your office. More private, if you get my drift."

This guy gave me the creeps. "Call my office. We'll schedule an appointment."

He sneered. "I don't think so. I'll be by tomorrow afternoon." It wasn't a statement. It was a threat.

CHAPTER 12

The dreams came that night. At 3:10, I woke in a sweat, sheets tangled around me. Eddie rested his head on my hand and whimpered. He sensed it was bad.

I'd been reliving my visit to the wrecked van in the police lot. There amidst all the other wrecked and impounded cars, a silver van with the front horribly caved in. Only shards of window glass remaining. The front passenger door cut away. The front seat stained with blood. On the floor by the brake pedal, one of Claire's sandals. Across the seat, Michael's backpack on the floor. Seeing the car, I'd realized the horror of their last moments.

Eddie licked my hand. I let him for a moment, then rubbed his ears. I wondered if dogs dreamed. Was that why Eddie was always awake by the side of my bed?

I untangled from the sheets, got up. I went into the bathroom and splashed water on my face. I was a bundle of nerves. Something about that blond guy had frightened me. Eddie padded in after me, looked up, and yawned.

"I agree," I said to him. "It's too early to be up." I headed to the kitchen, raided the fridge for a glass of wine, took it to the library, read for half an hour.

Eddie was snoring when I put the book down and went back to bed. I slept fitfully, finally waking for good at five-thirty. At seven, I called Dr. Swarthmore.

"Matt," she said when she came on the phone. "Good to hear from you although I didn't expect it to be so soon."

"I didn't either. But I had another dream last night." As I recounted it for her, I heard her making notes.

"Let's talk about the good and bad," she said when I finished. "This dream was farther along a time continuum than many of your other ones. I think that may be significant, an indication you're in the final stages of the grieving process. I am concerned, however, that this dream came so close to your last one. You said you felt your friend Joe's death triggered the last dream. What do you think triggered this one?"

I told her about the churning charges, my court appearance, the fellow who'd threatened me.

"That's a lot of stress for anyone, Matt. I'm not qualified to advise you on your professional issues, but I do think you need to find relief, an outlet for some of this stress. Can you take a day off? Go fishing?"

"I've never been much of a fisherman. I do play golf."

"Perfect. Get up a foursome. Do it today."

Why not? A little client golf might be just the ticket. I could relax, do a little bonding with some of my better clients, maybe even avoid any further bad news or threats.

At the office, I booked a one o'clock tee time at the Longboat Key Country Club. In three more calls, I had my foursome: Luis Santoro, prominent antique dealer. Tom Westerkamp, retired ad guru. Greg Alwes, real estate developer. A good, congenial group.

I worked like a banshee the rest of the morning, skipped lunch. Eddie and I bolted out the door at twelve-thirty. "Have a good time," I heard Rosemary call after us.

We met in the clubhouse, walked to the first tee together. Next to me, Eddie pranced around like a pup.

I was the last to hit. I took a couple of practice swings with my driver, cleared my mind. Took a cleansing breath. Swung. From behind me, Eddie took off like a rocket. Joyfully, he ran down the fairway after the ball, tracking it down, positioning himself next to it to let me know where it was.

"I knew about bird dogs," Greg said watching him, "I've never seen a golf dog before."

"You should get one," Luis said, his voice soft, resonant. "Maybe, you wouldn't lose so many balls."

"The way Greg hits 'em, any dog would be worn out after the first hole," Tom added, laughing.

Caught up in the banter, I felt myself relax. Dr. Swarthmore had been right. I'd needed this. So had Eddie.

We played nine, had drinks and told stories in the bar, went into the dining room for dinner. Told more stories over dinner. At one point, Tom had me laughing so hard that tears streamed down my face. I hated for the meal, the camaraderie to end. After saying good-bye to each of them in the parking lot, Eddie and I got in the Saab, headed to the office. I wanted to see what had gone on this afternoon.

Pinned to the back of my desk chair so I couldn't miss it, I found a note from Rosemary:

Matt, Two things you should know. Fowler called. Wants you to call him at his office as soon as possible. He said to call even if it's late. Wouldn't tell me what this was about. Also, a strange man came looking for you. When I said you weren't here, he got really angry. He said you knew he was coming? I couldn't find an appointment. I tried to make one, but he stormed out. Sorry. R.

He'd kept his threat. Whatever he wanted, I had a feeling, I'd just made it worse, even if I was following doctor's orders.

CHAPTER 13

I couldn't do anything about him then, but I could take care of Fowler. I looked in the rolodex for his card, found his office number and dialed it, thinking he wouldn't be there and I'd leave a message.

To my surprise, he answered. "Mr. Seattle, thank you for returning my call. I wonder if you might clarify something for me."

"I'll try."

"Mr. Jesso's records indicate a thousand shares of P&G purchased on April 6th and sold on May 12th. Two-hundred-fifty shares of Dell purchased on June 1st and sold July 1st. Three-hundred-fifty shares of G.E. purchased June 23rd and sold June 30th. Six-hundred shares of Pfizer purchased on June 28th and sold on July 10th. What can you tell me about those transactions?"

"I don't think I can tell you anything. Those aren't transactions I executed for Joe. Maybe someone else made them for him."

"Are you sure? They have your number on them." He was referring to the identifying number assigned each broker.

"My number? Can't be." I switched on my computer, called up the trade blotters that detailed Joe's file. I knew they wouldn't be there. They weren't.

"You say they're on my buy/sell confirmation forms?"

"They're not on your forms, no."

"Well, that's it then," I said confidently. "Somebody is throwing those trades my way." Throwing a trade was how brokers described giving someone else credit for the transaction. Usually, it happened if you had someone in your office who was sick or needed additional income for some reason. Even though you made the trade, you put their number on the transaction so they earned the commission. "What's the company? Maybe we can clear this up."

"I'm afraid it's not going to be quite that easy."

"Why?"

"It's your old firm—"

"Merrill Lynch in Detroit?"

"Merrill Lynch here in Sarasota."

"That doesn't make sense. They helped me when I first moved down here, but since I set up my brokerage I haven't had any dealings with them. I'm a local competitor."

"That may be, Mr. Seattle, but the fact is these transactions have your number on them."

"What about dates? What about Merrill's blotters? This is all trumped—"

"Mr. Seattle, please, my purpose in calling you was to shed light on these transactions. At the proper time, you'll have your chance to refute them."

I wasn't so sure about that. There wasn't any mystery to me about why these transactions had suddenly surfaced. Nevitt must have calculated I wasn't to the four hundred percent automatic loss of license yet, and had someone throw some trades my way. I had Fowler repeat the buys for me, asked him to fax me copies of the slips. When we were finished on the phone, I did the math. Sure enough. I was at four hundred and two percent.

I went back to my rolodex, found Tory's number. She could uncover who threw the trades. I dialed her number, got her machine. At the beep, I said, "Tory, it's Matt Seattle. I could use your help again. I need to find out who at Merrill Lynch made some stock transactions and put my broker's number on them. Can you give me a call and let me know a time we can get together. Thanks. 'Bye."

I hung up the receiver, started to check my voice mail, changed my mind. "C'mon, Eddie," I said. "Let's go home."

Back at the condo, I changed into my workout clothes, headed down to the gym. I did an hour on the machines, hour on the treadmill. By the time I finished, I felt it. Eddie and I went for a quick walk. I took a shower, and went to bed.

I didn't have dreams that night but woke to a torrential downpour. August was the rainy season, but that August was unusually wet. I stood and looked out the bedroom window. Rain fell in sheets. Eddie didn't like going out any more than I did, but he cooperated with a very quick walk. Didn't help, we still got soaked.

The drive to work was a mess. With Florida's poor drainage, the roads—especially the ones around St. Armand's Circle—were flooded, water often half way up the Saab's wheel wells.

Eddie, sitting in the front passenger seat, was trembling. He didn't like the noise of the high water under the car. I reached over and patted him. "Not a fit day out for man or beast, I know, but we'll get there."

We got our second soaking of the morning making the dash from the car to the front door. Inside, Eddie shook. My third soaking. Finished, he gave me kind of an oh-did-I-do-that look and trotted into my office.

I went to the kitchen, dried myself off with paper towels, made coffee, and carried a cup back to my office. I heard the squeak of the front door opening, the flap, flap, flap of some one shaking out an umbrella, followed by a distinct sniff, sniff, sniff.

"It's wet dog I'm smelling," Rosemary announced as she appeared in the doorway of my office. I watched her sniff, sniff, sniff, again. "Wet owner, too."

I laughed. "She's making fun of us, Eddie. Go shake next to her."

"Don't ya dare. I'm a mess already." She fluffed her hair. "Look at my hair. I'm a fright."

Fluffing hadn't helped. Her blond hair hung limp. "I'd give you some of my curl if I could. You know that."

She waved a hand at me. "Oh, go on. Rub it in." The telephone rang, and she left to get it. "Took me forever and a day to get in; now they're probably calling to tell us to evacuate."

I looked out the window. The rain didn't look like it had let up a bit. Niagara Falls was pouring off the roof.

I was busy that morning, the day's normal business plus catch-up from yesterday's time out of the office. I was placing a list of orders when Rosemary buzzed me. "Your friend Tory on two."

"Got your message," Tory said. "I hope this is something we can discuss over the phone."

I looked at the copies Fowler had faxed to me. It would be difficult to explain about thrown trades over the telephone. "I've got stuff you need to see. Is there a time we can meet?"

"You want to go out in this? God, it must be an emergency. Hang on." She put me on hold. Came back a minute later. "I wasn't planning on going out today."

"What a wuss."

She laughed. "I may be a wuss, but you're going to have to come to me."

"Where?" I asked.

"Pier Grille? About four?"

"Good choice. If it doesn't let up, I can get there by boat."

I'd said it as a joke, but as I drove to Anna Maria Island, I wished I had a boat. Low areas that had been puddles on my drive in that morning were lakes. Stalled cars marked most of the deep spots. The Saab hit a couple I thought would do us in. It took us a while, but we made it to the Pier Grille, only to find their entire parking lot under water. I parked as close to the door as I could in what I hoped was the shallow end of the pool. I stepped out of the car and water rose above my ankles. Eddie was happy to stay in the car.

I probably looked like a drowned rat by the time I made it inside. I spotted Tory in the same booth by the window. She looked pleased with herself—and dry.

I dripped my way over, slid into the booth, wiped water off my briefcase.

She laughed at me. "You're sure we couldn't have done this over the phone?"

"What? And miss all the fun I had getting here? No way." I reached into my briefcase, took out copies of the Merrill Lynch orders, spread them out on the table between us, explained thrown trades.

"So you want to know who at Merrill Lynch bought and sold these stocks and put your number on them?"

"Exactly. The other thing I need to know is that person's connection to Nevitt. If we can find that, I can get these churning charges dismissed."

A waitress came over, asked me if I wanted anything. Tory had a cup of coffee in front of her. I asked for one, too.

After the waitress left, Tory asked, "Won't whoever did this at Merrill Lynch get in big trouble?"

"Kicked out of the business."

"So that person's not going to want to cooperate, and the company won't want this exposed."

Our waitress brought my coffee, refilled Tory's cup and left.

Tory frowned, focused her gaze on me. "I want to be upfront with you about this. I'll look into it for you, but I can't promise anything. This is fairly sophisticated stuff. I have to assume whoever did it wouldn't have made and won't make a stupid mistake. I don't think this is going to be easy or quick. I wouldn't even know what to tell you in the way of an estimate."

"Don't worry about an estimate. See what you can find." I took a sip of my coffee. "Do you need another retainer?"

She nodded.

"Thousand dollars?"

She nodded again, gathered up the papers.

I got a check out of my briefcase, wrote it out, handed it to her.

She took the check, dropped it in her black bag. "I'll call as soon as I know something." She left a couple of dollars on the table and departed.

I sat there, sipped my coffee. She'd been right. Nobody was going to fess up to this. The best I could hope for was finding a connection between one of the brokers and Nevitt. I left a couple of dollars for my coffee, started to slide out of the booth. My cell rang. I got it out of my briefcase. "Matt Seattle."

"Matt," Rosemary said. "That man who came yesterday? He's back. And he won't leave."

CHAPTER 14

I hustled out of there, sloshed through the parking lot, jumped in the car, and headed for town. From the passenger seat, Eddie cocked his head and looked at me. Probably wondering why I was so agitated. I stroked his head. "It's back to the office, fella. Quick meeting, then we'll go home."

An agonizing hour later, I pulled the Saab into the parking area, turned off the ignition. Eddie and I made a run for the front door.

Inside, Rosemary sat rigid behind her desk, the stranger stretched out nonchalantly on the lobby sofa. He got up when I came in, grinned at me.

"Didn't I say call for an appointment?"

His eyes narrowed. "You should have been here yesterday when I told you I was coming," he said, an edge to his voice.

"Well, I'm here now. What do you want?"

He tugged at the bottom of his vest, smoothed his tie. "Think we could talk in private?"

I would have preferred to stay in the lobby. But Rosemary looked so terrified I decided it might be better to get him away from her. "C'mon back to my office."

I took my seat behind the desk. He sat in one of the visitor's chairs across from me.

"Okay, it's only you and me here."

He smiled, showing his pointy teeth again. Looked around the office. "Not bad." He noticed Eddie, who watched him from his spot by the side of the desk. "What a great dog. Yours?"

I nodded.

"You and your dog gotta really be close for you to bring him to work with you."

I nodded again. "Tell me about Joe." I wanted to find out what this guy knew and get rid of him

He wasn't in any hurry. He slouched down in his chair, smiled, adjusted the crease in his trouser leg, shot his cuffs. Gold cuff links, a monogram, W.W., on his right cuff. He tapped his fingers in front of him, touched them to his chin a couple of times. "Joe, he was a good old guy. I liked Joe. I think we all liked Joe. We being the guys that worked with him. We passed the hat when he retired, got him a nice present. A fancy watch. I wouldn't a wanted it, but he seemed to like it. I'm telling you this so you know we liked Joe." He paused as if waiting for me to say something.

"I liked Joe, too," I said to keep things moving. "But you're going to tell me something I'm not going to like about him, aren't you?"

His eyes got harder. "You think you're smarter than me? You think you know what I'm going tell you?"

I sat back in my chair. "No, I'm just waiting for the other shoe to drop. You gave me the good news, now give me the bad news."

He studied me for a minute, reached some sort of decision, and visibly relaxed, even gave me a little smile. "Like I was saying, everyone liked Joe. Liked him a lot. So imagine how everyone felt when they learned Joe stole from them—"

"Who's 'them'?"

"Doesn't matter. Better you don't know, actually. What matters is it was stolen money he invested with you." His eyes got hard. He delivered the threat in a flat, unemotional voice. "We want that money back." His mouth clamped shut, and he sat there glaring at me, eyes hard, face set, waiting.

I sat back in my chair, took a deep breath. "Look, I don't know who you are or what you are expecting. But even if Joe did steal money, those stocks are part of his estate. I can't do anything about that." I stood, indicating our meeting was over. "I can't help you," I said with what I hoped was finality. "You need to leave."

He remained seated. His face changed, the facade replaced by hatred. "What do you take me for? You stand me up? You blow me off? You think I came here not knowing anything? You think I care about his estate? You're going to move those stocks from his account to our account."

"I can't take those stocks out of his estate. You were at probate court. You heard that judge. I'm not even the executor anymore."

"You're doing it. Don't give me any crap that you can't." He dug a piece of paper out of his coat pocket and threw it on the desk in front of me. "Transfer them to that account."

I shook my head. "I told—"

"Shut up. Give me the papers on his account so I've got the cusip numbers. We'll transfer 'em."

He surprised me by demanding the cusip numbers. They were the Depositors Trust Corporation book numbers for stocks not issued but held in an individual's account. I shook my head. "No."

He stood up, so mad his body was almost twitching. "You're going to move that money. Until you do, I'm going to make your life miserable."

I didn't say anything, stood very still. He was like a live grenade that could go off at any second.

"I'll be back," he snarled and stormed out.

I heard him walk out, the front door slam, hard, followed by the patter of feet coming toward my office. Rosemary appeared at the doorway, her eyes wide. "Oh my God, Matt. What was that about?"

I tried to sound calm. I probably didn't succeed. "Mr. D'Onifrio's organization wants Joe's money back."

CHAPTER 15

"Should we call the police?" Rosemary asked in a high, frightened voice.

I hesitated. "I don't know. We should, but that'd make this public. If the N.A.S.D. heard I'd been investing drug money, they'd pull my license for sure."

"We've got to do something."

"We will." I stood, walked out to the lobby. She followed me. Eddie padded along behind us. "Let's start by locking the front door again." When we'd first opened the office, we'd kept the front door locked, used a buzzer to admit people. I threw the lock. "Don't admit anybody you don't know. That'll buy us a little time."

"Time for what?"

"We need to know what we're dealing with here. Find out about D'Onifrio. His organization."

"Find out what?"

"I don't know. The worst. Prepare for it."

"You make it sound like researching a stock."

"Same principle. I'll call Tory, see what she can find out for us." In my office, I picked up the phone, dialed her number. To my surprise, she answered.

"You again." She must have had caller I.D.

"Afraid so. Listen, I need your help on something else."

"As long as we can do it over the phone. I am not going out

again."

"We can. A stranger was just here at the office. He confirmed what you suspected, that the money Joe invested with me wasn't his. Then he said they—he never said who they were—wanted their money back. I don't know what he expected; I can't give him that money back. It's in the estate. It's just not poss—"

"He didn't want to hear that, did he?'

"That's when he threatened me, said he'd make my life miserable."

"When he threatened you, did he say anything specific? Did he give you a sense of what he might do?"

"He said he'd be back."

"Then you don't want me. You want the police."

"I can't do that." I explained what this would do to me with the N.A.S.D.

"But you didn't know it was drug money."

"You know that. I know that. The N.A.S.D. doesn't. They hear accusations of churning. They hear involvement with drug money. They think, hmmm, this guy doesn't sound upstanding. Better for the profession to be rid of him. No police."

"I can't protect you. I'm not a bodyguard."

"That's not what I want. I need to know as much as I can about D'Onifrio's organization—"

"Why?"

"So I can figure out how to resolve this. I don't know what I'm dealing with here. I feel like I'm trying to hit a golf ball with my eyes closed."

"Bad sports analogy. This isn't a refinement to help get you out of the rough. You're dealing with killers." She paused. "You're clueless, aren't you?"

"I wouldn't have said it that way. I need information."

"I'll get you some background, general information. Enough so you know what you're up against. That's all."

"That's all I need. I don't want you going after information that would put you in danger."

"You're probably in a hurry for this, too, aren't you?"

"I'm afraid so. This doesn't make me toxic, does it?"

"It's not helping you any. Your choice in playmates is really bad." She sighed. "Let me see what I can do. I'll get back to you." She rang off.

"You're sure this is the right thing to be doing?" Rosemary asked.

"Right now, I just want to avoid doing the wrong thing."

Since I was at the office, I stayed late, got some work done. Driving home, the rain was still heavy, the skies dark and foreboding. Matched my mood.

We navigated the waters to the Watergate club, parked the car, headed up to the condo. The first thing I wanted to do was change into some dry clothes. I'd been damp all day.

I did that and put a chicken breast in the oven to cook. Poured Eddie his dog food. While we ate, I turned on the weather channel.

"We've had significant rainfall," the good-looking female anchor said.

"That's' right," her equally good-looking male counterpart added, "six to seven inches in some areas, which has caused a good bit of low-level flooding." Tell me about it.

"Rains should lessen tonight, clearing skies tomorrow morning." That was all I wanted to know. "We needed this rainfall," the female anchor said before I clicked her off.

The sun was out when I woke in the morning. I hoped that indicated a better day. I fed Eddie, fixed myself a quick breakfast. Eddie danced around the kitchen with his leash. He'd had a hurried walk the night before. I made sure he had a leisurely walk to make up for it.

The commute to work was easier. There were still low spots filled with water, but thanks to the intense Florida sun, most of the roads were dry. Even roadside lakes had diminished. I parked the Saab in the lot, unlocked the front door, made sure Eddie was in, locked it behind me.

"Do we think that man will be coming by today?" Rosemary asked by way of a greeting.

She verbalized what I'd been worrying about on the drive in. "If he looks like he's going to give us any trouble, call 911. Say he's harassing us. We'll let the police deal with him and vice versa."

She beamed. "Be happy to."

The morning passed without incident. By noon, the sun and a good business day had me feeling I might have overreacted.

Amanda, from Julian's office, called at one-thirty, booked a prep session with Amy for four o'clock the following day. That was my only non-business call until quarter to five, when Tory called.

"I've got some information," she said cryptically. "When can you meet me?"

I wanted to say right then, but I had a few things I needed to finish before I left. "How about at dinner?"

"Where and what time?"

"Seven? At Moore's?" A restaurant on Longboat Key, not far from her.

"Why there?"

"It's one of Eddie's favorite places."

"Oh. See you at seven."

Eddie and I were there at seven. She wasn't. She breezed in at seven-fifteen. Once again, head to toe in black, the ubiquitous black bag over her shoulder. She spotted me immediately. The place was empty, just a few summer people, a group who'd been fishing.

I stood when she came to the table. "Sorry," she said. She took off her sunglasses, put them in her bag. I had a source call me back just as I was leaving."

"No problem. I had a glass of wine while I was waiting. Want one?"

She shook her head. "No, thanks. I've got a lot to tell you." She took a thick folder out of the black bag, put it on the table in front of her, hesitated. "How do we want to do this?"

"Let's have a bite to eat first. Talk over coffee. How's that?"

"Good." She reached for a menu. I didn't. I knew it by heart.

Our waiter came. Tory ordered the mahi-mahi, I had the crab cakes. We made small talk over dinner. Once the dishes were cleared away and coffee served, she got down to business.

"Let's start with D'Onifrio." She pulled a photocopy of a newspaper page out of the folder, turned it so I could see the photo. "This is the guy."

The head-and-shoulders shot showed a strong face, dark straight hair brushed back, broad forehead, dark penetrating eyes, roman nose, lantern jaw.

"Guy looks like he could be a bruiser."

"He's big, six-two maybe, and muscular."

"What's that by his ears?"

"Hearing aids. His hearing is seriously impaired. I'll get to that, but let me give you a little background first. He's forty-three, grew up in Miami, the second son of two Menendez mules." She looked at me. "You know what mules are?"

"Drug transporters."

"Mom and Dad were good at it. They used the swallow-the-condom-full-of-cocaine method. Probably wouldn't have gotten caught except Mom got sick on a flight from Columbia to Miami. Dad panicked, had her rushed to a hospital. He must have thought a condom broke. It turned out to be acute indigestion, but the hospital authorities became suspicious and called the police. Mom and Dad ended up in prison. All this happened while son Don was attending the University of Miami, working on a degree in finance."

"Are his parents still in prison?"

"Mom still is. Dad died in 1994."

She took a sip of her coffee. "D'Onifrio got his undergraduate degree, added a master's in finance, and went to work for the cartel investing money. He was good at it, rose in the organization, and attracted the attention of the top bosses. During a trip to Columbia in 1992, he was in a limo with Enrico and Ernesto Menendez. Attacked by a rival cartel, Ernesto and two bodyguards were killed. During the shooting, D'Onifrio covered Enrico's body, saved his life. Two bullets meant for Enrico struck D'Onifrio in the right shoulder. As a result of those injuries, he has limited use of his right arm. The gunfire also irreparably shattered his eardrums, leaving him deaf." She paused, took a sip of her coffee.

"Where did you find this stuff?"

"Most of this came from a source at the D.E.A." She took another quick sip of her coffee. Enrico considers D'Onifrio a son for saving his life. As a reward, D'Onifrio was given authority over all the cartel's money laundering operations and investments. It's an important position within the cartel, but D'Onifrio's real source of power is his relationship with Enrico. He has direct access to the top guy."

Our waitress came with more coffee; she refilled Tory's cup. Mine was still full, cold. "Why don't you bring me a fresh cup?" She nodded and left.

"D'Onifrio returned to the states to look for a base of operations. He was looking in Miami mostly, but when Shore Bank and Trust got into trouble in 1997 and came on the market, he jumped on it. When he bought the bank, it had 330 employees. Today, it has 840."

"Big increase."

She nodded. "The D.E.A. estimates that 20 of those people work full time for the cartel. Shore, as a parent company, owns or has significant positions in eighteen businesses."

"Here in Sarasota?"

"No. Spread around—Miami, Orlando, Tampa, Jacksonville. That's one of the things that worry the authorities. D'Onifrio's building an empire, getting more powerful. Twice, the D.E.A. has tried to infiltrate his operation and gain enough information to convene a grand jury. Both times the operatives disappeared." She closed the folder, her face grim. "Now do you understand why I told you he's bad news?"

I nodded. "Did you run across any vulnerabilities?"

She shook her head. "My guy at the D.E.A. had two words for D'Onifrio—smart, ruthless."

Our waitress set coffee in front of me, departed. I picked it up, took a sip. "Anything about his personal life? Married? Kids?"

She smiled. "He's not married, don't know about kids. I do know his place is rumored to be Playboy Mansion South, complete with a live-in harem. Don't let that mislead you. This is a guy you don't want to mess with. People who anger him disappear."

Good advice. But it came a little too late. I'd already angered him. What I didn't know was how badly.

CHAPTER 16

I was on the phone the next morning when I heard the front door rattle, Rosemary scream. "It's him."

I put my hand over the receiver. "Call the police," I yelled to her. "Sid, I'm going to have to call you right back." I raced out to the lobby, peered out the door window. No sight of him.

The police arrived three minutes later. I let them in, explained that we were being harassed by a blond stranger. They listened, walked around the outside of the building, reported no sign of anyone, and left.

As soon as their cruiser pulled away from the curb, the phone rang, startling us both. "Seattle on Stocks," Rosemary said, picking it up. Her face drained of color, her eyes widened. "It's him. He's demanding to talk to you."

"I'll take it in my office." I headed back, picked it up.

"We want our money, Seattle," the voice said.

"I told you it's part of the estate. I can't help you."

"Screw that. Transfer the damn stocks or give us the cusip numbers. You've got twenty-four hours." The line went dead.

"What are we going to do?" Rosemary asked from the doorway.

"We don't have any choice. I'm going to the police, file a complaint, get protection from this guy." Of course, that was easier said than done. It took three hours—filing a statement, answering questions, looking at mug shots—before they agreed to watch my building for the next twenty-four hours.

Back at the office, I played catch-up until three-thirty then headed to Julian's for our four o'clock with Amy.

They were both in his office when Eddie and I got there. Julian played host, asking if he could get anybody anything. When we declined, he got down to business. "I've talked to Nevitt, and the news is not good. He's filing to recover ninety-five thousand in brokerage commissions and asking for two million in damages."

The amounts staggered me. "Ridiculous."

His face was grim. "You'll probably be served tomorrow."

"We'll follow the same defense we used in probate court, won't we?" Amy asked.

Julian nodded. "Pretty much. I think we show the closeness of Joe and Matt's relationship, point up the brevity of the marriage, finish with Janet Jesso's questionable past."

"We may have something else." I filled them in on the thrown trades Tory was investigating.

"If she can trace those back to Nevitt or Wakeman, there's no question this'll be dismissed," Julian said.

"How soon will she know something?" Amy wanted to know.

I shook my head. "I don't know."

"Then we prepare assuming we don't have it," Julian said.

And we did. For the next hour and a half, we filled in the skeleton Julian had outlined earlier. He had another appointment at six. We quit at five-thirty, which was fine by me. I was starving.

"Let's go get something to eat, Eddie," I said to him as we got back in the car. The Salty Dog was on our way home so we stopped there. The temperature was cooling off. There was no humidity, a blue sky. It was a good night to eat outside on their deck. They fixed Eddie his bowl. Grouper sandwich for me. I lingered over a glass of wine, trying to relax, enjoy the nice evening. At seven, Eddie started dancing around, letting me know he needed to go for a walk. We went across the street to the grassy area in front of Mote Marine Lab. Eddie was quick. We crossed the street and walked through the parking lot to our car to go home.

He stepped out from behind a van, blocked our way. He had his right hand in the pocket of a light blue sharkskin suit. "You don't plan on giving us those stocks, do you?"

Lying wouldn't have done any good. "No."

I started to walk past him to the Saab. He took his hand out of his pocket. It held a gun.

The gun made two soft shoo, shoo sounds that were followed by a single yelp of pain.

Both bullets struck Eddie in the head. One by his left eye. The other in the top of his head. There was no question he was dead.

An immense feeling of loss seized me, a flood of emotion. Eddie had been my link to my family. My constant companion. He'd watched over me, kept me going when I didn't think I could go on. He was gone.

"You've got fourteen hours left, Seattle." The blond man put his gun back in his pocket, walked away, laughing.

Crying, I picked Eddie's warm little body up, cradled him in my arms, carried him to the car. Somehow, I drove us home, found a shovel in the gardening shed, buried him under a flowering tree on the front grounds.

"I know you're in heaven with Michael and Sarah. I know they're happy to be playing with you. You were always there when I needed you. I'll never forget you, Eddie." It was as much of a eulogy as I could manage.

I walked the beach that night, remembering, grieving, feeling sorry for myself. When it grew dark, I wandered back to my apartment, picked up the phone, and called Dr. Swarthmore at home.

"Adelle," I said when she answered. "He's dead. Eddie's gone."

She listened as it all poured out. "I'm sorry, Matt," she said when I finished. "I know how much he meant to you. To lose him unexpectedly in this way has to be devastating. You're going to have to work through the grieving process again, fight falling back into depression."

She was right. Already, I was feeling that what's-the-use feeling. People were after me, I was being investigated, sued. Why go on?

"Matt, I'm concerned about your situation. There's something I don't understand. The people responsible for Eddie's death? Why are they bothering you? If this is about Joe Jesso's securities, why aren't they talking to his wife?"

Hell of a good question.

"She'd be the logical person for them to deal with. As it is now, you're caught in the middle in a lose/lose situation."

Her insight triggered an absurdly crazy idea that might flip things to win/win.

CHAPTER 17

The dreams came that night. I was in a cramped interior room with no outside light. The air was heavy, suffocating. Beside me, a balding man in a dark blue suit was wringing his hands as he talked, his voice soft, reassuring, as he explained the various grades of caskets. Wood vs. metal. Rounded corners vs. squared corners. Crepe vs. silk. I wasn't really listening. I couldn't focus. The man kept talking anti-corrosion protection, air-lock seals. "It's important to make the right selections for your loved ones," he said.

Claire and I had never talked about this, about what we wanted. Death was something that came after old age, after a lifetime together. I started sobbing. I wanted to talk to her. Ask her. Find out what she wanted for Michael and Sarah.

I woke. My hand reached for Eddie. Found nothing.

I was alone. Totally alone. I fought back tears, looked at the bedside clock. Four o'clock. Six hours to the deadline.

I got up, took a long shower, dressed, ate a big breakfast, thought about what I needed to do. My plan to move this from lose/lose to win/win hinged on D'Onifrio. If I could get him to go along, the rest would fall into place. If I couldn't, it was time to go to the police. The place to pitch my idea was his office. A business meeting. Talk dollars. Convince him of the best way for him to get his money. I grabbed my car keys, headed out.

Shore Bank and Trust was located in a five-story glass office tower on the southern edge of Sarasota. At a little before six in the morning, the sun wasn't up, and neither were any of the bank's workers. The parking lot looked empty, the building dark. I was too early.

I parked the car and walked to a coffee shop across from the Shore building where I could watch the place, wait for my opportunity. I slid into a booth by the window and picked up a menu.

A waitress wearing a white dress with blue trim and a hairnet, carrying a small pad of paper and pencil, hovered next to me. "Morning. What can I get you?"

"Just coffee, thanks."

She nodded, scribbled something on the pad, left.

Across the street, people began arriving for work. Lights went on, people went to their desks. Within an hour, the sun was up, a steady stream of people coming and going. By then my eyeballs were floating. I'd just gotten refill number four when I saw a black BMW 7-series with tinted windows turn into the parking lot and park in a spot near the building's entrance. The driver's door opened and a dark-haired man wearing sunglasses and carrying a slim briefcase got out, walked confidently into the building. Don D'Onifrio had arrived.

My plan, which had made such sense back at the condo, now seemed foolish. All the warnings Tory had issued about D'Onifrio reverberated in my head. My heart started beating faster. If I sat there a minute longer, I'd chicken out. I paid my check, summoned my courage. I slid out of the booth, headed across the street to pay my respects.

I kept telling myself I wasn't walking into a den of evil. I was going into a bank, a normal work place with lots of people. Anything out of the ordinary—especially something bad—would be noticed. They didn't want that. They didn't want to attract any attention.

I rationalized my way through the revolving doors and into the bank's lobby. Inside, Shore looked like any other bank. Against the back wall were the tellers; in front by the windows the desk personnel cordoned off by a waist-high railing. I walked to an opening in the railing and stood there until one of them, a young black woman, waved me over. She indicated a visitor's chair in front of her desk. "How may I help you?" she asked with a smile.

I gave her an even bigger smile and one of my business cards. "I need to see Mr. D'Onifrio concerning some stocks. I don't have an appointment, but I know he wants to see me. So if you could just let him know I'm here."

Her eyes immediately became wary, her smile a frown. "Mr. D'Onifrio has a very busy schedule. I'm afraid he won't want to be interrupted."

"Don't worry," I assured her. "I'm not selling anything. This is business he wants to talk about. Believe me, he won't mind."

She looked dubious.

"Please."

She hesitated, took a breath, reached for the phone. She watched me. "Ann, I have a gentleman here to see Mr. D'Onifrio. He doesn't have an appointment, but he says Mr. D'Onifrio wants to see him." She glanced quickly at my business card, still in her hand. "Mathew Seattle. Can you check?"

I kept smiling while we waited.

"I'll tell him." She hung up, looked over at me. "Mr. D'Onifrio says he will see you. Ann will be down to get you in a moment."

Ann turned out to be a young blond girl in a tailored gray suit. "If you'll follow me, Mr. Seattle," she said in a melodious voice.

I did. To the elevator. Up to five. Down the hall to a corner office. The door was closed. She knocked lightly, opened it.

"Come in, Mr. Seattle," a refined voice said. I stepped through the doorway into a large, well-appointed office. D'Onifrio sat behind a carved Mahogany desk. The picture Tory had shown me of him didn't do him justice. Even seated, he had a powerful presence that exuded strength and authority. Part of that was his size. He was bigger than I expected. Part of it was his looks. His gaze was intelligent, penetrating. He wore a dark blue shirt, deeper blue tie. He held out a hand indicating one of the visitor's chairs. "Please, have a seat. Would you like some coffee?"

I took the seat, declined the coffee.

"Ann, hold my calls. Mr. Seattle and I do not wish to be disturbed."

"Yes, sir." I heard her say, followed by a soft whoosh and click of the door closing.

We were alone. With the door closed, there was an odd, irritating high-pitched hum in the room. It took me a second to realize it was coming from his hearing aids.

D'Onifrio studied me, smiled, a condescending smile. The smile of a predator toying with prey.

I resisted the temptation to turn and flee, took a deep breath. I had to get this on an adult-to-adult basis. If I dealt with him from a frightened-child position, I was dead meat. "Thanks for seeing me." I tried to sound confident. "I think you and I need to talk about Joe Jesso's stocks."

The smile lost a little of its amusement. "I'm listening."

"Over the past couple of days, I've learned it might have been your money Joe invested with me."

No reaction.

"If that's true, I can understand why you'd be upset. What I came here to tell you is I didn't know it was your money and there's nothing I can do to help you get it back."

The smile lost any remaining amusement. The eyes glared. I thought he might come across the desk and throttle me. When he spoke, however, his voice was calm.

"Listen carefully. It was not my money. It was my depositors' money. They are demanding an accounting. They don't want to hear your excuses. They want their money back. If you do not give it to them—" he shrugged his shoulders. Amusement returned to his smile. "Well, I cannot be responsible for what happens to you."

I had the feeling his depositors weren't Mr. and Mrs. Joe Lunchbox of Sarasota. "That money is part of his estate—"

He shook his head. "These stocks are under your control."

"I can't take assets out of his estate. I'd go to jail."

He laughed. "You think I care if you go to jail?"

"I'm sure you don't, but there's no way I could transfer those stocks into your name that the money couldn't be traced. You'd go to jail, too."

"No one will ever trace it to me. I know how to move money so it disappears."

"You can't make it disappear when the N.A.S.D. is watching."

His eyes narrowed to slits. "Why would the N.A.S.D. be watching my money?"

I laid it out for him. "Joe's new wife brought charges against me with the National Association of Securities Dealers so she could have me removed as executor of his estate. Now that I'm no longer executor, she has control of that money."

D'Onifrio's face registered disgust. He sat back in his chair, rubbed his chin with his hand. "That may be, but you know the cusip numbers. All I need are those numbers. I can do the rest."

"Won't work. With the N.A.S.D. watching those stocks, they'd have us both arrested for securities violations."

Anger flushed his face. His hands balled up into fists.

"But I know how you can get your money, and it will be perfectly legal."

"Tell me," he barked.

I took a breath. "Right now, that money belongs to Joe's wife, Janet Wakeman. Janet's a gold digger who marries older men for their money. That's why she married Joe." I watched his face. "So if one of your associates married her, that money would be joint property. You could take it without a problem."

D'Onifrio burst out laughing. "That is the stupidest thing I've ever heard. Why would I do that?"

"For one reason only. It's legal."

He threw up his hands in a dismissive gesture. "I want my money now. I don't want to play some game to get it."

"Why risk having a bunch of regulatory agencies breathing down your neck so you can have it now. You haven't had that money for two years. What's a month more to get it back without any complications?"

He picked up a pen, tapped it against the desktop, threw it down, studied me. Silence. Again I noticed the irritating hum. "I'll think about it." He stood.

I remained seated. "Thinking it over doesn't work for me. You killed my dog—"

"I am sorry about that. My associate should not have hurt your dog."

"I appreciate your saying that, but it won't bring him back. I don't want to end up dead because I gave you time to think it over."

"I assure you that will not happen."

"All I want is a yes or a no. What's there to think about? I'm told you're a powerful executive. This should be a simple decision for you."

"Don't goad me, Mr. Seattle, or you will join your dog. There are issues to consider beyond your understanding. I will review this and let you know my decision. End of discussion."

I stood. "Well, thanks for listening at least." I headed for the door.

When I opened it, Ann was waiting for me.

She smiled nicely. I was back among normal human beings. "I'll show you downstairs, Mr. Seattle."

"Thanks." I gratefully followed her to the elevator banks. She rode down to the lobby with me. Each floor dinged as we descended. On the fifth ding, the door opened. We were back at the lobby.

"Have a great day," she said as I stepped out.

"Oh, I will," I replied optimistically. The meeting with D'Onifrio had been such a disaster my day couldn't get any worse.

Or so I thought.

CHAPTER 18

"Where's Eddie?" Rosemary asked lightly when I entered the office.

"He's gone, I'm afraid."

"Gone?"

"He was killed last night."

Her face fell. "Oh, Matt, I'm so sorry. What happened?"

It was hard to talk about it. I choked up as I told her about the shooting in the parking lot, carrying Eddie home, burying him. I got myself under control and told her about my visit to D'Onifrio.

She listened sympathetically. When I was finished, she said, "As if you haven't had enough trouble, I'm afraid there's more." She handed me an envelope. "That came a wee bit ago."

I glanced quickly at the front of it. Registered mail From the Sarasota County Court. "Julian warned me this was coming." I ripped open the envelope, looked at the papers inside.

"What's it say?" Rosemary asked.

"Says I'm being sued by Janet Jesso. She's asking the return of ninety-five thousand dollars in investment fees and two million in punitive damages." I handed her the papers.

"My God," she said as she read them. "Can they do this?"

I nodded. "Julian says they can."

"For so much money?"

I nodded again. "Afraid so." If they won, I'd be out of business. Bankrupt.

"Matt, how are you holding yourself together? Losing Eddie. Now this."

I thought about what Dr. Swarthmore had said last night, warning me not to slide back into depression. She'd been right that it would be easy to let go, let the darkness surround me. But somebody had to pay for Eddie. I wasn't about to let his death go unpunished. This hadn't been an accident. This time I wasn't totally helpless. I held Nevitt and Wakeman as responsible for his death as D'Onifrio. "You know, Rosemary, as bad as this is, I'm going to get through it."

"You know I'll do anything I can to help."

"I appreciate that, Rosemary." I headed to my office. Waiting for me were voice mails, pink message slips, emails. I ignored them all, dialed Tory's number, got her machine. After the beep, I said, "Tory, it's Matt Seattle. Sorry to be calling you so often. I know you don't like that. But we need to talk as soon as possible. There have been major new developments and I need your help."

I cradled the receiver, sat there watching it not ring. After fifteen minutes, I decided I was kidding myself to think she'd call back quickly. I went to work, returned calls, booked transactions, did paperwork. At six, Rosemary stuck her head in, said she was leaving. By seven, I'd done all I could do. I got up, stretched, turned out the lights, and walked to the front door. I'd just finished locking up when I heard the phone ring. I set a new record for getting back inside, picked up the line at Rosemary's desk. "Hello."

"Catch your breath," she laughed. "You sound winded."

"Winded and worried."

"Winded is your problem; worried is mine. What's the matter?"

"I need you to find out about a guy for me."

"Why? What'd he do?"

"He shot my dog."

"The spaniel—the one I petted? This guy shot him?"

"Killed him."

"How horrible. I'm sorry for you, but you don't want me, you want the police."

"I've already talked to the police. I spent yesterday afternoon with them, looking at mug shots, trying to get protection. Lot of good that did me. Eddie's dead."

"I'm sorry," she said softly. "If the police couldn't help you, I probably can't either."

"Yes, you can. This guy works for Shore. You had all that information on Shore. You can find out about him."

"That was general information, not specifics. I'll be honest with you; I'm not sure I want D'Onifrio's organization knowing I'm poking around, looking at their people."

The tone in her voice told me she didn't want to get involved. Who could blame her? Why put herself at risk to find out who shot a dog? "I understand. I shouldn't have bothered you." I started to hang up.

"Wait," I heard her say.

I put the phone back to my ear. "Yes?"

"I didn't say I wouldn't help, but I need to know what I'm getting into."

"That's fair. You want to talk over the phone, get together, what?"

I heard the tap of fingers on a computer. Probably kept an electronic calendar. "How's ten o'clock tomorrow?"

"Fine. You want to come here?"

"I'll do that."

I headed out for the second time. This time, however, the phone didn't ring. I put the top down on the Saab, drove to Publix, picked up a salad for dinner. After dinner, I went for a walk on the beach, worked out for an hour and a half in the gym. Without Eddie, it was a long, lonely evening.

At ten until ten the next morning, I heard the door rattle, Rosemary use the buzzer. Early, again.

"Good morning," Rosemary said.

"He's expecting me," Tory said. "I can find my own way."

She appeared in my doorway; I waved her in, closed out of a computer program. She sat in the same visitors' chair she'd occupied on her last visit. "Sorry about Eddie," she said. "Having him shot in front of you had to be painful."

"Thanks," I shook my head sadly. "It was pointless. Mean."

She got a legal pad and pen out of her black bag. "What can you tell me about the shooter?"

I pictured him in my mind. "Young, early twenties. Sort of baby faced with short-cropped blond hair and a wispy, hardly-there blond moustache. That the kind of stuff you're looking for?"

She nodded.

"About five-eight, 125-pounds—thin, really thin. He wore a fancy suit, probably Italian, with all sorts of fancy goo-gas on it you don't see in a normal suit. Expensive or cheap, I don't know." I thought for a second, picturing him in our first meeting. "He had a monogram on his shirt sleeve. WW."

"Yeah. That gives me something to narrow this down. Anything else about him?"

I shook my head.

"You said you talked to the police, looked at mug shots. Tell me about that."

"I don't think they took me too seriously. I gave them his description. They put me at a computer terminal, had me look at mug shots. After an hour of that, I'd looked at everybody who fit the description. I didn't see him."

She made a note on her pad, looked over at me. "Did you tell them this guy works for D'Onifrio?"

"No."

"Too bad. They'd have taken you real seriously. Might have made a difference."

"It might," I agreed. "I didn't think I needed to name-drop to get what I wanted from the police."

She arched an eyebrow at me. "What exactly did you want?"

"Twenty-four hours of protection."

"Why twenty-four?"

I dropped back, explained about the stranger's attempt to get in the front door, his phone call after the police left.

"His threat was to deliver the securities in twenty-four or else," she said after I finished. "That was what? Forty-eight hours ago? Aren't you afraid you're living on borrowed time?"

"I'm okay," I assured her. "I talked to D'Onifrio and—"

"You what?" she asked incredulously.

"I talked to him. I went to his office."

"How could you be so stupid? Remember? People who bother him disappear."

"Well, I'm here. So my idea must not have bothered him too much."

She looked at me warily. "Your idea?"

"There is one way D'Onifrio can legally get his money back. I bounced it off him."

"What is it? What did he say?"

"Having one of his people marry Janet Wakeman. He'd get the money as joint property."

Her face registered shock. "That's the craziest idea I've ever heard."

"Crazy or not, he's considering it."

She shook her head, her eyes wide. "I am not believing this."

"I'll probably hear from him today."

"He'll say no. Think about it. What are the chances Janet Wakeman would marry one of his people? One in a gazillion, maybe less."

"She's a gold digger. Dangle a rich, older guy in front of her—"

The intercom buzzed. "I know you wanted me to hold your calls, but there's a Mr. D'Onifrio on one. I told him you were in a meeting. He told me to interrupt it."

CHAPTER 19

"Mr. Seattle," he said, his voice formal. "I have given your suggestion serious thought and would like to discuss it further with you. Can you come to my office tomorrow at nine o'clock?"

Not a yes. Not a no. Possibly a trap. "Mr. D'Onifrio, let me share my biggest concern. I show up at your office at nine and I'm never seen again."

There was an amused chuckle at the other end of the line. "I give you my word; you will be seen again."

"I'd rather have a simple yes or no."

"I'd rather have further discussion." His voice had turned cold. "Be here at nine." He hung up.

"Well, what'd he say?"

"You pretty much heard it. Be at his office tomorrow at nine."

"Are you going?"

I nodded. "He gave me his word it wasn't a set up."

"You believe that?"

In an odd way I did. If he'd wanted me dead, he'd have made it happen. He could get to me no matter how careful I was, how much protection I had. "I think I'm okay for this meeting. If it doesn't go well, I'll go straight to the cops."

She looked dubious, shifted in her seat. "With your meeting tomorrow, you still want me to find out about this guy?"

"Yeah, I want to know who he is."

She started packing up her stuff. "I probably won't know anything before nine, but I'll get the information to you as soon as I can." She left, obviously freaked out.

Rosemary came in, occupied the seat Tory had left. She handed me a stack of pink message slips. "It's a slow day we're having. Do you want me to help you prepare for your meeting in the morning, see if I can find you a bulletproof vest?"

I gave her a disapproving look. "Very funny."

"I'm serious. I'm with Miss Haughty—"

"Miss Haughty?" It wasn't like Rosemary to ridicule.

"Ms. Knight," she said, disapproval evident in her voice. "I'm agreeing with her that this is a meeting to which you shouldn't be going."

Despite their concerns, the next day at exactly nine, I entered the lobby of Shore Bank and Trust. Ann, the blond who had escorted me to D'Onifrio's office last time, was waiting for me.

"Good to see you again, Mr. Seattle. Follow me, please," she said pleasantly. We rode the elevator up to five, exited. She led me down the corridor to his office. Again the door was closed. She knocked and opened it. D'Onifrio was at his desk, again in shirt and tie, this time smoking a cigar. "Come in, Mr. Seattle," he said and sent a cloud of blue smoke toward the ceiling. "Sit down. Let's talk."

I entered, heard the door close behind me, took the same seat as the time before.

D'Onifrio leaned forward, the irritating hum of his hearing aids increased, and his eyes seemed to bore into me. "I have some questions for you."

I wanted to say shoot but bit my tongue and nodded instead.

He blew a smoke ring to the ceiling, watched it for a second. "Janet Wakeman, the woman Joe married, what do you know about her?"

I relaxed a little. He'd lobbed me an easy one. "I had a private detective look into her background. Janet, we discovered, is a professional black widow. Joe was her fourth husband. She has a lawyer working with her. Guy by the name of Greg Nevitt, whose job is to change the will or estate to leave everything to Janet."

"Nevitt did that with Joe's will?"

"He didn't have time. Joe'd only been married a week when he died. His will still named me executor. Nevitt had me removed as executor so he could control Joe's estate."

D'Onifrio blew another smoke ring at the ceiling, frowned, sat forward. "Where are my manners? Would you like a cigar?"

He wanted to be buddy-buddy now. That scared me. "No thanks, I'm fine."

"Coffee?"

"I'm fine."

"You're sure?"

I nodded. "Thanks, though."

He sat back in his chair, puffed out smoke. "This marriage plan you mentioned yesterday was based on what you learned about Janet's background?"

I nodded.

"Be honest now. Do you think this marriage could be arranged?"

"I think it's possible, yes."

"Possible doesn't sound very positive." Behind the cigar smoke his face changed.

I saw whatever chance I had slipping away. Sell, I thought. "She's a black widow. I'm positive that if you dangle a wealthy older man in front of her, she'll go after him."

That must have been what he wanted to hear. "Good," he said. "I have decided to give your plan a try."

That wasn't what I expected to hear. The expression on my face must have telegraphed that.

"You seem surprised?"

"Well, I guess I am. You threatened me. Why aren't you threatening them?"

"With you, I had hoped to force a fast resolution." He shook his head dismissively. "That's gone. Now, I think it is in my depositors' best interests to do this without attracting undue attention. Of course, if that fails, I will use force, take the money. First, though, we will see how you do."

"Me?" I said, alarmed. This wasn't what I intended at all. I wanted to pit the two of them against each other, end their involvement with me. "You don't need me. You know who she is. You can do this by yourself."

He blew a smoke ring in my direction. "It was your idea. Who would know better how to bring it to life?"

I saw my opportunity to get out of the middle vanishing. "I can tell you how to do it. You really don't need me."

He smiled at my discomfort. "You forget, you have no choice in this matter. I'm appointing you matchmaker."

He was on a roll. I nodded.

"By tomorrow, I will give you someone who can be this woman's new husband. Be here—" he leaned forward, flipped over the page in his planner, studied what rape, pillage, murder, and torture filled his calendar. "Ten o'clock tomorrow morning. Got that?"

"Got it. See you at ten," I said as I stood to go. Maybe I could still get this to work out. "When I pull this off, will you do something for me?"

His eyes narrowed. "I'm listening."

"The brother—the shyster lawyer—has accused me of churning…"

He made a face, waved his cigar in the air. "You churned Joe?"

"No, I didn't." I explained carefully. "Joe was my friend. This guy, Nevitt, is an ambulance chaser. He's falsely accused me of making lots of commissions off Joe. Essentially he's blackmailing me, trying to get money he doesn't deserve. I don't suppose, if I make this marriage happen, you could convince the brother to drop his complaint?"

He chuckled. "I'll say this for you, you have nerve. No one asks me for favors. They do favors for me." He paused, studying me. "But you amuse me. If you pull this off, I'll fulfill your request. I will convince Mr. Nevitt to drop his action against you and never bother you again. How is that?"

"That would be wonderful. Thank you." I started to back out the door.

"A warning—if my amusement turns to anger—" he waved a finger at me. "Very unhealthy."

I left before he could say more.

Ann was waiting for me in the corridor outside his office. "We'll be seeing you tomorrow at ten?"

"Yes."

"I'll walk you down." She led me back to the lobby. Left me with a word of caution. "He has given you a lot of rope. Don't forget that one end is tied around your neck."

CHAPTER 20

Even Ann's warning didn't faze me. I was elated. I'd taken a big first step in getting the various factions fighting each other instead of me. I wasn't out of trouble by any stretch of the imagination, but I hadn't had anything positive to build on in so long that I wanted to savor this.

Maybe that's why, when Tory called at four o'clock to let me know she had information on the guy who shot Eddie, I impetuously asked her to dinner.

She didn't jump at the invitation. "What's this about?"

"I had my second meeting with D'Onifrio. I'm still among the living and feel like celebrating my good fortune. Dinner by myself won't be much fun. We need to talk. Why not over dinner?"

She hesitated. "All right."

"Charlie's Crab at eight?"

"How about eight-thirty? That would be better for me."

"That's fine. I'll meet you there. Thanks, Tory."

I finished what I was doing, drove back to my condo, took a shower, and changed into some fresh clothes. Even taking my time, I was at the restaurant by eight-fifteen.

Charlie, owner and host, greeted me. He was a small man with slicked-back hair and a waxed moustache, as always dressed in a tux. "Mr. Seattle, good to see you." He looked around by my feet. "Where is Eddie?"

The pain returned like a fist to the chest. "I lost him," I said, trying not to turn maudlin. "An accident."

"I am sorry. Dinner is on me tonight."

"Thank you, Charlie, but you don't have to do that."

"I insist. Please."

"I am meeting someone, so—"

Charlie's eyes lit up. "A woman. Even better. I will have a bottle of champagne sent over."

"No. No. No. Charlie, this is a business dinner. She'll get the wrong idea if champagne shows up."

He nodded. "I understand. Dinner for you both, however, is on the house. Let me show you to your table." I followed him to a secluded spot by a window with a bay view. "Is this businesslike enough?" He grinned impishly.

"It's great. Thanks."

"I will watch for your business friend." He stroked his moustache. "I'm sure she's fat, ugly, with warts."

I laughed at his feeble ploy to pry information out of me. "Then you'd be wrong. She's attractive. But this is a business dinner."

He put his hands up by his face as if to say I believe you even though it was obvious that he didn't. When he brought Tory to the table, it was even more obvious.

She didn't look like a business dinner. She was dressed in black again. A tight black tank top, black stretch pants, black heels. She was wearing gold hoop earrings, hot pink lipstick, her hair pulled back and tied at the base of her neck with a pink scarf. Hardly business attire.

She took her seat, Charlie presented her with a menu, took drink orders—water with lemon (hers) and Diet Coke (mine)—and departed.

She glanced at the menu, looked up at me.

"Let's order," I suggested. "We can talk while we eat. Dinner is on

Charlie, so don't be shy. He likes women with appetites."

"Really? I would have thought women were not what Charlie found attractive."

"Wow, you are a detective."

"It's a gift, these powers of deduction."

"What else can you tell me about him?"

"He likes you."

"Too bad. The powers have failed you. He liked Eddie."

"The powers tell me it wasn't Eddie. Anyway, he's a cat man."

"Cats? You think Charlie has cats?"

"Absolutely."

The waiter arrived with our drinks. I asked him if Charlie could visit the table for a moment. The waiter left, and Charlie materialized in a flash.

"Charlie, I have a question."

"But of course."

"Do you have cats?"

"Cats?" He gave each of us a puzzled look, stroked his moustache. "Yes, I have three cats. Why?"

I looked at Tory. She was trying to keep a straight face.

"Ms. Wright," I nodded at Tory, "was recommending I get a cat. What do you think?"

Charlie looked at me, squinted his eyes, pursed his lips. Finally, he said, "No, I don't think so. I don't see you as a cat person. Sorry."

"Thanks, Charlie."

"Let me know if I can be of any further assistance." He turned, and sashayed away.

Tory was trying not to laugh or look smug.

"Okay, you win."

She broke into a broad smile. "The three magic words every girl wants to hear."

I opened my menu.

"What do you recommend?" Tory asked.

"I think I'm going to have the grilled grouper."

She started to put her menu down. Our waiter, ever vigilant, arrived at the table the moment her menu closed. Once we'd ordered and the waiter had departed, I said, "Tell me about the shooter."

She dug in her black bag, pulled out a legal pad, studied it. "That monogram you spotted identified him. WW stands for William Wilder." She looked over at me as if that name should mean something to me. Not getting a reaction, she continued. "He's also known as Wild Will or Willie the Kid. He's got quite a reputation as a hit man. The police think he's been responsible for more than twenty deaths the last three years. D'Onifrio reputedly uses him to get people out of his way."

"Out of his way? What does that mean?"

"These businesses around the state that Shore now owns weren't all smooth acquisitions. If a major stockholder or officer of the company objected, he or she disappeared or had an accident. Wilder's work. It's also believed he's responsible for the deaths of Judge Richard D. Clayton and State Senator Mark Kraski, who headed a committee looking into organized crime in Florida. The D.E.A. believes he killed three of their operatives who tried to infiltrate D'Onifrio's organization."

"Was he arrested for any of those deaths?"

She shook her head. "Never charged. No evidence. The D.E.A. knows D'Onifrio has other professional killers in his organization. They can't be one hundred percent certain it was Wilder."

Our waiter returned carrying a bottle of wine and silver bucket of ice.

"What's this?"

"Charlie said you didn't want champagne, but he thought a good white wine would accent your dinner." He placed the ice bucket on the table, presented the unopened bottle, used his corkscrew, and splashed a taste in my glass.

It was good.

He filled both glasses, put the bottle in the ice bucket, and departed.

"Listen," there was an edge in Tory's voice, "I thought this was business. If you've got something else in mind, I'm not interested. I've been burned. I'm not going to let it happen again."

"I hear you. Let me assure you this is business. Charlie knows I'm by myself. He's trying to play matchmaker. That's all. I'm not looking for a relationship."

"As long as we understand what the rules are here."

"Strictly business."

The assurances seemed to settle her a little. "Tell me about your meetings with D'Onifrio."

I needed to settle down, too. Her revelations about Wilder and overreaction to the wine had unnerved me. Talking was as good a way as any to regain my composure. "I was expecting D'Onifrio to be the kind of bad guy you see on TV. He wasn't. He's more polished, more intelligent. At our first meeting, I was surprised by how pleasant he was. Of course, he probably thought I was there to deliver the stocks. When I floated my marriage idea instead, he got angry. Said something cryptic about outside forces I didn't understand. After that, he calmed down, said he'd consider it."

"So you had a second meeting."

I nodded. "Again, he was very pleasant, offered me a cigar." I took a sip of wine. "He told me his depositors wanted the money back but didn't want to attract a lot of attention, so he was willing to give my marriage idea a try. When I heard him say that, I thought I was out of the woods."

"It's never that easy."

"No, it's not. I thought D'Onifrio would use my idea, have his people execute it. He had a different take. He said because it was my idea, I'd pull it off better than anyone else."

"Some truth to that."

"I don't know. Having an idea is one thing. Making it work— especially when it involves one of D'Onifrio's people, our potential groom—is something else entirely."

Our salads arrived.

"So what are you going to do?" she asked around a bite of salad.

I played with my fork. "I don't have any choice. I've got to arrange this marriage."

"Can you do that?"

"This woman is a professional gold digger. If we dangle a very wealthy—I mean very wealthy—old guy in front of her, I think she'll pounce on him."

"Don't you think it's too soon?"

I finished a bite of salad. "You mean because she's a bereaved widow?"

She nodded.

"Consolation in her grief, that's what our guy has to offer her. Maybe he's lost all his brothers to heart attacks and knows he doesn't have much time. Wouldn't hurt to have him casually mention something like that."

"You mean like, 'Hi, I don't have long to live. Would you like to marry me and my millions?'"

I grinned. "Something like that, but more obvious. I'm convinced that if we set the bait properly, we'll hook her fast."

She put her fork down. "You keep saying we, like I'm involved in this. I'm not."

She had me on that one. Subconsciously, I had been including her.

Presumptive on my part. But not a bad idea. She'd make a great collaborator. "Sorry. I shouldn't have assumed you'd be willing to help. This thing could turn dangerous."

She gave me a doubtful look.

"Not hooking up Janet and our groom. D'Onifrio. This guy Wilder."

Her eyes became knowing. Her mouth curled up at the corners. It was the confident expression of a card player who held a full house, knew her opponent only had a paltry two of a kind. "I might do it if the money was right."

I sat back in my seat, took a sip of my wine, studied her. As much as I could have used her help, I wanted to make sure she knew the risks. "It could get ugly. D'Onifrio or Wilder could—"

Her smile broadened. "What pitiful negotiation skills. You're making the price higher."

"I just—"

Dinner arrived, along with Charlie. He fussed over our table. Actually, he fussed over Tory. "You have not touched your wine. It was not acceptable?" He made a sad face.

"Oh, no. It's wonderful," she assured him. "I just got caught up in—talking." She grinned at me, picked up her glass, took a sip. "Wonderful."

He beamed. Man of a million emotions. "Bon appétit, then."

"Thanks, Charlie," I said as he departed.

Tory leaned over the table. "Let's say you agree to the outrageous fee I'm going to charge. Tell me why it's so important that I'm a part of this."

"You bring a woman's perspective. Which is important. You know Sarasota better than I do—"

She shook her head. "Not to be overly critical, but neither of those is worth the big bucks."

"You're right. But there's something else. They don't know you. Janet saw me in court. Nevitt has seen me twice. You can get close to them. I can't."

"Get close to do what?"

I leaned over the table, said conspiratorially, "You're going to be catalyst who sets everything in play."

CHAPTER 21

Over the rest of dinner and coffee, we talked through what needed to happen. It may all have been wishful thinking, but by the time we went our separate ways, I felt better. I had Tory on board. Tory had to be feeling pretty good, too. She'd negotiated a fee that would pay off the mortgage on her little house on Anna Marie Island. Good help doesn't come cheap.

We'd agreed to meet tomorrow at nine-fifteen at the Pier Grille and drive over together to meet the groom. On my way home, I called the office and left a message for Rosemary that I'd be late coming in, not to worry. I tried to make my voice light, untroubled. Not that she'd buy it for a minute.

Back at the condo, I changed clothes and headed to the weight room. I was still wound up from dinner. What Tory had told me about Wilder had finally registered. I'd assumed he was some punk I could punish for what he did to Eddie. I hadn't expected him to be D'Onifrio's top killer. If the authorities hadn't been able to do anything about this guy, I wasn't sure what luck I'd have.

I used the weights for forty minutes, ran for another forty. It helped. Not enough that I got any sleep. I was still too agitated. I watched the clock creep from one to two to three to four to five to six to seven. At seven, I got up, took a long shower, had some breakfast, and dallied at reading the paper until a little after nine.

Tory was waiting for me in the parking lot, standing next to her car. Again, dressed in all black—black turtleneck, black skirt, the ever-present large black bag over her shoulder. I wondered if all her clothes were black. She waved when I turned into the parking lot. I pulled the Saab into the space next to her VW Jetta, black, of course. She opened the passenger door and got in.

"You look like shit," she said cheerfully.

I put the car in reverse, backed out of the space, and headed for Shore. "I worried all last night, didn't sleep a wink."

She looked over at me to see if I was kidding, caught me yawning. "Don't go. Call it off."

"Believe me, I'd like to. But I figure it's better to have D'Onifrio working with me than against me. If we work with him, one of two positive things could come out of it. We could pull off this marriage. Or we could find out something about D'Onifrio we can take to the authorities."

"Like what?"

"I don't know."

"That's comforting," she said, an edge to her voice. "Stir things up. See what happens. That's your plan?"

I looked over at her. "No. Things are already stirred up. I want to take what's stirred up, settle it in a way that I'm out from under it."

"We're going to have to have a better plan than that to get out from under anything."

I nodded, didn't argue with her.

She adjusted her shoulder bag on the floor by her feet. "This meeting is to give us the groom, right?"

It was a nervous question. We'd talked through everything at dinner. "Yeah, I just hope it isn't groom and doom."

She groaned. "How can you make jokes at a time like this?"

"Keeps me from being so scared my voice goes up three octaves."

"I know what you mean. I can't believe I'm actually going to meet

D'Onifrio."

I looked over. "You can change your mind. Not go. I don't want you to do anything that makes you uncomfortable."

She dismissed my concern with a shake her head. "I can handle it. I'm a big girl. I'm not going to do anything stupid."

"What if it gets rough?"

"What if this groom guy's a dud?"

She'd ducked my question, struck a nerve. My biggest fear was that this guy would be a jerk, wouldn't cooperate. I sighed. "Well, I guess we'll need to figure out how to make lemonade."

We rode in silence the rest of the way. I parked the car in the bank's surface lot, got out, opened Tory's door for her. "He needs us to do this for him. We shouldn't have any trouble in this meeting." I think I said it as much for my benefit as hers.

Inside the bank, Ann was waiting for us in the lobby. She eyed Tory, sized her up. To me, she said, "Mr. Seattle, right on time. Let me escort you up."

We rode the elevator to the top floor. When the door opened, Ann stepped off briskly, led us down the hallway to D'Onifrio's office. She knocked on the door, opened it, closed it hurriedly. "He's on the phone. Shouldn't be but a minute."

We stood in the hall and waited. A minute passed. Two. Five. Ten. Twenty. At the forty-minute mark, we heard a muffled, "Ann," from inside.

She opened the door, stuck her head in. "Bring them in," we heard him say. She opened the door all the way, indicated we should enter, closed the door behind us.

D'Onifrio was seated behind his desk. In addition to a white shirt, foulard tie and braces, he wore a tired expression. I would have liked to believe he'd been up all night worrying about this meeting, but he probably had bigger, more sinister things to worry about. He frowned, acknowledging us, stood, came around his desk. "Mr. Seattle, introduce me to your friend."

He came up close to her, held out his hand. I made introductions over the hum of his hearing aids. "Mr. D'Onifrio, this is my associate, Ms. Wright."

Tory looked like she wanted to bolt. She didn't. She shook hands with him, smiled.

D'Onifrio released her hand, gestured to his left. "I believe you're already met my associate, Mr. Wilder."

I had to turn to see him. He was seated on the sofa by the door we'd just entered. He didn't get up. He grinned, showing us his pointy teeth, then adjusted the crease on one trouser leg of his light blue sharkskin.

Maybe that was why we'd been kept waiting. He was discussing my death with Wilder. "What's he doing here?"

D'Onifrio went back to his desk chair. "Let's just say he's the groom's best man."

"This isn't going to work—"

"It works the way I say it works," he said, a hard edge to his voice. So much for the friendly meeting I'd hoped for. "Sit down."

As we sat, he stared at us. "Don't get the idea because I'm letting you do this for me that I'm not in control. You're going to do what I say, when I say. Understood?"

He was trying to intimidate us. The scolding parent talking to unruly children. I needed to keep this on an adult-to-adult level. "I thought you wanted your money back," I said calmly.

"I do," he scowled.

"We're going to need some room or this isn't going to work."

The scowl deepened. Not the obedient child he'd been expecting. "Listen to me, you ever talk to me like that again, I'll have Wilder turn you into fertilizer."

"I'm not trying to cause you trouble," I said evenly. "I'm trying to keep this on a business-like basis. Threatening me isn't helping. Turn me into fertilizer, and you'll never see your money."

I thought that would provoke another outburst. It didn't. He leaned back in his chair and stared at me. His eyes narrowed. The frown turned down even further. A look meant to terrorize. I sat there quietly, hoping all the squirming my insides were doing didn't show.

After an eternity, his gaze shifted to Wilder. "Get Fish."

Wilder got up from the sofa, left the room. He came back followed by a second man.

As soon as I saw him, I understood the Fish reference. He looked exactly like Abe Vigoda, the guy who played Fish on the old Barney Miller cop show. He had the same sad sack face—deep dark eyes under black, bushy, out-of-control eyebrows, thin no-lip mouth, heavy jowls, thinning brown hair. He wore a short-sleeved white dress shirt, cheap striped tie that extended only mid-paunch. Brown polyester pants a good two inches too short revealed light blue socks.

His gaze went from D'Onifrio to us. "Hello," he said in a fog-horn voice.

D'Onifrio got up from his seat, walked around the desk, put an arm on the man's stooped shoulder. "Fish, here, has volunteered to marry this woman. Haven't you, Fish?"

"Always wanted to try marriage," Fish agreed matter-of-factly. Since he didn't have any lips, his mouth barely moved. His jowls quivered.

I had a feeling I knew why he was still single. I had a feeling I was going to get very good at making lemonade. I put all that out of my mind, stood, held out my hand. "Matt Seattle, good to meet you." Tory stood as well. "Tory Knight. I work with Mr. Seattle."

"Frankie F. Fontaine," Fish said as we shook hands. "Pleased to meet both of you."

D'Onifrio clapped him on the back and went back to his seat. "Fish is your guy. Tell me how quickly you can have him married."

I shook my head. "Hard to say. If we get lucky, within a month."

"Get lucky, get very fucking lucky. I don't want to wait a month for that money. If it goes a month, your time is up. Do you understand what I'm saying?"

Back to threats. "We'll do our best."

D'Onifrio dismissed me, looked at Fish, who was standing there looking very ill at ease. "Go with them, Fish. If they give you any trouble, just raise your hand. Wilder will be watching."

"I'll be fine, boss."

"Let's get a cup of coffee and talk," I suggested.

Fish nodded and walked heavily to the door. Tory and I followed.

I was almost to the hallway, when Wilder said, "Remember, Seattle, I'll be watching." He pulled a gun out of his pocket and pointed it at me. "Waiting for an opportunity to put a bullet between your eyes."

His laugh followed us down the hallway.

CHAPTER 22

The Tropical Breeze Café, a lunch counter Fish frequented, was a short two-block walk from Shore. We took a booth in the back. Fish sat on one side, Tory and I on the other. A waitress arrived with menus. Fish took one. I waved mine away. "Just coffee."

"Diet Coke," Tory said.

We looked at Fish, hunched over the menu studying it intently. He looked up at the waitress. "I'd like a grilled cheese sandwich—not too burnt—with a couple of those pickle slices. And coffee with cream." He handed her his menu.

"So," I started in, "should we call you Fish, Frank, Frankie?"

He shrugged. "Doesn't matter. I don't know why everybody calls me Fish. I've seen the TV show, and I don't think I look like the guy."

They could have been twins, but I wasn't about to argue. "Tell us a little about yourself. Are you from around here? What do you do at work? What do you like to do on your time off?"

He rested his arms on the table. After a thoughtful pause, the deep voice rumbled out slowly. "I grew up in Bradenton. I've been a delivery driver for Shore for almost six years now. It's not a great job, but it's okay. I like to bowl."

Not a conversationalist. "What made you decide to get involved with this?"

"You mean this marriage thing?"

"Yes."

"The boss told me I had to."

"You didn't volunteer?"

He shook his head.

"How do you feel about it now?"

"I'll do my job."

"It's a little different than a job. We're going to need you to court this woman. Can you do that?"

He stared across the table at me. "My last date—this girl and I went to dinner—she told me she had to go to the restroom and never came back."

"Was that recently?"

"I think it was in 1990."

I smiled reassuringly. "Well, that won't happen this time."

"I don't know. I'm not very good with women."

"You don't have to be. We're going to let this woman know you're worth close to ten million. She'll be all over you."

His bushy eyebrows flew-up in surprise. "You think?"

I nodded sagely.

Our waitress arrived with our drinks. Fish began opening cream container after cream container, pouring one after another into his coffee. He should have ordered a glass of milk. The waitress came back with his grilled cheese sandwich. He inspected it closely. "You've got to be careful. They hide the burnt side on the bottom. After you take a bite, they tell you it's too late to send it back."

I took a sip of my coffee. Fish took a bite of his sandwich. I waited until he swallowed, asked, "Think you can act like our ten-million-dollar guy?"

He nodded, ate one of his pickle slices.

"We're going to need to take a look at your wardrobe. See if we have to add some things to make you look wealthy," Tory said.

"We ought to take a look at your place, too. See if it works. Where do you live?"

He chewed, swallowed, took a sip of coffee. "I've got a doublewide out at Bee Ridge Estates. Close to the highway."

Swell. I'd have to find him a place.

"Do you go out much?" Tory wanted to know.

Fish looked at her blankly.

"You know, socialize."

"I'm in three different bowling leagues. I get out now and then."

"Ever been to A.A.?" I asked him pointedly.

His brow furrowed. "Alcoholics Anonymous?"

I nodded.

"Naw." He ate another of his pickle slices. "I usually stick to beer. Never had a problem. You only rent beer, you know."

"Tonight, we're going to an A.A. meeting to observe," Tory explained to him. "The woman we're interested in goes to A.A."

"She's got a problem?"

"No. A.A. seems to be the place she hooks up with guys. We're thinking it's the place where we can introduce you."

"Tonight, we want to get a sense of the place. What the room looks like. How many people attend. Where she sits. That kind of thing."

"The lay of the land. I can handle that," he said, finishing off his grilled cheese.

"Right. At the next meeting, we'll put the two of you together."

Fish pushed his empty plate away. Burped softly. Pulled his coffee cup closer. "You're going to be there with me, right?"

"We'll be there," Tory assured him. "You think you'll know anybody else there?"

"You mean, like, friends?"

She nodded.

He shrugged. "It's possible. But I kind of doubt it."

"If you don't think you'll run into people you know, we could give you a different name and background. If you could handle that, it might make things easier."

"What did you have in mind?"

"She's not dumb. She'll check up on you. Knowing that, we can create a background that will pass inspection. We make you someone from out of town who has just recently moved here. That way we can limit how much she can find out about your assets."

His jowls quivered. I took that as an okay.

I took a sip of coffee. "I can get friends at my old brokerage in Detroit to create a shell identity. When she checks it out, they'll be very guarded, passing along only the information we want her to know. You'll be the new rich guy in town, the one with a drinking problem, a drinking problem that may have damaged your health."

"Bad liver?"

"You could be borderline transplant. I've got a doctor client I bet will help set that up."

Our waitress appeared at the table. "Get you anything else?"

"Just the check," I said.

She wrote it out, tore it off her pad, placed it on the table.

"Should we look at wardrobe for tonight?" Tory asked.

I slid out of the booth and stood. She followed. "Why don't we divide and conquer," I suggested. "You do clothes. I'll set up the background identity. What time is the meeting?"

"Eight. In town."

"Let's meet back up at the Pier Grille at six. How's that?"

She nodded. "Are you going to change your appearance? You'd better if you want to go to the meeting."

She was right. If they recognized me, the whole thing would fall apart. "I'll do something. See you at six."

I watched them leave, paid the bill, and headed back to the office to use the phone. The first call was to my old brokerage in Detroit. When I hung up an hour later, we'd figured out how to set up accounts for Fish without violating any securities laws. I had enough trouble with the N.A.S.D. already. I didn't need more. Anyone who checked would discover an executive checking account, equities account, bond account, Roth IRA, and R.E.I.T account—all with substantial balances. What they'd actually be accessing were fictional accounts for an upscale investor created for use in a new packet of promotional materials.

The fictional name on the accounts was Frank Ford. Even the name seemed to suit Fish.

Now that he had money, I started calling to set up Frank Ford's medical history. That took longer. Even when you handle a doctor's investments, it's hard to get one to call you back. Both the doctors I needed—one in Detroit, one here in Sarasota—eventually called, reluctantly went along with creating a medical record showing chronic liver damage for Frank Ford.

My next call was to yet another client, this one a real estate owner with properties on Longboat and Siesta Keys. Since it was summer, he had lots of furnished units available for lease. I rented the flashiest one, a penthouse condo at the Sovereign, in Frank Ford's name for a month with an option to renew for a month.

I was down to my last call. Edith Hellsberg was an older lady who lived in my building at the Watergate and handled costuming and makeup for the Sarasota Actors Theatre. She thought it would be great fun to help me alter my appearance, said I should come to the theatre where she could work on me.

I saw her as soon as I entered the theatre lobby. Wearing a white smock, she was a small, gray-haired lady with a big smile. She rushed over, shook my hand, and pulled me along to her work area. "I love makeovers. By the time I'm done with you, your own mother won't recognize you."

We reached her area. "Sit on this stool," she said. As soon as I was situated, she tied a cape around my neck, spun me around to face a lighted mirror. "How different do you want to look?"

I had a feeling she was going to pile on the stage makeup. That wasn't what I wanted. "I need a few tricks, Edith. Simple things I can do and undo to alter my appearance."

She frowned. "On-and-off stuff, huh. Let's think what we can do." The frown was replaced by a smile. "I know. Hold on. Let me get a few things." She dashed out of the room.

I waited, thinking going there might have been a bad idea. There wasn't any reason I had to be at the A.A. meeting. If I didn't go, none of this would be necessary.

Edith returned, arms loaded. "Wait till you see what I've got," she said happily. She dumped it all on the counter. "Let's start with the shoes. Take yours off. Try these on.

I put them on and was suddenly three inches taller.

"Lifts," she explained. "Are those shoes big enough?"

"They're a little tight—"

"Suck it up," she said, digging in the pile for something else. "Sit down. Take your shirt off and put this on."

I took off the cape, then my shirt. This thing she had me putting on was like a vest, but with padding at the bottom that gave me a huge gut.

"That's perfect," she said more to herself than to me. "You're taller and we've changed your shape. Now we need to work on your face." She pulled a brown wig out of the pile. "Try this."

I tried to put it on. It wouldn't fit.

She watched me, shaking her head in amusement. "You've got a big head, Matt. Try this." She handed me a different one.

This one I could get on. It felt tight, confining.

"Let's see what we can do." She pushed, pulled, snipped, and brushed. Finally, she quit fussing, stood back, and admired her work. She spun the stool so I could look at myself in the mirror, asked, "What do you think?"

Gone was the salt-and-pepper curly hair. In its place was long brown straight hair. "Edith, it's great. I look like a different person. It's perfect."

"You're sure?" Concern showed in her face.

"Absolutely. Can I hold on to this stuff for a while? I may need it for a couple of weeks."

She waved a hand at me. "Keep it as long as you like. The theatre has so much, we never use half of it."

I gave her a kiss on the forehead. "Thanks, Edith. I owe you for this."

"Yes, you do." She smiled as she led me back to the lobby. "From now on, when it storms, I know who to call to take my plants in from the porch."

The acid test of my new look came an hour and a half later when I walked into the Pier Grille. From the doorway, I saw Tory and Fish sitting in a booth. I slid into the booth next to her.

Annoyed at the intrusion, Tory glared at me. "Don't—" she began. Then it dawned on her. "Oh, my God. You look so different."

"I know. I looked in the mirror, couldn't believe it."

I was studying Fish. Tory had worked magic on him, too. His hair had been stylishly cut, and he was dolled up in expensive but not pretentious clothes. They had to be new. I was sure Fish had never bought a genuine Polo shirt in his life. The little polo-player emblem made him look a little more upscale.

I nodded. "You look expensive. Do you feel rich?"

"What I feel is itchy. Must be the new duds."

Not the positive answer I'd hoped for. I smiled anyway. Think of it as homespun character, man of the earth, I told myself. "Well, itchy, let me fill you in on your new life, because the way this is set up, you've got some scratch."

"For real?" His eyebrows flew up

"For appearances."

"Oh." They lowered again.

Over dinner, I filled him in on his new identity as Frank Ford. By the time the check arrived, he seemed comfortable with his new identity. "Think you could get up in front of the group, introduce yourself as Frank Ford, say you're new in town?"

"You mean tonight?"

Our waitress arrived. I dug out my credit card, handed it and the check to her. She left. "Be great if you could. Rather than wait until the next meeting."

He gulped. Flushed.

"You can do it, Frankie. I know you can," Tory coaxed.

"I'll try," he said without conviction.

I signed the credit card receipt, left what I was supposed to leave, took what I was supposed to take. We departed.

We were off to our first A.A. meeting. The thought of it made me want a drink.

CHAPTER 23

The A.A. chapter Janet Wakeman trolled met twice a week in a converted storefront next to St. Mark's Lutheran Church. The sign next to the door identified it as the St. Mark's Multi-Purpose Building.

Inside, it was a single, large, open room. Neat rows of chairs faced a lectern at the far end of the room. A large coffee urn and stack of cups were on a table by the wall to the left. Over the pulsing hum of a stressed air conditioner, I could almost hear piped-in music. Thirty to forty people were already there. Mostly clustered in small groups. Several by the coffee urn. A few had already found seats.

Fish was one of those seated. By design, he was the first of our group to enter. We wanted him up front and visible. Tory had been next. She was standing by the coffee, surveying the room. I went in last, sat in the back row, tried to be invisible.

From the front of the room near the lectern, a bearded man with a large paunch said loudly, "If you want to go ahead and take seats, we'll get this evening's meeting started."

The buzz of conversations picked up as people finished their chats then died as they moved to sit down.

I looked for Janet. She wasn't difficult to spot. She stood out like Pamela Anderson at an AARP convention. She wore a tight red top that revealed plenty of cleavage, white slacks, a lot of gold jewelry. She had two older men trailing after her as she headed to her seat. I watched carefully. Since I was counting on a quirk of human nature, it was important to know exactly which seat she considered hers. People usually take the same seat time after time. If that was the case with Janet, we could plant Tory in the seat next to her.

She took the aisle seat, six rows from the front. Tory watched where she landed, too, took a seat several rows in front of her.

"It's good to see you all tonight," the bearded man intoned. "I see some new faces in the group. For you new people, we don't put on a lot of airs. We just get up and tell our stories. I was talking with Walt earlier—," he glanced around the room. "Walt, will you start us off?"

Walt, an older man in an ill-fitting suit, stood and headed to the lectern. He was followed by Grace, Allen, John, Jim, Helen, and Fritz. I kept waiting for Fish. The plan was for him to testify mid-program, introduce himself, say a few words. He didn't. Fish was still glued to his seat when the bearded man thanked everyone for coming and ended the meeting.

I left quickly. At the car, I fumed as I waited for Fish to return.

Tory arrived at the car first; she opened the door, and climbed in the back seat. Fish arrived right after her, settled in the passenger seat and hung his head. "I let you down. Sorry."

"Sorry doesn't cut it," I said. "Why didn't you do what you were supposed to?"

"I froze," he said slowly, quietly.

I started the car and pulled away from the curb.

"You couldn't even say a few words?" Tory asked.

He shook his head sadly. "I couldn't make myself get up there. I was afraid."

"We've got another chance in two days," Tory said to smooth things over.

"Think you can do it then?"

His head was still down. "I'll work on it. I'll be able to do it."

We rode the rest of the way to the Pier Grille in silence. If he couldn't say a couple of lines in front of a group, he wasn't going to be able to do the rest of what we needed him to do.

I pulled into the parking lot. Tory's Jetta was parked in front of the restaurant. I pulled into a space next to it. When I stopped, she said, "Frankie, I'll call you tomorrow and we'll work on what you need to do. Okay?"

He nodded glumly, got out of the Saab, lumbered to his car, an old Ford Monarch.

"You and I need to talk," Tory said pointedly as she moved from the back to the front passenger seat. When she was settled, she looked over at me. "Tell me there's more to this than hooking up Frankie and Janet. You saw him tonight. If he's our only option, we're dead meat. I am not feeling good about this."

I knew what she meant. I had trouble picturing Janet and Fish together, no matter how much money he supposedly had. "We need him to get better, that's for sure. Maybe we expected too much from him the first day."

That wasn't what she wanted to talk about. She shook her head. "Do you have a back-up plan if this goes boom?"

"Not so much a plan, more of a question."

"That's it? A question?"

I looked over at her. "Yeah. Something has been bothering me for a while now. How much money does D'Onifrio move in a year? Ballpark."

"The D.E.A. stuff I saw talked about hundreds of millions of dollars, maybe more. Nobody knows for sure."

"Then why is he so intent on getting back the three hundred and fifty thousand Joe took? It's peanuts to him."

"I don't know about that. Maybe he has to account for every penny."

I nodded. "He probably does. But this money was taken two years ago. They've closed the books on that fiscal year. So what triggered this? And why now?"

"Joe's death. That's your trigger, your why now."

"I don't think so. The trigger had to be on D'Onifrio's side. Something in his organization caused this."

"And you think this little charade with Frankie is going to help us find out what?"

"It's possible. He's pretty low in their organization to know anything. But by acting out this little charade, as you call it, we've at least bought some time to learn more."

"You're going to want me to do some digging?"

I nodded. "I think we need to work this on two fronts—dig for information, try and arrange this marriage. Either way, it's going to come down to the same thing."

She looked over at me. "What's that?"

"We've got to get ready to get lucky."

CHAPTER 24

I wasn't feeling lucky the following day. What I was feeling was harassed. The Dow was up twenty points, but the Nasdaq had fallen eighty. All the leading tech stocks—Microsoft, Cisco, Intel, IBM, Oracle, Dell—had dropped like stones. Most of my clients had some tech position. My phone rang like a banshee. I fielded one urgent call after another.

At one-thirty, Rosemary buzzed me. "Don't forget you're meeting with Julian at two."

I glanced at my planner. Damn. I finished executing a buy, grabbed my car keys, headed out.

On the drive over, I used the car phone to call Tory. "I'm on my way to meet with Julian," I said when she answered. "He's going to ask me if you've had any luck finding a connection between Nevitt and anybody at Merrill Lynch"

"Not yet. I'm working on it, but there are seventeen brokers, ten associates, and twelve clerical in that office. That's a lot to work through."

"Keep looking."

"I am. That's what I'm doing today. While I've got you on the phone, what time do you want to meet with Frankie tomorrow?"

"How much time do you think we need?"

"A bunch. He's got questions I can't answer. Where does he live? What kind of a car does he drive? How does he pay for stuff?"

"How about one-thirty at my office? We'll take care of all that stuff before the A.A. meeting."

"We'll be there."

I'd reached the parking garage of Julian's building. "Gotta go," I told her. I negotiated the turns of the garage, found a spot, parked, and took the elevator up to Julian's floor.

Julian was on the phone when his associate showed me into his office. Amy wasn't there yet. He waved me to a chair, wrote one word on a pad of paper and held it up. *Nevitt.*

I nodded, tried to follow the one-sided dialog.

"Sure, I understand," Julian said. "And I'm sure you understand that I will make an issue of Mrs. Wakeman's past marriages as well as your ongoing involvement with her." There was a long pause. "I think it's extremely relevant; I think a Judge will, too." Another long pause.

Behind me, I heard the door open. Julian waved. Amy took the other visitor's chair.

"That's a chance you'll have to take, isn't it?" Another long pause, during which Julian stood and paced behind his desk. "No, that's not acceptable. We want the suit dropped, the churning charge withdrawn." As he listened, anger colored Julian's face. "Don't get greedy, Nevitt," he said hotly. "You got what you were after. My client is no longer executor. Stop while you're ahead." More listening, and the pace of his pacing increased. "We'll come after you, expose this scam the two of you are running. You don't want your pictures on the front page of the paper. Drop the suits, we'll back off. Consult your client, counselor." He rang off, looked over at me, angry. "This guy is slime."

"What was that all about?" Amy wanted to know.

Julian plopped down in his desk chair. "Before you came in, I let him know we knew about their background and would paint her as a black widow. Sometimes that's enough to make them back off. Didn't seem to bother him." On his desk, he found a manila folder, opened it, rifled through the contents, handed Amy several sheets of paper. "He's filed for damages." He looked over at me. "Were you served?"

I nodded.

Amy looked up from what she was reading. "Big bucks. He's going for the gold."

"I called Tory on my way over here to see if she'd found any connection between Nevitt and those thrown trades from Merrill Lynch. So far she hasn't."

Amy shook her head. "But these peers who'll evaluate the churning charges against you—they'll see through the thrown trades, won't they?"

I shrugged. "Who knows. I'd like to think they would. I'd like to think Fowler knows they're trumped up. But the fact that they're thrown almost makes me look more guilty, like I knew I was going over four hundred percent and tried to hide it."

Julian's face was grim. "Let me call him, sound him out. We might learn something."

I gave him Fowler's number. "Would telling him Nevitt and Wakeman's backgrounds do any good?"

He stood, started pacing again. "Absolutely. The question is when we play that card."

"I say we play it as quickly as possible. The more people who know about them, the better," Amy said quickly.

He quit pacing, looked over at me. "I agree with her. When we finish here, I'll call Fowler, see if I can get on his calendar for a meeting. I'd rather deliver that kind of information face-to-face than over the phone."

We spent the next hour working through organization and details, much of which was Julian and Amy talking case law, precedents, cites. We finished at four. I retrieved my car from the garage, drove back to the office.

Rosemary's weary expression spoke volumes. "The Nasdaq dropped twenty more. The Dow plunged a hundred before the closing bell. Your voice mail is full." She handed me a mass of pink message slips.

I took the slips from her, glanced at them. "I'll tell Julian not to schedule any more meetings when the markets are in turmoil."

The phone started ringing. "I'd be ever so grateful," Rosemary said before answering it.

I was there that evening until almost seven, drove home, had a quick dinner, went for a walk on the beach. It was still light out when I left. I walked a mile and a half, turned around. The sun dropped quickly on my walk back. It was a spectacular sunset, white clouds at the horizon line turning pink and orange as the sun slid into the Gulf.

I covered the last half-mile in the dark, found my sandals on the pool deck, went up to the condo, changed into my workout clothes. I spent the next two hours in the gym, an hour lifting, an hour running. I took a long shower, went to bed.

The following afternoon, I was on the phone with a client when Rosemary showed Tory and Fish into my office. I nodded to them, indicated they should take seats, continued talking. "Your Pfizer is doing better than Merck right now. And I'd leave your AIM funds alone. They're doing just fine."

"When are we going to get back on the course?" my client wanted to know. "We haven't played in a while." Finally, the real reason for this call.

"The way the market's acting, things have been hectic. Let's see if we can't get out toward the end of the week."

"You got it. See ya, Matt."

I buzzed Rosemary, asked her to hold my calls, put down the receiver. Both of them were grinning at me. Something was up.

Fish surprised me by extending his hand. "Frank Ford," he said, his jowls quivering. "Moved down here for my health. Docs told me some time in the sun would do me good. The stress of running a corporation ate up my insides." He picked up my coffee cup, held it out in front of him. "Actually, this is what ate me up." He shook his head sadly. "Drink has been tough for me to give up, which is why I go to A.A." He pretended to take a drink. Smacked his lips. "Damn, that's good. Even if I do have chronic liver damage—life threatening, at that—I like to drink and spend money. Hell, what's the point of croaking rich? Cheers." He pretended to gulp the rest of his drink.

I sat there my mouth hanging open.

"What do you think?" Tory asked. "Isn't he great?"

"Amazing," I finally managed to say.

"It was just a matter of finding the proper motivation," Tory said.

"And what might that be?"

"I told Frankie if he got this right, he'd get laid."

CHAPTER 25

We talked through what we could at the office, mostly money issues, and headed out. Our first stop was the Sovereign, where I'd leased the penthouse apartment for Fish. On the way, I asked Tory how she'd fared with her Merrill Lynch inquiries.

She made a face. "Not well. You can usually find somebody with an ax to grind who'll talk. Not this time. Everybody's very closemouthed. So I've been working the financials, seeing who received money about that time. Turns out two brokers did: Regina Caswell and Ron Stoops. There was also a broker let go—Trey Brown. Same time period. I'm looking into all three of them."

"Wouldn't hurt to look deeper into Nevitt, too. Might help make the connection."

She nodded. "His financials might be very revealing."

I turned into the driveway that led to the Sovereign. "Your new crib," I said to Fish.

"Never thought I'd live on the beach," he said as we parked the car and headed to the office. "Smell that salt air."

"You're just leasing this place until you find something to buy," I expanded on the Frank Ford cover story. "I wouldn't be surprised if she wants to see where you live. You'll need to make the right impression."

We found the office, and I held the door for the two of them to enter. "This place would make the right impression on me," Tory said as she walked past me.

Inside, an older, balding man seated at a desk looked up from his paperwork. "Can I help you?"

"I'm Matt Seattle. I've rented one of the penthouse units for a month."

"Yeah, Glen mentioned you might be comin' by." He shuffled paperwork on his desk. "Here it is: 14-A." He stood. "Let me find some keys. I'll take you up, show you the place." He found keys in a wall cabinet. "Two sets enough?" he asked over his shoulder.

"That's fine."

"Follow me, please." He led us out of the office, providing a commentary on amenities as we went. "Pool's out that way, exercise room to your left, party room to your right."

We reached the elevators, rode to 14. He led us into the unit. "Living room," he announced, walking quickly through. "Kitchen's in here." He turned on the light, headed down a hall. "Bedrooms are this way; each has a bath. Linens are here in this closet." He came to a momentary stop in the master bedroom, turned. "Any questions?"

Without waiting to find out if there were, he retraced his steps to the living room. Like lemmings, we followed along.

"Here are the keys," he said, handing them to me. "If you think of anything you need, I'll be in the office. Name's Allen. Number's in the directory by the phone." He smiled. "Enjoy." With a wave of his hand, he ducked out the front door and shut it behind him.

I was a little taken aback by his quick departure although it was actually better this way. We could get to know the place on our own. Each of us wandered off in a different direction. Tory went into the kitchen. Fish sat down on the sofa, put his feet on the coffee table, got comfortable. I went out on the balcony. I wanted to make sure the view here wasn't better than mine. I stood at the rail, surveyed the panorama, decided I liked my view better. Satisfied, I went back inside.

Fish was still sitting on the sofa. He now had a remote in his hand, pointing it at a big-screen TV. He surfed until he found something he liked—wrestling. Grunts, groans, and screams emanated from the screen; it set my nerves on edge.

"If I marry this woman, would I be rich enough to live here for real?" Fish asked over the noise.

"Sure." I grinned. "I can see you two lovebirds living here." I walked over and picked up the remote. "Of course, if you really wanted to live here, you wouldn't be watching wrestling." I clicked through channels until I found a golf tournament.

He frowned. "Hey, I was watching the Rock."

"You're now watching the Tiger. You have to remember who you are. A person of your wealth and stature doesn't watch wrestling; he watches golf."

Tory emerged from the kitchen, talking. "I can smell what the Rock's cookin'—" She saw the look of disapproval on my face. "Oh, I mean, the Rock smells. Is cooked. Golf. Hey, now that's exciting. Go Tiger," she finished with a lame arm gesture.

"Suck up," Fish said snidely.

I couldn't keep from laughing. "As much as I'm enjoying this witty banter, we've got a lot to do before the A.A. meeting tonight. Let's get you some wheels; then with whatever time is left before the meeting, we'll get you moved in here."

"Sounds like a plan," Tory agreed.

Two hours later, Fish drove out of Mercedes of Sarasota in a red SLK 230 two-seat roadster. It was actually my car. I'd leased it in my name, figuring I'd use it after this was over. Fish, of course, was thrilled. He drove like a kid with a new toy, led us on a merry chase to his doublewide.

We packed up his more acceptable clothes, a few necessities, loaded them in the Saab. The trunk of the Mercedes, we quickly discovered, would hold very little.

We took off again for the Sovereign, where we unloaded Fish's worldly possessions, got them organized in the condo, and celebrated by going out for something to eat. Over dinner, Fish previewed for me what he was going to say at A.A. He made a few gaffes. Wasn't always fluid. Still, for the most part, he seemed to know his new persona. Tory and I tried to nuance a few areas, but overall I was pleased with his performance.

Back at the condo, we split up. Fish taking the Mercedes, Tory and I going in the Saab.

The last thing I said to Fish before he drove off was, "You feel good about this now, don't you?"

I expected him to say "piece-of-cake" or "no sweat."

He said, "Not really," and drove off.

Just as quickly, my confidence evaporated.

The multi-purpose room at St. Mark's Lutheran Church didn't look much different than it had two nights before. The chairs were arranged in the same way; the big coffee urn and cups were on the same table. The air conditioning still gasped for air. People talked in small groups.

The bearded man who had run the last meeting hauled the lectern front and center, tapped on the microphone, said, "Testing, testing."

Fish had found his seat in the front row.

It was déjà vu all over again except for one thing. Janet Wakeman was nowhere in sight.

"We're earlier than we were last time," Tory said in a whisper.

I looked at my watch. Maybe a minute or two earlier, not more. I felt my anxiety rising. "She may not come tonight."

"She seldom misses a meeting." She touched me on the arm. "I'm going to get in position."

I watched her take the seat next to the one Janet had occupied at the last meeting. With any luck, Janet would take her regular seat and Tory would be right next to her.

I found a seat in the back and settled in to worry, dinner a heavy lump in my stomach. Mentally, I cataloged all the things that could go wrong. I was up to number twenty-three, Fish forgetting and using his real name, when the bearded man strode to the podium and said, "Good evening. Let's go ahead and get tonight's meeting going. Sally, will you start us off?"

Sally was an older gray-haired woman in a blouse and slacks that didn't go well together. As she talked, a late arrival—an older man— took the aisle seat next to Tory, the one where Janet Wakeman usually sat. Tory looked back at me, made a face.

I knew what she was thinking. Our plan was beginning to fall apart.

Sally finished, relinquished the mike to Al. Still no sign of Janet.

Al finished his turn and turned it over to Ethel, an overweight woman with an irritating voice and a propensity to giggle uncontrollably. Ethel was in the middle of one of her giggle fits when, from behind me, I heard the sound of the outside door opening. It swung shut with a slam, followed by the click, click of high heels, the slap, slap of flats. Dressed in white capri pants and a tight red and white striped top, trailing an older man as if she had a hook in his nose, she swept down the aisle. When she neared where she usually sat, she stopped, put her hands on her hips in a how-dare-you gesture. Her seat was occupied. With a look of annoyance, she and her male friend took seats directly behind Tory, two rows back.

Tory's head turned as she looked to see who was causing all the commotion. At least she was aware of what was going on. Fish stared straight ahead.

Ethel finished with a fit of giggling and was replaced by Phil, a muscular bald guy in a golf shirt. I started worrying about Fish. Now that Janet was here, he needed to get up and give his talk.

Ed was followed by Marv. Fish still hadn't made a move. He looked frozen. Shelley came after Marv. Again, Fish didn't move. Worse, I had a feeling we were getting to the end of the program.

Tory looked back at me, as if asking what to do.

The bearded man was looking around the room, as if sensing the group was running out of speakers.

Get up, Fish. Get up.

Marv was winding down. The bearded guy stood, took a few tentative steps toward the lectern. This was it. This was the end. We'd wasted two more days, let a prime opportunity slip away.

I glared at the back of Fish's head, willed him to get up. Nothing.

The bearded guy was ten steps from the lectern.

Eight.

Six.

Tory looked back again. She knew it was over, too.

Four.

Fish wasn't moving.

I stood and headed for the mike.

CHAPTER 26

The bearded man saw me, gave a slight nod of his head, stopped where he was. I took the outside route to the front of the room as opposed to going down the center aisle. It was a little longer and allowed me to pass right in front of Fish. As I went by, I surreptitiously kicked him in the shin.

"Upphh," he said under his breath, glaring at me.

I glared back at him. "Sorry."

At the podium, I took a deep breath, surveyed the room. I didn't see anyone staring at my disguise, but standing there in the wig and fake spare tire, I felt absolutely ridiculous. I started in, altering my voice. "My name is Todd Kelter." I borrowed the name of a broker friend in Detroit. "And I'm an alcoholic. Been sober twenty-two days now. I lost some loved ones in my life, uh, started drinkin' and, well, it, uh, got out of hand, you know. The church helped get me straightened around and suggested I come to these meetings although I ain't much for speaking. Hearing you all, uh, has given me strength. Thank you." I looked hard at Fish.

He was watching me, his eyes wide with fear.

I started toward him.

He stood.

I smiled as we walked past each other.

As I took my seat, I heard him say: "My name's Frank Ford." His voice was low, quivering with fear. "I'm an alcoholic. I've been sober for seven days. I'm new in town, moved here from Detroit for my—"

Tory didn't wait. Her job was to set things in motion, and even though Janet wasn't sitting next to her as we'd planned, this was her chance.

Tory turned her head and leaned over to the man next to her as if to whisper something in his ear. "Jesus," I heard her say, "can you believe that dork is worth over ten million bucks?"

If I could hear her, I was sure Janet Wakeman, just two rows back, got an earful.

Fish flushed noticeably. "—health. The docs thought the change in climate might lower my stress level—that with a lower stress level, I wouldn't drink so much." He'd been looking down at the podium. Now he looked up at the audience. "But you know, there's a lot of stress to moving to a new place where you don't know anybody." He took a deep breath, blew out. "Makes me want to drink again, which is why I'm here. I can't go back to drinking. The temptation is so bad, yesterday, I called my sponsor in Detroit eight times. He told me in no uncertain terms I had to get in a program here. So here I am. Thanks for listening." He fled the podium for the safety of his seat.

The bearded man stood, walked to the podium, said, "Mr. Ford, a lot of us know your temptation. We'll help you, won't we?"

The group voiced affirmation. One male voice, louder than the others, stood out, "We sure will."

"We're a family," the bearded man continued. "We're here for each other, and we'll be here for you. Thanks, everybody."

People stood, pushed their chairs back. Informal groups started to form again. There was a buzz of conversation. Fish had three men gathered around him, talking. It wasn't Fish I was watching, though, it was Janet Wakeman. We'd put the bait in the water. Everything depended on whether she nibbled.

She stood, leaned close to her male companion, said something. I couldn't tell what. He nodded and she moved away from him to the coffee. She poured herself a cup from the urn, carried it a step to the right where Tory was putting cream and sugar in her coffee.

I couldn't hear what Janet said to her, but Tory made a face, shook her head, said, "I shouldn't have said anything. I'm sorry." She started to walk away. Janet said something else. Tory turned back to her and laughed. "As much as that guy's worth, all he has to do is say something and my boss would fire my ass in a minute. I'm getting out of here before I get in any more trouble."

Janet watched her head for the door. Fish had just left. I headed out, too.

Tory and I met at the Saab. She was grinning big time. "She went for it," she said excitedly as soon as I got in the car.

I grinned back at her. "What did she say?" I turned the key in the ignition, pulled the car away from the curb, and eased into traffic.

"She came up to me and asked why I said that man was worth over ten-million dollars. She said she knew he wasn't."

My excitement faded. I didn't like the sound of that. "You think she said that because she knew Fish, knew he wasn't worth ten million?"

"No. No. No," Tory said quickly. "I think she was trying to get me to tell her more, to prove I was right."

"Which you didn't do."

"Of course not. It wouldn't be believable. It's believable that I made an inappropriate comment. Blabbing more wouldn't be. Clamming up will make her think it was legit." She gave me a big smile. "Trust me, she's hooked. I saw it in her eyes."

"I'm glad that part's done. Tonight looked like it was going to be a fiasco."

She laughed. "I couldn't believe you got up there and talked. Where did that come from?"

"Desperation."

"You kicked Frankie on purpose, didn't you?"

"He needed a kick," I said as I slowed to enter St. Armand's Circle. The tourists who frequented the shops and restaurants around the Circle routinely stepped out into the street without looking. Tonight was no exception. A young man and woman, hand in hand, stepped out in front of me. I hit the brakes. The driver in the car behind me had to slam on his brakes to keep from rear-ending me. I glanced in the rearview mirror to see how close he'd come.

The distance I saw didn't bother me. The driver did. William Wilder.

CHAPTER 27

The following day it rained, a steady downpour that showed no signs of letting up. The kind of rain that drives tourists crazy, the kind the Florida Tourist Board swears never happens.

I had the Saab's windshield wipers on high as I drove to the office and still had trouble clearing off enough water to see the cars ahead of me. Our parking lot was a small lake. My shoes were drenched before I made it to the door. My umbrella did little to keep the rest of me dry. As quickly as I could, I unlocked the front door, stepped inside, and closed the door behind me. The office was dark. It wasn't six o'clock yet. I was in early to make up for being out the afternoon before.

I flipped on lights. I had just dumped the coffee in the filter paper when the phone rang. My watch said five 'til six. Somebody must have spent a sleepless night worrying about their stocks. I picked up the phone in the kitchen. "This is Matt Seattle."

"Matt, Julian. Listen, I've got to leave for Orlando in a few minutes, but I wanted to call and fill you in on my meeting with Fowler."

"What did he say?" I asked as I put the filter tray in the coffeemaker and hit the brew button.

"I'm afraid it wasn't good."

"Oh." Suddenly, I had that sick feeling in the pit of my stomach.

"Fowler interviewed all the brokers at Merrill Lynch. As you might expect, no one knew anything about those questionable trades."

I wasn't surprised. It would be one thing to admit throwing trades to help a friend who was sick or down on his luck. Admitting you threw trades for money or ill purposes would be career suicide. Worse, because those buys had my broker number, they wouldn't show on the Merrill Lynch blotters. There was no real evidence that could be used to force an admission. Unless that person came down with a bad case of the guilts, he or she was untraceable.

"That's pretty much what Tory discovered. What else did Fowler say?"

"He did ask each person he interviewed if they knew you."

"A couple of them probably said they did."

"Right. He asked if they knew Greg Nevitt and—"

"No one knew him. Surprise. Surprise. How did Fowler react to that?"

"He didn't really say. Judging by his tone of voice, I think he found about what he expected to find. I don't think it hurt us. I don't think it helped us. He said he'd share his findings with the arbitration panel and leave it up to them."

"Then it hurts us. Fowler should know this smells. For him to be neutral amazes me. He should be throwing this out. These are questionable buys we're talking about."

I agree with you," Julian said calmly. "When Fowler brought up Nevitt, I used that as an opportunity to ask if he knew anything about Nevitt's background. He didn't. I filled him in on Nevitt and Wakeman."

"What was his reaction to that?"

"It rocked him. I saw it on his face. He's an ivory tower guy, wants to keep his hands clean. I think he realized he might be dealing with somebody who doesn't play by the rules and might get dirt on him. Fowler didn't like that. Listen, I've got to run. Amanda will call you to set up our next session with Amy."

"Thanks, Julian." I hung up the phone, filled my cup, walked back to my office. By the time Rosemary arrived at eight, I'd gotten through most of the backlog. By mid-morning, I was caught up. The markets were taking a breather after yesterday's frenzy of activity. Our phones were quiet. It was the kind of day—if it hadn't been raining—I would have tried to get away for some client golf.

Instead, I wandered out to the lobby, stood in front of the window, watched the downpour.

"Two weeks and Rebecca will be here," Rosemary said from behind me.

I turned to face her, smiled. "I know you'll be glad to see her."

"That I will." She took a deep breath. "Dan and I were wondering if you'd like to come to the house, have dinner, meet her."

This was an invitation I shouldn't refuse. It would hurt Rosemary's feelings. I didn't hesitate. "Love to. What night?"

She looked at her calendar. "Well, she gets in on Monday. I was thinking Wednesday, maybe."

I got my Blackberry out of my pocket, found the date. It was clear. "Let's do it." I entered dinner at Rosemary's.

"You two will hit it off; I know you will."

"I'm sure we will," I said with a smile and turned to stare out the window again. Dr. Swarthmore would approve. I wasn't sure, though, that I was ready. Behind me, I heard the phone ring, Rosemary answer.

"Tory on line one."

I took it in my office. "Can you be available for a meeting tomorrow morning at ten?" she asked hurriedly.

I assumed this was about the thrown trades. "Sure."

"Call you right back." She was gone. Three minutes later, she was back.

"Okay, it's set. Paul Raines—he's a D.E.A. special agent—has agreed to an off-the-record meeting. We're going to meet out of town. I'll pick you up at your office at nine."

"I'll be ready," I assured her. And I was. At eight-fifty the next day, I was watching out the window for her. Instead of the steady rain I'd watched the day before, it was only spitting. Dark clouds mixed with flashes of blue sky, intense sunlight.

At eight-fifty-five, she pulled into the parking garden. "Hold the fort," I said to Rosemary as I went out the door. I got in the passenger seat of her Jetta. She put the stick shift in reverse, backed up, pulled out onto the street. "See if any of your playmates are behind us," she said as she turned from Palm to SR41.

I turned around in my seat, watched. "There's a white van, blue Ford Taurus."

"Keep watching them."

She turned off SR41 at Beneva. The white van kept going, the blue Ford followed. "We've still got the Ford."

She took Beneva down to Ellerby, turned left. On my right was Sarasota Memorial Hospital. The Ford was still following. She turned right into the hospital drive, pulled up to valet parking at the main entrance. "Where's the Ford?"

"He pulled up to the curb, half-a-block back."

"Time to change cars." She opened her door, got out. I exited my side. She gave her keys to the valet, got her ticket. We went in the hospital's main door, followed the signs to the main parking garage. We rode the elevator up to level six where a red Ford F150 pick-up truck was parked. She unlocked the doors, and we got in. "See if you can scrunch down out of sight," she said as she tugged on a ball cap.

I got down in the foot well as best I could, felt the truck spiral down the ramp, the bump as we leveled off.

"Okay, it's safe to get up," she said after we'd driven a few minutes. She took off the cap, threw it behind the seat. "See if anyone's following us now."

I watched as she pulled back on SR41, headed south toward Venice. "I don't see anybody."

"You're sure? Paul will be pretty annoyed if we bring a tail."

I watched out the rear window again. "I think we're clean." I turned back around.

She was staring out the front window, both hands gripping the steering wheel. She took a deep breath, blew it out. "Good." Her hands loosened a little. "Let me tell you about Paul before we get there. He's been investigating the Menendez cartel for over three years. Probably knows more about the inner workings than anybody. Paul got me the information I shared with you about D'Onifrio. When I followed up with him yesterday, said you thought something was going on, he agreed. I didn't think he'd be willing to meet with us, but he agreed to that, too. He's expecting you to ask a lot of questions. He'll give you as much information as he can. All off the record, of course."

I nodded. "Did you tell him my theory about Joe's money?"

She looked over at me. "I told him what you told me the other day."

"What did he say?"

"He didn't." She'd started watching out her left window. "We're looking for a NationsBank branch."

I started watching, too. "There it is. I see the sign."

She pulled in the parking lot, turned off the engine, and we walked into the bank.

"Can I help you?" an older, gray-haired lady, probably the manager, wanted to know.

"We're here for the ten o'clock meeting," Tory said.

"Oh, yes. Right this way." She led us to a small conference room in the back of the building. Once we were inside, she stepped outside, closed the door. I expected Paul Raines to be there already. He wasn't.

He arrived fifteen minutes later, stepped quickly into the room, shut the door behind him. He was a medium-sized man with short dark hair, graying moustache, hard dark eyes. He wore a white polo shirt, wrinkled khaki trousers, a cell phone on his belt. His gaze swept us, the room, returned to Tory. He extended his hand. "Tory, we've talked on the phone. Good to finally meet you." They shook. He turned to me. "You must be Matt Seattle. Good to meet you." We shook as well. "Sorry to make you come all the way out here, but it's a secure location. The room is soundproof, so we won't be overheard." He looked over at Tory. "I watched. No one followed you."

"I think we started with somebody, so the measures you recommended worked," she said.

He smiled, turned to me. "Matt, tell me how you got mixed up with D'Onifrio. Tory gave me a little bit. I want to hear it all."

I told him about Joe, Janet, Nevitt, Fowler, Wilder, the whole sordid mess. By the time I was finished, he was shaking his head.

"You befriend a guy and this is what happens to you. Jeez, that's awful." He stroked his moustache absent-mindedly. "I can't help you with any of that, but I can help you understand what's going on with the cartel. It's an interesting time right now. Enrico Menendez, who has been in sole control of the cartel since his brother's death, is getting ready to relinquish some responsibility. He's 83. Not in good health, knows it's time for him to name a successor. Since Enrico didn't have any children, the leading candidates are Ernesto's two sons: Ernesto, Jr., called Little Ernie, and Eduardo. Both have come up through the ranks. Both are tough, ruthless. But both have some baggage. Little Ernie's a hothead, prone to fly off the handle if he doesn't get his way. Eduardo likes to flaunt his power, make people uncomfortable."

"Great choice," Tory said sarcastically.

"Well, that's the problem. The word within the organization is that Enrico can't choose between them. Also, he doesn't want to have one be the winner, the other the loser."

"Why doesn't he have them share control?" I asked. "He and Ernesto did."

"Enrico doesn't believe his nephews get along as well as he did with his brother. He thinks they'd fight constantly and the cartel would suffer from the infighting." Raines paused, leaned forward. "Enrico has told a few of his key advisors he's looking beyond the nephews—"

"D'Onifrio," Tory said softly.

Raines looked at her, smiled. "Exactly. Enrico's adopted son." He stroked his moustache reflectively. "D'Onifrio has some baggage, too. Some of the senior council members question whether he's ruthless enough to head the cartel. So until Enrico makes the decision, D'Onifrio's under a microscope. They're looking for anything and everything. Knowing that, D'Onifrio is trying to find any perceived problems and eliminate them before they become issues with the cartel."

"You think that little bit of money Joe took would have been an issue?"

"Oh, yeah. First, it raises the leadership question. If you're a good leader, your people are loyal to you. They don't steal. Second, D'Onifrio didn't realize the money was missing, didn't immediately correct the situation." Raines made a face. "Sloppy. They won't tolerate that. Third, three hundred grand isn't a little bit of money; it's a chunk. More importantly, it's a chunk of their money. You don't trifle with their money."

I nodded. "D'Onifrio made a comment to me about it being his depositor's money."

Raines reacted with surprise. "You talked to D'Onifrio?"

"I had to," I said and told him about Wilder, Eddie's death, the deadline I was facing, and the plan I'd come up with.

"Sorry about your dog. I've got a black lab, myself. I know how I'd feel if that happened to him." He stroked his moustache. "I find it difficult to believe D'Onifrio would go along with this marriage idea."

"He said he was willing to give it a try because it wouldn't attract attention."

Raines grimaced. "Still doesn't make sense. There's no guarantee he'll get his money. No time limit."

"He said I had a month."

"Enrico and the nephews are due in town for a big powwow about then." He thought for a second, frowned. "He could be setting you up to show them how ruthless he can be."

CHAPTER 28

"What do you mean?" I asked, nervously.

His gaze darted to Tory, back to me. "I don't mean to frighten you, but the timing bothers me. D'Onifrio could be planning on killing or torturing you in front of Enrico and the nephews. Be a hell of a way to overcome objections he's too soft."

Tory's eyes were wide. "You don't really think he'd do that?"

"Yeah, I do. He's working hard to present the right image. Let me give you an example. D'Onifrio was about to receive a national award for his generosity in helping deaf Latina children. He's donated over a half-a-million of his own bucks for hearing aids, operations, whatever helps. He was scheduled to be honored in Miami last week. Two days before he was to pick up his award, he canceled. Why? So he didn't look caring. Wrong image if he wants to run the cartel."

I was only half listening, replaying the meeting with D'Onifrio in my mind, looking for something to disprove Raines theory. There wasn't anything.

"What do you think we should do?" Tory asked.

Raines thought for a moment, looked directly at me. "The first thing you've got to do is realize it's his agenda, not yours, that's being followed. He's playing you for a fool. Your only chance is to get away. Go to the police and ask for protection. If you don't want to do that, disappear. Move to Montana. But don't think you'll win against D'Onifrio. You'll lose—and when you lose—it's going to cost you your life." He looked at his watch.

I glanced at mine, too. Eleven-twenty. An hour had flown by.

Raines got a business card out of his pocket, slid it across the table to me. "That's how you can reach me if we need to talk. Never call from a cell phone or your own phones. Too much chance of being overheard. Call from a pay phone; I'll call you right back." He stood. "You guys go ahead. I'll leave in a little bit."

Tory and I stood.

He extended his hand, first to her, then to me. "Good luck," he said when we shook.

On the ride back to Sarasota, I stewed over what he'd told us. I had more information, not necessarily more answers.

"Want me to call Frankie and cancel tonight?" Tory asked.

If I took Raines' advice and got as far away from D'Onifrio as possible, there was no need to go through the motions at the A.A. meeting. I could load the few things I needed into the car, leave for parts unknown. If I left, I'd lose the brokerage, quite possibly Nevitt's suit for damages.

"Did you hear me? Do you want to cancel tonight?"

"No."

Tory looked over at me, surprised.

"We go on as planned."

Although Tory argued against continuing, eight o'clock found us back at St. Mark's for the nightly A.A. meeting. If this thing was going to work—if Janet had been intrigued by Frank Ford's money—I was counting on her initiating some sort of contact tonight. The good news was that she was already there when Tory and I arrived. I didn't have to worry about whether she'd be attending the meeting or arriving late.

Fish was already there, too.

The bad news was that Janet, standing by the coffee table, had three men buzzing around her. Fish sat, all by his lonesome, in the front row on the opposite side.

It seemed an insurmountable gulf. So far, I hadn't seen her even glance his way. Still, I wasn't ready to panic. The meeting wouldn't start for another ten minutes. Tory and I found seats in the back and settled in to watch the show. And that's certainly what she was putting on. Her act was almost musical, an ever-changing combination of three notes: hair fluff, boob jiggle, derriere wiggle. That night her costume consisted of a tight leopard skin-patterned top that showed plenty of cleavage, tight black capri pants, and silver stiletto heels. On a couple of jiggles, she almost came out of her top. Those guys couldn't get close enough to her.

"Can you believe this?" Tory whispered.

"She's a tease, all right."

"Tease? That one guy is sporting such a woody he's going to poke a hole in his pants."

I shook my head. "She hasn't even looked Fish's way."

Fish's shoulders were hunched. He looked like he was getting ready to throw up.

"He isn't exactly looking her way, either," Tory said.

"It may be sacrilege to suggest this here, but maybe we should have loosened him up with a couple of beers before we came over."

"Might not hurt. He's way too uptight to make a move on her."

"The move Fish would like to make right now is out the door."

Tory shrugged. "He said he could do it, Matt. We've got to give him a chance."

"Look at him. Does he look like he can do it?" I didn't wait for her answer. I nodded in Janet's direction. "Look at those guys. They get off just being around her. Fish is terrified." I shook my head. "Still, I don't know what choice we've got. I can't go up and kick him again."

The bearded man made his way to the podium. Every couple of

steps, he stopped to take a sip of his coffee.

"We rehearsed what he needed to do. He knew it backwards and forwards," Tory whispered. "She just needs to make the first move."

"Good evening, everyone." The bearded man held his coffee cup with both hands as if to soak up the warmth. "If you could find seats, we'll get started."

Janet fluffed her hair one more time, said something to the three men, and sashayed—alone—to a seat on Fish's side of the aisle.

Tory leaned over. "See," she whispered in my ear.

She saw Janet's choice of seats as an indication she was getting closer, getting ready to approach Fish. To me, Janet was still six rows away from him. They weren't playing kneesies yet.

The program started. One by one, members of the audience got up to talk. I was beginning to recognize some of the regulars—Sid, Ethel, and Don.

To my surprise, Fish got up. He gripped the sides of the podium with his hands. His eyes showed terror. "I'm Frank Ford, and I'm an alcoholic," he said in a deep, quivering voice. "I'm new to Sarasota. Been sober since I got here—twelve days now. Really don't know anybody yet. Oh, I met a few people, sure—doctors mostly. Them I gotta know. But I don't know any, you know, real people. It's pretty lonely. I guess, cause I'm lonely, I want to drink, which I know I shouldn't do." He paused, surveyed the room, his heavy brows knitted. "I learned something from this, something important. Friends are like a bypass operation, you need 'em to keep you going." As abruptly as he'd gotten up, he sat down.

"See," Tory leaned over and whispered. "Surprised you, didn't he?"

Stunned was more like it. His pathetic plea had been perfect. Unfortunately, two long-winded talkers followed Fish to the podium. The first man was bad, the second awful. So bad, in fact, the bearded man stepped in and announced they were out of time.

Nobody complained. Some people stood and began moving around, Janet among them. She scooted down the aisle, turned the corner, and intercepted Fish. They stood there talking. Or rather, she talked. Fish might have said a word or two. She smiled. Fish nodded. Something was decided. She took his arm, and they headed out together.

I tried not to stare as they walked by.

"Oh, my God," Tory said as soon as they were out the door. "It worked."

"C'mon," I said, standing up and following them. "We need to see what happens."

She hurried to keep up with me. "You want to spy on them?"

"I prefer to think of it as chaperoning."

Out on the street, we saw Fish holding the passenger door of the Mercedes open for her. She got in. Fish closed the door and headed for the driver's side. We walked hurriedly up the sidewalk to where I'd parked the Saab.

With the head start he had on us, I was afraid we'd lost him. Five blocks down the street, however, we spotted the Mercedes parked at the curb in front of a Starbuck's. That made sense. I remembered Tory's comment about how they'd gotten to know each other over coffee.

"Aren't we going in?" Tory wanted to know when I continued past.

"Starbuck's is a little too cozy for the four of us. I think we'd do better to watch from out here." I put my left turn signal on, waited for a car to pass, turned left into a driveway. I backed out, drove to a spot on the opposite side of the street from Starbuck's. From where we were parked, we saw Fish and Janet carry their coffee to a table by the window.

After only a few minutes, Tory groaned. "This is like watching paint dry."

I looked over at her, surprised. "Wait a minute. I'm the one who should be bored. You're the P.I. You should be extolling the virtues of stakeouts."

She gave me a pained look. "You are so full of crap."

"Moi? Your employer?"

The pained look continued. "Stakeouts went out with the Rockford Files. Nobody has time to sit around and hope they see something."

"And your alternative would be?"

"How about changing our appearances? You've done it once. I'm sure I can come up with something."

"I had a friend in the theater who helped me. I'll call her and see what she can do for you."

Tory nodded. "That's better than sitting in the car all the time. I feel like a stalker."

Fortunately, their coffee didn't take long. Forty-five minutes later, Fish escorted her to the car, they got in, and he drove her back to where her car was parked. After that, we thought he'd head back to the condo. He did, with one stop on the way, a liquor store, where he bought beer. Lots of beer. A celebration?

CHAPTER 29

We sat around the condo's kitchen table drinking beer. "She said she knew what it was like to be alone and didn't want me to have to go through that kind of pain." Fish was giving us the play by play, word for word. "I said, yeah, I feel like I don't have a friend in the world. She smiled when I said that, said she'd be my friend."

Gag me with a spoon.

"It was your speech," Tory said. "It showed your vulnerable side."

Fish nodded, swallowed some beer. He put the can back down on the table, leaned forward, and looked at her, his bushy eyebrows arched high. "You think?"

"I'm sure you impressed her," Tory assured him.

"Let's let Mr. Sensitive tell it—without coaching," I suggested.

Tory frowned at me, sat back in her chair.

Fish took the hint. "Yeah, well. She said she always went for coffee after these meetings and asked if I wanted to come with her. I said what I could really use was a beer." He paused, expecting a reaction. When he didn't get one, he said, "She thought it was funny."

"Hilarious. Continue."

He shrugged. "I drove to the coffee place—a Starbucks. Gave me a chance to show off the car. She thought it was nifty."

"Did she ask if you had other cars?" Tory asked.

"Yeah, she did. Like we rehearsed, I told her my big Mercedes was in Detroit. This one was just to tool around in down here." He shook his head. "Actually, she pumped me pretty good. She asked how I came to Sarasota. I told her by plane." Again, he gave us the look, waiting for a reaction.

I sighed, exasperated by his attempts at humor. "You didn't tell her you came here because your doctor recommended it?"

His brow furrowed, causing his eyebrows to collide. "A wealthy guy like Frank Ford wouldn't just do an information dump. A guy with that much money, well, he'd be a little more sophisticated. I thought that's how you wanted me to act?"

I smiled. The humor was Fish's attempt at sophistication. At least he was trying. Fish was only doing what he thought we wanted. It was important not to dump on him. Better to encourage him. "That's exactly how I want you to act," I said. "She gave you the perfect opening to talk doctors. I just wanted to make sure you took advantage of it—within character, of course."

His brow unfurrowed. His jowls quivered. His version of a smile. "Exactly. I was asking myself what's my motivation here? And I was thinking Frank Ford has a confidence about him, a sense of humor. He's not the kind of guy who would just blurt out his medical problems. I mean, he's a tough business guy, right? He'd be a hard case. She'd have to pull information about his doctors out of him. So that's what I made her do."

"You did?" I asked incredulously.

"Absolutely. She had to work to get Dr. Clark and Dr. Jarrett's names."

"But she got them?"

"Eventually."

"What else did she have to pry out of you?"

"She asked about family—if I'd been married, had children. I told her I was still a virgin and gave her one of these." He scrunched up his eye in what might pass for a wink.

"What did she say about not having any family?" Tory asked.

"Nothing."

"Nothing?" I repeated.

"Nothing," he said, finishing his beer, and leering at each of us ecstatically. "What she said was she didn't believe a guy like me could still be a virgin, but if I was, she'd have to do something about that."

CHAPTER 30

I had trouble getting to sleep that night. Once I did, the dreams came.

We'd just arrived at church for the funeral. Dad had driven. Mom had tried to make small talk. I'd sat in the back, dazed, withdrawn, Eddie by my side. Dad parked the car. I didn't want to get out. He helped me, put his arm around my shoulder. "We'll get through this, Matt."

Every step I took from the car to the church was slow, labored. The priest met us outside, said a prayer, escorted us in. Friends and family were there, a sea of sad faces. In front of the altar, three caskets in a row.

I saw it all but none of it registered. What got my attention was the music, the church organ groaning a somber dirge. Claire would have hated it.

"Matt, where are you going?" I heard my mother say as I walked off down the aisle to talk to the organist.

I startled the poor lady. She stopped playing, ending with a couple of abrupt, strident notes.

"Do you know In This Very Room?" I asked her, tears streaming down my face. The song had been one of Claire's favorites.

She nodded, began playing.

A lone voice starting singing. Others joined in. I tried. The words wouldn't come. Just tears.

I woke. The hurt as deep as ever. I looked over at the bedside clock. Five a.m. I knew I wouldn't get back to sleep. I got up, took a shower, had some breakfast, went in to the office.

At seven-thirty, I called Dr. Swarthmore, got her machine, left a message. She hadn't called back by ten, when Rosemary buzzed me. "Julian on line one."

I picked up. "Hello, Julian."

"Hang on one second." I heard him give instructions in quick, authoritative bursts to someone in his office, probably Amanda. "Sorry," he said coming back on the line. "Our mediation session has been scheduled for tomorrow at one o'clock here at my offices. You don't have a problem with that time, do you?"

All the things I'd rather be doing flashed through my mind. "No; let's get this over with."

"I agree. This is going to be a total waste of time. But at least it will get their demands on the table."

Unfortunately, the mediator was powerless to resolve anything. The mediation session was simply a required step to make sure there were issues to be resolved when the case went to arbitration. Nevitt, of course, would insist the issues were huge, setting the stage to ask for major damages. Julian would downplay things, field a trial balloon on how much Nevitt wanted to end this thing. Nevitt would get a figure out on the table. We'd laugh at it and the case would move on to arbitration.

"Nevitt give any clues when you talked to him?"

"Not really. He knows I've filed a motion to dismiss his civil suit. He ran his mouth about that. Judging by the way he ranted, tomorrow could be ugly. You prepared for that?"

"Guess I'll have to be. Who's the mediator?"

"Sue Ann Tansky. Know her?"

"No."

"Seemed nice enough on the phone, but I'm not expecting

anything from her. We just need to get through this."

"See you at one." I rang off, entered the event and time in my Blackberry.

Rosemary buzzed again. "Dr. Swarthmore on two."

"Adelle, thanks for calling back so quickly."

"Not a problem. More dreams?"

"Afraid so," I said and filled her in. As I did, I heard the scratching sounds of a pen on paper, pages being turned.

When I finished, she said, "I have a group session in just a few minutes, so I can't talk long. This dream, like all the others, Matt, was your mind processing information. The fact that you've now processed this information—that you have more of the grieving process behind you—is positive. These last dreams have happened in close proximity to each other. Almost in a cluster. Indicating, perhaps, a final burst to completion." I heard paper rustling, pages turning. "That's consistent with the progress you've made. You are far more interactive with people than you were six months ago. This dream cluster may be an indication you're getting ready to allow friendships to deepen into relationships." I heard the sounds of a door opening, people talking. "I'm afraid I have to go, Matt. Would you like to schedule a time when we can talk longer?"

I hesitated. "Let's see how things go the next couple of days. Then I'll call and schedule something."

"That's good. Take care, Matt," she said as she rang off.

I worked steadily the rest of the day. Left the office at seven, grabbed a bite of dinner on my way home, went for a long walk on the beach. I needed to think through what I'd learned from Raines.

His theory that D'Onifrio planned to use me to demonstrate his ruthlessness made sense. That's why he'd gone along with my crazy marriage idea. Not because he thought it would work or because he didn't want to attract attention. It was because he could turn it to his own benefit.

The question was could I turn it back? That's what I needed to explore. Ever since the meeting with Raines, something had been nagging at my subconscious. As I walked along the edge of the water, letting the waves wash up on my feet, I tried to get that something to reveal itself. I walked about a mile and a half, turned, and walked back.

That night, at two in the morning, I woke up knowing what that something was.

Better yet, I knew how to use it to my advantage.

CHAPTER 31

The next morning at the office, I told Rosemary I was going to run a quick errand, left the building, and found a pay phone. I dialed the number Paul Raines had given me.

"Yeah," a voice answered.

"This is Matt, I need to talk to Paul," I said trying not to reveal much.

"Give me your number. He'll call you right back."

I read him the pay phone number, hung up, waited. No more than a minute later, it rang. I picked it up.

"You needed to talk?" It was Raines.

"I've got a couple of questions that need answers."

"Not over the phone."

"No. I was hoping you'd meet with me again."

"You're out on Longboat, right?"

"Yes."

"You know where the dry dock boat storage is?"

"Yes."

"Go there tomorrow. Ask in the office for Mike. He'll get you to me."

"What time?"

"Be there at ten."

"I will. Thanks." I hung up, walked back to the office. I had two hours before our meeting with the mediator. I used the time to put through a batch of transactions, caught a quick lunch at The Bagel Stop, arrived at Julian's office ten minutes early.

I thought I'd be the first one there. Amanda, Julian's associate, assured me I wasn't. "They're all in the conference room," she told me as she led me back.

"Probably yukking it up in there, right?"

She looked back at me over her shoulder and rolled her eyes. "This is not the fun bunch, no." We reached the conference room doors. "Good luck."

"Thanks," I said as I opened the door. Inside, all three—Julian, Nevitt, and Sue Ann Tansky—turned and watched me. I tried to read their faces. Julian was smiling. Nevitt was scowling. The mediator, an older brunette wearing heavy glasses and a high-necked suit, showed a grim expression I took to be her I'm-objective-this-is-serious face.

I didn't let that deter me. I walked over, extended my hand. "Ms. Tansky, I'm Matt Seattle."

She offered a limp handshake and mumbled something that sounded like, "Havaseat."

I took the seat next to Julian and facing Nevitt. Tansky was to my left at the head of the long table, an open legal-sized folder of documents in front of her.

Julian looked at his watch. "Now that we're all here, I think we can begin." He looked at Tansky, who had her head down, studying documents.

She continued to read, apparently oblivious to our waiting. Finally, she looked up. "Let's try and make productive use of our time here." It was a schoolteacher's chiding voice. "The first thing I need to know is whether there's still a dispute to be mediated."

Nevitt snorted. "We think there is."

"We don't," Julian added firmly.

Tansky looked up from her papers, smiled slightly. "Those

answers add up to a yes. We'll move forward." She looked at Nevitt. "Mr. Nevitt, it looks like your client, Mrs. Jesso, never actually dealt with Mr. Seattle. Is that right?"

Nevitt nodded. "That's correct. Mr. Jesso handled all the couple's financial affairs. He told his wife he felt Mr. Seattle was taking advantage of—"

"That's enough Mr. Nevitt. I was just trying to understand why Mr. Jesso didn't bring these charges."

"He was about to," Nevitt volunteered, "when he died."

"That's hearsay, of course," Julian added smoothly. "Not the fact he died. That's indisputable. However, there's no evidence of any dissatisfaction on Mr. Jesso's part."

Tansky took a deep breath, blew out. "This will go more quickly without these little posturing exchanges," she chided, giving both Julian and Nevitt hard looks. "I need to get your positions on the table. Let's see if we can do that without starting a debate. Mr. Nevitt, state your position."

"We're looking for the return of all commissions, the total dollar figure is $95,000, I believe."

"Mr. Ockerman," she said to Julian, "what's your position?"

"We want a complete dismissal."

"Back to you, Mr. Nevitt. Is there anything else you require before this case goes to arbitration?"

Nevitt thought for a moment, frowned, shook his head. "I don't think so. No."

"Mr. Ockerman, is there anything you require."

"As a matter of fact, there is. You may have noticed that there are trades in question that originated at Merrill Lynch."

Tansky nodded. "Yes, I was aware of those."

"It's been alleged Mr. Seattle made those trades. He says he didn't, which calls into question who did. Since Mr. Nevitt's client is the one who stands to benefit, we'd like to review her financial records for the last year."

"That's ridiculous," Nevitt shouted. "She's the victim here. You're trying to harass her."

Julian smiled, handed Nevitt an envelope. "That's a court order. If you don't deliver complete financial records to me in two weeks, you'll he held in contempt. If my CPAs tell me something—anything—is missing, I'll go back to Judge Bruegger and you'll do thirty days."

"This is ridiculous," Nevitt repeated. "You can't—"

Tansky had started packing up her files. She paused. "I'm afraid he can, Mr. Nevitt. The only way to not comply would be to settle now. Do you want to try and negotiate?"

"No, we don't," Nevitt sputtered.

Julian stood. "Two weeks, Nevitt. If anything's missing, I will have your ass thrown in jail."

Nevitt, face red, jaw jutting, got up, glared at Julian. "Think you're so smart. You're not. You're only making things worse."

I felt like cheering as I watched him leave the room. It was the first time I'd seen Nevitt off balance. "Can you really get him thrown in jail?"

Tansky chuckled under her breath.

"Probably not," Julian said. "But he can't know that for sure. Might make him a little more motivated to cooperate."

Tansky stood, clicked her briefcase closed. "I believe I'm finished here."

Julian walked her out. I stayed. There were things I wanted to know. When Julian came back, I asked, "If we find something in these financial records, can't we get this whole thing dismissed?"

Julian smiled. "The proverbial smoking gun. That sort of thing?"

Okay, so it was wishful thinking.

He shook his head. "They're not going to turn over anything

incriminating. Nevitt's too shrewd to do anything that self-destructive. Meanwhile, though, we've bought ourselves a little time."

Time. I looked at my watch. I had a lot to do before I met Tory for tonight's A.A. meeting. I stood, walked over, shook Julian's hand. "Great job. Keep after them. I've got to run."

"Where are you off to in such a hurry? Hot date?"

"Just business."

"I don't believe it," he said, smiling.

Surprisingly, I wasn't sure I believed it, either.

CHAPTER 32

I'd arranged to meet Tory at Columbia, a restaurant on St. Armand's Circle. I was sitting at the bar with a really good glass of wine, making notations on my Blackberry, when she arrived. She took the stool next to mine, shook her head. "How can you drink before an A.A. meeting? Don't you feel guilty?"

After what I'd dealt with that day, I felt I deserved a glass of wine. I gave her a big smile. "Not at all."

The bartender arrived. "What can I bring you?"

"I'll have what he's having," she said, pointing to my glass.

"Very good," he nodded and headed to the bar.

"Talk about two-faced," I chided her.

"Yeah, whatever." She shrugged off my criticism with a smile. "I've had a hard day. I looked at the financials of everyone at Merrill Lynch. Do you know how long that took?"

I shook my head.

"Eight tedious hours." Our waiter arrived, placed her glass in front of her. She looked up. "Thank you." To me, she said, "Do you know what I found?"

I shook my head again.

"Zip. Zero. Zilch."

"Any luck connecting somebody to Nevitt?"

She took a sip of her wine, shook her head. "I've got a few things left I want to check. But so far—nada." She took a deep breath, blew out. "Then there's Frankie. The man's a constant interruption. He wanted direction on what to do in every situation. If he takes her to dinner, where should he go, how should he pay?"

"Did you tell him to use the credit card?" I'd arranged for a credit card tied to the Merrill Lynch accounts he was supposed to have in Detroit.

"Yeah. But then he wanted to know if there was a limit on what he could spend. You know, don't order an entrée over $12.00. That kind of thing."

"What you're telling me is Frank Ford the multi-millionaire is a tightwad. That plays, I guess."

"Anally-retentive tightwad," she corrected me.

"So is the anally-retentive tightwad primed to ask the loose woman out to dinner tonight?"

She laughed. "This is serious."

"I know."

She took another sip of wine. "She intimidates him. He is so off balance, he doesn't know what to do." She shook her head. "He ends up saying whatever pops into his head. So far that's worked out okay. Will he ask her out to dinner? I think he'll blurt it out at some point, yes."

I shook my head. There was no telling what else he might blurt out either. "On that cheery note, I suggest we order another round so we're fortified for this evening's festivities, or lack thereof." I held up my hand and signaled the bartender.

We ended up ordering another round of drinks and dinner. It turned out to be a very pleasant meal. We didn't talk business, just made small talk. Movies. Florida. Sports. Likes. Dislikes. I don't know whether it was the wine or thinking about something other than my sorry situation, but I actually relaxed for a few minutes. Still, one eye was on my watch. I made sure we got to the A.A. meeting on time.

Fish was in his usual seat in the front row. Janet was in her usual seat halfway back. However, there was a guy sitting next to Janet with his arm around her shoulder. Every so often, he leaned over and whispered something in her ear.

"Maybe it's not as bad as it looks," Tory said quietly as we found seats in the back.

"It looks bad enough to scare Fish off. Romeo there is practically kissing her neck."

As the meeting continued, he rubbed her shoulder, fiddled with her ear, hugged her to him. She didn't return his attention, but she didn't smack his hand, either. Fish may have known what was going on between the two of them. He didn't get up to speak; he just sat there, hunched over, staring straight ahead. I sat slouched down, dejected, waiting for the meeting to end and Janet to jiggle and wiggle out with her new lothario. The end, mercifully, came quickly. The bearded guy closed the meeting.

People stood, milled about. A few headed for the door.

I watched Janet. She and lover boy stood. He was talking to her, a smirk on his face, his hand on her upper arm, guiding her down the aisle. That was it. I looked over at Fish. He was still sitting there motionless.

"'Atta girl," I heard Tory say under her breath.

I looked back to see what had happened. Janet had shaken off lothario's hand, and they were having words. I couldn't quite make out what was being said, but the annoyed expression on her face spoke volumes. He tried taking her arm again. She pulled it back angrily. There was another verbal exchange I couldn't catch; Janet walked away from him. He went the other direction, toward the door. I did catch one word. "Bitch."

As he passed where we were sitting, Tory leaned over to me and whispered, "Look at the comb-over on that guy. Yech."

He was money, though. Neatly-tailored designer clothes. Kissy sandals. Flashy jewelry. Facelift. Should have spent a little more and joined the hair club for men.

I turned my attention to where Janet had headed, spotted her up front with Fish. She was talking, explaining probably. Fish was nodding. She finished. They both smiled.

"Yes," Tory said as we watched them leave together.

We ducked out ahead of them and hurried to the car. As we got closer, something about the Saab looked wrong. I walked faster. The closer we got, the more apparent it became. The convertible top had been slashed, leaving a huge hole. Strips of canvas dangled into the passenger compartment.

"How awful," Tory said.

I studied the damage, noticing the slashes were all at angles. That's when the ah-ha hit. "Wilder did this," I said angrily. "These slashes are in the shape of a "W." He cut his initial so we'd know it was him."

Tory shivered. "Let's get out of here."

I couldn't drive with the strips blocking my vision. I had to put the top down. The torn top folded awkwardly. It took me three tries to get it so things weren't hanging out, flopping around.

I raced to Starbucks, trying to make up lost time. When we arrived, I didn't see the red Mercedes parked outside, Fish or Janet inside.

"They couldn't have finished that fast," Tory said, peering into the shop.

"Is there another coffee place around here?" I asked.

She shook her head. "There used to be. Starbucks put them out of business."

I slammed my hand on the steering wheel. "Damn."

She looked over at me. "Don't get frustrated. Let's think where else they might have gone."

I pulled the car to the curb, put it in park. "Bar? Restaurant? His place? Her place? There aren't that many places they can go."

"There's a restaurant two blocks down. We can see if they went there. The car should be easy to spot."

I put the Saab in gear, pulled away from the curb. They weren't at that restaurant, nor were they at any of the other six places we tried before we gave up and drove to the Sovereign to wait for Fish's return.

Up in the condo, Tory got two beers from the refrigerator, handed one to me. "You look like you could use this."

I handed it back to her. "I don't like beer all that much."

"I do," she smiled and used a bottle opener to pop the top.

We waited in the living room. Tory got comfortable on the sofa, took off her shoes, surfed the TV. I paced. "Sit down," she said. "You're making me nervous."

"I'm too wound up. I can't sit."

"Just 'cause we don't know where Frankie is?"

That and the convertible top and Wilder and the meeting tomorrow and—

"Look," she said. "It's only nine-thirty. He's a grown adult. He might not come home until midnight. If he gets lucky he might not come home until morning. You can't pace all that time."

I continued to pace.

"Maybe you didn't hear me. Come here and sit down. Let me rub your shoulders."

I stopped pacing. "I'm all nerves tonight."

"Sit right here," she pointed to a spot on the sofa.

I sat. She kneaded my shoulders. It felt good.

"Jeez, no wonder you were pacing. You're one solid knot."

I laughed.

Fish picked that moment to walk in. "Whoa," he said and leered.

"Don't let me interrupt you; I'm just going to get a beer and go in the other room."

I sprang up. "You're not interrupting," I told him. "We were waiting for you, couldn't find you after the meeting."

He sauntered into the kitchen and got a beer from the refrigerator. "She didn't want to go for coffee. She wanted to get something to eat. We went to a place called Jewel's. Not bad. Pricey. But not bad."

"If you guys had dinner tonight, did you ask her out for tomorrow?" Tory asked.

Fish came out of the kitchen, chugged his beer, burped. "I'll have you know we're spending the afternoon together tomorrow. I'm picking her up at three o'clock; we're going to go to Mote Marine Lab and look at the fish. Stupid, if you ask me. But that's what she wanted to do. Then we're going to get something to eat at the Chart House. They got a band." He took a big drink. "She wants to stay and dance."

"Dancing. Way to go, Frankie," Tory said enthusiastically.

He shook his head sadly. "Her idea. Not mine. I told her I don't dance."

"Lot of holding and touching when you're dancing," Tory pointed out. "I think you're going to enjoy it."

"I'll enjoy the holding and touching part," Fish said, his sad sack expression betraying no emotion. "Not the rest of it."

"What time are you going to get there for dinner?" I asked.

His shoulders twitched. A shrug. "How long can it take to look at a bunch of fish? Bet we eat early. Six, maybe."

"You're doing great—"

"Yeah. You'll be in the sack in no time," Tory said with a smile.

Fish turned red. "I need another beer." He turned and went back in the kitchen.

"We need to go," I said to Tory.

"Okay." She put her shoes back on, got up. "I'm ready."

"Good luck tomorrow," I said to Fish as we headed out the door. "We'll catch up afterwards, see how it went."

On the ride down in the elevator, I asked Tory, "What do you think about this dinner and dancing thing?"

"Sounds like a woman with a plan. She's moving things along."

The elevator reached the ground floor, the doors opened. "That's what I'm thinking," I said, agreeing with her. We walked to the Saab, and I drove her back to the Circle where she'd left her car. On the way, I let her know I was going to meet with Raines in the morning.

She looked over at me. "You want me to go with you?"

"No. I'd rather have you concentrate on the Merrill Lynch/Nevitt connection."

She groaned. "I didn't realize you were such a slave driver."

I chuckled, pulled the Saab into a space next to her car. "I'll call you tomorrow afternoon; how's that?"

"I may have died from carpal tunnel by then." She grinned, got in her car, and drove away.

I drove home, worked out in the gym for an hour, took a shower, read for a little bit, went to bed. Unfortunately, although I was tired, I was also wound up. Too worried to fall asleep.

Everything hinged on what Raines had to say the next morning.

CHAPTER 33

At the dry dock office, I asked for Mike. He turned out to be a short wiry man wearing a wife-beater, faded swimming trunks, flip-flops. A cigarette dangled from the corner of his mouth. "Paul told me you was comin'. Boat's ready," he said, flicking his cigarette away.

I followed him out to the docks and a small fishing boat. He untied the lines, indicated I should get in. He jumped in after me, started the motor, guided us out into Sarasota Bay.

I wanted to ask where we were going, but the engine noise made talking difficult. I sat back, tried to enjoy the ride. We crossed the bay, ran north to Bradenton. Mike slowed the boat for a no-wake zone, entered a waterway, pulled up to a private dock. He nodded at the house. "Paul's inside."

I got out of the boat, started up to the house, hesitated. "Are you going to take me back?"

"Yeah, don't be all day."

I walked up to the back door, knocked, looked in. It was the kitchen of someone's home. Paul opened the door. "C'mon, in." He led me to the kitchen table. "Coffee?"

"Sure." I took a seat.

He poured two cups from a Mr. Coffee, handed me one, sat across the table from me. "Why aren't you a thousand miles away from here?" he wanted to know.

"It's not that simple."

"Life is never that simple. Survival is."

I gave him the Reader's Digest version of why I didn't want to go; he shook his head.

"You should leave," he said when I finished. "You can start over someplace else."

"I may do that." I took a sip of my coffee. "Couple of things I'd like to know first."

He nodded.

"You said Enrico and his nephews were coming to town. When exactly? Is this a special visit? Do they come often?"

His eyes narrowed, his jaw clenched. He looked like he was going to clam up on me.

"Please. I know it's sensitive information. I just need to know so I can make my peace with this."

His face relaxed a little. He stroked his moustache. "Enrico and his entourage will arrive in seventeen days. It's a regularly scheduled visit. They come twice a year to review the investments D'Onifrio has made on the cartel's behalf. The difference this time is that Enrico is going to make his decision. He wants all three of them present for the announcement."

"Do you know where they'll be staying?"

"They always stay at the same place, the Colony Beach."

Figured. The Colony, just down the beach from me on Longboat Key, attracted the rich and famous from around the world. A contingent of South American businessmen wouldn't be out of place at all.

"How long will they be there?"

Raines took a sip of his coffee. "Their reservations are for two weeks."

"How soon after they arrive do you think Enrico will make this announcement?"

He looked at his coffee cup, frowned. "That's hard to say. My guess is he'll want to go over D'Onifrio's resume with a fine-tooth comb, make sure there's nothing there that could prove embarrassing. How long will that take?" He shrugged. "If D'Onifrio passes muster, I think Enrico will go ahead, quickly make the announcement. This has been hanging over his head a long time. I think he wants to get it over with."

"What would happen if something embarrassing turned up?"

"Depends on how embarrassing."

"Say this stolen three hundred thousand dollars D'Onifrio missed."

Raines stroked his moustache, thought.

I took a sip of my coffee, waited. This was payoff time.

"You've got a couple of factors," he said finally. "Enrico has already told key advisors on the senior council that he favors D'Onifrio. How invested that makes him, how betrayed he'd feel, I don't know. I do know that in their culture you don't make the big guy look bad without suffering the consequences."

"What kind of consequences?"

"Could be anything from demotion to death. Although—even if D'Onifrio embarrassed him badly—I don't think Enrico would have him killed. You don't kill somebody who saved your life. The nephews, on the other hand, would kill D'Onifrio in a heartbeat. They'd jump on an opportunity to eliminate a rival."

"Which nephew is the bigger threat?"

He grinned. "Depends on whether you'd rather be shot or have your throat slit. They're both dangerous."

"Let's say the nephews decided to eliminate him. Would it happen immediately? Would they do it here? Or would they do it in Columbia?"

"Little Ernie's a hothead. He'd try and do it the day of the announcement. Eduardo might, too. I don't think either of them is worried about the U.S. authorities, if that's what you're asking." He stood, walked over to the Mr. Coffee, held up the pot. I shook my head. He poured some in his cup. "D'Onifrio won't go down easily, either. He'll be prepared for anything, probably armed to the teeth."

"Are you saying the nephews might not be able to kill him?"

He walked back to the table, sat down. "Be tough. Even with all the firepower in their entourage, and they're bringing fifteen bodyguards."

"But they can't bring guns into the country?"

"They have people here for that. By the time they get in cars to leave the airport, they'll be fully armed."

I finished my coffee. "Does Enrico speak English?"

"A little. The nephews are fluent." He smiled. "Television."

"Where do they hold their meetings?"

"Usually at Shore. Although one year when Enrico was ill, they used a meeting room at the Colony." Raines must have sensed I was running out of questions. "Listen, I don't know what you're thinking. But I hope what I've told you makes you understand it's a bad idea. Get away from these people. They've killed four of my men. They won't hesitate to kill you." He stood.

I did, too. "Thanks for meeting with me." I held out my hand, we shook.

"Sorry to bother you at home."

"This isn't my house. It belonged to one of my operatives. They tortured him to death last week."

CHAPTER 34

I had a ton of work waiting for me when I returned to the office. "It's all this gallivanting around you've been doing," Rosemary said, summing up the problem.

She was right. I'd been out of the office way too much. The clients had to be wondering. Worse, I didn't see how the situation was going to get any better for the next couple of weeks.

I'd had talks with a young broker at Smith Barney, Saul Badgett, about joining the firm. He was a sharp young kid who'd be great to help out and "grow the business." But I hated to bring him on with Fowler and the N.A.S.D. hanging over my head. It wouldn't be fair to Saul to have him join, then go out of business.

So I chained myself to my desk and worked. At six, Rosemary stuck her head in to let me know she was leaving. "I'm impressed," she said. "You got a good bit accomplished."

I still had a pile in front of me. "Guilt," I told her. "I don't want the clients feeling I'm neglecting them."

She smiled. "Well, I haven't heard any talk about stringing you up by your thumbs yet."

"Only because you've covered for me so beautifully."

She blushed, made a face. "Oh, go on."

"Just want you to know I appreciate all you're doing."

She beamed. "See you in the morning." I heard her lock the front door as she left.

I went back to the stack, was almost to the bottom when the phone rang.

I picked up the receiver, hit the button. "Seattle on Stocks."

"Matt. Tory. I wanted to call and let you know I've done all I can on this Merrill Lynch investigation. I haven't found anything. Sorry."

So was I. If she'd found something, anything, I could have gotten Nevitt off my back. "You said it was going to be tough."

"I tried everything I know to try. Whoever's guilty has hidden it really well."

"The Nevitt connection. Anything there?"

"I'm afraid not. I cross-referenced him with everybody at Merrill Lynch. No matches."

"Thanks for trying," I said, discouraged.

She rang off.

I tried to go back to work. But after her phone call, my heart wasn't in it. I turned off my computer, left for home. I stopped at Publix, picked up a salad. In my present mood, I needed something simple. No preparation. No cleanup. Back at the condo, I ate my salad right out of the plastic container, washed it down with wine in a plastic cup. Dinner over, I rinsed the plastic, put it in the recycling bin, and got out my Blackberry. I wanted to enter what Raines had told me while it was still fresh in my mind.

When everything was entered, I stared at it, tried to sort it out. My plan had been vague at best. Get information about D'Onifrio's sloppiness to Enrico and crew, see if I could start a fight between them. What Raines had given me confirmed that was possible, not probable. I wasn't going to be able to get anywhere near Enrico or the nephews.

I worried about it for more than two hours. Frustrated with myself, I got up, put on a pair of swim trunks and a tee shirt. It wasn't the first time I'd gone for a midnight walk on the beach to sort things out. I left my shoes by a chair on the pool deck and walked to the Gulf's edge. It was a warm night with a sky full of stars, just a touch of a breeze. I walked on the wet sand, letting the waves wash over my feet as they ran up on the beach. Usually, a walk at the water's edge relaxed me. Tonight, my mind was too confused, conflicted to enjoy this simple pleasure.

"Well, well. It's just you and me. How about that?"

William Wilder stood ten feet in front of me, a gun in his hand.

I froze.

He took a couple of steps forward. He was dressed in a fancy shirt and tie. Braces held up his trousers. His concession to being on the beach was no suit jacket. He was grinning wildly.

"What do you want?" I was scared, but I was also tired, and that made me irritable.

He laughed. "Oooh, getting brave are we? You won't feel so brave when I tell you want I want." He raised the gun and pointed it at my head. "I want to put a hole right between your eyes." He pretended to pull the trigger. "Poof, you're dead." He put the gun down. "You're lucky. Tonight is not about what I want, it's about what Mr. D'Onifrio wants. He wants to see you."

"Great, I'll call him in the morning, go by the bank." I started to turn to walk back to my condo.

"Not tomorrow. Now."

I stopped, half turned around. "What if I don't want to go now?"

He grinned. "He said I could pistol whip you, not so bad you couldn't talk, but pretty bad."

I didn't doubt him. In fact, he was probably hoping I'd give him trouble so he could hurt me. I took a deep breath, blew out. "Where are we going? I don't have any shoes on."

"Poor baby, doesn't have any shoes. You're going to have to walk over broken glass, too."

I followed Wilder to his car, thankful I was walking on sand, concrete, and asphalt. He drove us to D'Onifrio's house, a huge, walled estate on the water south of town. A guard opened the gate at the end of the driveway. Wilder pulled up in front of the house, stopped, turned off the engine. "Ring the door bell. He's waiting for you." I got out and walked up to the door. The driveway was loose gravel that felt like broken glass. I reached the door, pressed the bell.

Ding dong, ding dong, ding ding ding dong, it echoed inside.

The door was opened by a young blond woman wearing a man's white dress shirt and nothing else. I could tell there wasn't anything else because she only had the very bottom button buttoned. Ann, the girl from the bank.

"Close your mouth and come on in," she smiled at me. "He's waiting on you, and he doesn't like to be kept waiting."

I shut my mouth, remembered Tory's description of this place as the Playboy mansion South.

"This way." She led me down a long hall to a media room in the back of the house. A porno flick was playing on a projection TV system with a screen so large the assembled body parts looked life-size.

D'Onifrio was sitting on a leather sofa, watching. Ann tapped him on the shoulder. He turned, looked at her, then at me. "Sit." He pointed at a chair next to the sofa.

I sat. Or rather, perched. Nervously.

He stared at me, his face tired, his hair disheveled. He was wearing a black satin robe. I don't think he had anything else on. Not even his hearing aids. There was no whine. "Fish tells me his involvement with this woman is going well. Wilder tells me he thinks it's going well. I want to know what you think."

I swallowed. "I think she's bought the idea that Fish is a multi-millionaire and she's starting to put the moves on him. It's actually going faster than I thought—"

"How fast?" he said, his face turning more intense.

"Pretty fast, I think." I fumbled for words.

He scowled. His eyes looked away from me, back to the screen, back to me.

"They went to dinner and dancing together. She suggested the dancing. I think that's pretty good, considering she's only known him a couple of days."

"How much longer will it take?"

I shook my head. "The way she's acting, I don't think it's going to be too much longer."

"Not good enough," he glared at me, his eyes narrowing. "My depositors are demanding an accounting. Every day the money is not where it belongs makes them angrier."

"I'm trying to—"

"I want you to feel the pressure I feel," he shouted at me. "What do I need to do to make you move faster? Do I need to torch your business? Do I need to hurt one of your friends? Do I need to hurt you? I will do whatever I need to do to get the money back. Understand?"

"I hear you," I said quietly.

Now that he'd threatened me, he smiled. "Good." He turned away from me, watched the screen.

I assumed that meant he was through with me. I stood and returned the way I'd come in. Wilder was waiting for me outside, standing by the car. When he saw me, he got in, started the engine. I didn't want to be anywhere near him, but I wanted to get home. Reluctantly, I opened the passenger door and got in.

We rode to Watergate in silence. He pulled in the entrance, stopped the car, looked at me, grinned. "End of the line."

I felt lucky to be home. I opened the door and climbed out.

"Last guy I killed took two days to die," he told me before I closed the door. He laughed hysterically, hit the accelerator. The car threw gravel on me as he pulled back out on Gulf of Mexico Drive. I turned and walked down the drive to my building.

As I walked, I tried to assess what had just happened. D'Onifrio had wanted to personally pressure me. That had to mean the pressure on him was getting really intense. Confirmation of what Raines had told me earlier in the day.

My watch said two-fifteen when I entered the condo. I closed and locked the door behind me, poured myself a glass of wine, took my second shower of the evening, got into bed, and tried to will myself to sleep. I tossed and turned, becoming more and more agitated until the shrill ring of the phone shattered the night's quiet.

The bedside clock read three-fifty as I grabbed the receiver off the cradle. No phone call at this time of night is good news. "Hello."

"Is this Mr. Matthew Seattle?" a male voice asked.

"Yes, what is it?"

"Mr. Seattle, this is Sarasota Metro Fire Department."

CHAPTER 35

It felt like somebody had hit me with a truck.

"We're calling to notify you that a fire is in progress at a property we believe you own on Palm near Coconut."

Thirty minutes later, I turned the Saab off SR41 onto Palm. I went only a block on Palm before being stopped by police barricades. I slammed on the brakes, pulled to the curb, got out of the car. A policeman stopped me almost immediately.

"That's my building that's on fire."

He nodded, let me continue on. Ahead, I saw what was left of the building illuminated in the eerie white light of halogen spotlights. There was a haze of smoke, the smell of wood burning in the air. I didn't see any flames, but that was because there wasn't much left to burn.

Most of the roof was gone. All of the windows and the front door were gone. Big black scorch marks ran up from the openings. The yard and the parking area were littered with charred remains—a sofa, a visitor's chair, wallboard. Firemen walked around with hoses, squirting things that still smoldered. Exhaust fans blew a constant stream of smoke and noise from the building.

I stood on the curb and watched, feeling helpless and angry. D'Onifrio hadn't needed to do this to make me feel the pressure.

A fireman in full gear came over, stood next to me. "Are you Mr.

Seattle?" he shouted over the noise of the exhaust fans.

I nodded.

"I'm Captain Harris. Sorry about your place. We got here less than two minutes after the alarm was turned in. Flames were already shooting out the roof. Not much we can do when it's that far along. It's going to be a total loss, I'm afraid."

I knew he was right.

"There's a fireproof safe in the back left room," I shouted, telling him where my office had been. "Is that safe okay?"

He shrugged. "If it's fire rated, it should be. When things cool off, we'll take a look. In the meantime, there's a man who needs to talk to you." He pointed to a group of men standing by one of the fire trucks. "See him? The guy with the windbreaker that says Sheriff's Department. He's the arson investigator."

I nodded, headed over, and introduced myself.

"Jack Fines. Arson," he said and handed me his card. "Let's go over to my vehicle, get out of the noise. It'll be easier to talk."

I followed him over to a police cruiser. He got in the driver's side, I got in the other side, pulling the door closed behind me. He was right; it did cut down the noise.

"Mr. Seattle, I don't mean to alarm you," he said, "but this fire was set. Do you know of anyone who might want to harm you?"

I shook my head, tried to look bewildered and buy a little time to think. I couldn't tell him anything about D'Onifrio. That would only make matters worse. Saying I couldn't think of anyone who had a grudge against me sounded fake.

"Think back. Has there been any trouble at work? At home?"

A terrible idea surfaced. One I should have rejected immediately. Instead, I put everything I had into selling it. "Actually, there has," I said tentatively. "But I can't believe he'd do anything like—"

"What kind of trouble?"

"Well, it's really sort of a misunderstanding. I can't believe it has anything to do with this."

"It might. Tell me about it."

I made him pull the story of the Wakeman/Nevitt suit out of me a detail at a time. Each time he got a nugget of information, he wrote it down in a small notebook. "You say you had this meeting with the negotiator just a couple of days ago," he repeated, writing furiously. "What was her name, again?"

"Sue Ann Tansky. She'd be a good person to talk to. She can tell you how upset Nevitt was when we asked for financial documents."

He finished writing, looked over at me. "Any other problems or people you can think of?"

I pretended to ponder that for a few moments. "No, I can't think of anything else."

"We'll start looking into this. Is there a number where we can reach you if we have further questions?" I gave him one of my cards. He looked at it, tucked it in his notebook. "If you think of anything else, you've got my card." He opened his door. "Thanks for your time, Mr. Seattle."

"Thank you. I appreciate your effort to track down whoever did this."

He gave me a final we'll-get-'em nod and got out of the car. I did, too.

I stood on the curb and watched the firemen pull things out of the building and throw them on the lawn. It was still too soon to go back into the building, and watching didn't seem very productive. I looked at my watch. Four-twenty. It had been a long night. It was probably going to be an even longer day.

I headed for my car. I needed to let all my clients know what had happened. The easiest way would be a fax alert. I could do that from my machine at the condo. As I walked, I considered headlines:

"Seattle's Stock Picks So Hot, Building Burns."

Or

"How Can You Be Sure Seattle Has The Hottest Recommendations?
Hey, Who Else Has Had A Building Burn?"

Or

"Seattle's Stock Picks Are On Fire.
(Oops, The Building Just Went Up In Smoke.)"

When it came time to actually do it, however, I chickened out, used the more bland:

"Building Destroyed By Fire.
Won't Stop Seattle Service."

In the text, I told everyone to contact me at my cellular number and that we'd be back in touch as soon as we had a new location. I turned the fax program on send and went to the kitchen to get something to eat.

I made coffee, dumped Cheerios into a bowl. As I poured a glass of orange juice, my hand shook. I was used to getting a bad night's sleep, not to getting no sleep. I sat, ate, tried to hold myself together.

At seven-thirty, I called Rosemary at home and broke the news to her.

"How horrible," she said angrily. "What can I do to help?"

"I don't know yet. I'll know more after I talk to the insurance company. I'll call you back."

I hung up and dialed Shelby Simms, my agent, gave him the details. He had a plan of action.

"Here's what we'll do. I'll have a portable office trailer brought to your location. Fully furnished—desks, phones, computers, fax. You'll be back in business by noon. Let me get going on that. Once we get that set up, we'll start on your claim. How's that sound?"

"Sounds great, Shelby. Can you let Rosemary know when the unit will arrive? She'll get things going on our end."

He agreed. I called Rosemary back and filled her in on the plan while I had my third cup of coffee. Tired and wired.

As soon as I hung up, the phone rang. It was Tory. "Matt, I just saw your building on the morning—"

"Yeah, it was a pretty bad night."

"Do they know who did it?"

"They don't, but I do. It was D'Onifrio."

I heard a little gasp at her end, then she said, "I'm afraid I've got more bad news, too. Frankie fell off the wagon last night."

CHAPTER 36

"I just got off the phone with him. He is really hung over. Apparently, he had a couple of beers before he met her because he was nervous. A couple more while they were eating, a couple more while they were dancing."

"How many is a couple of couples?"

"I asked him that. He thinks he may have had fifteen or sixteen beers. He really doesn't remember."

I groaned. "He's supposed to have chronic liver damage. He can't drink like that."

"Well, he did."

I tried to think. My head felt like mush with a lump of pain behind my eyes. "Can you call him back? Tell him to stay in the condo, not take any calls or make any calls to Janet. Maybe we can turn this to our advantage."

"How?"

"By pretending he's deathly ill. That's going to take a plan. Could we get together over lunch, put something together."

"Where?"

"The Pier Grille is easy. Quarter to twelve?"

"See you there."

I hung up and dialed Julian's number. "He's taking a deposition," Amanda said. "Can I help you?"

"I need to fill him in on some late-breaking developments. Have him call me as soon as he can, will you, Amanda."

"Sure."

"Oh, and tell him to call my cell number. The office burned down."

"What?"

"One of those late-breaking developments I need to talk to him about."

"I'll definitely have him call you."

I poured my fourth cup of coffee, looked at it, dumped it in the sink. I set the timer on the oven to go off at quarter after eleven, went into the living room, and stretched out on the sofa.

Brang, brang, brang brought me back to reality. The damned oven timer. Still groggy, I jumped up, shut it off, went to the bathroom, splashed some water on my face, brushed my teeth, tried to feel human.

It wasn't working. Looking back at me in the mirror was a drawn and haggard face. I didn't dwell on it; I had more to worry about than my appearance.

Tory was waiting in a booth, iced tea in front of her. Her hair pulled back in a ponytail, wearing a Day-Glo orange tee-shirt. I slid into the other side of the booth.

She made an exaggerated face. "You do look like hell."

"And just think, I look better than I feel."

Our waitress arrived and handed me a menu. Tory already had one. I handed it right back to her. "Cheeseburger and a Diet Coke."

"Want fries with that?"

I shook my head.

"You, ma'am?"

"Cobb salad, please." She watched the waitress leave with our orders, then turned to me. "What happened?"

I started with my meeting with Paul Raines, moved to the

evening's abduction on the beach, finished with my conversation in the police cruiser with Jack Fines.

She laughed at the last. "Nevitt is going to be pissed."

That made me laugh, too. "I hope so. I hope they haul him down to headquarters, work him over with rubber hoses."

Our food arrived. We ate in silence for a few minutes, then I asked, "Were you able to get Fish to stay inside and not answer the phone?"

She finished a bite of salad. "Yeah, he didn't care. Said he'd stay in and watch the tube. What are you thinking?"

I swallowed a bite of hamburger. "For a guy who wasn't supposed to drink, he put away a lot of beer last night. If he were sick, he'd have had a reaction to all that beer. I'm thinking that we make it look like he spent the day at the hospital."

"How are we going to do that?"

"We need just a few trappings to draw the picture—a hospital bracelet around his wrist, a home health nurse at the condo."

"I'm not sure I see where you're headed with this."

I took a drink of my Diet Coke. "We need to accelerate the marriage. D'Onifrio torched my building to let me know he was serious about not waiting any longer."

"You're sure about that?"

"Absolutely sure. It's what Raines warned me about. D'Onifrio's turning up the heat as the meeting with Enrico gets closer. I'm also sure his next hurry-up message will be something worse. I'm thinking we use Fish's drinking and the resulting illness as a way of letting Janet know he could die at any time."

"You think that will hurry her up?"

"Can't hurt. If she thinks she might lose a big score, she might move things along faster. Especially if Fish dangles some money in front of her."

"Like a big diamond ring?"

I took a bite of burger, chewed, thought. "A ring feels like rushing things. Maybe we have him start looking at really expensive houses. Maybe he tells her his condo is only temporary, he's looking to buy a place, but he wants to know if she'll share it with him."

"Back into a proposal. That might work."

"If she thinks she's picking out a million-dollar house—"

Tory nodded a couple of times, digesting what we'd just talked about. "When are you thinking all this is going to happen—her seeing him sick and all?"

I swallowed the last of my hamburger, pushed my plate aside. "I'm hoping when she can't reach him today she'll wonder what's going on. When he finally answers the phone—or better yet, when the home health care person answers it—I'm betting she'll want to come over and see how sick he really is."

"So you're thinking tonight?"

I wanted to do as much as I could as fast as I could. "It would be good if it happened tonight. If it did, we could do the real estate tomorrow."

Tory finished her salad, took a drink of tea. "You want me to hire a nurse, prep Frankie and the condo?"

I nodded. "That'd be great. I'll arrange for a realtor who can take them to some expensive houses tomorrow."

"What time do you want him to start taking calls again?"

I shrugged. "I don't know. Seven?" I looked at the check, left money on the table. I slid out of the booth. "I've got to go check on my new digs."

She stood. "I'll call you when I've got it lined up."

I thanked her as we headed out to the cars.

From the Pier Grille to the office was a thirty-minute drive. I talked on the phone the entire way. By the time I turned onto Palm and got my first look at the trailer, I had a realtor friend clearing her schedule for the next day.

I pulled the Saab to the curb and parked. The trailer was larger than I'd expected, probably thirty feet long. It took up the entire length of our little parking garden. Rosemary was standing in the doorway. She waved when she saw me pull up, walked down the three steps, and headed my way.

I met her half way. "It's bigger than I expected."

"It's not half bad inside, though right now it's hotter than blue blazes. They're working to hook up the air conditioning. The man who will hook up the computers said he'd come back when we've got air. It's too hot for computers now; he said they'd fry."

I nodded. "How about phones?"

"He was a real man, not afraid of the heat. They're hooked up."

I looked over at the burned-out building, roped off with yellow accident-scene tape. "Anybody here about the building?"

She made a face. "A gentleman from the building inspector's office was here. He looked at it from his car, condemned the place. Said it'd have to be bulldozed." Dislike was evident in her voice.

"How about Shelby?"

"He's been here all morning. You just missed him."

"Many client calls?"

"A good many. Everyone calling to say how shocked they were to hear the place burned. A lot offered help."

"Any business?"

"A bit. I didn't know when I'd see you, so I had your friend in Detroit handle the trades."

A flatbed truck carrying a port-a-potty pulled up. The driver leaned out the window. "Anybody know where they want this?" He said gruffly.

I pointed to the far side of the trailer. "Put it over there. Thanks."

Rosemary shook her head. "A loo. He thinks of everything, that Shelby does."

"Well, I'm going to see if the fireproof safe really was." I stepped over the yellow tape, around the debris in the yard. Inside the shell of the building, the smells of burned wood and wet plaster were almost overpowering. I made my way to what had been my office. There wasn't much of it left. The sofa and chairs had been thrown outside the night before. Some charred wood was probably what was left of my desk and credenza. Surprisingly, several of the photos that had been on the wall above the credenza were still there. Grimy, soot covered, glass broken, but still hanging.

I made my way to the closet. The door was gone. The safe had fallen part way through the floor, but it looked intact. I unlocked the top drawer, pulled it open. The computer backup disks weren't discolored from the heat. I took a handful, carried them back to the trailer.

"It worked," I told Rosemary as I dumped them on one of the desks. "Best five hundred dollars we ever spent." By the time I had the contents of the safe transferred to our new workspace, the air conditioning was working, the technician had hooked up the market feed on my computer and was working on Rosemary's.

I sat at my desk and took stock of my new domain. It had all the ambience of a tin can, was noisy as hell, and smelled of industrial cleaner. I was thrilled to have it.

CHAPTER 37

I spent what remained of the afternoon calling clients, reassuring them. By six-thirty, I'd talked or left voice mail for everyone on our client list. I told Rosemary to call it a day, locked the place up, and headed home for a much-needed shower and dinner.

As I drove, my cell phone rang. "You want to come over to Frankie's and see how we've set things up?" Tory asked. "I think it looks pretty convincing."

"I'll swing by. Has Janet called?"

"Eight times so far. I think she's calling every half hour or so now. Wait until you hear the messages she's left. They're hilarious."

"Like what?"

"Like 'Poor Frankie baby, I'm so worried about you. I can't bear our being apart all this time.'"

"Really?"

"Would I make up stuff like that?"

"No, but I'm sure she didn't say it in the baby-talk voice you used."

"Baby talk, smooches, the whole nine yards."

"I'll be there in fifteen minutes. I'm driving through St. Armand's Circle now." I negotiated the day's maze of tourists, crossed New Pass Bridge, and drove down Gulf of Mexico Drive. In ten minutes—record time—I pressed the intercom buzzer at Fish's condo.

"C'mon up," he said, and the door buzzed.

I took the elevator up. Tory met me at the door. "Janet just called again, left another icky message."

I smiled. "By icky, do you mean smarmy?" I asked as we walked into the condo's living room.

"The concern in her voice is so fake."

"Oh, she's concerned. About his money."

Tory led me to the kitchen. "I want you to meet Helen; she's our home health nurse."

Helen was a slightly plump older woman with short gray hair and a round face. She wore a white uniform. "Good to meet you, Matt," she said as we shook hands.

"Good to meet you, Helen. Thanks for doing this, especially on such short notice."

"Glad to help. I had an uncle who got involved with a sweet young thing like this. He didn't have much." Her smile turned to a frown. "But what he had, she took."

"I'm sorry."

"Don't be. It was his own fault. Everybody warned him. He wouldn't listen to any of us." The smile returned. "I know my part. Want to quiz me?"

"Sure. Who are you and why are you here?"

"I'm Helen Montgomery, a home heath care nurse. Mr. Ford didn't want to be admitted to the hospital, so Dr. Clark asked me to watch him today."

"What's wrong with him?"

"I really shouldn't say. You should talk with Mr. Ford or Dr. Clark." She looked over at Tory. "How was that?"

"Perfect," Tory told her. "Make her pull every bit of information out of you."

"Right, but when she finally pulls it out of you what are you going to tell her?" I asked.

"That he's suffering from acute liver damage, recently inflamed by alcohol poisoning. He could die if he drinks more—"

"Die when?"

"In days," she said with a sad shake of her head.

Pretty convincing. You just didn't expect this kindly older lady to be scamming you. "You're wonderful, Helen." She beamed. "Where's your patient?"

"In here," a male voice called from the den.

I went in and found Fish wearing a white bathrobe, sitting in a recliner with his feet up. He clicked off the television before I could see what he was watching. Wrestling, probably. He fixed me with an unhappy stare. "How do you expect me to get any nookie with that woman out there?"

"You're ill, Fish, very ill. Tonight's not nookie night. Tonight's sympathy night, the perfect set-up to make tomorrow nookie night."

"Well, I guess that's all right," he grumbled.

"Wait a minute. What's that I smell?" I asked, sniffing the air.

"Nothing."

"It's beer," I told him accusingly. "You've got beer in here."

"No, I don't."

I looked around his chair. Sure enough, two Bud cans on the floor. "Tory," I called. "Get all the beer out of the refrigerator and throw it down the garbage chute."

I picked up the two empties. "If she smells beer on your breath, everything's ruined."

"She won't smell anything, trust me," he groused.

"Why wouldn't she? I did."

He sighed heavily, got up from his chair, walked out of the room, and returned carrying a large bottle of Scope. He screwed off the top, chugged a couple of swallows, came over, and exhaled in my face. "How's that?"

"Better. In fact, minty fresh. Keep it that way."

"You worry too much. It's going fine." He sat back down in the recliner. "When will nurse Ratchet out there start taking calls?"

I looked at my watch. "Let's start the festivities at eight. You know the plan for tomorrow?"

"House hunting, yeah. Am I well enough to do something tomorrow evening?"

"Dinner and a movie. How's that sound?"

"Boring. I was thinking of asking her back here to see my etchings."

"Go for it," I said. Must have surprised him. His eyebrows shot up. "Tomorrow evening, over dinner or after sex, I don't care which, you need to tell her you love her and don't want to live without her."

His brows fell, knit together in concentration. "You want me to pop the question?"

"No, don't mention marriage. Just tell her you want to live with her—in one of those million-dollar-plus houses the two of you just looked at. Dangle that out there, see if she doesn't bring up the subject of marriage. Okay?"

He nodded.

"Anything else you need before I go?"

He shook his head, clicked the TV back on. This time I got a look. Happy Days. No wonder he'd clicked it off so fast.

I found Helen and Tory talking in the living room, joined them.

"What time do you want Helen to start answering the phone?" Tory asked.

"Eight o'clock. When Janet leaves, after her visit, give her fifteen minutes then you can leave, too." To Tory, I added, "Could we talk for a few minutes?"

She looked at me quizzically. "Sure."

"You folks run along. We'll be fine," Helen told us in her

motherly voice.

"I'll call you tomorrow, find out how it went," Tory said as we left.

We rode the elevator down to the lobby. I looked out on the pool deck. It was deserted. "Want to talk out by the pool?"

"That's fine."

I opened the door, held it for her.

"What's this about?" she asked as she passed by.

"Second thoughts."

"Oh."

We took seats at a table with an umbrella. She eyed me expectantly.

"I'm worried about D'Onifrio's next hurry-up message. He's already burned my business. His next threat was to hurt one of my friends. I don't want that to be you. I'm thinking the best thing for us to do is part ways. I'll give you a check for the fee we set. That should give you enough money to get away from here for a while."

Surprise showed on her face. "What are you going to do?"

"I'm not sure, exactly. I'm going to try to use Joe's missing money as a way to get D'Onifrio in trouble. Remember how Raines said Menendez would be upset about that?"

She nodded.

"I just need to come up with a way of getting the problem in front of Enrico."

"When are you going to do all this?"

"According to Raines I've got a little under two weeks."

She nodded. Didn't say any more.

I waited, uncertain what to say next.

She looked directly at me, searching my face. "Why are you telling me this now?"

"I told you. I don't want you to get hurt."

"Why? I'm a hired gun. What do you care if I get hurt?"

"I just do," I said softly, meeting her gaze.

She didn't say anything after that, but I sensed something changed. Her attitude was different. "If this is two weeks off, I don't have to go yet. I can help you a little longer."

"You're sure?"

"I can take care of myself, remember. When the time comes to leave, I'll leave. Until then, what do you want me to do?"

I sat back in my chair. "We need to know more about D'Onifrio. There has to be a chink in his armor somewhere. Something we can use to stir things up."

She smiled. "Penetrating armor is my specialty."

"Thanks. We probably ought to get out of here. I don't want to bump into Janet in the lobby."

We didn't.

I drove back to my condo, had a late bite, tried to read for a little bit. Couldn't concentrate enough to get through a single page. Gave up. Went down to the gym and worked out. If there was going to be a confrontation, I wanted to be in shape. After an hour on the machines, an hour running, I'd had enough. I went back upstairs, took a shower, went to bed. If my alarm went off in the morning, I didn't hear it.

Bright Florida sunlight streaming in the window roused me. The bedside clock said eight-forty.

It was close to ten when I arrived at the trailer. Rosemary, phone to her ear, handed me a stack of pink message slips. There were five desks lined up in a row. Rosemary was at desk one—closest to the door. I walked back to desk four—closest to the air conditioning.

I accessed the markets on my computer, scanned the pink slips, began returning calls. A little after eleven, Rosemary turned, looked back at me. "Tory's on one."

"Just got off the phone with Helen," she said after I picked up.

"She thinks it went perfectly. Janet asked Helen about Frankie's condition—had to pull it out of her—and Helen told her if he had another bender like that he'd be dead in twenty-four hours of acute alcohol poisoning. His liver couldn't handle it."

"What did she say?"

"Helen said her face sort of lit up. I think it gave her ideas."

"Good. How about the house hunting?"

"Helen said they set it up. The real estate agent will call you afterward, right?"

"Yeah, I'll call you and let you know what she says."

"I'll be here. I'm working on you-know-who. Nothing wonderful yet. The good stuff usually takes some digging."

"Keep after it."

"I am." She rang off.

I went back to work. Around one-thirty, activity trailed off and I ducked out and brought us back Chinese. Desk two became our lunchroom. I placed the white takeout containers in the middle of the desk and we loaded up our plates. I used a fork. Rosemary was adept with chopsticks.

"So how are your extracurricular activities coming?" she asked around a bite of rice.

I made a face. "Hard to say. I'll know more tonight. With any luck, we could have our first marriage discussions."

She waved her chopsticks in the air. "That's great news."

I nodded over a bite of sweet and sour chicken. "Yeah, we're making progress. I don't know if it's enough to suit D'Onifrio."

"What do you mean? He should be thrilled with what you've done."

"He's not. He burned our building because we weren't moving fast enough. I'm worried about what he'll do next."

Her eyes got big.

"I don't want to scare you, but it might be good if you and Dan went on a vacation. Visit Rebecca instead of having her come here. That way you can see your mom and dad. Don't worry about what it costs; it's on me."

"Oh, Matt, you're too generous. We couldn't."

I smiled. "You can. In fact, I insist."

She hesitated. "Let me talk to Dan, see what he says."

"Tell him I won't take no for an answer."

She ate a bite of shrimp, mulled the possibilities. "I'd love to see my mum and dad. My cousins. Dan's never met some of them."

I was pleased that she'd focused on the trip rather than the threat. She was still bubbling about what they'd do, who they'd see, when Margo Cohen, the realtor, called later in the afternoon. "They just left," Margo said breathlessly. "It went so well I couldn't wait to call."

"Don't skimp. Give me all the details."

"Oh, where to start. I took them to the Thone house on Bayridge first. That wasn't for them. Too beige. We went to the Nelson's house in Plantation Estates. Too ordinary. Then we went to 3423 Gulfside—that big house that's been on the market forever—and they loved it."

"Isn't that the one that's outrageously priced?"

"You think seven million is outrageous?"

"Yes."

"Well, your couple didn't," she said excitedly. "She loved it. He loved it." Her voice became sarcastic. "Of course, she thinks it needs a new kitchen, and the pool? Well, the pool is 'way too small."

"So then what?"

"I showed them the Fishburne house on Lake Forest. Too confining. The Tallit house on Taragon Way. Too dark. Then we went back to Gulfside."

"How did they act? What did they say?"

"I was getting to that. They walked around a lot and talked, you know, the way you do when you're trying to figure if your stuff will fit. I sat on the lanai waiting. Finally, they came out, and he said he wanted to make an offer. I went through the motions of writing up a contract for seven mill. I showed him where he needed to sign. But instead of signing, he tossed the pen over his shoulder, turned to her and told her he wanted the house but he wouldn't live in it without her. It was so romantic."

Yes! "What did she say?"

"She went over and hugged and kissed him. But then she told him she wouldn't live with him—she wasn't that kind of woman. He didn't bat an eyelash, Matt, he got down on one knee and asked her to marry him."

I could feel my heart beating faster, adrenaline pumping through my body. "What did she say?"

CHAPTER 38

"What could she say to such a romantic guy? She said yes, of course."

I felt a huge weight lift from my shoulders, I gave Rosemary a thumbs-up.

"I told you we were due for some good luck," she called over.

"They were going to have dinner together tonight and talk about the wedding," the realtor continued.

"Thanks, Margo. I owe you one."

"You sure do. Make it the next Microsoft."

I started to ring off.

"Matt, Matt, wait a minute. What do you want me to do with this contract?"

"Tear it up."

"Let's rethink that. I could see you in—"

"In your dreams, Margo. 'Bye." This time I did hang up. I dialed Tory's number. "He proposed, she accepted," I told her as soon as she answered the phone.

"Already?"

"Happened house hunting just the way we thought it would, only quicker. Janet said she wouldn't live with him, so right on the spot Fish got down on one knee and proposed."

"How romantic."

"I think they're going to set the date at dinner tonight."

"What if she wants a big, expensive wedding?"

"She won't. She won't want the exposure. She'll want to keep this fast and low key."

Rosemary signaled me. "Julian's calling on line two."

"Gotta go, Tory. I'll call you back." I hit the button for the other line. "Hello, Julian."

"Matt, I've just gotten the strangest call from Nevitt. Has something happened?"

"Why? What did he say?"

"He wanted an extension on supplying Janet's financial information. The strange part was that he was positively jubilant on the phone. Every other conversation I've had with him has been hostile. Today, he was Mr. Happy."

I took the call as a good sign. Nevitt's mood had to be caused by Janet's engagement. The timing was too coincidental for that not to be it. "What did you tell him?"

"I told him if he didn't have his shit to us when he was supposed to, we'd go to the N.A.S.D. and demand a dismissal of the charges. He didn't give you any warning when they came for your stuff. No reason we have to give him extra time."

"What did he say then?"

"That was strange, too. I thought he'd be pissed, start shouting. The way he's acted in the past. Instead, he said something like, well, we'll see. He didn't seem upset at all. That's why I was wondering if something happened?"

"My guy proposed. Janet accepted," I explained, gave him a little detail on Fish and Janet. "They think she's about to make a big score. Julian, I'm small potatoes compared to what they think they're going to get from this marriage."

"That explains why he was Mr. Happy on the phone with me. But remember, he hasn't let you off the hook yet."

"But if he's about to make a big score and I'm a big nuisance, why bother with me?"

"Money," Julian answered simply. "He's greedy."

He was probably right. It was wishful thinking on my part that Nevitt would back off. "Well, keep pushing him," I said encouragingly. "Delivering those records has to be a hassle when they want to concentrate on this wedding."

"Let's hope," Julian said before he rang off.

I felt like celebrating. Rosemary, however, wanted my nose to the grindstone. She had three callbacks for me, all of which turned out to be large, profitable transactions. Sometimes you have stretches where every time you pick up the phone, it's money.

In fact, we did such good business that I was humming to myself as I left the trailer to go head home.

Back at the condo, I took a long, cold shower. I needed it. Even sitting next to the air conditioner, I felt I'd spent the afternoon being broiled alive. I dried off, threw on some clothes, called Tory back.

"You sound happy," she said.

"I am. It's been a good day."

"Frankie's pretty excited, too. Since I talked to you, he has called three times. Once to fill me in, twice with questions about tonight. They're going to have dinner after the A.A. meeting, talk about a date."

"Did you tell him the sooner, the better."

"Sort of. I checked on what he needs to do. With the application for the license, blood test, the earliest they can have a justice of the peace wedding is Friday. I told him to shoot for Friday or Saturday."

"Good."

"His other call was about a ring and a honeymoon. Two things she's asking him about. Any ideas?"

"Have him tell her he's getting his mother's ring out of the safety deposit box in Detroit."

"How about the honeymoon?"

"He should defer to her, ask her what she wants to do. That should buy us a little time."

"I'll tell him."

"When do you think he'll be back at the condo? I'd like to know what they decide for a date. If this wedding actually happens, it changes the situation with D'Onifrio."

"My guess is it'll be late. Frankie's been invited back to her place—as he put it—to talk about the arrangements."

"Really. And what do we really think is going to happen at her place?"

"Well, Frankie has it in his mind he's going to get laid. I told him not to be too disappointed if she doesn't come across."

"Women," I said lightly. "Here he's ready to give her millions and she won't give him a little nookie."

She tossed it right back at me. "You men. It's all about immediate gratification."

"We're pigs. I admit it. But let's get back to you women, for a minute. Inviting him back to her place makes no sense. She should be stalling, telling him no sex until after the marriage."

"I agree with you. I'm just telling you what Frankie told me."

I was beginning to get a bad feeling about the evening's activities. Might not hurt to watch over the lovebirds, find out what was going on. "How would you feel about doing a little chaperoning tonight?"

"I'd be afraid Janet would recognize me. We never did anything about a disguise."

Darn, forgot about that. "Let me call you right back."

I hung up and got out my Watergate directory. Looked up Edith's number, punched it in.

"Hello," she answered demurely.

"Edith, Matt Seattle. You don't by any chance have a woman's wig I could borrow, do you?"

"I have several. Why?"

"Yours or the theatre's?"

"The theatre's."

"I have a friend I need to disguise, much the way you did me. I was wondering if I could borrow one of them?"

"Of course you can, dear. Why don't you have your friend come by? I'll help her make one of these work."

"Thanks, Edith. Let me talk to her, call you right back." I hung up, dialed Tory's number. "Tory," I said as soon as she answered. "Edith says you can have your choice of wigs. She'll even fit it for you."

"She doesn't need to do that."

"She wants to. C'mon over. It just takes a few minutes."

"I guess," she said reluctantly.

I gave her my address, called Edith, let her know it was a go.

Twenty minutes later, the buzzer rang. It was Tory. I buzzed her up, met her at the elevators, walked her to the unit.

"Nice place," she said when we were in the living room.

"Make yourself comfortable." I indicated the couch and leather club chairs. "I'll call Edith." I headed for the kitchen, stopped, turned. "Can I offer you something to drink?"

She turned, smiled. "A glass of ice water would be great."

In the kitchen, I made my call, then returned with her ice water in a tall glass. She was looking at the view. I joined her, handed her the water.

"I bought the place for the view."

"It's wonderful. If I lived here, I'd be looking at that view all the time." She turned, looked back at the living room. "Not that your place isn't something to look at. It's so, so—"

"Unused looking?"

She smiled, shook her head. "No, that's not what I—"

"So Pottery Barn?"

"Sort of." She made a face. "So put together, I guess. I mean that in a good way."

I grinned. "Thanks. I think."

She walked over to a grouping of stand-up picture frames on a long stainless steel table. "Is this your family?"

I followed, picked up a picture, held it as I talked. "Claire and I on the beach at Grand Cayman—we were celebrating our second wedding anniversary." I replaced it, picked up the next one. "Michael in his Hornets uniform with Eddie. Being drafted by the Hornets meant you were really good." I put his photo back. "And this is Sarah," I said, my voice cracking as I picking up her photo.

Tory looked from the photo to me. "She looks like you."

I nodded although I saw more of Claire in Sarah than myself. Just looking at her photo made me smile. "She was such a loving child. There was so much goodness and caring in her." I put the photo of her down and picked up a picture of the entire family. "This was taken on a skiing trip to the U.P. over Christmas break. It was the last photo of all of us before the accident."

"You all look so happy."

"We were. You take it for granted that it's always going to be that way; then without warning, it's gone. In an instant, all you're left with are the things you wanted to say, the hopes and dreams you'll never realize, a hole where your heart used to be."

"I'm sorry," she said, softly

"No, I'm the one who should be sorry. I don't usually get this maudlin. Forgive me. This isn't what we're here for tonight." Fortunately, the doorbell rang. "That should be Edith."

It was. She had three wigs. Two blonde—one curly, one straight. One redhead. After I introduced the two ladies, Edith had Tory try on all three wigs. I would have chosen the redhead. Surprisingly, the blond curly one fit best, looked best. Edith fiddled with it while I went to change clothes, put on my disguise.

When I returned, Tory wore the wig and a doubtful expression. "What do you think?"

"You look like a completely different person."

Edith took that to mean mission accomplished. She beamed. "Well, you children have fun. I've got to be going."

I walked her to the door. "Thanks, Edith."

She gave me a motherly pat on the cheek. "I like your friend, Matt."

I'm sure I blushed.

Once Edith was gone, Tory said, "We need to be going, too."

I looked at my watch. Twenty 'til. We'd just get there for the start of the meeting. I grabbed my car keys. "I'm ready."

On the elevator ride down, she took papers from her black shoulder bag. "We've got some things to talk about. I got more information on D'Onifrio."

We walked to the Saab. I held her door for her, got in my side, started the engine, and drove out of the complex.

"I've been looking into the companies he's bought to launder money," she said as we drove. "Trying to see if there were irregularities that would allow us to call in the authorities, create a stink in the press." She had a stack of papers, held together by a big metal clip. "You'd probably be better looking at this stuff than I am."

I looked over at her. "Good idea. I'll go over them tonight."

"I've also been looking for a disgruntled worker at Shore, someone with whistleblower potential."

"Let me guess—there aren't any to be found."

"You're right. For a bank, Shore has a very high accident rate—some even fatal. But if we could find someone—"

I shook my head. "It's a good idea, but I don't think it's going to pan out."

She turned in her seat. "Here's the one I like best," she said excitedly. "Remember Raines told us D'Onifrio was to receive an award for helping deaf children?"

I nodded.

"I found the organization. It's the Foundation for Latina Speech and Hearing Services, headquartered in Miami. And guess what? They'd still like to present it to him. They'd even be willing to come to Sarasota."

She was right. This was the best of all. A humanitarian award D'Onifrio had actually earned, not something trumped up, and the Foundation would do all the work. "Perfect."

She smiled broadly. "I'm thinking we give them a list of the people—D'Onifrio, Enrico, the whole bunch—that should be invited to the award ceremony. When they arrive, we use the opportunity to get information about Joe's money to Enrico, Little Ernie, and Eduardo. Maybe we disguise it to look like a program."

We were at St. Mark's. I started looking for a parking place. "What if he doesn't come? What if they don't?"

"Are you kidding me? The Foundation told me they'd do media promotion for the event. D'Onifrio would look like an ingrate if he didn't attend. If he attends, I'll bet the rest of them do, too."

I pulled over to the curb, parked the car. "I'm impressed. I've been thinking about this for days and haven't come up with anything. You work on it for a day and come up with something brilliant."

She looked over at me. "Thank you." Her expression said the compliment pleased her.

We talked about the details of making her plan work as we walked the block and a half to St. Mark's. We found seats together in the back, continued talking.

"Oh, my God! Look at her," Tory said, glancing at the entrance.

CHAPTER 39

Fish and Janet had just made their entrance, and what an entrance it was.

She had on a white silk blouse, open at the throat. The way the silk moved revealed that she wasn't wearing anything under it. With it, she wore a short, short beige skirt. I wondered if she had anything on under that. I had a feeling that when she sat down, half the room would find out.

Fish had her on his arm, a shit-eating grin on his face. Maybe he already knew the answer. He had on a garish-looking Hawaiian shirt—lots of palm trees and hula girls—tan slacks, sandals.

"Can you believe how she's dressed?" Tory whispered. "She might as well not be wearing any clothes."

"I can't believe how our boy is dressed. Where did that shirt come from?"

She winced. "From his place. I told him not to bring it. He insisted."

"It's got hula girls on it."

"I know."

"Someone worth ten million dollars wouldn't wear a shirt with hula girls on it. Jimmy Buffett might. Warren Buffett wouldn't."

"Would it make any difference if I told you he has worse?"

"Impossible."

She gave a throaty little laugh. "Believe me, it's true. Nobody's looking at him, though; they're all looking at her."

I looked around the room. She was right. Everyone was staring.

Our chubby moderator was aware of that, too. He stroked his beard nervously several times, cleared his throat loudly. "Everybody, please take seats. We'll get going in just a minute."

People began finding seats and the staring lessened. Within minutes, the meeting was in session, a steady procession of folks making their way to the podium to testify. As they droned on and on, I felt myself getting drowsy.

An elbow bought me back to reality. "This is winding up," Tory said quietly. "Let's beat the crowd."

We got up and went out the door. "Good idea," I told her as we walked to the car. "They don't need to see us here and at the restaurant."

Marina Jack's was only a short drive away. Located right on the edge of town, surrounded by boats anchored in the Bay, it was particularly picturesque.

The host must have liked Tory. The table he took us to was perfect. On one side, we had a view of the marina. On the other, we had an unobstructed view of the room. No matter which table Fish and Janet had, we'd be able to observe them.

"Can I start you off with something to drink?" our waiter wanted to know.

"Glass of wine to celebrate your great idea?" I suggested to Tory.

She nodded. "Sounds good." She looked at the waiter. "A white wine—something dry."

"Make it two," I added.

He left. I watched the door.

"Don't worry. They should be right behind us."

They weren't.

Ten minutes passed. Twenty minutes passed. When half an hour had gone by, I decided they'd gone somewhere else.

"Relax. He said she wanted to come here," Tory said although she was intently watching the door, too.

Forty-five minutes had gone by when the door opened and they walked in. Here, too, Janet's outfit had people looking. I watched as the maitre d' escorted them to a secluded table where she wouldn't draw too much attention.

Once they were seated, I relaxed a little bit. Tory seemed more agitated.

"Something wrong?"

"No," she said softly.

She could deny it, but something was bothering her. "Did I do something?"

She shook her head, seemed flustered. "It's this restaurant."

"Bad meal?"

"Bad memories. This is where I told my husband I wanted a divorce after I found out he was having an affair."

"I'm sorry. I didn't know." I signaled for the waiter. "We'll go."

"No, she said quickly. "I'll be fine. I didn't think it would still bother me. Maybe it was all the waiting. Let's just eat and get out of here."

Fish seemed to be in a hurry, too. He asked for the check almost before Janet finished her meal and rushed her after dinner coffee. I had a feeling he was anxious to get to Janet's place for dessert.

"I think they're getting ready to depart," I said.

"I'm ready if you are."

I got our check, paid quickly in cash, and we left ahead of them. From the Saab, we watched them play kissy face in the parking lot on the way to Fish's car. When they reached the car, Janet leaned languidly against the rear fender while Fish unlocked and opened her door for her. Instead of getting in, Janet put her arm around his neck and pulled him to her. Fish pressed his body hard against hers, did a few pelvic thrusts.

Tory saw it, too. "Good thing you didn't lease him a Lincoln Town Car."

The clinch broke, and she got in. Fish closed her door and walked around to the driver's side. Even from where we were, we could see the bulge in his pants.

"The way she's dressed, the way he's acting, I have trouble thinking she's going to be able to hold him off," I said as I put the car in gear. I pulled out of the parking space, prepared to follow them.

"That'll certainly make Frankie happy. When I talked to him about what they were doing tonight, all he wanted to talk about was the best way to get her into bed."

They pulled out of the parking lot into traffic. I followed about six or seven car lengths back. We were only about twenty minutes from where she lived. At the speed Fish was driving, it didn't take long. He was there in ten.

From a block away, we watched as he pulled into her drive, got out of the car, opened her door, and escorted her up the walk to the front door. She used her key and they went inside.

"Think they're tearing each other's clothes off in there?" Tory asked.

"Scary thought," I said. Headlights illuminated the interior of the Saab. "Get down," I ordered.

The car passed us, turned into Janet's driveway, and parked next to Fish's Mercedes. We sat back up.

"Who's that?" Tory wanted to know.

The driver's door opened, and a dark-haired man got out. "Nevitt."

"What do you think he's doing here?"

Nevitt looked at Fish's Mercedes, strode quickly to the front door, rang the bell, and waited.

"My guess is he's here to provide coitus interruptus."

Nevitt rang the bell again. The door finally opened. Looked to me like Janet was wearing a robe. Nevitt stepped in and the door closed again.

"Now what?" Tory wanted to know.

I wasn't sure. I hadn't expected Nevitt to show up. Judging by the way he'd arrived right after they'd gone in the house, this had to be arranged, and it had to have a purpose other than keeping Fish from boinking Janet. I just couldn't figure out a good reason for forcing a meeting like this.

"Now we wait," I said.

We didn't have to wait long. No more than five minutes passed before the front door opened and Fish strode angrily down the walk to his car. From the doorway, Janet waved good-bye.

Fish backed recklessly out of the driveway, gave her a quick wave, and sped down the street.

We followed him to the Sovereign, found him chugging a beer in the kitchen. He finished that one, chugged another, looked over at us, his eyes wild.

"Frankie, what happened?" Tory asked, obviously concerned.

"Hell if I know. She's got her hand in my pants on the ride to her place. We get to her place, go inside, she takes off her blouse, starts rubbing up against me with those big breasts." He threw up his hands. "The damn doorbell rings. I tell her to forget about it. But no, she puts on this robe that was on the sofa and answers it."

"She just happened to have a robe right there?"

His jowls went down, his version of a frown. "She lets in this guy she introduces as her brother, Greg Nevitt. He congratulates me on the engagement, tells me he's an attorney, wants to know if he can help. Help? The only help I need is for him to leave. I say no, everything's wonderful, thanks for stopping by. He don't take the hint.

He says he knows paperwork can delay things and if there was any paperwork holding things up, he'd be glad to expedite it. Again I say no, everything's wonderful, thanks for stopping by. Turns to Janet, says he needs to talk to her about some family matters. She gives me a peck on the cheek, tells me to be a dear and call her tomorrow. Instead of getting screwed, I get screwed over."

"Frankie, remember? I told you tonight wasn't going to be the night," Tory said.

Fish's eyebrows shot up. "Yeah, but she was telling me different. Then boom, she cuts me off, right at the balls."

It was pretty obvious that this whole little encounter had been staged to smoke out whether Fish wanted a prenup. That had to be the paperwork Nevitt was referring to. "What date did you and Janet end up setting?"

"Friday. Next week."

I'd expected him to say this Friday or Saturday. "She couldn't do it this weekend?"

"I don't know. I asked her for next Friday."

"We talked about this Friday or Saturday," Tory said, reminding him.

"That don't matter. The boss told me the date is next Friday."

"D'Onifrio told you?"

Fish nodded.

"Why then?" Tory wanted to know.

Fish shrugged.

I knew. D'Onifrio had timed the wedding for two days after Enrico's arrival. I viewed it as confirmation of Raines' theory that D'Onifrio had gone along with my wedding idea because it fit into his plans with Enrico. Which meant the other part of Raines' theory might be accurate as well.

D'Onifrio was planning on grabbing me at the wedding.

CHAPTER 40

At nine the next day, Tory came to the tin can and worked the phone from desk three. Posing again as Oliva Lopez—mother of a child who had benefited from D'Onifrio's help—she re-contacted the Foundation for Latina Speech and Hearing Services in Miami and spoke with Executive Director, Bill Perez.

While they talked, I wrote a document that detailed Joe's theft, how long it had gone undetected, that it hadn't been repaid. I made the document as sensational as possible. What I didn't know or wasn't quite sure about, I made up.

After a lengthy conversation with Perez, Tory hung up, looked over at me. "Good news and bad news. The bad news is they can't do it next Thursday. They can't quite put it together that fast, and even if they could, several of their key people have other commitments for that particular night."

That was bad news. I was working on the assumption that D'Onifrio was going to grab me at the wedding, serve me up to Enrico. I wanted the awards ceremony before the wedding to preempt D'Onifrio and serve him to Enrico.

"Bill said Friday night would be the best for them. I know that's the same day as the wedding, but here's the good news. If it's Friday, he can hold this at Asolo."

I was impressed. The Asolo Theatre was a 500-seat turn-of-the-century opera house built in Dunfermline, Scotland, and reconstructed in the Ringling Museum. In season, it was home for a repertory company whose performances ranged from classics to new plays. "The Asolo's a lot more upscale than a meeting room at the Holiday Inn."

She smiled. "You know when I first mentioned the idea that D'Onifrio might accept the award if it was presented here in Sarasota, Bill jumped on it. He doesn't think small. He has a Miami Spanish-speaking television station broadcasting the event and wants to do public service announcements in Tampa, Orlando, Miami, and Sarasota. Said he'd have something ready to air by tomorrow."

"What time on Friday? Did he say?"

"Seven. The wedding should be over by then."

Seven would work. I wasn't concerned about the time of the wedding. No matter when it was, I wouldn't be anywhere near it. "What did he say about contacting the guest of honor?"

She grinned. "You'll love this. I told him D'Onifrio refused the award before because he didn't want to seem immodest. I said he might tell them again he didn't want it, but he really did. Bill said he could bring enough peer pressure on D'Onifrio that he wouldn't refuse. He's going to call him today, call me back when he has a confirmation."

"Think Bill can get him there?"

"He sounded pretty confident. They're planning on putting on the presentation whether D'Onifrio is there to accept his award in person or not. I gather when they broadcast something like this, donations go through the roof." She looked over at my computer. "How's the write-up coming?"

I printed it out for her. Let her read it over. We were making revisions when Rosemary said, "Bill Perez on line three for Oliva."

Tory's gaze met mine as she picked up the receiver, put it to her ear. "This is Oliva." She listened for a moment, smiled. "I didn't expect to hear from you so soon, Bill." More listening. "He did." She nodded her head. "Fantastic." More listening. "Definitely. We'll stay in touch." More listening. "You know I'm more than willing to help. Thanks, Bill. 'Bye." She hung up. "He accepted. Didn't protest a bit. Bill says he's looking forward to it."

What did that mean? This was contrary to the ruthless image he was trying to establish. He shouldn't have agreed, much less so easily.

Tory's cell rang. She reached in her black handbag, pulled it out, looked at the caller number. "Frankie," she said to me. She put the phone to her ear. "This is Tory."

Even across the trailer, I heard her phone emitting low foghorn rumblings.

"Tell her it's coming." More rumbling. "She's messing with your mind, Frankie. You can't demonstrate your love every minute of every day. We've got eight long days to go before the wedding." More rumbling. "We'll work on it. I'll call you back." She hung up, shook her head, smiled. "This woman is good. She's got Frankie thinking she's going to call off the marriage because he hasn't given her a ring yet."

"As soon as she gets the ring, she'll want to know about the honeymoon. As soon as she knows about the honeymoon, she'll want to know about the house. Every day until the wedding, it'll be something, some demand," I said.

"Disgusting."

"I agree. But what else can we do?"

"What if we don't do anything? Pitting Enrico and the nephews against D'Onifrio is the important thing. The wedding has become incidental."

She tilted her head, frowned. "I don't think it's quite that simple. The wedding is the way D'Onifrio thinks he's going to get his money back. If the wedding gets called off, or if Frankie feels like we're not supporting him, D'Onifrio's going to hear about it, and he's going to come after you." She shook her head. "The wedding has to happen."

From the front of the trailer, Rosemary said, "I agree with Tory, Matt. If you change direction now, it's going to look like you're up to something. Better to lull them along."

What they said made sense. Maybe instead of viewing Fish as a liability, I should be looking at him as an asset. He obviously talked to D'Onifrio from time to time. Maybe we could use him to gain and plant information. I looked at Tory. "I guess we need to come up with a ring."

She smiled. "Yes, we do. And not just any ring. Remember, you set it up as Frankie's sainted Mother's ring."

I nodded, remembering, "An antique ring." I thumbed through my rolodex, found the number for Luis Santoro, dialed. One of the sales staff answered and I asked for Luis.

He came on the line. "Hello, my friend. How have you been?" His voice was soft, musical, with just a touch of an accent.

"I'm good, Luis. Thanks for asking. I'm calling with an unusual request."

"Ah, I was hoping you were calling about playing golf."

"Actually, I'm looking for an antique wedding ring."

I heard a sharp intake of breath on the other end of the line. "Congratulations, my friend. I had no idea. Of course, you were right to call me. I have the best, you know. Unfortunately, I must be away for an appraisal this afternoon. Will this keep until tomorrow? Or do you wish to meet me at the store this evening?"

"Tomorrow's fine, Luis."

"It would be my great pleasure. Your lady friend, she will be with you, yes?"

I looked over at Tory. "Yes, I believe she'll be with me. What's a good time to meet you, Luis?"

"Would two o'clock be acceptable?"

"Perfect."

"What did you tell him?" Tory wanted to know as soon as I hung up.

"It's what I didn't tell him. He thinks the ring is for me." I smiled. "I didn't correct him because, well, it's too complicated for one thing. For another, I'll probably get a better deal this way."

She eyed me skeptically. "What else?"

"He asked if my fiancé would be accompanying me."

She got a smug look on her face. "And let me guess what lucky girl might get to play that part."

"You win," I said, smiling broadly.

"It's the part of a lifetime, right?"

"Actually, it is. And just think, you don't have to sleep with the director. There's no gratuitous nudity required. All you have to do is try on diamond rings and say things, like, 'Oh, sugarbunny, I'm afraid this three-carat diamond isn't big enough.'"

"Sugarbunny? You want me to call you sugarbunny?"

"Stud muffin?"

Her eyes rolled back in her head.

"I'm sure that between now and when we meet Luis, you can come up with an acceptable term of endearment." I picked up my Blackberry, noted the appointment and time, looked back at Tory. "The other person we need to talk to is Raines. We ought to fill him in on what we're doing, see if he can help us get the information to Enrico and the nephews."

Tory's face turned serious. "He might not want anything to do with this."

Easy way to find out. I called him. Used a pay phone two blocks north on Palm. Like my last call to him, the person I talked to had him call me back almost immediately.

"You still haven't left town?" he asked in greeting.

"Soon. I've got an idea I want to run by you first. Can you meet with me one more time?"

He hesitated. "Is this necessary? I don't—"

"You need to hear this."

"I'll call you back at this number in twenty minutes." He hung up.

Exactly twenty minutes later, the pay phone rang. I picked it up. "It's Matt."

"Here's what you do. This afternoon at four, go to the Cortez Boat Brokerage on the right side of Cortez Road after you cross the bridge from Anna Maria to Bradenton. Tell them in the office you want to see The Rarely Used."

"That's the name of a boat? The Rarely Used?"

"I'll be on board." He rang off.

At four, Tory and I followed one of the Cortez sales staff down the wooden dock to a forty-six foot older yacht. "This is the Rarely Used," the salesman said, indicating the boat with his hand. "Look her over for as long as you like, let me know what you think. I'll be in the office."

We boarded, found Raines seated in the galley drinking a Mountain Dew. He looked tired, wary. With a nod, he indicated seats across from him. "What's this about?"

We took turns filling him in. When he'd heard it all, he looked directly at me. Our gazes met. "I had a feeling you'd try something stupid. Although frankly, this isn't as dumb as I expected. Did you bring the write-up?"

I handed it to him.

He read it carefully. "This all true?" He asked when he finished.

"Not entirely. I embellished a detail or two."

He snorted, drained the last of his Mountain Dew, threw the plastic bottle in the wastebasket. "Here's what I want you do. Keep talking to your guy at the Foundation. Keep me posted on what's happening. Any changes, I want to know fast. Same drill, call from a pay phone. Got that?" He looked at each of us.

We nodded.

"This thing goes down on Friday, I want you both out of town on Wednesday." Again, he stared directly at me. "You didn't leave last time I told you."

"I'll leave," I said quickly.

"If you don't, they'll kill you." He frowned. "I'd put a guy on you to protect you, but they'd spot it, know something's going on." He paused, glanced at my write-up. "You coordinate the show programs. I'll make sure the write-up gets into the hands of Enrico and the nephews. Anything else we need to discuss?"

Tory shook her head.

There was something I wanted to know. "I'm curious. I thought you'd be furious with us for arranging this. I thought you'd tell us to call the whole thing off. You're not. Why?"

Raines' eyes narrowed. He stroked his moustache. "It's too late. This thing is in play. The only thing I can do now that you've stirred things up is try to direct the explosion, keep you guys alive."

CHAPTER 41

I had dreams that night. We were at the cemetery. My father walking beside me, his head bowed. Eddie running ahead. We walked through the grass between tall trees, in and out of the shade, to a clearing where three caskets waited for us. Small groups of people watched us approach. Family. Friends. The priest. It was quiet, so quiet I was aware of birds chirping, the sounds our shoes made on the grass.

We reached the gravesite. The priest began reading from the Bible. I didn't listen. Mentally, I said good-bye. I reached out, put my hand on each casket. My hand rested on Claire's the longest. The hardest good-bye.

My Dad put his arm around my shoulder, said, "Let's go home, Matt."

My hand pulled away from the metal.

I woke. My hand out.

I lowered my arm, wiped my eyes, the image still vivid in my mind. My hand coming away from the casket. My letting go.

When I called Dr. Swarthmore at seven-thirty and related what I'd experienced, she seemed cautiously elated. "Matt, the symbolism is so obvious. I have to believe this is your subconscious bringing finality to your loss. Even after the dream, your feeling of your hand coming away from the casket suggests that you're through the grieving process. The thing you need to ask yourself is why did this happen now? Is there a person or persons who have helped you heal?"

"I'm not sure," I said honestly.

"The answers will come to you. You've made significant progress. My one concern is your holding back, your unwillingness to open up emotionally with a woman."

It was a concern she'd raised before. As before, I didn't say anything. I hid in silence.

"Stay in touch, Matt," she said when I didn't say anything. "Good things are going to start happening for you."

I thanked her, rang off.

We were busy at the office that morning. Lots of calls. A ton of paperwork. At ten, Julian called.

I used my shoulder to hold the phone to my ear. "Hello, Julian," I said as I finished signing a stack of forms. "Have we got financials?"

"That's why I'm calling. Nevitt just dropped off a Jim Beam box full of stuff. Hard to tell what's here, what's missing. I've got Nathan Cohen, a CPA I work with, lined up to go through it."

"See anything in there that ties to Merrill Lynch?"

"I haven't looked that closely. Want me to rummage through?"

"Yeah, I'll hold."

He was gone a long time before he came back on. "Sorry, no Merrill Lynch. You didn't expect it was going to be that easy, did you?"

"I guess I didn't. There has to be a connection, though. I was hoping there might be something that would shed some light on how they pulled that off."

"Let's see what Nathan finds. The guy's a financial archaeologist. If it's there, he'll dig it up." Julian knew a good exit line when he delivered one. He rang off.

Nathan might be wonderful, but I doubted Nevitt was dumb enough to have given us anything incriminating. What might be telling is what Nevitt didn't deliver. Nathan might be able to put together a case based on empty spaces.

I buried myself in paperwork. Didn't get up from my desk until one-thirty when Tory arrived.

Once again, she was dressed in black. On her face, she wore a smirk. "Oh, Snugglebear. Time to go ring shopping."

Rosemary tried to hide a giggle.

I stood, headed down the aisle. "Snugglebear? That's the best you could come up with?"

She took my arm, grinned.

"We'll be back," I said to Rosemary. "Hold the fort."

There were a number of cars—Mercedes, Lexus, Cadillac—in the antique store's parking lot when we arrived. The most notable, however, was a white Rolls convertible with a Florida vanity plate that read, Luis. I parked the Saab two spaces over. It was like docking your cabin cruiser next to the QEII.

I got out of the car, walked around, opened Tory's door for her, and together we walked to the front door of the shop. It was opened before we got there by a beaming Luis Santoro. He was a tiny man with olive complexion, silver hair brushed straight back, a thin, jet-black moustache, perfect white teeth.

"Matt, good to see you," he said warmly, extending his hand. "Please introduce me to your lady friend."

"Luis, this is Tory Knight."

Tory started to shake hands. Luis surprised her with a kiss on both cheeks. "You are delightful. Matt, he is a lucky man. Please, come into the shop."

We followed him in. He closed the door, led us to his private office. He indicated chairs, "Please be comfortable." He took his seat behind the desk. Between us, displayed on a square of black velvet, were five diamond rings—each more stunning than the next.

Luis watched Tory's reaction. "Tell me, my dear, which one makes your spirit soar?"

Tory reached for a ring with a large oval-cut stone. It was by far the most distinctive ring on the table. "I've never seen anything like it." Her voice had awe in it.

Luis smiled. "She has wonderful taste, Matt. This ring is an excellent choice, the cut and clarity—" He kissed the tips of his fingers. "Perfection." He reached across the desk, took the ring from her. "May I, my dear?" He took her other hand and slipped in on her finger.

Tory gave a little gasp as she looked at it on her hand.

"It is yours now. My wedding gift to you."

I hadn't expected this. "Luis, I can't—"

He stopped me with a stern look, an angry wave of his hand. "You have made a humble shopkeeper a rich man. You are more than my advisor. You are my valued friend. This is my gift. To argue with me about this will be futile." He stood, came around the desk, again kissed Tory on both cheeks. "I wish for the two of you a long, loving life together." He turned and hugged me. "My friend, I am honored you called me to share in your happiness."

I patted him on the back. "Thank you, Luis. I'm the one who is honored. You're a true friend." We separated. I looked him directly in the eyes, aware he was more than a business associate. More than a friend, even. He'd become part of my extended family. "That's why I can't do this."

"What?" He asked, his face confused.

"Tory, let me have the ring, please."

Reluctantly, she took it off her finger and handed it to me.

"Let me share something with you, Luis," I said as I placed the diamond on the black velvet square. I launched into a sanitized version of my predicament.

"I understand," he said as I finished. "This ring is not for your lady. It is for this black widow."

"I didn't want to involve you in this. I just wanted to buy a ring. But I can't mislead you. Please accept my apologies and let me know what I owe you for the ring." I took my checkbook and a pen out of my pocket, got ready to write him a check.

"This ring," he held up the one Tory had chosen, his face stern, "is not for sale." His face changed into a smile. "This ring I will hold for the two of you. Perhaps one day, it will grace your hand again as my present to you."

He picked up one of the other rings. "This one, I think, will be good for your black widow. It was worn for many years by the mistress of a South American dictator. A fitting choice, don't you think?"

He opened a desk drawer, took out a ring box, placed the ring inside, and handed it to me. "Put your checkbook away. I will not take your money. It is in my best interests to help you out of this situation in which you find yourself. This will be my contribution to your cause."

"Thank you, Luis," I told him sincerely as we did the hug and back pat thing again.

"What a great friend," Tory said when we reached the car. "He obviously thinks a lot of you."

I nodded as I opened her car door for her. "Luis is a gentleman of the old school. They don't make them like him anymore."

I got in my side, started the car, waved at Luis standing in the doorway, and backed out of the parking space. "Now that we have the ring, Fish needs to make a dramatic presentation to her."

CHAPTER 42

Tory and I met with Fish that evening. We found him lounging on the sofa, dressed in polka-dot boxers, a wife-beater tee-shirt, black socks pulled to mid-calf. His hair wasn't combed. He hadn't shaved. "'Lo," he said. His gaze never left the TV.

I went over, found the remote, clicked the TV off. "Why aren't you and Janet out tonight?"

He looked annoyed. Probably more at my turning off his TV than my question. "She didn't want to. I think she's mad at me."

Oh, good. A lover's spat. I got the ring box out of my pocket, opened it in front of him.

"Holy smokes," he said, his eyebrows shooting up, his jowls quivering.

"This is your mother's ring," I said, coaching him. "Your father, the trucking baron, searched Detroit to find the most beautiful ring in town. This is that special ring. He gave this ring to your mother, and now you'd like to give it to her."

Fish swallowed. "If you say so."

"What I want you to do is present it with some drama. Don't just give it to her, let her know it's special. Make her feel special."

"Snugglebear," Tory said, grinning. "Right idea, wrong direction." She looked over at Fish. "Frankie, repeat after me—the way to get in a girl's pants is romance. Say it with me." He did. When they'd finished, Tory said, "What Matt was trying to tell you is if you want to get anywhere with Janet, you have to romance her. This ring is a tool to

234 \ JAY GILES

heat up your romance. If you just hand it to her," she shook her head, "you'll get nothing. But if you present in a romantic way, guess what you're going to get?"

"In her pants," Fish finished.

"Can you do it, Frankie? Can you be romantic?" Tory asked softly.

Fish's jowls began to quiver. "I'll be so romantic she'll want to hop right in the sack"

"'Atta boy," I said and handed him the ring box.

"Call her. Ask her out to dinner tomorrow night. Tell her you have something special you want to give her," Tory said.

He hopped right up, went out to the kitchen, called. We eavesdropped on the half of the conversation we could hear. When it was over, he padded back out to the living room. "It's on. She said this has all happened so quickly, she's still sorting it out. That's why she's been acting the way she has. But she said she knows she loves me and wants to spend her life with me."

"Touching." I tried not to laugh. "Tory and I want to share in this happiness. We're planning on being at the wedding. That's okay with you isn't it?"

"Sure," he said, brows knitting together in sincerity.

"I'm asking because I don't want this to get too big. Will your boss be there?"

"Mr. D'Onifrio?"

I nodded.

"Yeah, I talked to him this afternoon. He wanted to know the exact time and place. I told him Friday two o'clock at City Hall, room 410. He told me he'd be there."

"Just him? Or will other friends come along?"

"The boss won't come alone. He'll bring a car full, at least. Three, four guys."

"We'll be there, too. Let him know that, okay?"

"Sure. No problem."

"I'm glad he's coming. I know he's pretty busy that day."

Fish scratched his belly. "Yeah, he's getting some big award that night. Kinda surprises me, him doing that during meeting time."

"Meeting time?" Tory asked innocently.

"His bosses are going to be in town. Happens a couple of times a year. Everybody has to walk around on eggshells, treat 'em like they're kings, do whatever they want. They're a real pain in the ass if you ask me."

"Timing's perfect, though. D'Onifrio will get his award while his bosses are here. They'll be there to see it, won't they?"

"Don't know. Them guys don't tell me what they're doing."

"We've got to be going, Frankie," Tory said. "I'll call you tomorrow, and we'll talk through what you're doing tomorrow night."

He went to the couch. As we stepped out the door, I heard the TV click back on.

"What do you think?" I asked Tory as we rode down in the elevator.

"You planted we'd be at the wedding. That worked. I didn't expect he'd know anything about Enrico."

The elevator deposited us in the lobby. "I'll call you tomorrow morning," she said at her car.

I walked to the Saab, drove back to my condo. I changed into exercise clothes, went down to the gym, used the machines for an hour, ran for an hour on the treadmill. I took a long shower, rewarded myself for exercising with a glass of Chardonnay. I carried my glass of wine into the library, stretched out, read for a bit. At eleven, beginning to nod off, I marked my place and headed to bed.

My drowsiness lasted until I walked into the bedroom. On the bed, I found a cat that looked as if it had been skinned, tortured. Pinned to the head with a knife was a note.

CHAPTER 43

The note read: *A preview of what's coming.*

A sick feeling began in my stomach and spread. I wondered if Wilder had left me other presents. I went room to room. Didn't find anything. I got a garbage bag from under the sink, took it back to the bedroom, gathered bed sheets, cat, knife, and note. I stuffed it all in the bag, took it out, and dropped it down the garbage chute. Even as I got rid of everything Wilder had touched, the point of his visit stayed with me. He could get to me anywhere.

I wedged a chair under the door handle. Balanced a glass on top of the knob. Tricks I'd seen in movies. Only after I rigged every possible access to the place, did I remake the bed, try and get some sleep.

As you might imagine, it was not one of my better nights. When I finally did drop of to sleep, I had nightmares, but not of Claire and the kids. These were of faceless people jumping out of the darkness, grabbing me.

When I awoke terrified for the fourth time, I gave up and got out of bed. I showered, shaved, dressed, got myself a bowl of cereal and a glass of orange juice. I was in the office by five.

At eight-forty-five, the trailer door opened, Rosemary rushed in, closed the door behind her, plopped her bag on her desk, and said, "Sorry I'm late. The oddest thing happened this morning."

I knew what she was about to say, felt awful. "Your cat disappeared."

She nodded. "Did Dan call and tell you? We can't understand it. That cat never leaves the house. This morning, she's nowhere to be found."

"Rosemary, have a seat. Let's talk for a moment."

She walked down the aisle, settled in my visitor's chair. "I can't gab long, I'm late and I've got work that needs doing."

"Last night, someone left a dead animal in my bedroom as a warning. It was a cat," I said gently.

Her eyes went wide. Her mouth opened.

"I'm sorry. I didn't know it was your cat."

Her mouth closed. In her lap, her hands were clasped together, the knuckles white. "Someone was in my house? Took my cat?"

"I'm afraid so."

Her gaze searched my face. "Why? Why would somebody do that?"

"I can't explain it. It doesn't make any sense. They didn't have to kill Eddie, either. But they did. I can't do anything about your cat, but I want to make sure you're safe. We talked about you and Dan going to England. Now's the time."

"We can't do it. I've been meaning to tell you, he can't get the time off."

"Call him, talk to him, see if he can't get the company to reconsider." Dan was a CPA. This wasn't his tax time. Someone could cover for him. "I'd like the two of you to go as soon as possible. Today, even."

She didn't say anything, didn't move.

"Rosemary?

Her eyes cleared, she looked at me. "It's so mean, Matt. So hurtful." She stood. "I'll call Dan."

She looked shaky as she walked back to her desk. She sat, composed herself, picked up the phone. Dan wasn't available. She left a message for him to call as soon as he was out of his meeting.

At ten-thirty, he called back. Rosemary poured out what happened to the cat, their need to leave. When the conversation ended, she turned in her seat to face me. "Dan said he'd see what he could do."

At eleven, he called back. Rosemary listened. "I wouldn't feel right about going by myself," she said finally. "I'd be worried the whole time." More listening. She turned, looked at me. "Can you pick up?"

I picked up the phone. "Hello. Dan. Sorry I got you guys in such a mess."

"This wasn't your fault, Matt. I was just explaining to Rosemary, there's no way I can leave. I've got a deal closing middle of next week. But I think she should go."

"I'd be worried if he stayed here by himself," Rosemary said adamantly.

"I'll be fine." Dan sounded like a kid with an overly protective mother.

"Tell him he needs to go, Matt."

Uh, oh. Mom telling Dad to discipline junior. "I'm most concerned about you, Rosemary. Dan's a step removed. He'll be okay. I'd like to get you on a plane out of here, today if possible."

"Go ahead, hon. Matt's right. You'll get to see Rebecca, your folks."

The look Rosemary gave me said she wasn't convinced. "Oh, all right," she said hesitantly. "I'll call, see about flights."

"Bye, Matt," Dan said.

I hung up. They talked a while longer. When she hung up, I said, "Call A-One Travel. Charge it to the company."

She made a face. "You don't have to pay for my trip."

"Call," I told her and went back to work.

"It's done," she said, twenty minutes later. "I fly out tomorrow at five-twenty."

"Nothing sooner?"

She shook her head. "Best I could do."

"Between now and then, I want you to be careful. Don't go anywhere by yourself. Stay in crowds. Does your house have an alarm you can set tonight?"

"You're beginning to scare me, Matt."

"Good. If you're scared you'll be careful."

"I'm going to be fine. I'm leaving. It's Dan I'm worried about."

"I'll check on him, make sure he's okay."

"So will I. I'll be calling him every night." She stood, came down to my desk, hugged me. "I should be calling you every night, too."

A tear ran down her cheek.

I smiled. "Don't cry. There's nothing to cry about."

She pulled away, dabbed at her eyes with a tissue. "What do you mean? If ever there was a time for a good cry, this is it."

We got through the rest of the day without more tears. Not that there weren't moments. It wasn't a particularly busy day—the markets were quiet in anticipation of a Fed meeting the following week—so Rosemary had time to dwell on unpleasant possibilities. I didn't. I used the time to send a fax alert to all our clients, letting them know the office would be closed the following week.

At five, we called it a day, turned off the lights and computers, locked the door to the trailer. As we walked to our cars, I said, "Just to be safe, let me drive you home."

She shook her head, made a face. "You don't need to do that. It's out of your way."

I insisted. I wasn't about to let her drive home alone. I was glad I did. When we arrived at her house, Dan wasn't there yet. I sat with her until we heard the sound of his tires on the gravel driveway.

He came in the front door, tie loosened, suit coat over his arm, briefcase in hand. We talked for a few minutes. When I said I had to go, Dan said he'd walk out to the car with me.

"You really think she's in danger?" he asked.

I nodded. "I think you are, too."

He frowned. "Rosemary doesn't know, but I've got a gun. I'll keep it handy."

I nodded, opened the door to the Saab. "I'll call you. We'll get together for dinner one night."

"You're on," he said and waved as I backed out of the driveway. During the drive back to town, my car phone rang. I hit the button. "Matt Seattle."

"Matt, it's Tory. Fish is ready for this evening. He's going to be very romantic."

I laughed.

"I've also talked to Bill Perez, the Foundation guy, twice this morning. Everything is confirmed for Friday. He has Asolo booked, big name to MC, promos start airing tonight. This guy knows how to put an event together. He's impressive."

"Did he say any more about D'Onifrio?"

"He said he's talked to him several times, mostly answering questions. What time does he need to be there? How long should his acceptance speech be? What else is on the program? That kind of stuff."

"If he's asking those kinds of questions, sounds like he's planning on being there. You haven't heard any more from Raines, have you?"

"No, why?"

"Getting Joe's information to Enrico and the nephews still worries me."

"Raines will take care of it," she said confidently.

I turned onto the causeway, slowed; the drawbridge was up. A sailboat mast bobbed up and down as the boat made her way past.

"We ought to touch base tomorrow. See how Fish's evening went, what else we need to do for him."

"You want to meet at his place?"

"Around eleven."

"See you then."

I hit the off button, waited for the bridge to lower, traffic to clear. On a whim, I stopped at the Holiday Inn for dinner. Fridays they had a seafood buffet. I ate a leisurely dinner, got back to the condo about ten, went for a walk on the beach, was in bed by midnight.

Saturday was overcast, windy—a good day to get my top fixed. I called the Saab dealer, dropped the car off. I drove the loaner, a silver sedan, to Fish's condo for our eleven o'clock meeting.

"I just ordered pizza," Tory said when I let myself in. "Frankie's starving. He said she loved the ring."

On the sofa, Fish gave us his version of a grin. "She was ecstatic until after dinner. Then she started asking me about the honeymoon."

I laughed.

"It's not funny," he said in his foghorn voice. "What are we going to do?"

I pulled a chair up facing him. "What's the boss say you can do?"

"What do you mean?"

"This marriage was to get him his money. Is he planning on taking it right away? Is he going to give you guys a little time together? Have you talked about this with him at all?"

"No."

"No, what?"

"No, we haven't talked about it."

"Why don't you find out what he's planning. That way we'll know what to do about the honeymoon. Why don't you give him a call now?"

Fish stared at me, as if deciding whether making that call was a good idea. He got up slowly, went into the study, closed the door behind him.

The pizza man arrived, Tory buzzed him up. I met him at the elevator, paid him, carried the two large pizzas back to the kitchen.

Fish was in the kitchen waiting on food.

"What'd he say?" I asked.

Fish took one of the boxes, opened the lid, pulled out a slice. He took a big bite, talked with his mouth full. "As soon as we're married, he's taking his money. He don't care about the honeymoon. He said if I want to take one with her, that's fine with him." He opened the refrigerator with his free hand, got out a beer.

"That's not going to work," Tory said. "She's going to be expecting a honeymoon. By the end of the week, she'll be obsessing about it."

I put a slice of pizza on a plate, got out a napkin. "I agree. We're going to have to do something. Quickly."

Fish swallowed a mouthful of pizza. "A cruise. She keeps talking about a cruise. There's got to be a cruise we can take that leaves Saturday."

"Let me look into it," I said reassuringly. "I've got a couple of clients who are travel agents. They might be able to find you something."

"She'd like to cruise the Greek Isles," Fish said pointedly

Tory almost choked on a bite of pizza. "Wouldn't we all? Let Matt see what he can get. You're awfully late to be leaving on Saturday."

I didn't learn much else. Fish and Janet were going to a movie Sunday afternoon. Tory was following up with Bill Perez and his people.

I went back to my place, worked the phone. The first call was to Richard Seagle at A-One travel. He wasn't in. Next, I tried Sandi Halblien-French, who owned Pier 'n Plane Travel. She was.

"What happened to my GE stock?" she wanted to know when she

came on the line. "It's down eight points."

"Keep repeating: volatility is your friend," I counseled her. "The market is going through a period of ups and downs, might go sideways like this for the rest of the year."

"Just buy me the ones that always go up. Is that too much to ask?"

"Hey, for you, no problem. I'll throw in the winning lottery ticket, too."

She laughed. "I'm going to hold you to that, wise guy. In the meantime, what can I do for you?"

"I need to book a cruise for two leaving next Saturday."

I heard fingers tapping computer keys. "Who's the lucky woman?"

"This isn't for me. It's for a client."

"Must be a pretty good client," she said absentmindedly. "You know, Matt, I'm not seeing much here. Can I call you back on this?"

"I'm at home." I gave her my home number, my cell phone number.

"I'll call you this afternoon."

I rang off. Paced around the condo. Felt cooped up. Decided to go for a walk on the beach. I put on a swimsuit, grabbed a towel, and headed out. I walked for an hour, letting the waves wash over my feet. I found three shark's teeth, two tiny ones, one almost an inch in size.

When I got home, I dropped them in a glass bowl, almost half full with the little black teeth, went in the kitchen for a glass of ice water. The phone message light was flashing. Sandi probably. I hit the button. The Darth Vader voice said: You. Have. Two. Messages. First. Message. Saturday. Two. P.M. "Hello Matt. It's Sandi. I think I've found a couple of things that might work. Give me a call. I'm here until five."

I punched in her number. "Sandi," I said when she came on, "It's Matt."

"Good. I've found two cruises for you. Both leaving Saturday out of Miami. The first is a Holland American ship and goes to San Juan, St. Thomas, and St. Croix. Six days, five nights. The second is a Princess Lines cruise that goes to St. Thomas, Aruba, and Cozumel. Five days, four nights."

She ran off the prices. Neither was to the Greek Isles; both were expensive. Since there was a good chance this cruise would go unused, I opted for the less expensive of the two.

"I'll book it. Whose name shall I use?"

"The lucky couple are Mr. and Mrs. Frank Ford. And Sandi? Can you put some literature on this cruise in the mail to me?"

"I sure will. A bill, too."

I hung up, feeling good that it hadn't been more painful. I hit the play button for the second stored message. Second. Message. Saturday. Two. Twenty. P.M. "Matt, this is Dan. Have you seen Rosemary? She went to Publix this morning and hasn't come back. I'm worried about her. Call me if you know anything. Thanks. 'Bye."

I felt sick. If Rosemary still wasn't home, most likely D'Onifrio had grabbed her.

CHAPTER 44

I called Dan. He picked up before the first ring finished.

"Dan, it's Matt. I just found your message. Is Rosemary home yet?"

"No. She went to the grocery at ten. Hasn't come back." If he was trying not to sound frantic, he wasn't succeeding.

"Why the grocery? Why didn't she stay home?"

"She said she wanted to get a few things so there'd be food in the house while she was gone."

"Why didn't you go with her?"

"Publix is only three miles from the house. I didn't think I needed to. I'm scared, Matt. Is this part of that trouble?"

I didn't want to frighten him more. "I'm not sure. Have you called the police?"

"Not yet. I keep hoping she'll walk in the door."

"Call them. Don't wait. Tell them what's going on, get them looking for her. That's the best thing to do right now."

"I will. Thanks, Matt."

I hung up, feeling awful. I grabbed the keys to the loaner car, and went out to find a pay phone. The closest one was at a CVS Pharmacy, a short drive away.

I put thirty-five cents in the slot, punched a number I was getting to know all too well. "I need to talk to Raines. It's an emergency," I said to the woman who answered.

"He'll call you right back," she said.

I stood there guarding the phone for half an hour. When it finally rang, I jumped, grabbed the receiver. "This is Matt."

"What's the emergency?" Raines' voice was tense.

"They've kidnapped my associate."

"Tory?"

"No, a lady who works in my brokerage, Rosemary Shears. I just talked to her husband, Dan. Rosemary went to the grocery this morning, never came home. He's got her. I know he does. What do we do?"

"You're sure about this? She isn't out shoe shopping or something?"

"No."

A deep sigh ended in, "Shit. I'll check, see who knows something about this. Has the husband gone to the police?"

"He was about to."

"Find out who's working the investigation, let me know. Give me a number where I can call you. Land lines. No cellular."

I gave him my home and work numbers.

"Seattle, I have to tell you this. She could be dead already. If she's not, it's because they're going to use her to get to you. Anything you hear, call me. Understand?" He hung up.

I got back in the loaner, used my cell phone to call Tory. Her answering machine picked up. I left a cryptic message, told her to call me. I pulled into the Watergate. Not recognizing the car, Ehrlichman stopped me.

"Oh, Mr. Seattle. New car, huh? Sorry to have stopped you."

If only he was real protection. I rode the elevator up to the condo, went to the kitchen, got a glass of ice water. I drank deep gulps, tried to calm down. I was jazzed with adrenaline. The phone rang. It was Tory.

"Matt, what's wrong?"

"D'Onifrio's got Rosemary."

"What?"

"He kidnapped her. I want you to get away before something happens to you. Pack a bag. Go somewhere for a couple of days."

"What about you?"

"I have to stay. Raines thinks D'Onifrio may have taken Rosemary to trade for me."

I heard a gasp at the other end of the line. "You can't do that. They'll kill you both."

"I can't not do it. I couldn't live with myself if they killed Rosemary. I'm going to talk to D'Onifrio—"

"Matt, you can't—"

"Through Fish. Fish can call him, deliver a message for me. I'm going over to his condo now."

"I'll meet you there."

"No, you need to leave, too," I said, but she'd already hung up.

I slammed the phone down on the receiver, grabbed my keys, headed out again.

Fish was sprawled on the sofa when I charged into the room. Surprised, he jumped. In five quick strides, I was to the sofa. Snatched up the remote, clicked the TV off. "Listen to me," I said sternly. "We've got problems. Your boss has kidnapped a lady I work with."

Fish's eyes got big, frightened.

I walked to the kitchen, grabbed the cordless phone, took it back to the living room, thrust it at him. He fumbled with it, didn't want to take it.

"Here's what we're going to do. You're going to call him. Tell him to release her. If he does that, I'll turn myself over to him at the wedding."

Fish stared at me, his mouth hanging open.

"Call him," I yelled.

Fish sat up, dialed. "I need to talk to the boss." He listened, covered the receiver with his hand. "I don't think he's there."

"Tell them to find him."

He took his hand off the receiver. "This is important. You better find him."

He looked up at me, his eyes wild. We waited. His head jerked. "Yeah, boss. Sorry to disturb you, but Seattle told me to call, said you grabbed one of his people." He closed his eyes, clamped his jaw shut. "The thing of it is," he said, opening his eyes. "He says he'll turn himself over to you at the wedding if you release the woman." He listened, looked up at me, shook his head.

I grabbed the phone away from him. "Let her go. She doesn't have anything to do with this. I'll drive over to your place right now, if you agree to release her."

This brought amused laughter. "I don't want you. Yet. You still have work to do for me. This woman is my insurance policy that you make sure this marriage happens. If it doesn't, she will die. I haven't decided about you yet. I may put you through a torturous ordeal. Or I may just let you die. How much pain you suffer depends on how you perform, Mr. Seattle."

"Let Rosemary go," I said again. "I'm going to do what you want."

"I'm sure you will. I am not an unreasonable person. I will not hurt your friend before the wedding. But if things start to go wrong, do you know what I will do?"

My throat closed. I could only imagine. I couldn't speak.

CHAPTER 45

"I will start cutting her up, sending you pieces as reminders of how you have failed me. Perhaps a hand to start. An eye. The tongue, I am given to understand, is very painful."

"There won't be any problems. Things will go smoothly."

"Thank you, Mr. Seattle. I thought you might see things my way." He rang off.

"I'm sorry, man," Fish said from the couch. "I didn't know anything like this was going down."

I needed air. I put the phone down, walked out on the deck, leaned over the railing. I felt sick.

From inside, I heard a door open, close. Voices talking. Steps. "Are you okay?" Tory asked, leaning next to me on the rail.

I was so low I didn't know what to say even though my throat had relaxed a bit.

"You can't blame yourself. There was no way you could know this was going to happen."

But I should have. He'd even warned me that night at his house, the night he torched my offices.

"They'll find her. Raines will get her back. You can't give up now, Matt. You have to keep your head in the game. That's her only chance."

She didn't have a chance. D'Onifrio wasn't going to let her walk away, a witness to what he'd done.

"C'mon, you've got to snap out of it. Let's get moving." She pulled my arm. We went back into the condo. "What did Raines have to say?"

Fish was standing there watching us. Having her ask about Raines in front of him brought me back to attention. "Rosemary's husband, you mean?"

For a split second, her face showed confusion. Her mouth opened as if to say something, closed quickly. "Yeah. Isn't that his name?"

I nodded. "He just wants her back. He's frightened. He doesn't have any idea what's behind this."

Fish was still standing there. He looked uncomfortable. "Guys, if there's anything I can do to help, let me know. You know I'll do it for you. I feel awful about this."

I went over, patted him on the shoulder. "Thanks. What we need you to do is get married. Make sure Janet doesn't do something goofy to delay things. I almost forgot. I booked you a cruise. You leave Saturday from Miami, visit San Juan, St. Thomas, St.Croix. Six days, five nights. Looks like a good time."

"Thanks. I really appreciate you springing for that, especially with how the boss is treating you."

"I appreciate you making that call to him."

His jowls quivered in a frown. "I'll tell him when I talk to him—this ain't right."

"Wouldn't hurt to call Janet," Tory suggested. "Tell her you've booked a cruise. Position this as a little excursion, the best of what's available on short notice. Tell her you'd like to take a big trip with her first of the year. I'll call you tomorrow, make sure everything's going okay." She looked over at me. "We need to talk to Rosemary's husband."

"Fish, if you hear anything—anything at all about Rosemary—will you call me?"

He nodded.

When we were going down in the elevator, Tory hit the door with her hand. "I can't believe I mentioned Raines in front of him. I'm sorry."

"An easy slip to make. We've gotten to thinking of Fish as a friend."

She hit the door again. "Damn."

It opened on the ground level revealing two little old people, each holding a bag of groceries. They scurried out of Tory's way.

"What did Raines tell you?" she asked as we walked to our cars.

"Not much really. He said he'd look into it. Told me to call when I found out who was handling the police investigation. I'm going to call him now, fill him in on my conversation with D'Onifrio."

"I'll follow you."

I drove to that same pay phone at CVS, called Raines, got the call back. "I don't know anything yet," he said in a gruff voice.

"I'm calling because I talked to D'Onifrio. He confirmed what you suspected. He's holding her to get me."

"Only way this makes any sense."

"I tried to get him to let her go. He wouldn't. I tried to set up an exchange at the wedding. He wouldn't agree to that, either. But he's going to be at the wedding. If something's going to happen, it'll be then."

"When's this wedding?"

"Friday. Two o'clock. City Hall. Room 410."

"And you think he'll have her there?"

"I don't know, no. But I said I'd be there. If he lets her go, he can take me."

"Matt, you can't do that," Tory said adamantly.

From the earpiece, I heard Raines say, "I agree. Let's play it like you're going to make the trade, but not plan on going through with it. I'll have people there. We'll get the woman away from them, get you out of there."

I desperately wanted to believe he could pull that off.

"Can you get me a picture of this woman?"

"Yes."

"A guy named Rusty is on his way to your place to sweep your phones. Give him the picture. Call me with any news." He rang off.

I hung the receiver in its cradle, turned to go.

Tory stood in front of me, arms folded in front of her, a concerned look on her face. "Tell me you're not going to do that."

"Raines said to play it like it's going to happen but not to go through with it. He'll have people there."

Her face softened a little. "Good."

I headed for the car, away from further confrontation. "Raines has somebody on his way to my place. I need to get back."

"I'll come, too," she said to my surprise.

As I pulled up to the guardhouse, Ehrlichman stepped out. I stopped, leaned out the window, and explained I had a guest following in the car behind me. If I hadn't, he'd have assumed Tory was an intruder and given her a full body-cavity search. Instead, all she'd get from him would be a goofy leer.

"Service guy came by for you, Mr. Seattle," he said when I'd finished. "I rang your place. You weren't there, so I couldn't let him in. He said he'd come back at five."

I looked at the car's clock. Four-forty-five. "Sorry I missed him. Send him on when he comes back."

"I sure will, Mr. Seattle."

"Thanks." I raised my window, drove on.

Actually, the delay helped me. I knew I had a picture of Rosemary. I'd used it in an announcement when she joined the brokerage. But what had I done with it?

I parked my car in the garage, waited at the front of the building for Tory. She arrived a minute later. Parked in the visitor's area. We walked in, rode the elevator up to twelve. "Make yourself at home," I said to Tory as I opened the condo's front door. The answering machine was beeping, I went there first, hit the play button.

You. Have. Two. Messages. First. Message. Saturday. Three. Twenty. P.M. "Matt, it's Dan. Rosemary still hasn't come back. I've called the police. You haven't heard from her, have you? Call me back." He sounded desperate.

Second. Message. Saturday. Four. Ten. P.M. "Mr. Seattle, this is Lieutenant Brock Ellsworth of the Sarasota Police. Rosemary Shears, who I understand works for you, has been reported missing by her husband, Dan. Mr. Seattle, if you wouldn't mind calling me at this number at your earliest opportunity, I'd appreciate talking to you. Thanks."

I wrote down his name and number. Headed into the library. If Rosemary's picture was here, it would be with the office stuff in my desk. Sure enough, in a file marked announcements, I found it. A five-by-seven glossy.

The downstairs buzzer sounded, I headed for the intercom.

"It's Rusty," a voice said, "you should be expecting me."

"C'mon up." I buzzed him in.

The doorbell rang moments later. "I'll get it," Tory said.

Rusty was a young guy with red hair and a goatee. He had on overalls that said Central Service, carried a large gray metal toolbox in each hand. "Raines told you I was coming, right?"

I nodded. "Said you were going to sweep the phones?"

"Yeah, want to show me where they are?"

I showed him the three phones. "One of D'Onifrio's people was in this condo," I said as I showed him the phone in the bedroom.

"Really? I better sweep the whole place." He opened his tool kits, took out a bunch of gadgets. Tory and I watched him as he worked.

Half an hour later, he packed his stuff back up. "You're clean. You can call Raines from here now. I've put a scrambler on your phone. It activates when you call him at this number." He handed me a card. I got Rosemary's picture, gave it to him. He put it in his tool kit and departed.

"I'm going to call Dan back, then Raines," I said to Tory. "Find out what he wants to do about the police."

Dan must have been right next to the phone. "Hello," he said in a frightened voice.

"Dan, it's Matt. Any news?"

"No. The police just left. They've been here all afternoon."

"There was a message on my machine to call a Lieutenant Ellsworth."

"He's the one in charge."

"What'd he say?"

"He told me not to panic. Said she could still turn up. He's wrong. Something's happened. I know it."

"Let me call Ellsworth. See what he needs. What can I do for you? Want to go get some dinner together? Bring something by your place? What sounds good?"

"Thanks, Matt. I can't eat, I'm too worried. Call Ellsworth. If you hear anything, let me know."

"Poor guy. He has to be beside himself," Tory said after I hung up.

"Rosemary and Dan are the nicest people in the entire world."

"I didn't say that to make you feel bad. You're a nice guy, too. Very few people look out for others the way you do."

"Thanks." I smiled a little self-consciously, dialed the scrambler number. A man answered, got Raines.

"Yeah," he said.

"It's Matt Seattle. You said you wanted to know who was in

charge of the investigation. There's a message on my machine from a Lieutenant Ellsworth. He's the guy, and he wants me to call him back."

"I'll call him, tell him we're involved. He may still want to talk to you, but I want to talk to him first. Anything else?"

"I don't think so."

"My guys are alerted. No word on your friend yet."

He rang off. I put my phone down, feeling vaguely unsettled by the conversation with Raines. The last thing I needed was a turf war.

Tory slung her bag over her shoulder. "I've got to leave."

I rode down in the elevator with her. "I know you meant leave the condo, but you should leave Sarasota. Take off before D'Onifrio grabs you, too."

She looked at me, her face resolute. "He's not going to come after me. It doesn't make any sense for him to take another hostage. Besides, you need the help."

I didn't think anything else I said would change her mind. We rode in silence the rest of the way. The doors opened when we reached the ground level. "Thanks," I told her before we stepped out and headed to our cars.

On the way back to my place, I made a quick trip to Publix, picked up some chicken from the deli counter. I ate in the kitchen, one eye on the phone, wondering who my next caller would be.

It turned out to be Ellsworth. He called at seven. "Mr. Seattle, I've talked to Paul Raines. I'd like to talk to you."

I tried to read between the words, but couldn't tell if the conversation with Raines upset him. "Sure. When do you want to meet?"

"How about now?"

"Where?"

"Police headquarters. Fourth and Main. Tell them at the front desk you're there to see me. They'll have someone escort you up."

Forty minutes later, I was sitting in the visitor's chair across a battered green metal desk from Brock Ellsworth, a short, muscular man with big shoulders, a big neck, a shaved head. His features were regular enough until you got to his eyes, which were cold and distrusting. He wore a patterned tie over a brown short-sleeved dress shirt, the sleeves rolled up. To show off his biceps, I guessed.

Every inch of his small office was in use—photos pinned to the walls, cardboard boxes stacked against walls, files everywhere.

Ellsworth had sent the girl who walked me to his office to get us coffee. She surprised me when she brought back two large cups from Starbucks.

Ellsworth gulped his eagerly, said, "I hate the crap we've got here."

I took a sip of mine, smiled. "It's very good. Thank you."

"Don't mention it. Thanks for coming right over. I told you I talked to Raines. He asked me to cooperate on this. I told him the department always cooperates with the D.E.A. But you know what? I'm a lot more concerned about Rosemary Shears than I am about Don D'Onifrio." He drank more coffee, put the cup on his desk, leaned forward. "I want you to tell me everything you know about this, 'cause I don't want Rosemary Shears dying because this guy Raines has a hard-on for D'Onifrio."

I told him what I knew. Didn't leave anything out. While I talked, he finished his coffee, threw the cup in a wastebasket where it joined others.

"Let me get this straight," he said when I finished. "You're going to this wedding thinking Raines is going to rescue you and this Rosemary Shears?"

I nodded.

He laughed contemptuously.

CHAPTER 46

"Raines doesn't care about you or this Shears woman. He's only interested in putting D'Onifrio away. He's on a personal vendetta because he's lost four of his men. Now he might be telling you he wants to get D'Onifrio on kidnapping charges, but if D'Onifrio kills you and the Shears woman, Raines can go after him for murder." He sat back in his seat, watched me, waited for my reaction.

If he was trying to frighten me, he was succeeding. I tried not to let that show. "What should I do?"

He continued to watch me. "You walk into that wedding, I guarantee they'll carry you out in a body bag. He can't stop what's bound to happen."

"I hear you, but I don't see I have any choice. If I don't go, Rosemary's dead. Rather than warning me about Raines, the two of you should be working together, figuring out how to keep us alive."

Ellsworth smiled. "Didn't I tell you? The department always cooperates with the D.E.A. Stay in touch, Mr. Seattle." He handed me one of his cards. "It would be in your best interest to keep me very much in the loop."

He stood. I was dismissed.

I drove home in a daze. I had the bad guys fighting, the good guys fighting, the clock ticking.

Sunday the weather worsened. It was overcast, spitting rain. My mood darkened as well. In the afternoon, I had a bad conversation with Raines. He was annoyed with me for talking to Ellsworth and not calling to fill him in on the meeting. He was more annoyed when I told him what Ellsworth had said. He did little to assure me that Ellsworth was wrong. Most troubling, he never mentioned Rosemary. I had to ask twice before he told me they didn't know anything new.

That evening, I took Chinese over to Dan. We ate at their kitchen table. Dan wolfed his down as if he hadn't eaten in days. He looked terrible. His eyes were tired, bloodshot. He hadn't shaved or combed his hair. His clothes looked slept in. Twice during dinner he broke down and cried.

I tried to steer the conversation to happier times. He rallied a bit then slid back into sadness. After dinner, we played cards. He seemed to enjoy that. When I left at nine, he hugged me. "Thanks for coming, Matt. You don't know how alone I feel."

But I did. I knew exactly how he felt.

There were messages on my machine when I returned to the condo. The courtesy call from a carpet cleaner I deleted immediately. Ellworth was call two. I returned his call, learned he'd gone off duty. I left a voicemail that I was returning his call and would call him in the morning. Call three was Tory. She answered when I called.

"I was checking to see how you were doing. You were pretty low when I left yesterday."

"You don't know what low is. I just took dinner over to Dan."

"That was nice of you."

"He's a mess."

"I thought you might need a little cheering up, too. You want to have a drink somewhere?"

"Sure. Meet you at Tommy Bahama's at ten-thirty?" I named an upscale restaurant and bar on St. Armand's Circle.

She was already there when I arrived, seated at a table for two. A man was leaning on the other chair, talking to her. As he saw me approaching, he left quickly.

"A friend?" I asked, sitting down.

She smiled. "He'd like to be. He was sharing some interesting ideas on how we could get to know each other."

Our waitress arrived. Tory had a glass of wine in front of her. I ordered one, too.

"So how are you holding up?"

"I've had better days." I told her about the antagonism between Raines and Ellsworth.

Her face grew serious. "I was counting on Raines."

"I was, too. Now, I don't know if I trust either of them."

"Are you still going to the wedding?"

I nodded. "Have to."

She fiddled with the stem of her glass. "It's not fair. There are so many creeps out there—like that guy that was just hitting on me—I don't know why this had to happen to you."

"I'm not happy about it, either. In fact, I'm scared to death," I said honestly. "But I'm planning on getting through it. Somehow."

She started to say something.

I stopped her. "If I don't, I've had a good life. I had a great marriage. Two wonderful kids. A dog that looked after me."

She smiled at the mention of Eddie.

"A great career. Something good even came out of this mess—I met you."

She looked up sharply.

Maybe it was the wine talking. Maybe it was Dr. Swarthmore's voice in the back of my head urging me on. Maybe it was from my heart. Whatever it was, I did something I hadn't done in an awfully long time: I opened up. "I thought I'd never care about anyone again. I was sure I'd spend the rest of my life by myself. But you've changed that. When I'm with you, there's an excitement to life. I don't know how you feel, but I know I'd like to see more of you." I stopped, unsure of her reaction. "I'm sorry; I've probably embarrassed you."

Her gaze found mine. "You couldn't embarrass me. You are the kindest, most considerate man I've ever known, and I'm terrified I'm going to lose you."

My spirits, which had been plumbing the depths, soared. I smiled, reached out, took her hands in mine. "We have to make a pact. I'm not going to lose you. You're not going to lose me. When this is over, we'll both be around to spend time together."

CHAPTER 47

Monday, Raines called me. "Seattle, we're going to scout City Hall, take a look at the area where this wedding actually takes place, see what we have to work with. It would be good to have you along."

Of course, it couldn't be simple as just meeting him there. I had to drive to a home in the gated community of the Longboat Key Club Estates, go inside the home, wait half an hour, leave via a van in the closed garage. My guide was a woman, Tara, who spent the half hour before we left watching out the window. In the van, she watched the mirrors. "We're clean," she said into a walkie-talkie as we drove over the causeway to the mainland. We drove to a back entrance of City Hall. Dumpsters and garbage cans lined the wall. She pointed to a door. "One of our men is waiting for you."

The man inside took me to a room on the third floor. Raines and nine other people were inside, looking over blueprints. He nodded to me when I came in, continued giving the group instructions. When he was done with his briefing, he sent them to the fourth floor in ones and twos. He said to me, "We're going to have three agents on four, six watching the street entrances, one coordinating from a set of floor plans. Once D'Onifrio and Shears enter the building, it'll be sealed. We'll have them."

I was impressed. Not the shoot-out at OK Corral Ellsworth had led me to believe.

Raines got something out of a backpack, handed it to me.

"What's this?"

"Bulletproof vest. Try it on. Make sure it fits."

I put it on, had trouble putting my polo shirt back on.

"Don't worry about that. Wear a bulkier shirt on Friday," Raines said. He took the vest from me, put it in the backpack, handed it to me. "Hold on to that."

"Will you be here Friday?"

"I'll be close by." He looked at his watch. "We can go up now."

Room 410 turned out to be two rooms connected by a door: a large waiting room and a smaller room where the actual ceremonies were conducted. Once couples were called into the ceremony room, they didn't return to the waiting room. They exited to the hall.

"We'll have agents at both of those doors," Raines whispered as we stood in the waiting room. "I want you over there." He pointed to a long wooden bench by the door to the ceremony room. "Any questions?"

"What time should I be here?"

"Wedding's at two. Be here at one-thirty. Don't acknowledge any of my people. D'Onifrio will have people here, too."

"How about Ellsworth? Have you coordinated this with him?"

Raines face hardened. "Ellsworth may have a leak in his organization. The less he and his people know the better."

I didn't like hearing that. "What if he asks me?"

"Tell him you don't know."

Guess I'd used up my last question. Raines headed for the door. Led me to the service elevator. "Tara will take you back."

We repeated our little charade at the home in the Estates. I drove back to the Watergate, went by the lobby to pick up my mail. Sure enough, there was a fat manila envelope from Pier 'n Plane. I carried it all upstairs, dumped it on the kitchen table. The answering machine was beeping. I ignored it, got a can of Diet Coke from the refrigerator, took it out on the balcony.

Looking out at the Gulf, I tried to sort things out. One of those calls on my machine could well be Ellsworth. If Raines was right, I didn't want to tell him anything. On the other hand, Ellsworth had been pretty convincing when he'd made his case against Raines. I worried it while I drank my drink, didn't settle anything. I went back inside, played my messages. There were two.

Julian was the first. "Matt, I have the report from Nathan Cohen, the CPA who reviewed the information Nevitt supplied. He said they didn't give us much, no bank or brokerage statements, no tax returns. It's a lot of fluff. I'm calling Fowler to set up a meeting, go over Nathan's report with him, ask for a dismissal. I'll keep you posted."

That was welcome news.

Tory was the second call. "It's Tory. Frankie just called and wanted more details about his honeymoon cruise. Janet's getting antsy again. He was hoping he'd have something to share with her. They're having dinner and going dancing tonight. Give me a call. Oh, I had a good time last night."

I smiled, dialed her number. Her machine picked up. I started to leave a message, but she picked up, out of breath. "Glad you called. I was on my way over to Frankie's to try and calm him down."

"Why? What's wrong?"

"Janet wants constant attention. Frankie doesn't know what to do with her. I told him I'd come over, help plot some things to get him through these days before the wedding."

"I've got cruise literature. If you're headed over to his place now, I'll meet you there. We can go over this stuff with him."

"Great. See you in a little bit."

I hung up, started out, hesitated. I'd told Ellsworth I'd call him. I hadn't. I went back to the phone, dialed his number. After four rings, there was a little hiccup, and I was kicked over to someone else.

"Suarez." A woman answered.

"This is Matt Seattle calling. I was trying to reach Lieutenant Ellsworth."

"He's not in right now. Can I help you?"

"I think I need to talk to him. Would you let him know I called? I'll try to call him back."

"Matt Seattle, got it."

"Thanks," I told her and hung up. I grabbed the envelope from Pier 'n Plane, headed out.

When I let myself into Fish's condo, Tory was already there. The two of them were seated at the kitchen table. On a big piece of wrapping paper, Tory had drawn out a calendar of the days before the wedding.

I peered over her shoulder to see what they'd filled in. Not much. "We're just getting started," she said.

Within half an hour, she'd penciled in an agenda for Tuesday, Wednesday, Thursday. In Friday's column, she had the wedding marked at two. She tapped that with her pencil. "We'll arrange for a limo to pick you and Janet up, take you to City Hall." She marked that down. "Friday night you can spend here or at her place. Saturday you leave for your cruise."

That was my cue to spread out the cruise literature. Fish studied it intently. He looked up, eyes wide, brows knitted together. "This is great. You don't know how much I appreciate you guys doing this for me."

While he was in an appreciative mood seemed a good time to probe for information. "What arrangements have you made with D'Onifrio for after the wedding? Might impact how we get you to this cruise?"

"The boss has thought through all that. He's going to have papers for her that look like she's getting access to all my accounts. Instead, they'll give us access to all hers."

"He doesn't have time for that, does he? The awards presentation is only a couple of hours later."

"He's planning on doing it right after the ceremony. I mean right after we say our 'I do's.'"

"Did he say any more about Rosemary?"

Fish's jowls quivered, his version of a frown. "I asked. He said he'd have her there like he told you."

That helped.

Fish held up the cruise literature. "Thanks again for this."

I smiled. I hoped I'd be there on Saturday to wish him bon voyage.

CHAPTER 48

On Wednesday, Ellsworth called. "Mr. Seattle," he said politely. "We need to talk." When I hesitated, he said, "Now."

On my drive to the police station, I copied what I'd seen Tara do. I checked my mirrors, watched the cars behind me, took a circuitous route. This late in the game I didn't want D'Onifrio's people seeing me going to the police.

Ellsworth didn't offer me Starbuck's, only a brusque "Sit down."

When I was seated, he handed me a stack of eight and a half by eleven black-and-white glossy photos.

"These were taken at Sarasota/Bradenton International Airport earlier this afternoon."

I looked at the top photo.

"That's Enrico Menendez." The photo showed a stooped, older man with a lined face and thinning hair walking across the tarmac from a private jet.

I went to the second photo.

"Little Ernie. Behind him, on the right, is Paso Diaz, head of security. They brought fifteen bodyguards on this trip. That's a lot of muscle, even for them."

I placed Little Ernie's photo on the desk next to Enrico's. Looked at the next one.

"That's the other nephew, Eduardo."

I put his photo next to Little Ernie's, studied the nephews. They looked like brothers; both had the same dark hair brushed back, the same round face, the same slash of a mouth. Little Ernie wore a goatee, Eduardo, a moustache. Little Ernie looked shorter and thicker than his brother. No one—in any of the photos—was smiling.

"The rest are close-ups of the bodyguards, shots of the limos that took them to the Colony."

I rifled through those quickly, placed them in a pile on the desk.

Ellsworth gathered the photos, put them in a certain order, set them on the side of his desk. He leaned back in his chair. "Did seeing them make these people real for you? Do you understand that each one of these men has been responsible for multiple deaths?"

I nodded, said nothing.

"Keeping you alive isn't going to be easy."

Again, I nodded, said nothing.

"Don't make it harder than it already is, Seattle. I know you're planning something; tell me what."

There was no mistaking the threat in Ellsworth's voice. "All Raines told me was he wanted to catch D'Onifrio with Rosemary. He didn't tell me how or where he planned to do that."

"Then why did you go to City Hall with him?"

"He wanted me to see the place. His idea was for D'Onifrio to bring Rosemary to the wedding, make the exchange there. But D'Onifrio wouldn't agree to it."

"Of course not. D'Onifrio's not going to put himself in a position where he can be caught with this woman. So what's the plan, now?"

"I don't know that there is one."

Ellsworth stared at me, frowned. "I could put you in protective custody, keep you alive."

"You could, but he said he'd kill Rosemary if I'm not there. If you want to help us, don't let them take us out of that building."

"Don't worry, I'll do what I need to do—even if you aren't leveling with me."

Having made his point, he told me to go. I did. I drove home hurriedly. In my condo, I paced from room to room. Maybe Ellsworth had been right; seeing those pictures did make it real. I was definitely more tense. I started to put on my workout clothes, picked up the phone instead, dialed Tory's number.

"Hello," I said after she answered. "I was wondering if you had plans for dinner."

"My plans included cold, left-over pizza."

"I can do better than that."

"I was hoping you could."

"How about if I pick you up in an hour?"

"I'll be ready."

When I pulled in the drive, she was sitting on her porch. She smiled, stood, walked down two steps to the drive. I got out of the car, opened her door for her.

"Thanks," she said as she slid in the seat.

I got in my side, backed up, headed for a place a mile or so down the beach from her place called the Sandbar.

"This is better than cold pizza," she said when I pulled into their parking lot.

The Sandbar had good food and a location that provided panoramic views of the beach. In season, we'd have had to wait an hour for a table on the deck overlooking the Gulf. In August, five minutes.

"What prompted this?" Tory asked when we were seated.

"We probably have some business that needs discussing, but mostly, I wanted to see you."

She smiled.

Our waiter arrived, gave us menus, took drink orders, and left.

Tory reached in her black bag, took out a five-by-seven printed booklet, handed it to me. "A stack of those came today from Bill

Perez. I dropped off two dozen with Raines."

I examined the booklet. The cover was dark blue, the logo of the Foundation for Latina Speech and Hearing Services imprinted in silver. Inside, on the left-hand page, was the agenda for the evening. The page on the right included a photo of D'Onifrio and a bio listing his accomplishments. The next left-hand page showed the rest of the evening's award recipients. Five smaller awards were also being handed out. The rest was about the organization.

"Raines thinks he can fit my little write-up in this?"

She nodded. "That's what he said. He'll have people positioned as ushers who'll watch for Enrico and the nephews, hand them the doctored programs."

Our drinks arrived. I raised mine. "Here's to pulling this off."

She clinked glasses with me. "It's going to go swimmingly. I know it is."

I took a sip, put my glass down on the table. "Ellsworth wanted to see me today. Showed me pictures of Enrico, Little Ernie, and Eduardo walking from their private jet. Questioned me about what Raines was planning."

"You say that like he's planning trouble."

"He might. He says they'll cooperate, but there's something between him and Raines."

"Raines seemed pretty confident when I talked to him. He has forty agents working on this. He said he had D'Onifrio under twenty-four hour surveillance, scenarios for everything that could possibly happen. He also suggested I spend Friday at his headquarters. He said I might be able to help and would be safe there."

It felt reassuring to hear that Raines had forty agents, more reassuring to know Tory would be safe. Some of my doubt about Raines vanished.

"The lovebirds seem happy, too. Frankie has been taking Janet places, spending money on her. That seems to be what she wants, constant attention."

"No chance she'll stand him up at the altar?"

"The limo's to make sure that doesn't happen."

Our waiter returned. "Have you folks decided yet, or do you need a little more time?"

We opted for more time. We weren't in any hurry.

"Has he had any more conversations with D'Onifrio?"

"They talk every day. My sense is things must be getting better. Frankie seems more upbeat and confident that he's actually going on his honeymoon."

"Nothing more we need to do for him?"

She shook her head.

"Anything more we need to do for anybody?"

"Not that I know of."

"Then the business part of this meeting is adjourned; on to more pleasant topics."

She grinned. "And what might those be?"

"You and me, of course," I said lightly. "I want to know all about you."

We traded stories over dinner and coffee. Went for a walk on the beach. Talked more. It must have been eleven by the time I drove her home. Even then, we sat in the car talking. Neither one of us wanted the evening to end.

I walked her to the door. She leaned forward and kissed me. It was a kiss meant to be quick. It quickly turned into something far more. Reluctantly, we parted.

"There'll be time for us once this is finished," she said, smiling.

CHAPTER 49

Thursday morning at seven-thirty I called Dr. Swarthmore.

"Matt, good to hear from you. Things are going well, I hope?"

"That's why I'm calling. I think they are going well. I've met someone, a lady by the name of Tory Wright." In the background, I heard the scratching sound of her pen taking notes.

"The two of you are attracted to each other? You have told her how you feel?"

"Yes. To both. I surprised myself. I opened up."

She gave a little dry laugh. "Felt good, didn't it?"

"You know, Adelle, it did."

"And you don't feel guilt, do you?"

"No guilt. Uncertainty. But no guilt."

"It's natural for you to feel some uncertainty. However, if you are attracted to each other, the uncertainty will work itself out as your relationship deepens. This is the best kind of therapy for you, Matt."

"Sure feels like it. Adelle, thanks for getting me this far. I want you to know I appreciate all you've done, all these phone calls you've taken at odd hours of the day and night."

"Thank you, Matt. That's very kind. Stay in touch."

"You know I will. Bye, Adelle." I rang off.

I made myself some breakfast. Cheerios, half a grapefruit, orange juice, coffee. Went over my plan for the day. Workout, walk on the beach, visit with Dan, maybe play a little golf. I'd just finished breakfast when the phone rang. I carried dishes over to the counter, picked up the receiver. "Matt Seattle."

"It's Raines. I think it would be good if we went over plans one final time."

"Okay."

"Here's what I want you to do. At eleven, be at Mote Marine Lab." It was a marine research facility on the south end of Longboat Key that had become a tourist attraction. "A woman will be waiting for you by the windows to the Manatee exhibit."

"I'll be there."

I looked at my watch. Eight. I punched in Dan's number. When he picked up, I said, "Dan, Matt. I thought maybe I'd stop by if you'd like a little company."

"I'm going crazy, Matt."

"I'll be there in half an hour, and you can tell me about it."

I hadn't seen Dan since Tuesday, when I'd dropped by in the afternoon. He looked more haggard, seemed more depressed. We sat in the living room.

"I think the police know things they aren't telling me," he said wearily. "I talked to Ellsworth yesterday afternoon, and he told me they'd know something Saturday. When I pressed him on why Saturday, he clammed up. What's that mean, Matt?"

"Sound like he's got a lead but won't know anything definite until then. He may not be hiding anything; he may just not want to get your hopes up."

Dan rubbed his face with his hands. "This waiting, not knowing anything, is eating me up."

We talked for another hour. I listened, tried to offer reassurance, got him talking sports. Dan was a huge Tampa Bay Bucs fan. I also watched the clock. At ten-thirty, I stood, told him I had to go. He walked to the car with me.

"Thanks for coming by," he said as I opened the car door.

"Hang in there. Things are going to get better."

He nodded, but the look on his face said he didn't believe me.

I had to hustle to get to the Mote by eleven. The place was filled with vacationers, from kids to empty nesters. At the Manatee exhibit a lone woman stood off to the side, watching. I started toward her. She nodded me off. I walked on to the main window, watched the Manatees swim.

She waited five minutes, walked over to me. "I needed to make sure no one was following you. We can go now."

She led me out an employee's entrance to a van parked behind the building. We got in. She drove nervously to the parking garage of a downtown Sarasota office building, parked, led me inside.

She took me to a large, windowless room on one of the building's upper floors. On the walls were maps, blow-ups of floor plans. In the center of the room, a large square table held computers, telecommunications equipment. Raines and three men were huddled together around one of the computers. He looked over when we entered the room, came over, shook my hand. "This is our situation room," he said by way of a greeting. "Everything that happens tomorrow we're going to monitor from here."

This is where Tory's going to be," I said making the connection.

He stroked his moustache, nodded. "She may be able to help. Her dealings with Bill Perez may come into play as the evening progresses." He went over to one of the computers, booted it up. "I want you to know what we'll be doing tomorrow." He patted the top of the monitor. "We'll be tracking D'Onifrio every step of the way. Any activity, any movement by his people will be reported here. Ten agents will be at City Hall. Thirty more will be ready to move as directed."

"Do you know where he has Rosemary?"

"No. We theorize she's being held at someone's house. If that's the case, there's no way to find her now. As things develop tomorrow, they'll have to move her. We'll be monitoring their activity and that'll tell us where they have her." He keyed something into the computer. "Here's our coverage in and around City Hall. We have agents stationed near all the exits. Nobody will be able to enter or leave without our knowing about it."

"Let me tell you my biggest fear."

Raines turned away from the computer screen, looked at me, his face expressionless.

"They don't bring Rosemary. The more I think about this, the more I think D'Onifrio's too smart to be caught with her. What happens then?"

"We have several scenarios in case that happens," Raines said matter-of-factly. "Remember, this thing has been billed as a trade. If they don't bring her, they'll have to talk to you, broker arrangements. Otherwise, there's no deal; you don't go with them. You don't leave City Hall. Once we know where she is, we'll get her, get you out of there." He turned back to the computer screen. "That's why we have agents in all these locations." He indicated agents spread from Bradenton to Venice. "Wherever she is, we want to be able to get to her fast."

Made sense. "Let me tell you my second biggest fear."

That got a wan smile.

"What if this awards presentation doesn't come off? What if D'Onifrio cancels at the last minute? If Enrico and the nephews don't show up? What happens then?"

"Nothing."

The surprise must have shown on my face.

"You've got to understand, my main concern is getting the Shears woman back and not having an incident at City Hall. If—and it's a big if—we can pit D'Onifrio against Enrico or the nephews, that's icing. I'm not counting on it. I won't be surprised if it doesn't work. This whole awards presentation, missing-money thing is flimsy at best."

Hearing him say his main concern was Rosemary helped me. In the back of my mind was Ellsworth's comment that all Raines cared about was getting D'Onifrio.

When I didn't say anything, he looked at me, half-smiled. "What? You aren't going to tell me your third biggest fear?"

"I just had the two," I said quietly. "You seem to have things under control."

"That's why I brought you here. To see for yourself that we're on top of the situation. We've got this thing mapped out. If anything feels wrong to you—at any time—let us know; we'll shut it down."

"How do I do that?"

"My people will be in room 410 with you. All you have to say is I'm not comfortable. They'll know to get you out of there."

"What if D'Onifrio has people there, too?"

"That's why you've got the vest."

On that happy note, the conversation ended, and Raines had the woman take me back to Mote. I drove home, changed into some trunks, and went for a walk on the beach. I walked hurriedly, fueled by tension.

If Raines thought seeing his operation eased my concerns, he was wrong. I didn't have a clear understanding of what he expected from me. Couldn't imagine how I was going to broker arrangements. Nor did I understand how he was going to liberate Rosemary. How was I going to alert Raines' people where she was being held? I should have asked more questions, pinned him down on exactly how all this was going to work. Maybe I hadn't asked because I really didn't want to know. If I knew the details of what was about to happen, I might not want to go through with it. The fact that Raines had given me the vest told me he thought there could be trouble.

I walked to the pier at the Colony Beach, where Enrico and his entourage were staying, turned around, headed back. I didn't worry on the way back. I watched for shark's teeth. Found one good one just as I reached the Watergate.

About six, I got hungry, made myself something to eat. After dinner, I called Tory.

"How are you feeling?" she asked.

"I just want to get tomorrow over with."

"I don't blame you."

I told her about the meeting with Raines, that he seemed to have things under control.

"That's what I got from him when I took him the awards booklets. He seemed confident that he had all the possibilities covered."

"We'll find out tomorrow," I said a little apprehensively. "Since I won't have a chance to see you tomorrow, I thought I'd see if you wanted to get together Saturday evening."

"I'd like that."

"Pick you up at six thirty?"

"See you then. Good luck tomorrow."

I hung up, aware of the real reason I'd called her. If I made plans for Saturday, that meant I couldn't die on Friday.

In spite of all Raines' assurances that nothing would happen to me, I kept seeing Wilder shoot Eddie. If Wilder got his hands on me, it wouldn't be as quick or painless.

I puttered around the rest of the evening, went to bed at eleven, slept well. No dreams. That morning I did comfortable, familiar things. Worked out in the gym. Walked on the beach. Mostly I tried to stay positive. The closer it got to two o'clock, the more nervous I became. By lunch my stomach was in a knot.

After lunch, I changed clothes, put on the bulletproof jacket, a bulky shirt to hide it. Before I left, I spent a long time looking at photos of Claire and the kids. At one o'clock, I put them away, went out to face whatever was waiting for me.

CHAPTER 50

The Room 410 waiting area was crowded when I arrived. I did a quick count. Twenty-four people. Some young. Some old. Virtually all couples. Made me feel odd walking in by myself. Fish and Janet, I noticed, were not among those present.

The wooden bench where Raines wanted me to sit was full. I found a spot, leaned against the wall and tried to figure out who belonged to whom. I knew three of the people in the room worked for Raines. D'Onifrio undoubtedly had a few people there. I'd have been surprised if Ellsworth didn't have a person or two there as well.

The door to the ceremony room opened, and a gray-haired woman in a rose-colored suit stood in the doorway. "Farr/Zelinski wedding."

A young couple jumped up. "That's us," the man said excitedly.

They went through the door. The woman in the rose suit closed the door behind them.

The process was repeated every ten minutes or so. People left to be married. New people arrived. I looked at my watch. One-thirty. I scanned the room again, looked at those who had been there when I arrived. I still couldn't quite tell who worked for the good guys or the bad guys.

At one-forty, Fish and Janet arrived. He looked ill at ease in a tuxedo that gave him a barrel-chested, bow-legged look. Janet had on a simple white dress that was stunning. She surveyed the room with disdain. I watched to see if there was any recognition when her gaze swept past me. Didn't see any.

The lady in the rose suit opened the door. "Martin/Taylor wedding."

A couple got up from the bench. I quickly took one of the vacated seats. Raines would be pleased. I was in position. Joining me in grabbing a seat was a young Latina woman and a pimply-faced man in an AC/DC tee shirt.

Two new couples arrived. Still no sign of Rosemary or D'Onifrio. The clock on the wall said one-fifty. I was becoming more anxious. If they were coming, they should have been there by then.

At two-twelve, the woman in the rose suit announced. "Ford/Jesso wedding." Fish and Janet walked into the other room, and the door shut behind them.

I assumed that once they were married, something would happen. I waited. Tense. Alert. Apprehensive.

At two-twenty, Peters/Halsbock were called, went in.

The Latina woman sitting next to me got a magazine out of her bag, opened it. On the left hand page, where I could easily see it, a note had been taped: *I have a gun. Go with me. Or the woman dies.* I looked at her, saw her hand in her handbag holding a gun.

Raines hadn't told me what to do in a situation like this. I felt my heart rate increase, sweat roll down my hairline. I saw the ceremony room door start to open.

"Get ready," the Latina woman whispered.

"You fucked my sister?" A blond, scantily-dressed woman across the room screamed. "You louse, how could you fuck my sister the day before our wedding?"

She started pummeling the guy next to her with her handbag. Everybody turned to watch.

He covered his head with arms sporting plenty of tattoos. "Baby, she came on to me," he whined loudly. "What could I do? She was askin' for it."

"Let's go," the Latina woman whispered and stood up. Her hand grabbed my arm, pulled me through the doorway. We pushed past the woman in the rose suit, into the ceremony room. I heard the door close behind us.

The justice of the peace lay on the ground, a pool of blood around his head. The man of the Peters/Halsbock party came up behind the woman in the rose suit, hit her in the back of her head with his gun. She crumpled.

I felt a sharp stick in the arm. Turned to look, caught a glimpse of a hypodermic syringe in the Peters/Halsbock woman's hand. In seconds, my vision went bad, and the room started spinning. I fought to stay conscious, but the blackness took me.

CHAPTER 51

I woke shivering, lying on a concrete floor. Hands tied behind me. Shirt and bullet-proof vest gone. I blinked open my eyes. Tried to focus. Only darkness, fuzzy shapes.

From behind me, muffled sounds. I wrenched my body around, looked. I saw faint light spots, stared, willing my eyes to adjust to the darkness. A wave of nausea hit me, forced me to close them. I fought to keep from being sick. Took deep breaths.

When I opened my eyes again, my vision was better. Sharper. I made out a seated shape. A figure. The light spots, hair and skin. Rosemary.

The muffled sounds increased. I used my elbow, propped myself into a sitting position. Tried to gather my legs.

From behind me, I heard the sounds of a key in a lock, a knob being turned, door hinges squeaking, a smack as the door hit the wall. Light flooded the room. Brightness forced me to close my eyes.

Sound of steps. Hands grabbed my arms, roughly hauled me to my feet. The rapid movement made me sick.

"He puked on my shoes," a man said angrily.

A fist slammed into my ear. I fell hard to the concrete. Was hauled to my feet again. My hands untied. Two men, one on either side, escorted me out the door into a larger room. I had to squint. The lights in this larger area were brighter.

The space looked like an abandoned manufacturing plant.

Concrete floors. Metal support posts. Ribbed sheet metal ceiling. Hanging tungsten lighting. The floor was littered with greasy shop rags, metal scraps, torn safety posters.

The two men pushed me forward toward a group of men standing in the center of the vast shop floor. To my right, I saw a yellow backhoe. The bucket rested next to a stack of concrete chunks and dirt.

As the group watched us approach, they shifted, forming two halves of a thirty-foot circle. I was taken to the center, spotlighted by a tungsten lamp directly overhead.

D'Onifrio, dressed in a tux, stood fifteen feet away to my right. Wilder next to him, in one of his gaudy three-piece suits. Minions arced out on either side of them.

An equal distance to my left, I recognized Enrico, Little Ernie, and Eduardo. Ten to fifteen more men to the sides of them. Chairs were brought for Enrico and the nephews.

As Enrico settled wearily into his seat, I could see the blue cover of the awards show booklet in his hand. He waved it in the air. "Dee, you may begin," he said in surprisingly good English.

D'Onifrio nodded, his face cold, expressionless, his voice strong. "Enrico, members of the council, we are at war. Our enemies will use any and every means to try and defeat us. In the past, they have tried to infiltrate our organization, shut us down, send us to jail. Always, we have caught these agents, killed them before they could do any damage. These deaths do not stop our enemy's efforts. In fact, it only makes them try harder. They send more agents, try more ingenious schemes. They know we are growing more powerful, and they are afraid."

Across the circle, Enrico nodded his agreement.

"Fearful men do stupid things." D'Onifrio pointed at the booklet resting on Enrico's lap. "They think they drive a wedge between us with their lies. They think we will fight amongst ourselves. They are wrong. We will not fall for their tricks. We are not fearful, we will not do anything stupid. We are strong. Strong men do smart things. For two years, I have had a man planted in our enemy's camp. That was smart. Everything they have planned—including this—we have known. Their leader, Raines, is this man's boss. Tonight, Enrico, to honor you, I have had this man Raines eliminated."

From behind D'Onifrio, two men carried Raines' dead body to the center of the circle, dumped it on the concrete next to me, returned to their group. Raines' face had been horribly beaten. A long red gash ran across his throat. His clothes were soaked with blood.

"This was all his plan, Enrico. A plan to make you think I was no longer loyal. It is no coincidence this is happening now; they knew you were deciding on leadership. They sought to discredit me."

Again, Enrico nodded as if in agreement.

"They have wronged me and they will pay with their lives. Enrico, I know that no guns are allowed in meetings, but if you will send for a gun, I will execute this traitor here and now."

Enrico turned his head, said something. A man went scurrying off, returned short minutes later with a revolver, handed it to Enrico. Enrico held it out in a trembling hand for D'Onifrio.

He strode across the circle to get it. "Down on your knees," he said to me as he passed.

I stood motionless, paralyzed by fear.

D'Onifrio took the gun from the old man's outstretched hand. Checked to see if it was loaded, turned. He walked toward me, grinning. I closed my eyes.

CHAPTER 52

Three shots rang out. I braced for the impact. The sound reverberated off the metal ceiling. People started yelling. I hadn't felt anything. I opened my eyes. Saw D'Onifrio's back. Bullet holes in the heads of Enrico, Little Ernie, Eduardo. D'Onifrio's and Enrico's people were only concerned with fighting each other. No one paid any attention to me.

I got down on the floor, slowly crawled away from the fighting. The route took me past the backhoe, the hole that had been dug in the concrete floor. At the bottom were three bodies. I recognized the woman who had met me at Mote Marine Lab. Realized they'd intended to dump all of us in this mass grave.

Using the backhoe as cover, I ran for the doorway where I thought they were holding Rosemary. Wrong door. I tried the next one to the right. It opened. In the darkness, I could make out Rosemary's shape.

I undid the gag in her mouth, worked on the ropes that bound her hands and feet.

"Oh, Matt," she croaked hoarsely, "I heard shots, thought they'd killed you."

"He had more important people than me to kill. Can you walk?"

She stood. Tried to take a few steps. Was unsure on her feet.

I put my arm around her waist. Half walked her, half carried her to a door I hoped led away from the shop floor. Locked. The top part of the door looked like painted glass. I grabbed the chair to which Rosemary'd been tied. Used it to shatter the glass. Reached through the shards, unlocked the door, walked her as quickly as I could down a hallway. We navigated that hallway, two more before we found a door that let us out of the building.

"Where are we?" Rosemary asked, looking around.

All I could see in the night's darkness was an expanse of parking lot, other industrial buildings nearby. There was a loud, roaring sound in the air. A commercial jetliner, gear down, flew very low overhead. "We have to be on the far side of the airport."

On the left side of the building were a series of big, green dumpsters. I ran over, took a look. One was garbage. One was metal scraps. But the last was paper. I boosted Rosemary into the one filled with paper. "Hide under the paper. You'll be safe there until help comes."

"What are you going to do?" she asked before I closed the lid.

"Find a phone. Call the police." I sprinted down the side of the building to the corner, stopped, peered around. Eight cars, three of them limos, were parked by a front office area. I didn't see any guards, but that didn't mean there weren't drivers waiting in the cars.

I bent down, ran over, hoped the commotion inside would last long enough for me to make the call. I reached the cars. Looked for heads. Didn't see any. I tried the first car. Open. No phone. Second car. Locked. First limo. Open. Phone turned off. Second limo. Open. Phone turned off. Third car. Open. Cell phone lying on the passenger seat. I snatched it up and ran to the building across the street, concealing myself behind shrubbery. I turned the phone on. Pressed 911.

"I need the police. Specifically, Lieutenant Ellsworth. This is an emergency," I told the operator.

"I'll patch you through to the police."

Across the street people were starting to come out of the building. D'Onifrio was easy to spot in his tux. He got in one of the limos and was driven away. A few others got in cars, drove away. Most franticly searched the outside of the building. I knew who they were looking for.

"Lieutenant Ellsworth's office, Officer Suarez speaking. How can I help you?"

"This is Matt Seattle. Ellsworth was looking for Rosemary Shears. I've found her. We're at an abandoned industrial building across from Harris Industrial Plumbing on the far side of the airport. Tell Ellsworth that D'Onifrio has twenty people. You've got to hurry; they're starting to leave."

"We're on our way."

I clicked off. Watched. The searchers had spread out. There may have been fifteen, sixteen of them. They moved erratically, running from place to place. Several ran past the dumpster where Rosemary was hidden. None stopped to check. Two came in my direction, circled the building. Another one stopped, not more than five feet from me. I could see the gun in his hand, hear his breath coming in big gasps.

A horn blared. Three short blasts. One by one, the searchers returned, got in the two remaining cars, drove off.

I stayed in the bushes, waited for the police. A good twenty minutes later, they arrived. Three cars and two vans pulled up and began unloading men in full riot gear.

I left my hiding spot, joined them. Ellsworth saw me, came over immediately. I gave him a quick overview of what had happened. He listened intently, sent two policemen to get Rosemary. Gathered the rest, told them how he wanted them deployed, sent them out.

Ellsworth got a bulletproof jacket from the van, handed it to me. "Show me the door you came out."

I put on my vest, led Ellsworth and three officers to the door. An officer opened it carefully; another ducked inside, pronounced it clear. We moved down the hallways to the door that led to the plant floor. Again, they went through the doorway carefully. Didn't matter. The big room was empty.

The lights were still on. The backhoe was still there. D'Onifrio's people were gone.

Ellsworth and I walked over to the hole. It was empty, too. The bodies had been removed. "I saw the body of a female D.E.A. agent down there," I told him.

His face was grim. "No bodies, but plenty of blood. See all those dark spots."

"More blood over here, Lieutenant," someone called out.

We walked over. "This is where D'Onifrio shot Enrico and the nephews." I pointed to where they'd had me standing. "Raines' body was right over there."

"Follow the trails; let's find out where they went with all these bodies," Ellsworth ordered.

"There's a lot of blood on the loading dock, trails leading in," one of the officers said.

"Show me," Ellsworth told him.

We followed the officer to an open loading dock door on the backside of the building. Pools of blood littered the dock floor.

"Jesus," Ellsworth exclaimed. He reached for his walkie-talkie. "Ryker, you're in charge. Red team stays, seals up the area. Blue team heads back. Get the crime scene investigation people in here. Tell them this is top priority, bring as many people as they can." He turned to me as he started to go. "You come with me."

I didn't move. "Aren't you going to have D'Onifrio arrested?"

Ellsworth stopped, smiled. "You mean the man who earlier this evening was recognized by the President of the United States, the

Governor of Florida, and numerous other dignitaries as one of the nation's leading humanitarians?"

"He did this. He killed people."

Ellsworth's smile disappeared. "I'm sure he did. But it's your word against his. By now, he has twenty witnesses who'll say he was with them all evening. This whole thing was carefully constructed. We're going to have to move cautiously."

Ellsworth took me back to police headquarters in his squad car. On the way, I asked about Rosemary.

"We called in the medics for her. Report I got was that she was dehydrated, otherwise okay. They started fluids, took her to Memorial for further evaluation. We notified her husband, had a cruiser take him to Memorial to be with her." He looked over at me. "Don't worry; we'll keep them both in protective custody until this gets sorted out."

Knowing Rosemary was okay made me feel better. "Thanks."

I was glad I asked when I did. Once we reached the station, I was taken to an interrogation room. Ellsworth had an officer bring me a shirt, something to eat and drink. Then, we went at it. He wanted every detail. I gave it to them. I talked as fast as they could type. When I was finished, they had me go over it again. When they thought they had it all, Ellsworth left.

He returned an hour later wanting additional detail on three areas:

Joe Jesso.
Raines.
The awards presentation.

I gave them what I could, but I was beginning to spit thin. They must have sensed that, too. We took a break, went down to the cafeteria, got coffee. Just walking, being out of that room, felt good. The hot coffee tasted wonderful. The respite didn't last long. He walked me back to the room, closeted me there for the next two hours.

Ellsworth looked as tired as I felt. "Couple more questions and we'll call it a night, okay?"

I nodded.

"When did Raines first know about the award presentation?"

I could picture us on board The Rarely Used, Raines drinking his Mountain Dew as Tory and I talked him through the idea. "Friday a week ago, why?"

"We're trying to piece together a timeline of what D'Onifrio knew when."

"Raines thought someone on your staff was leaking things to D'Onifrio."

Ellsworth scowled. "The leak was at Raines' end. Possibly a woman named Angelica Duartte. She's missing." He fixed me in his gaze. "Have you ever heard that name before?"

I shook my head. "No."

"Sometimes, she was called Angel."

I kept shaking. "Not a name I know."

"When he took you to City Hall, were there female agents with him?"

"Yes, but I couldn't tell you if one of them was this woman."

Ellsworth seemed disappointed. "Well, that's enough for now. We're—"

"Wait a minute. How did they get me out of City Hall? I thought all the doors were being watched, people were stationed around the outside of the building?"

"They were," he said brusquely. "We had people around the building, so did Raines."

"So what happened?"

"City Hall is undergoing electrical work. Electricians have been all over that building for the last month. We found a couple of them locked in a storeroom, unconscious. We're theorizing that D'Onifrio's men—posing as electricians—wheeled you out in a cardboard box, took you away in one of the trucks. Probably had you out of the building before anyone put together what was happening." He looked directly at me. Our gazes met. "This was carried out like a military operation. Everything executed perfectly."

I pictured the justice of the peace on the floor, the pool of blood by his head, the lady in the rose suit being hit in the head with the gun. "The people in the ceremony room? Are they okay?"

"The J.P.—can't think of his name right now—is in critical condition. The woman, the clerk, is fine." He paused. "We're going to have you stay here where we can watch over you. Your friend, Ms. Wright, is waiting to talk to you." He nodded at the officer who'd worked on my statement. "Hennings will take you to her and when you're finished, show you to your room."

Tory was in a similar interview room down the hall. When Hennings opened the door to let me in, Tory stood, came over and hugged me. "I was so worried about you," she said choking back tears.

I held her tightly. "I'm okay. It feels so good to be holding you."

Hennings closed the door, leaving us alone. As soon as we heard it click shut, our lips met. We kissed, long and hard.

"We've got to talk," I said softly and filled her in on what had happened to me. "What about you? Raines said you'd be with him today. What happened?"

"That was strange. I arrived at his situation room at nine this morning, the time we'd arranged. I expected he'd be there. He wasn't. No one knew where he was. They spent a lot of time trying to find him; when they couldn't, this woman took charge."

"Angelica?"

"Yeah, they called her Angel. She pretty much ran things. Then about one-thirty, right before the wedding, she walked out to get a soda, never came back. After that, the place got weird. I left. Got in my car, started home. Hadn't gone four blocks when I realized there were a bunch of guys in a van following me. I decided not to take any chances and drove straight here. Been here ever since."

"Have they been questioning you all that time?"

"Some. At first, they wanted to know what Raines was doing. Then as it got closer to the awards show, they asked me about that. Ellsworth and I watched it on cable. What a gala. Looked like the Oscars. When the show ended, they left me alone. Then you called and all Hell broke loose." She came over, hugged me. "Thank goodness it's over now."

"It's not. D'Onifrio's still out there."

She pulled away from me, her face alarmed. "They'll arrest him, won't they? You saw him kill those people."

"Ellsworth said they had to move cautiously."

Hennings returned. "Sorry to interrupt, but I need to take you to your rooms now. I'm going off duty."

I don't know what I expected. Certainly not the Ritz Carlton, but my room was a no-nonsense bed, toilet and sink.

Henning stood at the doorway. "I'm not going to lock you in. You're secure up here, but I'd suggest you stay in your room. Someone will be by in the morning, bring you breakfast."

"Thanks."

The metal door clanked shut. I went over and tried the bed. Not bad. I got comfortable and immediately went to sleep.

Day two in protective custody started early, was slow, tiring. At six a.m. I was awakened, a breakfast tray placed on my bed. When I tried venturing out into the hallway, I was told to return to my room. When I asked for Ellsworth, I was told he wasn't available. Whatever that meant.

I did call Rosemary and Dan at the hospital, made sure they were okay, apologized for what I'd put them through. Dan, bless his heart, thanked me for all I'd done.

I expected a tray for lunch, too. To my surprise, Hennings reappeared, walked me to the cafeteria. Tory was already there. I learned she'd been in a similar room, hadn't talked to anyone all morning, either. "What do you think is going on?" she asked when Hennings got up to get more to drink.

We got the answer at four that afternoon. Ellsworth, wearing a dark blue suit, white shirt, and red tie, met with us. He pulled the knot of his tie down, unbuttoned his collar button, rubbed his neck. "Paid a friendly visit on Mr. D'Onifrio early this morning. Asked him if he could account for his whereabouts yesterday evening. Of course he couldn't give me an answer right away. Had to ask why I wanted to know, that kind of stuff. Made me work to find out he was at a party thrown by an associate, a VP at Shore. He called this guy in. I spoke with him. Of course, he confirmed D'Onifrio's story, said twenty-five people were at the party. I got a list of names. We're checking them now."

"They're cartel people. They'll say whatever he wants."

"I know," Ellsworth said disgustedly. "I also met with Steve Shaffer, Raines' boss. He told me he got a call at home from Raines Thursday night. Said Raines was feeling depressed, burnt out, needed some time off."

"They made him make that call," Tory said.

"You know that, I know that. The problem is they have duress words, words that let the other person know you're being forced to make the call. Raines didn't use any duress words. Not one."

"That woman you mentioned—Angel—she'd know those words. She'd keep Raines from using them."

"Shaffer is adamant there is no traitor in the organization. Told me they were a hand-picked team, impossible for D'Onifrio to crack."

"What about her leaving the situation room and never returning?" Tory asked.

"According to Shaffer, she took a call about Raines' disappearance, went to investigate, was back in the office later that afternoon."

"That is so trumped up."

Ellsworth gestured with his hands. "Shaffer's covering his ass. He's not going to be any help."

"What about the blood? What about the bodies?"

"The blood is being analyzed. Bodies? We haven't found any yet. We checked with the Colony Beach. According to the desk staff, Enrico and the nephews checked out yesterday evening. Airport records show the jet left at ten for Miami."

I sat back in my seat, dazed.

"I met with Pat Armstrong, the D.A., this afternoon. Went over everything with him. He doesn't feel we have a case."

"What?" Tory and I said together.

Ellsworth used his hands to tick things off. "No bodies. No cooperation from Shaffer at D.E.A. No chance to break D'Onifrio's alibi. No winnable case." He put his hands down. "Armstrong's a political guy. Without something, he views prosecuting D'Onifrio as a P.R. nightmare."

"So where does that leave us?"

"Exposed."

CHAPTER 53

"What's that mean?" Tory wanted to know.

"It means we'll keep working on this. Keep trying to find ammunition for Armstrong to go after D'Onifrio. But I'll be honest with you. Unless we get a break, that could take some time. I can't keep you in protective custody forever. Sooner or later, you're going to have to be on your own."

Tory's expression said she didn't like what she was hearing. "You think D'Onifrio will come after us."

"I don't think he'll come after you, Ms. Wright." His gaze left Tory, settled on me. "He'll come after you, Mr. Seattle. You witnessed him killing Enrico. He won't leave you standing."

"You can't let that happen. You have to protect him," Tory said vehemently.

Ellsworth's tone was conciliatory. "We'll do what we can. Short term, we can keep you here a couple of more days. Long term, you should start thinking about what you want to do."

Start thinking about leaving Sarasota was what he was suggesting. Distance myself from the danger. What bothered me was I'd be distancing myself from it, not eliminating it. I'd always be looking over my shoulder, wondering if they'd traced me to my new location. "If I stay in Sarasota, what kind of protection could you provide?"

"I'd like to tell you I can give you good protection. But the reality of the situation is that I don't have the manpower. For twenty-four hour protection, I have to use a minimum of three officers. That's to have one person watch your back at all times. One person is not going to be able to stop them if they decide to come after you. I don't know that ten officers would stop them. See my problem?"

"What do you think your chances are of getting a break in this case? Arresting D'Onifrio?"

"Like I said, not good. Usually, if there's something to find, you uncover it quick. If you don't, it means they've covered their tracks really well. No telling how long it will take then. Without something, Armstrong won't do anything, either. He told me three judges and the mayor were at Asolo to see D'Onifrio accept his award. If he goes to one of those judges and says he wants to go after the guy who is so good to deaf children for murder, that judge is going to look at him like he's crazy."

I didn't know what else to say. Tory was quiet, too.

Ellsworth rubbed his neck. "I'm sorry. I know this is rough on you. But I wanted to tell it to you straight." He stood.

"I appreciate that," I told him.

"If I hear something, I'll let you know right away," he said as he went out the door.

"D'Onifrio can't get away with this. He can't kill that many people and not slip up somewhere," Tory said positively.

If there was a slip, two days of investigation didn't uncover it. As each day passed, Ellsworth became more somber. Tuesday afternoon, he gathered us for a meeting in his office.

When Tory and I were seated, he leaned forward, elbows on his desk, chin on his hands. "I've just met with Armstrong and my boss, Chief Greer. Bottom line, nobody wants to go after D'Onifrio right now. Lot of pressure coming down to make this go away. The mayor just got a donation from D'Onifrio of half a mill for a rec center in a low-income neighborhood."

Tory started to protest. He waved her off.

"The Chief knows it's hush money, but the higher ups don't see it that way."

He was cutting us loose.

"I can't keep you in protective custody any longer. If I do, it's going to start causing problems. We talked earlier about your going away. Have you thought any more about that?"

We both shook our heads.

"I think it's time," he said softly. "At this point, the best I can do is give you an escort to the airport and get you on a plane."

"When?" I asked.

"This evening if possible. Tomorrow at the latest."

I looked at Tory. Our gazes met.

"I don't see we have any choice," she said.

She was right. But agreeing to leave was the same as admitting D'Onifrio had won. I had trouble with that.

"Can you give us a minute?" I asked Ellsworth.

"Sure." He stood, walked around his desk to the door. "I'm going to make a Starbuck's run. What'll you have? I'm buying."

He was trying to be nice. "A decaf would be great, thanks."

"None for me, thanks," Tory said.

"I'll be back in ten minutes," he said, closing the door behind him.

"Why don't you want to leave?" Tory asked, the concern showing on her face.

I got up, paced around Ellsworth's tiny office, tried to make sense of the way I felt. "Lot's of reasons. I don't like leaving my friends, everything I've worked for here. I don't—"

"You don't like D'Onifrio winning, do you?"

I stopped pacing, looked at her. "No. I don't."

She stood, came over, put her arms around me. "I know it's hard to accept, but let's go while we've still got each other. He almost killed you on Friday; I don't want to give him another chance."

I hugged her, let go of my head trash about winning and losing. "I don't want to lose you, either. You're much more important than all the other stuff. Where do you want to go?"

She pulled away so she could look at me. "Have you ever been to Charleston, South Carolina? It's a beautiful, historic town. Warm all year round. On the water. Great restaurants. I think you'll like it."

"Charleston it is. Ellsworth's trying to get rid of us tonight, but I'd like to make some calls, go tomorrow."

When Ellsworth came back with the coffees, I told him what we'd decided. He nodded his head. "I think that's smart."

"Would it be possible to have somebody run us back to our places so we can pack up a few things?"

He hesitated, probably debating the risks. Finally, he said, "Yeah, we should be able to do that. Best time would be the middle of the night. They might not be watching."

That evening, I made my calls. There weren't many. Rosemary. Julian. My banker. The manager at the Watergate. The Saab dealer about my car, the loaner. I told them all that this was only temporary, that I'd be back shortly. I didn't want to admit I was leaving for good.

At two in the morning, three officers in an unmarked car drove me to the Watergate to gather my belongings. Another crew took Tory to her place.

I packed as quickly as I could. Clothes. Family photos. Laptop, Blackberry. Financial information. Cleaned out the food in the kitchen. Put it all in garbage bags, dropped them down the chute. Tidied the place as best I could. The manager would watch over it until I decided if I wanted to put it up for sale or do rentals. When I'd finished everything, I walked around the condo one last time. Looking. Remembering.

"Are you ready, sir?" the one officer asked.

I nodded. We rode down in the elevator, carried everything to the van.

As they loaded the suitcases in the trunk, I said, "One more thing I need to do. Just take me a minute."

I walked to the spot where Eddie was buried, bent down, placed one of his favorite chewy strips on the ground. "I won't forget you, Eddie."

I didn't sleep well after we returned to the station. Picked at my breakfast tray. Was annoyed that they made me stay in my room.

At ten, two officers knocked on the door, said they'd like to clarify a couple of areas on my statement. They asked question after question. Stupid stuff that we'd already been over again and again. It was a huge waste of time that contributed to my being out of sorts.

At eleven-thirty, Ellsworth arrived, sent them away. He suggested we have a bite to eat together before our flight at two. On our way to the cafeteria, we stopped by Tory's room and she joined us.

Over lunch, Ellsworth gave us the latest news—or more accurately, non-news—on the investigation. "It's not looking good," he said wearily. "No bodies have been discovered. Shaffer admits Raines has disappeared but isn't ready to say he's dead or that there were problems with his staff. D'Onifrio won't talk to us. Says talk to his lawyers. When we do, they start crying harassment. To top it all off, the mayor told the chief he thought we were wasting too much time on this investigation." He bowed his head for a second. "We're not going to stop investigating, but we're going to have to be more low key about it."

"You're telling us he's gotten away with it."

Ellsworth looked at me for a moment, nodded his head. "Pretty much."

I felt defeated. I had thought all along that something would come along, rectify the situation.

When we were finished with lunch, he gave each of us one of his business cards, told us to stay in touch. As we shook hands good-bye, he surprised me. "I didn't like you at first, Seattle," he said. "But you're an okay guy. Sorry this turned out badly for you."

I couldn't help smiling. "I didn't like you at first, either. But you've grown on me, Ellsworth. Crack this thing so we can come back. We'll all go out to dinner and celebrate."

That was the last we saw of him. We went back to our rooms, collected our luggage, carried it down to the motor pool area where an unmarked white Ford panel truck was waiting to take us to the airport. Two officers helped us stow our luggage in the back. When it was all loaded, we got in the truck's back seat; they sat up front. The driver started the truck, pulled out of the garage area into the bright Florida sunshine.

He surprised me by heading inland. "Aren't you going to take 41?" I asked. Once we got out of downtown, SR41—the Tamiami Trail north—would have been a straight, four-lane shot to the airport.

"I'm going to go 301," the driver said over his shoulder. "It's more direct, and this time of day, there's less traffic."

He may have been right. But State Route 301 was one of those highways with a traffic light every block. Drive. Stop. Sit. Repeat. After the fifth repetition, I decided going this way had been a mistake.

"What airline are you folks flying?" he asked, looking in the rear view mirror at us as we waited for the seventh light. He never heard the answer.

Simultaneous explosions sounded outside the truck. Both side windows shattered. Shards of glass flew inward. Blood splattered the windshield, ceiling. The two officers slumped together in the center of the van.

CHAPTER 54

We heard the crank of the door handles, the squeak of hinges as the doors were pulled open. Hands reached in from either side, pulled the dead officers out. Wilder climbed into the passenger seat, held a gun on us. Another man got behind the wheel, put the truck in gear, accelerated through the intersection, down the road.

Wilder turned in his seat so he could look back, waved the gun at us. "You weren't going to leave without saying good-bye, were you?" He grinned, showed us his pointed teeth. "I told the boss he should have shot you before he got rid of those Colombian assholes. Know what he told me?"

Didn't seem like a question he wanted me to answer.

"He didn't think you were that important." He laughed loudly.

The driver made a right at University Parkway, drove inland.

"The boss also wanted me to thank you. He really appreciated your help in setting up the Colombians. He would never have gotten a gun anywhere near them. Thanks to you, he wastes that sanctimonious old sack of shit, those two shit-for-brains leeches. Now he's got control of everything. Nobody can challenge him."

I watched the gun in Wilder's hand, thinking if he waved it close enough to me, I'd make a grab for it. Beside me, Tory was very still, tense.

The driver slowed, turned into the parking lot of a boarded-up 7-11 store, parked. The driver got out. Wilder kept the gun on us. The driver opened the door for us. Wilder's gun didn't waver, didn't get close enough to grab. We got out slowly. Wilder followed.

The driver unlocked the padlock on the boarded-up door, propped it open, got back in the van. "I'll lose the ride. You know where to pick me up after you finish with them?"

Wilder nodded to him. "Inside," he said, waving the gun at us.

Tory led the way. I was in the middle. Wilder behind me, the gun at my back.

Inside the 7-11, all that remained was the counter by the door, a few display racks jammed together on the right hand side. Parts of light fixtures, shelving, display cards littered the place. Against the back wall were three bags of concrete, mixing tools. A hole about six feet long, four feet wide had been dug in the floor. Wilder saw me looking at it, grinned. "We own this property," he said smugly. "Once you're buried, nobody will ever find you."

Tory stopped, looked at me, her eyes wide with fear.

I gave her what I hoped was a reassuring smile, walked three steps past her to put a little separation between us. If I could grab Wilder, screen Tory from him, she had a chance to get out the door.

I nodded at the hole, "This is the same thing you did at the manufacturing plant."

He responded by pointing his gun at my chest. "Seattle, I wanted to make this long and painful." He grinned, savoring the possibilities. "A bullet in each kneecap."

I heard him. But my attention was on Tory. Our gazes met.

"One in the nuts."

I tried to signal her with my eyes.

"Maybe, bury you alive."

Her eyes danced back. She was trying to tell me something, too.

I frowned, unsure of what she was signaling, not wanting her to do anything rash.

Wilder saw it. "Trying to save the girlfriend, Seattle? Set up some move to get the gun like they do in the movies?" He pointed the gun at Tory, grinned wolfishly. "Maybe I'll start with her kneecaps. Let you watch her die, before I do you."

Tory's gaze darted to the side. Whatever it was, she was about to do it.

"No," I said urgently, as much to her as to him. I took a step toward him.

Wilder swung the gun my way. Probably sensed Tory coming at him from the other side. He jerked the gun in her direction. Fired.

Tory screamed.

The bullet hit her in the shoulder, knocked her down.

I went at Wilder in a bull rush. Hit him in the stomach, chest high, drove him back. He struggled to keep his feet under him, but I had the momentum. He went over backward, landed hard on his back, grunted, as the air was knocked out of him. I got on top of him, straddled his chest, tried to wrestle the gun away from him.

He was a professional killer, but I had seventy pounds on him and had him in an awkward position. He bucked. Kneed me. Punched with his left hand. Tried to get the gun in his right hand pointed at me. Twice he pulled the trigger. Both bullets slammed into the ceiling.

I stayed on top of him, fought to get control of the gun. Even though I was using both hands on his one, I couldn't get any leverage. His arm was extended away from his body just enough that I was in danger of rolling off, letting him up.

I strained. Pulled. Yanked the gun. Tried to point it at him.

His other hand landed a hard punch to my ear. I felt the pain in my eyes.

I slammed my right fist into his nose as hard as I could. Blood spurted. I hit him again, felt the bone break. I hit him again, same place. Felt his whole body twitch. The hand that held the gun relaxed for a second.

I reached for it, yanked the gun around, forcing his arm toward his bloody face.

Inch by inch, the gun moved closer.

He pushed and kicked.

I concentrated on the gun. When I had it twelve inches from his face, I slammed my fist into his nose again. He yelled, his body involuntarily convulsing from the pain. I forced the gun closer. Only eight inches away.

He hadn't given up. He kneed me in the groin. A good shot that had me seeing stars. I lost my grip on his hand. He pulled the trigger, and something blew by the side of my head. I slammed his broken nose again, put everything I had into it.

He screamed in pain, grabbed my ear with his left hand, tried to rip it off. I used my right hand to pull at his fingers, break his grip. I bent a finger back, heard it snap. Still, he was tearing my ear. I pulled another finger back. When it snapped, he let go of my ear. I held on to his broken fingers, twisted them.

His screams intensified. I pulled at his gun hand, moving it, pointing it at his head. Our gazes met. What I saw was vengeance. He wasn't finished.

I used that to feed my rage, used both hands to drive the gun toward his head. The force must have surprised him. The gun barrel swung crazily, knocking into his pointed teeth. Two broke off.

He forced the gun back up, but only momentarily. I pushed it back down, drawing blood when the barrel smashed against his lip. This time, he wasn't able to force it back. I slammed the gun against his lip again, splitting it wide open. I slammed it against his mouth, breaking off more teeth. When he screamed, I jammed the gun barrel in his mouth, my hand over his on the trigger.

"This is for Tory," I told him. His eyes got wide, frightened. He knew what was coming. "And Eddie," I added at the last second. I squeezed his hand. His finger pulled the trigger. The explosion told me it was over. His body went limp.

Gasping from exertion, I got up, staggered over to where Tory lay on the sidewalk, a pool of blood forming around her right shoulder.

CHAPTER 55

I panicked. We were stranded. The next building almost a quarter-of-a-mile away. Too far to go for help.

Tory's black bag was on the floor next to her. I rummaged in it, searching for a cell phone. My hand felt something hard, rectangular. I pulled it out, turned it on, called 911. "This is an emergency. A woman's been shot. Send help. Hurry." I told them where we were.

"How was she shot?" the woman on the other end of the phone asked in a calm, dispassionate voice.

"Doesn't matter," I said, repeated the address. "Get somebody here fast. I'll keep the line open so you can tell me how long until help arrives."

"They're en route," she assured me. "Should be there in less than eight minutes. Are you where they can see you?"

"No. I'm inside a building."

I bent over Tory. The pool of blood looked bigger. I ripped off my shirt, pressed it on the holes where the bullet had gone in the front of her shoulder, out the back. If I could stem the flow of blood I might buy her a little more time.

"Hurry. Hurry. Hurry," I said out loud.

The lady on the phone must have heard me. "They're approximately five minutes away. Can you hear the siren?"

"No. I don't hear anything. Are you sure they know where we are?"

"They have your location. Keep listening."

I strained to hear. A distant whine, growing louder.

"The ambulance should be in sight now. Do you see it?"

"I hear it now. I'm inside, I can't see it."

"They see the 7-11," the voice said. "They should be there in seconds."

"Thank you. Thank you. Thank you."

I heard the ambulance screech to a stop. Doors slammed. Paramedics, a man and a woman, burst through the doorway, ran over to us.

"We'll take over now," the woman said, moving me out of the way. The man knelt over Tory. Into a shoulder walkie-talkie, he said, "We have a female with gunshot entry and exit wounds in the right shoulder." He pulled my shirt away from the wound, grimaced, looked at me. "You did the right thing minimizing the blood loss."

What he said hardly registered. I was watching Tory breathe. Her face was drained of color, her breathing now coming in small, faint gasps.

The man glanced over, saw Wilder. Into his walkie-talkie, he said, "We also have a deceased male. Let the police know."

"Should be there in seven-to-eight minutes," the voice from his walkie-talkie responded.

I watched him work on Tory. Bandaging her shoulder. Slipping an oxygen mask over her nose and mouth. Starting an IV. They began immobilizing her head. "Why are you doing that? What's wrong?"

The woman looked over at me. "She hit the back of her head on the concrete. There's external bleeding. We don't know yet about internal bleeding or brain damage."

Until I heard those words, I'd been operating on adrenaline. Suddenly, all that was gone. I was empty. All I could do was close my eyes.

I heard the sound of a siren. Doors slamming. Police came through the door.

"He's over there," the guy working on Tory told them. They went over to look.

A backboard was brought for Tory. They got ready to lift her on.

"Excuse me, sir," one patrolman said. "Can you tell us what happened?"

I watched as they lifted Tory onto the backboard.

"The dead guy is William Wilder. He killed two policemen who were taking us to the airport, tried to kill me, shot Tory." I nodded my head in her direction. Now that they had her on the backboard, they secured it to the stretcher.

"Sir, can you tell us how Mr. Wilder died?"

I stood. They were almost ready to move her. "In the struggle, he shot himself."

"Let's go," the female paramedic said. They started moving the stretcher to the ambulance. I went, too.

"Sir," the one policeman said after me, "we need you to stay here and answer questions."

Like hell. I turned back. "I'm going with her. Talk to Lieutenant Ellsworth. He knows me. I'm Matt Seattle."

I thought Ellsworth's name might spring me. It didn't. After a hurried conference, one of the policeman climbed in the ambulance with me and we made the forty-minute drive to Sarasota Memorial Hospital together.

A trauma team was waiting for us when we pulled up to the emergency entrance. They off-loaded Tory's stretcher, wheeled it in, headed down a long hallway, picking up men and women in white lab coats along the way.

At a set of double swinging doors, they told me that was as far as I was allowed to go. "We'll let you know," a woman with a nametag identifying her as Dr. Lora Kline told me. I must have looked like I was going to fall apart. "Don't worry; we'll take good care of her," she added.

I knew they would. Still, all the old memories of Sarah in the hospital flooded through me.

CHAPTER 56

Ellsworth easily spotted me in the crowded emergency waiting room. I was an island in the sea of people. No one wanted to get too close to the shirtless man covered in dried blood.

He eased himself down in the chair next to me. "How is she?"

"She's in surgery now. They're worried about brain damage."

"Tell me how it happened," he said, then apparently changed his mind, stood. "First, let's see if we can find you a shirt, get you cleaned up a little."

I stood, followed him out of the waiting area to an employee lounge. The place was empty.

"You can wash up in there." He pointed to a door marked Men's Locker Room. I'll see about a shirt."

When I returned, he had a scrub shirt, two cups of coffee.

"Decaf, right?"

I nodded. "Thanks, I appreciate this."

He waited until I put on the shirt and took a sip of coffee, then ushered me over to a couple of chairs. "Now I want to know everything that happened. Don't leave out a detail."

When I got to the part about the truck being hijacked, he said, "We found Barnes and Illig's bodies. We're still looking for the van."

"I'm sorry about your officers. They never had a chance; it happened so fast."

His head dropped a little. "They were good men," he said softly.

I sipped my coffee. Picked up the story.

When I finished, he said, "They'll try again, you know."

I did know. D'Onifrio would keep coming after me until one of us was dead. "Can't you arrest him for this?"

"I can question him. But I don't have enough to charge him."

"What about Wilder? He worked for him. Doesn't that tie him to all this?"

"Not enough." He took a long pull of his coffee, looked over at me. "I'm going to station four men here to watch over Ms. Wright. I'd like to use more, but I don't have them. You can go back with me. You'll be safe back at the station."

"I'm staying here," I said adamantly.

Ellsworth shook his head, frowned. "We can protect you better."

"I need to be here with her, know how she's doing."

He took a deep breath, blew out. He had to realize this wasn't an argument he was going to win. "All right. When you're ready, call my number. I'll have someone come pick you up." He stood. "I've got to go. With two officers down, there's a lot that has to be done."

I held up my coffee cup. "Thanks."

He fixed me in his gaze. "If I don't see you tonight, I'll want to see you in the morning."

"I understand."

He left. I walked back to the emergency waiting room, found a seat. This time people weren't scurrying to get away from me. I looked at my watch. Surprisingly, it was only seven-thirty. I drank the last of my coffee, wondered how long it would be before someone came out to talk to me.

I sat there for the next two hours. I was hungry, tired, achy, and that cup of coffee wanted out. Still, I sat. Knowing as soon as I left to go to the bathroom, they'd come to tell me something.

At a quarter-after-nine, I was rewarded for my patience. Doctor

Kline came looking for me; she sat down next to me, folded her hands in her lap. I braced for the worst.

"She's through surgery and in recovery," she said, speaking softly. They'll be moving her to ICU as soon as we can make a spot. There was brain hemorrhaging—"

"What does that mean?" It sounded awful.

She pursed her lips. "It means the brain experienced trauma—a strong blow—that caused bleeding. Dr. Guardio, one of the area's best neurosurgeons, operated to relieve the pressure. It's too soon to know anything. She's still in a coma from the trauma she sustained. The next twenty-four hours are crucial in seeing how she recovers." She stopped, looked at me. "Any questions?"

"How about the gunshot wound?"

"Not as troubling. The bullet passed through her shoulder. They've cleaned the wounds, stopped the bleeding. The concern is the head trauma."

"When can I see her?"

She gave me a sad smile. "Immediately, if you want. As I said, she's in a coma, but you can certainly be with her. It's good to have you there."

"I can go with her to the ICU?"

She nodded, started to get up, sat back down. "You don't look so hot, either, especially that ear. Has anybody taken a look at you?"

I shook my head. "I'm okay. Tory's the one to worry about."

She stood. "C'mon, I'll take you to her. On the way, I think I can round you up a couple of the hospital's ten-dollar aspirin." She grinned at her joke. "Might help the pain."

"Couldn't hurt," I agreed as I stood and followed her.

Sarasota Memorial is one of those hospitals where an addition was added to an addition added to an addition. Kline led down a maze of corridors and up a floor to surgical recovery.

She pointed to an empty spot along the wall. "That's where she was. They must have taken her up to ICU."

That entailed another elevator ride, several more corridors, before we arrived in a large square area with patient stations around the outside, a nurses' station in the center. Kline checked at the nurses' station, learned which spot was Tory's, and led me over.

It was like looking at Sarah all over again. Tory lay on her back, bandages around her head, a tube running out of her nose, a blanket pulled up to her chin, leaving only her head and the arm with the IV visible. Monitors and machines surrounded the bed. I stood there, thinking how pale and fragile she looked.

Kline brought me a chair, put it by the foot of the bed.

"Thank you. When do you think she'll wake up?"

She paused, as if calculating. "I think she'll sleep the night, probably wake sometime tomorrow. They gave her a good bit of anesthesia before the surgery." She looked at me. "You'd be fine going home, getting some sleep, coming back in the morning."

I shook my head. "Thanks, but I think I'm just going to sit with her. It's that holistic thing you mentioned. I think she'll know someone's here."

"Well, I'm off duty. I'm going home. If you want to get something to eat, Windows, the hospital cafeteria is one floor up and quite good. Just take "C" elevator and turn left when you get out." She pointed past the nurses' station. "There's a waiting room with chairs that turn into cots if you want to get a little sleep, phones, restrooms."

"Thank you. I appreciate your looking out for me."

"Glad to help," she said cheerfully. "That's why I got into this business. I'll check on you in the morning."

She left. I tried the chair. It was hard, uncomfortable. Good. That would help me stay awake. I had to be ready, alert. The hospital was too big; there were too many ways someone could avoid Ellsworth's four men. I planned to be right by Tory's bedside—the final defense.

Right now, however, I had to find the bathroom. I headed in the direction Kline had pointed me. Found the waiting room. Found the restroom. Unloaded the coffee. Splashed water on my face. It helped. I felt a little better, a little stronger. Refreshed, I left the restroom and went in search of something to eat.

The food in Windows might have been wonderful earlier. I tasted it after who-knows-how-many hours on the steam table. I wolfed down turkey, dressing, green beans, mashed potatoes, a bowl of fruit, and a large Diet Coke. Couldn't have taken me more than five minutes.

While I ate, I decided that there were a few phone calls I needed to make. I used the phone in the ICU waiting room. Dropped thirty-five cents in the slot and dialed Julian's home number. His machine picked up. After I listened to his voice telling me he wasn't there, the beep sounded, and I left my message. "Julian, it's Matt. Tory and I were ambushed on the way to the airport. Tory was shot and she's in intensive care—I'm here at Sarasota Memorial Hospital with her. The guy who shot Tory, William Wilder, I killed. It was self-defense. I've given Lieutenant Ellsworth a complete statement. Could you follow up with him in the morning, make sure everything's okay? I'm going to stay here at the hospital and watch over Tory. Thanks, Julian." I hung up. He was going to freak when he heard that message.

My next call was to Rosemary. "Dan," I said quickly when he picked up. "It's Matt. How's Rosemary doing?"

His voice sounded tired but happy. "Much better. I got her home from the hospital this morning. Where are you calling from? Rosemary said you were leaving town for a while."

"Didn't make it to the airport. There was some trouble." I looked down the hall toward the ICU. I could almost make out Tory's bed. "Tory's in ICU. She's got a gunshot wound and head trauma."

"Is she going to be all right?"

"They said the next twenty-four hours are crucial. That's all they'll tell me."

"We'll say a prayer."

"Thanks, Dan. I'll keep you posted. Tell Rosemary I've changed my mind. I'm not going to close the office."

"You two can talk about that later. Take care of Tory."

"I will."

For the next call, I dug out my calling card. Dr. Swarthmore was long distance and, if I reached her, this call might go awhile. I punched her home number, waited while it rang. "Hello," she said sleepily.

"Adelle, it's Matt. I'm sorry. I wouldn't have called so late if it wasn't an emergency."

"That's all right. Tell me what's the matter."

I told her about the hijacking, Tory's being shot, my struggle with Wilder, my fear. "Looking at Tory lying in that hospital bed, it's like seeing Sarah all over again. Adelle, I don't know if I can go through this again."

Her voice was calm, firm. "Tory and Sarah are two completely separate events, Matt, not the same event repeating itself. You have to recognize that, accept it. React to Tory's situation as if you've never been through this before. Don't predetermine the outcome. The timeliness of her treatment, the fact that the surgeons didn't observe and note brain damage, leads me to believe her prognosis might very well be favorable. It's important for you, during this period, to sustain your mental health. I'm very concerned about the level of stress you're experiencing. Overloaded with stress, we often make expedient decisions that may not be in our long-term best interest. If, as you say, you have people who are trying to kill you, I want you to weigh your decisions carefully. Make sure they lead you out of harm's way."

I heard her, but the words didn't reach me. I'd experienced that with her before when she'd talked about the grief, and all I knew was emptiness.

"Matt? Are you there?"

"I'm here. Just trying to take in what you've said."

Her voice changed. The clinical tone gone. "Matt, I'm concerned about you. I want you to call me every day until you're through this."

"I will. It'll be good to have someone to talk to."

"Don't try and shoulder this all on your own, Matt. You always want to do everything, make things right for everybody. Those are great qualities for a person to have. I never want you to lose them. However, this is a situation where you can't do it all by yourself. Let other people—Ellworth, for example—help protect you and Tory. Realize you can't please everybody. There's no win/win solution here. Do what it takes to get the two of you through this."

"I will. Thanks, Adelle. I'll call tomorrow."

"Do that. Take care, Matt."

I hung up the receiver. Told myself she was right. My job was to get us through this. To do that, I had to anticipate what was going to happen. By now, D'Onifrio had to know Wilder had failed and we were alive. That would only anger him more. He'd want us eliminated as soon as possible but probably wouldn't try anything while the hospital was busy. He'd come in the small hours of the morning.

I headed back to Tory's bedside, got ready to pre-empt the future.

CHAPTER 57

A nurse was taking Tory's vital signs. She seemed a little startled by my arrival. "How is she?"

"Heart rate, temperature, and blood pressure are good. We'll know a lot more when she wakes up. Are you her husband?"

"I think I qualify as a significant other," I said, smiling. "I'm planning on spending the night here." I put my hand on the chair. "Dr. Kline told me that would be all right."

She looked disapprovingly at the chair. "I'll see if we have something better than that." She showed me the nurse call button on the side rail of the bed. "If she needs anything, press this button." She left, returned a few minutes later with a chair that had padding and arms.

"Thank you," I said as we swapped chairs.

"You wouldn't have gotten any sleep on this thing," she said knowingly.

Little did she know—I wasn't planning on sleeping.

I positioned the chair so I could watch over Tory. Although there wasn't really anything to see. She hadn't moved. She seemed to be resting peacefully. I also positioned the chair so I could see anyone coming down the hallway. Once I had the chair where I wanted it, I walked back to the waiting room, got a cup of coffee from the machine, carried it back, and took my position.

I had the watch until dawn.

At one o'clock, coffee gone, backside aching, I stood, walked to the waiting room, got a fresh cup. It didn't taste very good, but it was something to do. I carried it back, sipping a little bit off the top so it wouldn't spill.

My watch said one-fifteen. I was the only thing moving. The floor was quiet, buttoned up for the night. Even the nurses in the center station had their heads down and were silently filling out paperwork. Every now and then, a monitor went off or there'd be a patient check, and one of the nurses would attend to it. But for the most part, the place was calm, peaceful.

It was just the kind of setting where someone could tiptoe in and—using a silenced gun or a knife—kill and get out without anyone noticing. Maybe that was an exaggeration, but sitting there in the dim light, lulled by a soft symphony of monitor beeps and buzzes, it sure seemed possible.

Worse, here I was sitting in a chair at the end of her bed, like hanging out a sign saying, here we are. The more I thought about that, the more sitting there seemed a really dumb thing to do. Especially since I was rapidly convincing myself that whoever D'Onifrio sent would get past Ellsworth's people.

I stood, stretched, carried my chair over to the nurses' station.

An older nurse with curly gray hair, working at a laptop, looked up at me. "Did you need something?"

I pointed over in the direction of the waiting room. "I was going to try and get a little sleep in the waiting room. Would it be okay to turn off the lights in there? They're kind of bright."

"Sure, the switch is right by the doorway."

"Thank you." I placed my chair against the wall, started for the waiting room. I had a thought and returned to the nurses' station.

She looked up again. "Yes."

"My sister is coming from out of town. I won't miss seeing her arrive because I'm in the waiting room, will I?"

"Well, you will if you're asleep. But to get here from either "B" or "C" elevators, you have to go by that waiting room, so conceivably you could see her."

"Thank you."

I yawned. She went back to updating the patient files. I went to the waiting room, found the light switch, flipped it off. The room was dark except for the soft glow of light from the illuminated fronts of vending machines. Anyone walking down the hallway would have a difficult time seeing who was inside.

My next task was to secure a weapon. I remembered the old TV show, McGyver, where the hero would defeat the bad guys by making a device out of whatever he happened to find handy—a comb, two paper clips, a hub cap. I walked around, looking, but nothing jumped up and said use me as a weapon. I finally decided to take an arm off one of the chairs. It was heavy wood I could use as a club. Not very ingenious. McGyver would have been disappointed.

With a dime, I unscrewed three of the four screws that held the arm to the chair. The fourth wouldn't budge. I pulled. Wiggled. Strained. Got nowhere. Frustrated, I made a loud sneezing sound and slammed it with my foot. The arm splintered at the end and broke away. I gave it an exploratory swing. The proverbial blunt instrument. It would work.

I made myself comfortable in a seat in the corner of the room that gave me the best view of the hallway. A round clock on the wall told me it was one-thirty-four. There'd be a shift change with lots of people coming and going sometime around five. If D'Onifrio was going to try something, it would have to be before then.

Of course, I had no idea how many people he'd send, how they'd be armed. Even with my chair arm, I didn't have any illusions I could best armed assailants. My only hope was to scare them off.

To do that, I was counting on the fire alarm box I'd discovered on the wall to my right. I theorized that once I pulled the alarm, sirens would go off, lights would flash, and D'Onifrio's people would scatter.

Not a great plan, but all I could come up with.

I tried to stay awake by watching the black hands creep around the white face of the clock. Every five minutes, I'd move, stretch, cross my legs—anything to mark time. It got old, of course. And it didn't keep me from dozing off. There was a stretch in there from about two to two-forty-five where I must have dropped off. I awoke with a start, suddenly alert.

I tiptoed to the doorway, my heart pounding, fearful of what I might see. I peeked cautiously into the hallway. It was empty. All was quiet at the nurses' station. I used the bathroom, splashed some water on my face, and went back to my seat.

That little bit of sleep had helped. I felt surprisingly refreshed. The clock on the wall said two-fifty. Two more hours, I told myself and tried staying awake by thinking of companies and their stock symbols. That seemed more effective than watching the clock, but by three-thirty, my eyes were once again getting heavy. I'd closed them—just to rest them for a second—when I heard that "dink" sound of an elevator's arrival followed by the whoosh of doors opening.

Through the glass portion of the waiting room hallway wall, I saw the heads and shoulders of two women in white—nurses probably—get off the elevator and head toward ICU. I almost ignored them. I'd been expecting D'Onifrio to send men. But something about the one woman, a blond, seemed vaguely familiar. Bam, it hit me. Ann, the blond from D'Onifrio's office.

Every nerve in my body tingled as I tiptoed to the doorway to make sure. They were halfway to the nurse's station, backs to me. My heart raced faster. The other one looked like the woman who'd sat next to me at City Hall.

There wasn't any doubt. Nor was there any time to go back and pull the alarm. They were almost to the nurses' station. I did the only thing I could. I charged.

I had the element of surprise going for me. Running up behind, I swung the chair arm as hard as I could at the side of the dark-haired woman's head. It connected with a solid thump, dropped her like a bag of rocks.

The nurses at the station screamed. To them, I was attacking one of their own.

"Call the police," I yelled back and dove for the dark-haired woman's purse. I was sure there'd be a gun in there. I jammed my hand inside, bumped into something hard.

Ann launched a kick that caught me in the kidney. Pain shot up my left side. Worse, my hand slipped away from the gun. She landed another kick to my ribs. Started to kick again. This time I saw it coming, grabbed the heel of her foot, yanked upward. She went down on her ass. I reached for the purse.

It was good I was quick. By the time I had the gun out of the purse and pointed at her, she was back on her feet, coming at me. She kept coming, daring me to pull the trigger. A dare she would have lost.

"Freeze. Police," a voice boomed from the end of the hall.

She looked around wildly. Realized she was sandwiched between us. The plainclothes officer walked closer, gun drawn, calling for backup on his walkie-talkie. When the backup arrived, he handcuffed her.

"You know her?" the first officer asked, nodding in her direction.

"I know she works at Shore for D'Onifrio."

"How about that one?"

"She does, too. She's the one who drugged me at City Hall."

He reached down, picked her purse off the tile floor, found her wallet, read from her driver's license: "Virlinda D'Onifrio. Looks like we got a relative. Too bad we didn't get him."

Virlinda wasn't moving. They handcuffed her hands behind her back anyway.

"Call this in to Ellsworth. He'll want to know," the one officer said.

The nurses at the station must have been calling, too. A young doctor from the emergency room arrived to look at Virlinda. He bent down, examined the back of her head, said, "Ouch, that's going to hurt."

"Is she going to be okay?" I asked.

He looked up at me, shrugged his shoulders. "Headache. Possible concussion. She'll live."

The officer who'd called Ellsworth returned. "He wants Gary and me to bring these two in. You guys stay. He'll have someone relieve you at eight."

The doctor struggled to roll Virlinda over on her back—an awkward maneuver with her hands handcuffed behind her. Her head rose, rolled, hit the floor with a wham. "Oh, Jeez," the doctor mumbled and quickly waved some smelling salts under her nose.

She wrinkled her face, groaned. As soon as her eyes opened, they hauled her to her feet.

"Get 'em out of here," the lead officer said.

Once they left, all I wanted to do was collapse. I couldn't believe how much that had taken out of me. I was tired, drained. Thank goodness it was over. I needed sleep.

But before sleep overtook me, I wanted to watch over Tory, talk to her, let her know I was there.

I carried the chair back over, put it at the end of the bed, walked to her bedside. I held her hand for a little bit, said what was in my heart. I desperately wanted to hear her answer me. It wasn't to be. She didn't move. She was quiet. The room was quiet. My words exhausted,

I went to the foot of her bed, settled into the chair. My eyes closed, my body relaxed. I could feel myself begin to nod. Still, some niggling thing was keeping me from sleep.

I was cold.

I tried to forget about it, settle back down, will myself to sleep. Instead, I found myself focusing on how chilled I felt. Unless I did something, I'd never get to sleep.

Annoyed with myself, I stood up, walked over to the nurses' station. A young black nurse looked up as I approached. "Is there a blanket I could use?" I asked her.

She smiled. "Sure. They do keep it kind of chilly in here." She stood up. "I'll get you one from the supply closet."

I started to follow her as she headed down the hall. We hadn't gone more than three steps when a monitor sounded. She stopped, looked at me, and pointed down the hall. "They're right around the corner. First door—marked 'clean supplies.' Take whatever you need," she said quickly and left.

I found it easily enough. It was a walk-in storage room with floor-to-ceiling shelves stocked with supplies. Ice buckets. Scrubs. Bed pans. Rubber gloves. Sheets.

Sterile dressings. Scalpels. Syringes. And, yes, blankets. The place had virtually everything. I took a blanket off the shelf, tucked it under my arm, turned out the light, and returned to the hallway. As I closed the door, the nurse's words—take whatever you need—ran through my mind. Wouldn't hurt to have one other thing I'd seen in there. I quickly reopened the door, took one out of the box, put it in my pocket, and returned to my chair.

I settled back down, pulled the blanket up around my chin, closed my eyes. Fell into a fitful sleep. My head kept bobbing up and down. My limbs twitched. My ear throbbed. Deep sleep never came.

The ICU monitors were especially troubling. A deep beep, beep,

beep or ping, ping, ping would shatter the quiet, jerking me awake.

I was almost asleep, when an odd, irritating high-pitched hum roused me. Wasn't a monitor. Was a sound I knew. But from where?

I knew the answer at the same time that I felt tremendous pressure against my face.

D'Onifrio's hearing aids.

CHAPTER 58

With my hands, I grabbed for what was over my face. Felt an arm. Something soft. The texture of fabric. A pillow. Pulled at the arm. Pulled at the pillow. Tried to breathe. Couldn't. The pressure continued. I pulled at the arm. Pushed at the corner of the pillow, trying to raise it up to get a breath. Couldn't get it far enough. No air. My chest felt heavy, my head light. I knew I didn't have long before I blacked out.

I tried to push the pillow away with my left hand, reached into my pants pocket with my right. My hand tightened on the scalpel I'd taken from the supply closet, wiggled it out.

I put everything I could muster into swinging the scalpel over my head. It struck something hard. The force of my jab caused the blade to skip along that hard surface until it buried itself in something soft.

An ear-splitting scream tore through the ICU. Instantly, the pressure on my face was gone. The scalpel was knocked from my hand. I couldn't worry about it. I yanked the pillow away from my face, jumped up from my chair, gulping at the air.

D'Onifrio stood there, slightly hunched over, hands trying to stop the blood that flowed freely from a rip that started on his left cheek and continued up to his ruined left eye. He must have come with the two women. Seen them botch it. Seen me, half asleep. Thought he could eliminate me quickly and easily. Despite the pain, he stared at me with his good eye, face contorted in anger.

I looked around, didn't see any sign of the two officers who were supposed to be protecting Tory. Nor did I see any nurses at the station. It was just the two of us.

He balled his hands up into fists. Took a step in my direction. "Wilder was right. I should have killed you before the old man," he snarled, blood streaming down his face.

Even hurt, he was dangerous. He was bigger and stronger than I was. I kept backing away, thinking the pain would slow him, help would arrive.

He lunged, lashing out with his fists. A right caught me on the side of the face.

I backpedaled. I wasn't a fighter; D'Onifrio was. He hit me in the face again. Where were the police? I backed up, bumped into the counter of the nurses' station.

He saw he had me against the ropes, smiled wickedly, slowly closed the distance between us.

This was it. I got my hands up. Did the thing he'd least expect. Attacked.

I stepped forward, put my weight into a right to the face. He blocked it. I followed with a left, caught him on the ripped cheek. He growled. Swung a hard right at my head. I moved and the blow glanced off.

My right connected with his good eye. He retaliated with a flurry of blows, forcing me to cover my face with my hands. I didn't know what to do. My back was against the counter; there was no escape. Again and again, he hit me. Jarring blows that hurt me, drained me, frightened me. Unless I did something, I was finished.

I used the counter as leverage, pushed forward, tried to bowl him over. It worked halfway. Got me away from the counter. But it allowed him to grab me in a bear hug. He tried to throw me to floor, slipped on his own blood, took us both down hard. I landed on my right shoulder, immediately felt burning pain. D'Onifrio landed on his back.

I was up first. Hit him with a hard right to the face as he struggled to get to his feet. He fell back. I went after him. Hit him with another hard right to the face. Hurt my hand. He tried to get up, again. I went after his injured eye. Hit him with a left. Another left. He yelled. The gash on his cheek spewed more blood. He turned his back to me, got to his feet.

We squared off again.

He didn't act as strong now, wasn't as aggressive, wasn't as steady on his feet. My right arm was useless. Pain ran from my shoulder to my hand. He threw a clumsy right at me. I easily avoided it. That gave me confidence. He was weakening. Even with the useless right arm, I was stronger.

I kicked him in the side of the knee. He bent over in pain. I followed with a left hand to the face. Caught him on the cheek. He went down on all fours, breathing heavily.

"You're finished, D'Onifrio. Give it up." I wheezed.

"Not until you're dead."

I kicked as hard as I could. The blow caught him in the face. He went over on his back, lay still.

The only sounds in the ICU were my gasps for air and the irritating hum of his hearing aids.

CHAPTER 59

"What happened?" A surprised Dr. Kline asked the next morning.

I'm sure I was a sight. My right arm was in a sling for a dislocated shoulder. My right hand was in a cast for three broken knuckles, two broken fingers. Cuts on my face had required nine stitches. Bruising was developing in various shades of purple.

"Fell asleep and fell off that chair you found for me." I tried not to smile. It hurt.

I saw a twinkle in her eye. "Try and help someone and look what happens. How's your lady friend?"

"They say she should wake this morning. Nothing, so far."

"Some people take longer. Has Dr. Guardio been by?"

"I haven't seen him. But I wasn't here for awhile. I was with the police."

That surprised her. "Police?"

"Investigating my chair fall."

An I've-been-had look appeared on her face. "I'll see if I can find you one with a seat belt for tonight." She smiled. "I'm on all day. Let one of the nurses know if you need me."

"Thanks. I appreciate your looking in on me."

Tory didn't wake that morning. She didn't wake that afternoon. Or that evening. I lived by her bedside, leaving only to get something to eat, use the phone, or go to the bathroom. By nightfall, the jubilation I'd experienced at surviving D'Onifrio's attack had worn off and

Tory's condition had me depressed and discouraged.

That evening, Ellsworth stopped by. "Thought you'd like a progress report," he said as we walked to the cafeteria to get coffee.

"I am kind of curious."

We got our drinks, settled into seats. "D'Onifrio's still here in the hospital—"

I choked on a sip of mine.

"Under armed guard," he added quickly. "They operated but couldn't save his eye. He also has a broken nose, some internal injuries—none of them serious. His lawyers are already trying to spin this, say he was attacked, get him released. Armstrong's not having any of that. He's going after him for murder."

"Why the change of heart?"

"Twice now they've planned to use graves in abandoned properties owned by Shore as a way of disposing of bodies. Looks like a pattern. We got a search order, started looking in other abandoned properties, found something that had recently been covered over. When it's excavated, we think we'll find Raines, Enrico, the nephews, maybe others.

"What happens if there aren't any bodies there?"

"We'll keep looking. A pattern this strong usually leads to something."

"Will they let him out on bail?"

Ellworth finished a sip of coffee, shook his head. "No. They know he'll leave the country. Remember, I told you Armstrong's political?"

I nodded.

"He knows he's got a juicy case. Lots of publicity. Could go national. He'll make sure this one is locked up tight."

I liked hearing the locked up tight part. Ellsworth talked a few minutes more, looked at his watch, said he had to go.

On my way back to the ICU, I stopped in the waiting room, used the phone, called Dr. Swarthmore.

"How are you, Matt?" she asked when she heard my voice.

I chuckled. "A lot has happened since I talked to you last night."

"Tell me."

I did. I thought she'd be freaked out, but she wasn't.

When I finished, she said, "While I know last night wasn't pleasant, it did give you closure. You no longer have the threat of this man hanging over your head. The fact that it happened so quickly is also beneficial. You no longer have two major concerns vying for your attention. One area of worry has been eliminated. You can now focus on Tory. What are the doctors telling you?"

"I haven't seen them."

Even over the telephone, I sensed her disapproval. "Until you talk to her doctors, you have no real sense of her condition. Find out when they make rounds, make sure you talk to them at length. Let me know what they have to say. In the meantime, stay positive. Don't dwell on the negatives; don't allow yourself to be pulled into depression."

"Thanks, Adelle." I replaced the receiver. She'd been a little curt at the end, but I felt buoyed by talking with her, much the way I had the night before. I needed that as I settled into my chair for my second night's vigil.

That night, I slept surprisingly well. I woke feeling that it was a going to be a good day, a feeling that lasted until I saw that Tory hadn't moved.

At nine-thirty that morning, Dr. Guardio, the neurosurgeon, and Dr. Henry, a consulting neurologist, came to look at her. The two of them examined her, talked mumbo-jumbo to each other, dictated some notes, turned to go.

"Doctor, there are a couple of things it would help me to know."

Guardio nodded.

"Is there brain damage?" I asked the worst question first.

Guardio, a big hairy bear of a man with a soft voice, shook his head. "We don't believe so. There was significant internal bleeding and the back of the brain was bruised, but preliminary indications are that there should be no long-term debilitation."

"All the nurses have said she should be awake by now. Why isn't she?"

"Normally, yes, she should have regained consciousness by now." He frowned. "However, comas caused by severe traumas such as the one she suffered often last for an extended period of time. The bruising of the brain may be the key here. She'll return to consciousness once the brain has had a chance to heal sufficiently."

"Are we talking days, months, years? Help me understand."

Henry, slight, stooped, with thick glasses, fielded his one. "Impossible to say for sure. In most severe trauma cases, we're talking in the range of five to seven days on the low end, twenty to thirty days on the high end."

"We've ordered some additional scans that may give us a better idea," Guardio said. "The fact that she hasn't responded quickly concerns me although the injuries don't indicate the coma will last for an extended period. The additional tests should prove valuable."

That was all I got out of them. At eleven a.m., two orderlies came to wheel her bed to x-ray.

"How long will this take?" I asked one.

He checked his paperwork. "Doc's ordered four scans—two regular, two with contrast. That's gonna take awhile."

I was torn. I wanted to stay with her, but I needed to get organized, too. I couldn't continue to live here like a homeless person. I opted for organized. If she was going to be gone and they didn't expect her to wake today, it was the time for me to be gone, too.

I followed them as they wheeled her bed down the corridor to the elevators, rode down in the same elevator. They exited on the second level for x-ray. I stayed to the ground level, feeling guilty for leaving her.

I walked through the main lobby and out into the sunshine. It must have rained during the night. There were still big puddles on the ground. But that blindingly intense Florida sun was out. I used my hand to shield my eyes, looked for a cab. I spotted one, waved my good arm, and it pulled over.

"Where to?"

I had him take me to my condo. The ride seemed long and slow. When we finally made it to the Watergate, I paid him, rode the elevator up to my floor, unlocked my condo door.

As I walked in, I had the feeling I'd been gone forever. It was replaced by a feeling of panic. All my family photos were in that police van. I went to the phone, dialed Ellsworth's number. I got one of his assistants, Officer Tuttle.

"We did find the van," he drawled. "I know there were belongings in the back. Suitcases, I believe. We have them here. If you want I can check, make sure we have everything."

I thanked him, told him what I had. He went to check.

"All here," he said when he came back.

"Good, I'll be over to pick it up." I thanked him again.

That finished, I headed to the bathroom, stripped off my clothes, jumped in the shower. God, did that feel good! I shaved, washed my hair, put on clean clothes—shorts and a polo shirt. I packed as much as I could get in a carry bag, took the bag into the living room, and left it by the door. Next, phone calls.

First call was to the Saab dealership. I arranged for my car to be brought to the condo.

Second call was to Saul Badgett, my stockbroker friend who worked at Salomon Smith Barney, a bright kid, lost in their big organization. We'd talked about his joining my brokerage before. Now was the time to bring someone in. I knew just how to do it—equity.

The phone at the Badgett house rang twice before a woman answered. I asked for Saul, and the woman—his wife, I assumed—went to get him.

"Yeah," he answered, "this is Saul."

"Saul, Matt Seattle. I've got a crazy idea I want to bounce off you. Got a minute?"

He not only had a minute, he didn't think the idea of starting work for me the next day was crazy at all. It probably wasn't, at the salary level we agreed upon. What clinched the deal was my offer of a 15% equity position after the first year. Even for a bright future star like Saul, those offers don't come along every day.

An agreement reached, I top-lined my situation for him, explained I'd be working off site, gave him my phone numbers, told him I'd drop off a key to the office that afternoon.

"I'll do you proud, Matt," he assured me before he rang off.

I was sure he would. In fact, I only had one reservation about Saul. He was already a better golfer than I was.

My third call was to Rosemary. I got their machine, left a message reinforcing that she should take some time off, however long she needed, that Saul would be starting with us tomorrow.

I would have done a fax alert to the clients, but my computer was with my belongings at the police station. Not a big deal; I could swing by the office, send it out on my way back to the hospital.

I grabbed a couple of books from the study, gathered up my carry bag, went down to the lobby to wait. I wasn't there long. My Saab pulled up with a new black top.

My first stop was Saul's, where I dropped off keys. Second was the police station. They loaded the luggage in the Saab's trunk and back seat. Third was the office. I faxed an announcement about our new associate. At my fourth and final stop, I picked up something I wanted to have—just in case—and returned to the hospital.

Total elapsed time for my whirlwind outing was three hours, thirteen minutes. I stopped at the nurse's station, learned Tory had only returned from x-ray twenty-minutes earlier.

"The bruising is more substantial than Dr. Guardio thought," Jane, an RN with short-cropped blond hair, told me. "The good news is they didn't see any new bleeding. As soon as they can find a room, he's going to have her moved to the neurology floor."

"How soon is soon?"

"My guess is they'll come get her around dinner time."

Dinner time came and went. It was closer to eight p.m. when they arrived to move her. Two orderlies wheeled her bed to a room on the seventh floor. It was a double, but Tory's was the only bed in the room.

Once she was settled, I introduced myself to the nurses and explained that I was going to stay, do whatever I could to help.

Leah, a short, chubby nurse with straight red hair, said, "If you're staying, we can get a sleeper chair for that room. Might make you a little more comfortable."

Around ten, an orderly came in with a chair that went flat and could be slept on. Most people would have found it uncomfortable, but after two nights of sleeping sitting up, it felt like heaven to me.

The next day, we settled into a routine that would be repeated day after day. Guardio, occasionally with Henry in tow, did rounds between eight and eight-fifteen. Physical therapy came at nine-thirty and again at two-thirty in the afternoon. Around that schedule, I did my brokerage work. The cell phone seemed attached to my ear. I was either talking with clients or with Saul on executing the trades and running the office.

When I wasn't on the phone, I did as much exercising as I could.

Walking and sit-ups, mostly. Did a little reading. In the evenings, Rosemary and Dan often stopped by, concern for both of us etched on their faces.

Every morning at seven-thirty, I called Dr. Swarthmore. As the days slowly passed, each like the previous one, my phone conversations with her became longer.

I was getting discouraged. Guardio and Henry didn't seem to have any answers.

As day seven turned into day eight turned into day nine, the feeling she'd never come out of the coma weighed more heavily on me. Adelle acted as my counterweight, kept me balanced, focused. Not an easy task as day nine turned into day ten turned into day eleven.

Day eleven, the unexpected struck.

CHAPTER 60

Leah, the nurse on duty that day, broke the news to me. "Did you see the paper this morning?" She asked, suppressing a grin.

I shook my head.

"I'll get you one."

She was back two minutes later with the day's Sarasota Herald-Tribune. On the front page, just below the fold, I read the headline, *"Modern Day Sleeping Beauty and Her Prince Charming."* What followed was a two-column, four-inch story on the front-page, finishing with a two-column, eight-inch story on the jump page.

It was a heavily romanticized version of what had happened. There was no mention of Wilder's death or the kidnapping. As the newspaper told it, Tory had tried to save my life, taken a bullet, and was now in a coma. I, in turn, had saved her life by stopping the bleeding from her wound then wouldn't leave her side at the hospital until she woke. Two young lovers sacrificing for each other. Written in a way to tug at those heartstrings, maybe even get you to shed a tear or two.

"It's so romantic," Leah said as I finished reading.

She wasn't the only one who thought so. Flowers started arriving. The phone started ringing. By day twelve, the room was so filled with flowers, balloons, and stuffed animals it was hard to walk. The nurses had pinned a copy of the article to the bulletin board across from Tory's bed. That evening, I asked Doctor Kline if she'd leaked the story to the press. She denied it, of course, but her protests weren't very convincing.

On day thirteen, Guardio picked his way through the flowers for his morning examination. Tory'd been experiencing muscle spasms, some head movement. "She's fighting to regain consciousness," he said encouragingly. "It could be any time now."

I watched and waited for the rest of the day, pretty much ignoring everything else. At five that afternoon, her eyelids opened and she mumbled something unintelligible before slipping back to sleep. At five-forty, her eyes opened again and stayed open. I called the nurse who brought some ice chips. Tory sucked on a couple of them for a minute and closed her eyes again.

She didn't wake again until nine-thirty. This time she stayed awake a little longer. She had a few more ice chips, managed to say a few words before slipping back to sleep.

At eleven-forty-five, she woke again, her eyes clearer this time. "Matt," she asked hoarsely. "Where am I?"

I sat on the edge of the bed, held her hand. "Sarasota Memorial Hospital. You've been here for almost two weeks."

"That long?"

"We've been worried about you."

"What's wrong with me? Why don't I remem—" Her voice trailed off as she slipped into unconsciousness.

She didn't wake again that night. For me, it was a night of fitful sleep. Half listening for her. Wanting to be there when she regained consciousness. When I woke in the morning at six-thirty, she was asleep, but it was a restless sleep. There was movement. Her hand. Her lips. I sensed that her eyes might flutter open at any moment. I sat on the edge of the bed and waited.

Mid-morning, her breathing changed, she gave a little gasp, and her eyes blinked open. She looked at me and smiled.

"Morning," I said, smiling back.

"I was hoping you'd be here."

"I wouldn't have missed this moment for anything."

For the first time, she seemed to see the flowers that filled the room.

"What's all this?"

I got up off the edge of the bed, took the newspaper article off the bulletin board, and handed it to her.

She took it, looked at it, shook her head, handed it back to me. "I can't see to read it. The type is all blurry."

I read it to her. Halfway through, she started to cry. When I finished, she said, "Oh, Matt, hold me. I was so afraid I was going to lose you."

"I've been afraid I was going to lose you." I held her tightly, reluctantly pulled away to get something from my carry bag. I brought it back to the bed. I opened the

little black felt box in front of her. It was the diamond ring Luis had saved for us. "I don't want to lose you ever. Tory, will you marry me?"

Tears welled up in her eyes. "Oh, Matt," she said, her lower lip trembling, "I knew I was falling in love with you, but I didn't want to be hurt again. Before, I would have told you no."

Her hand touched the newspaper article; her gaze took in the flowers in the room. "Now I know you're the one." Tears rolled down her cheeks. She reached out and hugged me to her. "Yes. Yes. Yes."

The next morning's Sarasota Herald-Tribune carried the front-page headline, *"Sleeping Beauty Wakes. Says Yes To Prince."*

EPILOGUE

I expected to talk to Fish after he and Janet returned from their honeymoon, but I couldn't reach him. I tried calling his doublewide, Janet's place, work. Didn't get an answer at either residence. A co-worker told me Fish hadn't returned. When I checked with the airlines, I learned that the tickets for their return flight from Miami had gone unused.

In October, I got a postcard from him with a Davenport, Iowa, address and phone number with the message: Call and I'll fill you in. I called and learned that Janet had greedily signed all D'Onifrio's documents in the limo following the wedding. Their first night on board ship, she'd tried to get him exceedingly drunk. When the alcohol didn't leave him at death's door, and after Fish insisted on, as he described it, non-stop sex, Janet must have realized she'd been had and jumped ship at first port.

Fish was a little bummed by her departure, but hooked up with one of two sisters taking the cruise together. Fish and the sister were living happily in Davenport. He didn't know what happened to Janet. But he cleaned out all her bank accounts before D'Onifrio had a chance to get to them.

The churning accusations against me were dismissed by the N.A.S.D. arbitration panel. The faulty financials Nevitt delivered and Janet's failure to appear helped, but basically the panel recognized there was no merit to the charges. Fowler even came close to an apology for what they'd put me through.

Nevitt, however, didn't give up. He tried to press forward with his lawsuit to recover commissions and damages. Armstrong heard about it, arranged a hearing before a judge, had the lawsuit dismissed. Even better, he started proceedings to have Nevitt disbarred.

Ellsworth's belief in D'Onifrio's habit of burying bodies in vacant buildings panned out. It took four digs before he hit the mother lode. The first three all had bodies, but not the bodies he wanted. Hole four yielded Enrico, Little Ernie, Eduardo, Raines, and two other D.E.A. agents. Until the discovery of the bodies, it looked like D'Onifrio's lawyers might be able to get him off. As details of how Raines and the other D.E.A. agents had been tortured and killed appeared in the press, his lawyers began plea bargaining with Armstrong. Ironically, D'Onifrio ended up serving a life sentence in the same prison where his father died.

Angel, the mole in Raines' organization, was arrested following a routine border stop. In the false bottom of the van she was driving, patrol agents found half-a-million in cash, fake Columbian and Mexican passports, and two handguns. She was extradited from Texas to Florida and tried as an accessory to murder.

Saul proved a great addition. His energy and enthusiasm were contagious. I made another smart business decision, too. With more business coming in, I hired a new receptionist, made Rosemary our business manager, gave her a five percent equity share in the business. The tin can became close quarters, but I had an architect's drawings for the new building, construction due to start.

Tory and I? A year after I proposed, we were married in a small private ceremony that included the two of us and our new little addition. Tory had given me a Springer Spaniel puppy as a wedding present. We named him Brock, in honor of Ellsworth, who served as my best man.

LaVergne, TN USA
17 August 2009
155050LV00003B/247/A